I0775547

South
of
Sepharad

The 1492 Jewish Expulsion from Spain

A Novel

by Eric Z. Weintraub

South of Sepharad © copyright 2024 Eric Z. Weintraub. All rights reserved. No part of this book may be reproduced in any form whatsoever, by photography or xerography or by any other means, by broadcast or transmission, by translation into any kind of language, nor by recording electronically or otherwise, without permission in writing from the author, except by a reviewer, who may quote brief passages in critical articles or reviews.

ISBNs: 979-8-9873191-1-6 (pb)
979-8-9873191-2-3 (hc);
979-8-9873191-3-0 (eBook)

Book Cover Design: The Book Cover Whisperer, OpenBookDesign.biz
Interior Book Design: Inanna Arthen, inannaarthen.com

Library of Congress Control Number: 2023933915
First Printing: 2024
Printed in the United States of America

Names: Weintraub, Eric Z., author.
Title: South of Sepharad : the 1492 Jewish expulsion from Spain : a novel / by Eric Z. Weintraub.
Description: [Roseville, Minnesota] : [History Through Fiction], [2024]
Identifiers: ISBN: 979-8-9873191-1-6 (paperback) | 979-8-9873191-2-3 (hardcover) | 979-8-9873191-3-0 (ebook) | LCCN: 2023933915
Subjects: LCSH: Jewish physicians--Spain--History--To 1500--Fiction. | Jews--Spain--History-- Expulsion, 1492--Fiction. | Spain--History--Ferdinand and Isabella, 1479-1516--Fiction. | Conversion--Spain--History--To 1500--Fiction. | Jewish families--Spain--History--To 1500-- Fiction. | Jewish refugees--Morocco--History--To 1500--Fiction. | LCGFT: Historical fiction. | BISAC: FICTION / Historical / General. | FICTION / Jewish.

Classification: LCC: PS3623.E4324485 S68 2024 | DDC: 813/.6--dc23

For Laura Cesareo
My inspiration and motivation

"It was a disastrous event, even though they may say the opposite in schools. An admirable civilization, and a poetry, astronomy, architecture and sensitivity unique in the world—all were lost, to give way to an impoverished, cowed city, a 'miser's paradise.'"

Federico García Lorca

CONTENTS

Foreword

The first germination of the idea for *South of Sepharad* spawned from a trip I took to visit my girlfriend, Laura, for the holidays when she was studying abroad in Granada, Spain. Immediately, I fell in love with a city that surrounded me with old-world Moorish architecture and ancient labyrinth-like alleyways, unlike anything I'd seen in my hometown of Los Angeles. That the food and wine were also exquisite (not to mention affordable) didn't hurt either.

Though the city charmed me, I never expected it would inspire me to write a novel. However, my attitude changed on January 2, 2016. As Laura and I walked along the city's main street, Calle Gran Vía de Colón, we encountered locals lining up for a parade.

"What are they celebrating?" I asked, assuming it was one of the countless Spanish holidays unknown to me in the States.

"They're commemorating the end of La Reconquista," Laura replied. She explained that for centuries the south of Spain had been controlled by the Moors. Over time, Queen Isabella and King Ferdinand (also known as the Catholic Monarchs) slowly conquered the Iberian Peninsula in the name of Spain and on January 2, 1492, they succeeded in capturing the last Muslim stronghold: Granada. But this crash course in Spanish history only interested me half as much as what she said next. After La Reconquista, the Catholic Monarchs expelled all the Jews from Spain. The event that created the Sephardic Diaspora that continues to this day.

The story of the expulsion surprised me. Despite growing up in a Jewish household and studying for years in Hebrew school, I'd never heard about the expulsion of the Jews from Spain. I knew Jews were persecuted often during the middle ages and frequently forced off their land, but heard few specifics beyond this generalization meant to account for several centuries of history. My understanding of the Spanish Inquisition was equally opaque, an event I knew mainly as a punchline to Monty Python skits and Mel Brook's *History of the World: Part I*. Although the expulsion of the Jews from Spain occurred over 500 years ago, the event sounded oddly current to me. It is a story of mass migration. A story of refugees fleeing war, of xenophobia, of anti-Semitism, of the forced separation of families. All qualities that feel contemporary in our time, in both 2016 and now.

Although my Hebrew school teachers never shared with me the story of the expulsion, they did impart another lesson I'll never forget: "Those who do not know history are doomed to repeat it." Because an event from 500 years ago felt contemporary, and because I'd needed to travel almost 6,000 miles to learn of it, I felt captivated to know more.

I at first gravitated to books to learn about the expulsion of the Jews. While I found a plethora of information on the Catholic Monarchs and the Spanish Inquisition, the books I first found on the expulsion were academic and only offered the vaguest description of the topic. While I slowly learned the basic story of what happened—that the Spanish Jews fled to whichever country was closest to them—academic history books could not provide me with the human questions I yearned to have answered. Who were these people? How did they leave Spain? What was it like to go through this experience? The famous quote of Toni Morrison's came to mind, "If there's a book that you want to read, but it hasn't been written yet, then you must write it." At that moment, I knew I wanted to write a novel about the expulsion of the Jews from Spain.

I chose to write a novel rather than non-fiction because I wanted to write about people caught up in this event. Although I chose to write fiction, I did not give myself the excuse to invent anachronisms at my convenience. After all, this began as a quest to learn history.

Books and websites related to the chronicling of the history of the expulsion, along with conversations with people in the Sephardic community, proved to be my greatest resources in my research.

Three books in particular provided me with valuable insight into the time period. *History of a Tragedy: The Expulsion of the Jews from Spain* by Joseph Pérez offered, to my knowledge, the most comprehensive work written about the expulsion that I've found. I discovered the book in the gift shop of a medieval torture museum of all places. Teofilo F. Ruiz's *Spain's Centuries of Crisis 1300-1474* provided a meticulously informative picture of the events of Spain leading up to the expulsion. Marcos Aguinis' historical novel *Against the Inquisition* dramatized the inner-workings and bureaucracy of the Inquisition in painstaking detail. I would encourage anyone interested in learning more about the events depicted in this novel to seek out these books and the works of their authors.

The main cast of characters in *South of Sepharad* are fictitious. However, several people mentioned at the periphery of the novel are real historical figures; many of them still very famous. Isabella I of Castile, Ferdinand II of Aragon, the Grand Inquisitor Tomás de Torquemada, the Emir Muhammad XII of Granada, Pope Alexander VI, the wealthy Portuguese man Isaac Abarbanel, and Christopher Columbus were all real people, most of them playing monumental roles in world history that have altered the course of humankind to this day.

Striving for authenticity, I tried to feature as many real-world locations in the novel as possible. However, several places in Granada have been altered. The Nasrid Great Mosque now supports the foundation of the Granada Cathedral. The Darro River that once ran through the city has been damned and relegated to the valley below the Alhambra. La Judería is long gone, transformed into the city center of Realejo.

Unfortunately, no primary accounts from the generation of Jews expelled from Spain exists—it would've been too dangerous to keep such records. Thus, the research for this novel is compiled exclusively from secondary sources. In addition to the three books listed above, which served as the foundation of my research, I have included a recommended resources section at the end of the novel, and History Through Fiction hosts a webpage containing a complete collection of my resources and references on their website.

Based on these many sources, this novel is my best conclusion for what happened to the people expelled. Any historical inaccuracies or anachronisms are my own.

I wrote this novel because I did not know this part of history. However, I have learned enough about this infamous event to propose that it has gone underexplored—perhaps not among Jewish communities and history aficionados, but I believe the details and importance of this story have passed out of the knowledge of the general public. Considering how much this event has in common with the present, it deserves renewed interest.

My hope is that this novel may play a part in stirring a renewed investigation into the history of medieval Jews, of the Spanish Inquisition, of the first Jews expelled from Spain in 1492, as well as the Muslims who would also be forced to convert and later expelled by the Spanish Empire in the following years.

I do not believe a book can cure the many ailments of today's world. However, I believe that if we all know a little more about history, we may be less inclined to continue to repeat it.

Book I

LA JUDERÍA

Chapter One

At the graveside, the mourners lowered into the burial pit the featherweight body of a girl swaddled head to toe in white linen shrouds. The groundskeeper had only dug a grave half the length necessary to inter a man or woman, for Vidal's daughter had never grown tall, dying a week short of her third birthday.

They laid Sarah to rest in a hole of excavated earth with her feet facing east, toward the rose-colored brick of the cemetery wall that doubled as the eastern most fortification of Granada, and beyond the wall, toward their banished home of Jerusalem. Vidal stood beside his wife and four remaining children to perform the kriah, tearing the left side of his black jubba in mourning as Bonadonna tore the left side of her black qamis. His two sons and two daughters tore the right sides of their matching clothes in unison. All were older than Sarah. None wept, still despondent that only one day earlier, their family had been whole.

The mourners who surrounded the family numbered into the hundreds, each of them balancing themselves on a spot of untouched grass, scarce among the glut of tombstones that marked the 500 years of residents laid to rest in La Judería's cemetery. Vidal was physician to Jews, Moors, and Catholics alike, all had answered his call to mourn the loss of his youngest daughter. He pulled a shovel from the mound of dirt beside the burial pit and filled the grave with soil. The occasion was a mitzvah, the rabbi reminded everyone, for burying the dead was a selfless task, one each mourner would do without expectation of reward. Vidal poured three shovelfuls into the pit until an archipelago of earth covered the milk-colored sea of the shrouds below. He then drove the shovel back into the mound and stood aside to allow his family to perform the mitzvah. Their shovelfuls fell onto the body with such force that Vidal feared the dirt might bruise skin. To him, the soft drops of earth hitting body sounded loud enough to wake anyone but the dead.

It'd only been a cough. As a father of five and physician to countless more, Vidal had come across countless illnesses like Sarah's. They were symptoms caused by rain or the plummeting of the temperature in early autumn, an inevitable consequence brought upon children who refused to wear shoes in the house or a coat outside. He'd examined Sarah's tongue, listened to her lungs, and prescribed Bonadonna to prepare hot tea with honey and lemon. Throughout the examination, Sarah asked what he was doing and why, only now reaching the age where the world made her curious. He told her he was working to make her healthy and instructed her to sleep, for time, rest, and all-knowing God could cure her illness with greater skill than the most learned physician. Before he left her room, she handed him an alabaster brush and asked him to comb her hair, something she always requested when she wanted his attention. Although he had many patients waiting for him in the city, he brushed her curls until they were as smooth as lake water at dawn. "Thank you, Father." The first time she'd been old enough to thank him for caring for her. The last words she'd ever speak.

He spent the rest of the day making rounds to see his other patients: people who suffered from heart disease, liver disease, madness, broken bones, arthritis, and the countless illnesses that plagued the elders. Bonadonna checked on Sarah every half hour while he was away, but when time came for her to make supper, she left their daughter alone to sleep in peace for an hour. Vidal would've done the same if he were home. By the time he returned from his rounds in the city and checked on his daughter, her chest lay at rest and her lips turned the color of eggplant. Though he could not determine how a phlegmatic illness killed her with such haste, his daughter had died from a circumstance his profession trained him to prevent. How could he forgive himself?

As others stepped forward to fill the grave, Vidal attempted to distract himself from his thoughts by listening to the whispers of friends and neighbors down the line. Although conversation was meant to be limited to the memory of the deceased, he heard two neighbors exchanging news from the east of an impending siege of Baza by Ferdinand's army. The kingdoms of Aragon, Castile and León had been attempting to invade Granada for over five years. Although they'd taken much ground in their campaign for conquest, they'd had no luck coming within fifty leagues of the city. But Vidal could not allow himself to grow worried with politics at a time like this.

Once earth packed the burial pit, he faced eastward with the rabbi as they led the mourners in a recitation of the Kaddish. People of all faiths recited Hebrew around him as if—for only a moment—the ancient language became their common tongue.

Chapter Two

Synagogues, churches, and mosques alike tolled their bells throughout the city. All of Granada stood at the sidelines of the parade route to witness a first glimpse of their new rulers. "Long live King Ferdinand!" they chanted. "Long live Queen Isabella!"

In the street, warhorses carried Castilian officers engulfed in bevors and battlefield armor down a route that began at the city walls and ended at La Alhambra. Military drummers beat in rhythm, accompanied by the cry of trumpets and whistles of flutes that proclaimed the majesty of the king and queen while keeping every soldier and stallion in formation. Flagbearers passed waving the red and gold striped sigil of Aragon and the symbols of lions, castles, and crowns that composed the banner of Castile and León. Despite the chill of the icy January air, the people danced and celebrated along the route, welcoming not only the conquering monarchs but also the end of a war that had consumed the Kingdom of Granada for the past nine years.

At the edge of the thoroughfare, Vidal stood beside his son Eliezer, where petals of red carnations thrown from the rooftops behind them fell over their shoulders like a gentle rain. Few were eager to cross the street, but as Vidal was a doctor, he could not neglect his patients in favor of celebration. He carried his leather instrument case filled with medical supplies and held down his woolen cap to keep the wind from carrying it away. He was well insulated from the frost thanks to his gray-streaked beard, his thickest wool coat, and the boots he'd acquired mere days before

Castile's siege of the city that'd commenced eight months earlier. Though his son was naked-faced and skinny as a peasant, Eliezer neither shivered nor hugged himself for warmth. The boy watched the parade with his mouth agape as if he were witnessing the procession of a king's harem.

Vidal attempted to let the excitement of the procession overwhelm him as well. Look at the splendor of this parade! Listen to the music they play to greet their new subjects! But his stomach carried a feeling no different than when he anticipated a grave diagnosis for a new patient. He'd read the Articles of Capitulation in the month preceding the surrender, terms signed by the new monarchs and Granada's soon-to-be exiled emir that assured no citizen of Granada would lose their home or the ability to practice their faith under new rule, but Vidal was dubious that the new rulers would keep their word. He'd heard horrors of how the Kingdoms of the Iberian Peninsula treated their Jews, of the murders of Jews in Jaén, Córdoba, and Sevilla. How could he celebrate their arrival when he held the sneaking suspicion that such barbarism might come to pass in his home as well?

Once a battalion of horses passed, a soldier signaled for those who needed to cross to do so with haste. Vidal took Eliezer by the arm and led him across the route, even as Eliezer stood on his toes for a final glance at what section of the parade would pass next.

A street south of the parade route, they hurried through an empty Granada overdue to call on the next patient. Houses made of plaster lined the streets, packed beside each other wall-to-wall, intact only because the emir had surrendered before a single projectile could be fired over the city walls.

They walked through a small yard of lemon trees to reach a manor made of marigold-colored bricks, the house where his daughter lived with her husband's family, and knocked on the cork oak door. His daughter Catalina—born Goyo before she converted to marry a Catholic—greeted them. At nineteen years old, Catalina was his oldest child. She wore a blue gown and her eyes the shade of black cherries reminded him of Sarah, gone now for nearly four years. If Sarah'd lived, would she have grown up to look like her sister?

16

Though anxious to solicit Catalina's thoughts on the arrival of the new rulers and learn of her congregation's attitudes toward the Articles of Capitulation, he treated the moment like any other house call and asked to be brought to the patient. Catalina led them to the second floor while listing the ailments her grandfather-in-law suffered: trouble breathing, sleep twenty hours a day, fatigue from so much as sitting up in bed.

Before she married, Catalina acted as Vidal's nurse, accompanying him on house calls until Eliezer was old enough to be his apprentice. Unlike the family members of so many other patients, she did not probe Vidal with questions or offer hypotheses of a diagnosis, but only brought him to the master bedroom where Aznaro de Zaniçeras lay in a featherbed propped up on silk pillows below a crucifix that adorned the wall. Señor de Zaniçeras, who'd seemed strong and masculine all of Vidal's life, now looked emaciated with an illness that left his body weak and his breath labored. With the lavender curtains closed shut and the room lit only by candles, the atmosphere felt as dour as if Catalina were sitting shiva for a man who had not yet died.

"Come, Señor de Zaniçeras," Vidal said. "It is a new year, and we have a new king and queen. Let us bring some sunlight into this room." Vidal drew the curtains, flooding the room with the silver light of the winter sky and the piercing brightness of the snowcapped Sierra Nevada mountains beyond the city walls. The celebratory sounds of drums and cheers traveled faintly over the ochre rooftops, allowing him to feel like he was still involved in the celebrations, only at a distance.

Vidal examined Señor de Zaniçeras while Eliezer stood beside an armoire that overflowed with clothes half-tucked into a drawer, observing the patient with the concentration he used to comprehend the Kabbalah. As Catalina had reported, Señor de Zaniçeras wheezed and coughed phlegm, unable to fill his lungs with the air needed to respond. Vidal put his ear to the patient's bare chest.

"Can he be cured?" Catalina asked.

"He's phlegmatic. Common for this season, but his case is severe." No one dared address that Sarah died from the same symptoms. Except for the anniversaries of her death when the family pilgrimaged to her grave, they spoke of Sarah rarely.

"Will it kill him?"

"What is it I always tell my patients?"

"We must remain hopeful. But you need to be honest."

"At the moment, I'm uncertain whether he'll recover."

"We can give him a remedy to improve his breathing," Eliezer said.

Vidal glanced at his son as if to signal a warning. "What did I tell you about suggesting treatments in front of a patient?"

"She's my sister."

"Señor de Zaniçeras is your sister as well? I hadn't known."

"Apologies, Father."

"We'll do what we can," Vidal told Catalina. "I would give him sumac but we've been short on medical supplies since the siege. I'll give him a remedy to ease his pain and dissolve the phlegm."

"As I suggested," Eliezer added, eager to receive any credit he felt owed.

"Enough, Eliezer. No one likes a brash doctor."

"He's right, little brother," Catalina said.

Vidal removed vials of ginger, garlic, and lemon from his instrument case—the only herbs left to pillage from his wife's kitchen—and requested that Catalina fetch a cup of water to dissolve the ingredients into a remedy. Eliezer produced a sponge he'd dusted with opium that morning and when Catalina returned with the water, he moistened the sponge and asked the patient to inhale. As Señor de Zaniçeras took in the opium, the sound of his breathing grew less obstructed.

Catalina took her leave while Vidal administered the remedy and Eliezer packed their supplies. They met her in the sitting room at the front door of the house where she mopped boot marks from the stone floor.

"Has his breathing improved?" asked Catalina.

"I assure you, he's comfortable."

"Will you stay for breakfast?"

"We don't eat with our patients' families."

"Please. I hate to think of either of you going hungry." Along with medical supplies, food remained scarce. For a week, Vidal's family had eaten dinners of asparagus and olives. But with the siege ended, the knot of hunger in his belly would soon loosen. He heard his son's stomach growl as well.

"If there's anything you can spare, we'd be most grateful," Vidal said.

"My father-in-law just slaughtered our last sow." Catalina backed away as if anticipating for her father to decline. "I could offer you a link of sausage…"

"You know we cannot eat that."

"Surely God will understand when there's so little to go around?"

Eliezer put his hand over his mouth as if pretending that only Catalina would hear him. "Fetch us some fruit."

"Of course. Apologies, Father."

Once she left, Vidal told his son he needed to have a word with Catalina in private and asked Eliezer to wait outside.

"Might it be relevant to my training?"

"No. And don't question me again."

Eliezer resumed the role of obedient apprentice and left his father. The boy was now seventeen and quickly becoming an expert at diagnosing symptoms and recommending the best treatments, but was still clumsy when it came to bedside manner.

When Catalina returned with apricots and slices of bread, Vidal asked her to keep their conversation confidential from her in-laws. "In your church, has your priest addressed any rumors regarding Ferdinand and Isabella's plans for the Jews of this city?"

"Not at all. What have you heard?"

"I've heard nothing."

"Something must have provoked this question."

"Merely curiosity."

"So you're asking about church gossip, Father?"

"I'm asking if you have any reason to believe your mother, siblings, or I will face consequences for being Jewish under this new king and queen?"

"Gabriel told me a condition of the emir's surrender was that the Jews and Moors go unharmed," she said, repeating her husband's words.

His daughter was one of the most trusting people he knew. She even believed that the leaders of kingdoms known for their wicked history of the treatment of Jews would leave him undisturbed. Yet he could not blame her. She followed his word when she lived under his roof and now she followed the word of her husband. Neither of them ever wronged her, why would a king do otherwise?

"Honestly, I've heard nothing, Father. But if Gabriel or I hear anything we'll come to you right away."

Vidal thanked his daughter and returned to the business at hand, instructing her to give Señor de Zaniçeras a mixture of ginger, garlic, and lemon every other hour and to contact him if the man grew more ill. They said their goodbyes and he met his son outside.

Eliezer consumed the apricot as they hurried to the next appointment. "What did you ask her?"

"You are not a physician yet. That means I cannot tell you."

For the remainder of the day, they hurried from Bib Rambla to El Albayzín to make house calls. By midday, the procession had passed, and they crossed the unobstructed main road back into La Judería as locals swept the fallen carnations and horse manure from the stone streets. Wherever they walked in the city, La Alhambra loomed in their view of the sky. The stone-built palace was the size of a small town and so entrenched in the side of Sabika hill that it seemed to have sprouted out from the mountain it rested upon. The sound of the procession now came from the palace itself, but because towers and houses obstructed even the road to the entrance, Vidal saw no sign of man, horse, or sigil.

Although he'd never know how they altered the emir's former palace, the idea of new rulers occupying the sacred Alhambra made him uneasy. Simply because his daughter knew nothing did not mean that Vidal's suspicions were unfounded. He wanted to ask every converso and Catholic he knew—his patients, Catalina's family—but imagined he'd seem mad for bringing up such a topic. This was not appropriate to discuss, especially when he had no evidence other than a feeling in his stomach and rumors of horror stories in faraway cities. The Articles of Capitulation proved his theory false. It was absurd to believe that the new monarchs would punish him for his faith or for his residence in Granada. Their armies had fought for control of Granada for nearly a decade and now found themselves exhausted, depleted, and in charge of a new kingdom. The monarchs were undoubtedly concerned with how to get supplies through the mountains, how to run the economy, how to govern the Moors, and how the irrigation system worked. He doubted they'd think to ask the emir anything before they banished him. Yet he should worry about his faith? He laughed every time he asked himself the question. What difference would it make? He was one man in a city of thousands.

Chapter Three

In the months that followed the arrival of the monarchs, Vidal watched Granada transform from a Sultanate to a Catholic Kingdom. One afternoon, while passing through the mirador at the summit of El Albayzín, he looked across the Valley of the Darro to see workers erecting a crucifix on the highest tower of La Alcazaba, the old stone fortress at the forefront of La Alhambra. A week later, he found himself in line at the money changer's bench in Plaza Bib Rambla to trade his gold dinars and dirham coins adorned with Arabic script for maravedis and reales embossed with the quartered sigils of Aragon, Castile and León. With supply lines reopened, he used the new coin to purchase meats, fruits, and grains imported from the neighboring kingdoms to replenish the necessary herbs and tools needed for his medical practice.

The sound of Castilian gradually overtook the more common tongue of Arabic. Every day, he noticed new vendors and faces in the streets, as people from throughout the Iberian Peninsula flocked to Granada to take up residence in the city and its surrounding towns. Fresh bread from the new bakers overwhelmed the scent of lemon trees when he walked in the street. The water level of the Darro River diminished as new farmers drew from it to grow their crops. He found himself late to call on patients every time the construction of a new church obstructed a plaza that'd been on his route since the years he apprenticed under his father. Where he'd once tracked his day by the number of times the adhan was recited by the Moors throughout the city, he now monitored the number of times a church bell tolled on the hour.

None of his concerns about the monarchs' intentions toward his faith came to pass, but rumors spread throughout La Judería that cooking with olive oil would be met with punishment—though no neighbors or friends could declare that they encountered any consequences for cooking this way. He would have switched to lard if not for the kosher restrictions; thus, he ordered his family to close all the windows and doors at night, for he did not want the smell of oil of all things to break the peace established between their neighborhood and the new rulers.

More soldiers arrived in the city, and the monarchs enforced a strict curfew that required all Granadinos to be home between the hours of sundown and sunrise. Though it seemed a punishment at first, in synagogue, Vidal joked with his neighbors that they should view the curfew as an accommodation, as it complimented the hours they must remain home for the Sabbath.

With this newfound time in the evenings, Vidal studied the Torah with his youngest son Asher, whose bar mitzvah would occur in August. Though twelve years old, Asher had the height and frame of a child half his age. Vidal had conducted dozens of tests to determine if his son might indeed be a dwarf, but Asher matched no descriptions or symptoms Vidal found in any medical text. The boy simply detested eating long before the siege took food off the table and never sat still unless it was time to sleep. Vidal could only determine that Asher expounded so much energy on a daily basis that his body retained no more to grow.

They sat beside each other at the family's chestnut wood table, worn and eroded from nearly a century of use, to analyze and rehearse from a prayer book by candlelight. The rabbi had assigned Asher an intriguing haftorah portion from Numbers, the story of Moses sending twelve spies into Canaan. Though Asher had learned Hebrew, practically raised on it along with Ladino, Castilian, and Arabic, he struggled to pronounce the words with the hard H sounds from the back of the throat and whenever he encountered an א, he pronounced the aleph like a Castilian N, arguing he could not tell them apart.

"No, no, no, Asher. The aleph signals the vowel that accompanies it. It's not meant to be read as a letter in its own right. This is the first thing they taught you in school."

"If I'm not supposed to speak it except in prayer, why learn Hebrew at all?" Asher bounced and wiggled in his seat as if he were trying to invent some new form of chair dance.

"Reread it from line twenty-six."

"If God knows what I'm trying to say, what's it matter if I say it wrong?"

Vidal could tell by the scarlet color of the boy's cheeks that Asher didn't care about the answer, and was only looking for a way for his father to dismiss him. He'd not so easily fall into the boy's trap.

"If you read the Book more carefully, you wouldn't ask such nonsense."

As Vidal ordered his son to continue, Bonadonna entered from the courtyard. She'd taken a bath in the bucket outside and though she wrapped her hair in a towel, water trickled down her neck into her red qamis. The bathwater flushed her face, making her olive skin glow in the candlelight. She was five years Vidal's junior and was married to him in a betrothal arranged by both their parents against both their wishes when she was only fifteen. Even though she'd bore five of his children and wore the hips to prove it, in the glow of the candlelight she still looked as youthful as the day they were wed. But he tried not to dwell on her physical appearance. Since Sarah's death, she'd shown little interest in intimacy, as if fearful that even a suggestion of lovemaking would bring another child into the world they would not have the skill to raise to adulthood.

"What's the matter, Asher?" she asked. "Why don't you want to study?"

"It's boring. Why do I need a bar mitzvah? What difference does it make?"

"Don't you want to be a man like your father and brother? Or do you want to be a boy forever?"

Asher groaned as if she'd beat him at a game of chess in two moves. "A man…"

Bonadonna put a hand on Vidal's shoulder. "Be patient. He's never going to learn with you screaming at him."

"Patience is why he hasn't improved."

"For someone who sees patients every day, you certainly have little of it yourself." He knew she was kidding, even if all of his wife's jests carried an air of truth.

"If you don't like my approach, why don't you help him?"

"You and I both know a woman cannot help with rehearsals for a young man's haftorah."

"Our new queen might say otherwise."

"I'll take my leave; you need to spend more time with the children anyways."

Once Bonadonna departed down the corridor to their bedroom, Asher recited the next two lines without error, until his knowledge of Hebrew seemed to fall away as swiftly as one forgets a dream after waking and Vidal berated him to focus again. His wife was right that he needed to spend more time with the children, but whenever he attempted to do so, their actions reminded him why he preferred the company of his patients, where he could practice the work God put him on this earth to do, and work to save lives, rather than have a son like Asher challenge his authority. If he'd behaved like Asher with his own father, the man would have beaten and starved him—may he rest in peace. For Asher to go before the congregation and recite from the Torah as if he'd never looked upon the text in his life was Vidal's greatest fear, so much that some nights he had nightmares of such scenarios, and would wake up winded and covered in sweat. Once he realized the events that transpired were confined to his dreams, he thanked God and prayed for reality to unfold differently.

Once April arrived and brought with it the late setting of the sun, a jovial mood journeyed through La Judería. Vidal rejoiced that they would have more hours outside thanks to the curfew's association with sundown. On a spring morning after a brief rain, where the streets dried within hours once the clouds' evaporation gave way to the sun, and the peach trees bloomed and the orchards bore their first figs and quinces of the year, Vidal enjoyed the rare opportunity to return home hours before the beginning of the Sabbath to nap and wash before dinner. But as he dragged the round cedar bucket filled with water into the courtyard guarded by the four walls of their house, and raised his physician gown covered in mucus, phlegm, and bile in anticipation of bathing beneath the blue sky, Bonadonna appeared in the doorway that led from the kitchen to ask where he'd placed the beef to cook that evening.

"I left you reales to make the purchase."

"You saw patients in the Albayzín. You could've brought the order home."

"I was very busy. There were many patients to see."

"You don't look busy with your bath."

"Bonita, I've been working since sunrise. You've been in the house all day; you can go to the market."

"Put aside the bucket, Vidal. We'll go to the butcher together."

She left the courtyard as abruptly as she'd arrived. He looked down at the pool of translucent water rocking back and forth in the bucket. The bath tempted him as much as an opportunity to bathe in the forbidden fountains of La Alhambra. But he knew his wife was right. His attention to his practice was no excuse to ignore the everyday responsibilities of life, a lesson she never missed an opportunity to remind him. He'd been a mere street away from the butcher when he called on a Moorish patient that morning. He could have purchased the beef needed for supper. He looked up past the courtyard walls, where the wind blew the clouds across the sky. A nice day for a walk with his wife.

He draped the soiled black gown back over his body and met Bonadonna by the front door, where she prepared to walk with Iamila, who'd reassumed the role of youngest daughter following Sarah's passing. The three made their way to the market along the gray stone-paved roads of La Judería so narrow that they could not walk beside each other at once. Iamila strode beside Vidal, holding his hand. She was only eight. She had curly hair and dark skin, looking like a spitting image of what Bonadonna had looked like when Vidal knew her as a child. Her short stature required

Iamila to hurry alongside Vidal, taking two steps for his one. As they walked, they made their way against a stream of Jews returning home from the city with meals wrapped in cloth and vegetables piled into wicker baskets to prepare their Sabbath dinners that evening.

"Can we go to the mirador today?" Iamila referred to the lookout at the summit of El Albayzín that hosted an eye-level view of La Alhambra from across the Valley of the Darro.

"We have no time."

"You promised last week you'd take her," said Bonadonna.

"We must prepare for the Sabbath. We'll take her to the mirador another time."

"But what if the queen leaves before we can go?" Iamila asked.

"You've already seen her." His daughter had glimpsed Queen Isabella during the parade that welcomed the new monarchs into the city in January and longed to see her again with the obsession of a lovestruck youth.

"But if she remembers me, maybe she'll ask me to be her handmaiden."

"I'm sure that role has been filled since her birth."

"It is exciting to think about, no? A woman ruling us. The most powerful woman the world has ever known. More powerful than Cleopatra. More powerful than Joan of Arc. Here, in our city."

"She is still only somebody's wife," Bonadonna said.

Something about Iamila's words struck Vidal. What would a woman do with the kind of power Queen Isabella wielded? Aside from the handful of edicts and decrees passed down from La Alhambra over the past four months, the queen had remained quiet in her new palace. After decades of war and conquering the Iberian Peninsula, would she finally rest?

They entered the dirt-covered alleyways of El Albayzín, pushing their way through crowds of patrons and vendors with long black beards who wore maroon-colored robes and white turbans. They went uphill passing storefronts with rugs hanging from their entryways, stained glass lamps imported from the Ottoman Empire available in every color imaginable, baskets of marigold, vermillion, and scarlet colored spices molded into piles that resembled the Great Pyramids built by his ancient ancestors, and the smell of teas that he'd never missed until their absence during the siege.

In a butcher's shop off the main street, where stacks of raw meat sat in baskets and a lamb carcass split rear to head was hung upside down spread eagle on the wall, Vidal ordered eggs, yeast, cooking oil, and meat. This butcher, in particular, had struck a deal with the rabbis of La Judería to sell kosher meat that'd been blessed in secret and provided a cut wrapped in white cloth, containing a glass vial of oil rolled within. When they paid the butcher with the silver real coins, he wished them a good Sabbath.

Once they returned home, Bonadonna kept the windows and doors shut to hold in the cooking scents. The thick, fatty smell of boiled meat mixed with cooking oil congested the air of the kitchen and wafted across the dining table at the other end of the room, down the corridor into the two bedrooms of the wooden house. The family took turns washing in the courtyard and dressed in their most elegant clothes: black gowns with gold trim and yellow caps for Vidal and his sons, and crimson dresses and cherry-colored headscarves for his wife and daughter. Once the sun set outside and the light that streamed through the courtyard windows faded into darkness, they sat for dinner to commence their weekly day of rest.

Bonadonna lit the fire from the hearth and gave the prayer for the lighting of the two Shabbat candles. "Barukh ata Adonai Eloheinu, Melekh ha'olam…" Though he stumbled through the pronunciation, Asher next recited the Shalom Aleichem and the Eishet Chayil, singing quietly, so that the soldiers down the street would not hear. "Shalom aleichem, malachei hasharet, malachei Elyon…" Vidal recited the Kiddush as he passed a cup of red wine around the table, then Bonadonna served boiled eggs, meat stew and bread, making trips from the cauldron on one end of the room to the table at the other. As they ate, they spoke of preparations for Asher's bar mitzvah in the month of Elul—August, as their new rulers called it.

"Will you be ready, Asher?" Iamila asked. "Or are you going to make a fool out of yourself in front of the rabbi?"

"You only wait until it's your turn," Asher replied.

"I already know Hebrew. I don't need to study."

"Enough," Bonadonna said. "Asher will do fine. He's been studying very hard."

"I was terrified of my bar mitzvah," Eliezer said. "Everyone I ever met coming to the temple just to watch me. To judge and scrutinize every word that came out of my mouth."

"And you succeeded without a single misstep," Vidal said.

"Because I knew no matter how many words I had correct, it only took one wrong pronunciation to invoke the congregation's wrath."

"In truth, no one cares if you make a mistake," Bonadonna told Asher. "It's a celebration of you becoming a man, not an exam."

"Nonsense," Vidal said. "Our community knows the Torah better than they know their way home. Everyone will hear if you sing a false note."

"It was worse when our grandparents were still here," Eliezer said. "Be grateful Grandfather Yehuda and Grandmother Yona aren't alive to attend."

"Eliezer ha-Rofeh," said Bonadonna. "We raised you better than to speak this way."

With the wine in his belly, Vidal did not hesitate to look up and address God aloud. "Adonai, forgive my son, for he disrespects Your fifth commandment."

"It's 'Honor thy father and thy mother,' not honor thy grandfather and thy grandmother," Eliezer said.

"The latter is implied."

"A joke, Father. You know I miss them as much as anyone at this table."

Vidal addressed Asher, "It's only a couple more months of such intense study. Once you are through with your bar mitzvah, we will devote more time to your apprenticeship."

"Will I dissect my first cadaver this year?" Asher asked.

"We're doctors, not surgeons. We diagnose our patients and

treat them with remedies. Surgery is as different of a trade from a physician as a king from a magistrate."

"In that example," Bonadonna said, "the surgeons are the kings."

"Bonita, you insult me in front of the children?"

"Simply being truthful."

"So we won't be cutting anyone open?" Asher asked. "No amputating of any limbs or trepanning?"

"Trepanning? Where did you hear of such barbarism?"

"What's trepanning?" Iamila asked Eliezer, and when he whispered the answer into her ear, she stuck out her tongue at the definition. "You don't do that, do you, Father?"

"No physician I've met engages in such a practice." Was it possible that new doctors moving into the city might? He could not dwell on the idea and took another drink of wine to help his mind drift from the subject.

"Thank God I was born a woman. I do not have the stomach for such procedures."

"Worry not, Sister. You won't be the one doing the drilling," Asher said. "In truth, it will be quite the opposite."

"Asher!" Vidal and Bonadonna exclaimed. Truthfully, Vidal did not know how or where Asher acquired such a macabre knowledge of the world. The next time he was near Asher's school, he would need to have a word with the boy's teacher.

"God help the poor souls who become your patients," Eliezer told his brother.

"Finish your stew, then it's off to bed," Vidal said.

"Apologies, Father," Asher said. "But what if I want to be a surgeon?"

"Learn your manners first," Bonadonna said. "Then we can debate your profession."

"First, you will learn the ways of a physician," Vidal said. "Then, if you truly believe surgery is your calling, we will speak about arranging further apprenticeships."

"And what will I be doing as your new apprentice?"

Nothing pleased Vidal more than the opportunity to talk

about his work, especially when he could do it around the dinner table with his children as a captive audience, but as he was about to give his son an itinerary of the next five to six years, a knock at the door startled Vidal as if a tremor had shaken the table. With their feast laid out, he felt as exposed and unprepared as if someone was calling on him to answer the door while he bathed. A Sabbath dinner was not forbidden in Granada. Indeed, if a neighbor called on them, they would think nothing of the sight. But as curfew was in effect and no Jews wandered the streets after dark, he deduced that it must be a soldier or official from the city. Someone in need of a physician at best, someone who smelled the oil in their cooking at worst. If a Catholic looked upon their ritual, they'd view it as exotic, perhaps even a rebellion against the crown.

He ordered his children to extinguish the candles and Eliezer licked his fingers to snuff out the wicks with saliva. At the other end of the room, Bonadonna picked up the glass vial of cooking oil that rested on the stone counter beside the hearth and threw it out the window. Eight reales worth of oil shattered on the ground outside.

The knock came from the door again, louder and more insistent. As his eyes adjusted to the dark, he could tell Bonadonna was looking from the hearth to the window debating whether to throw the food out as well. It would assure that nobody could prove they'd cooked with oil, but as the Sabbath dictated that they perform no work until the following sunset, they would have nothing to eat until the next sundown. He ultimately gestured for Bonadonna to keep the cauldron where it was. Even if the caller saw no food, the smell would linger.

From the door came the sound of a man's voice. "Señor ha-Rofeh. Señor ha-Rofeh, it's Gabriel."

The voice of Catalina's husband was as welcome a sound as music. He patted the sweat off his forehead and ordered Asher to open the door. Gabriel stood at the threshold out of breath and sweating in the cold night. His smooth blond hair, usually combed and well-kept, fell over his face. He cradled a furled paper in his hand like a baton.

Vidal invited Gabriel inside, and once his eyes seemed to adjust to the darkness, Gabriel looked at the plates of stew on the table, a banquet for many by the standards of post-war Granada, and apologized for his intrusion.

"No apology necessary," Vidal said. "Sit with us. We have meat and bread—"

"Señor ha-Rofeh, if I could speak with you in private?"

"Is something wrong?" Bonadonna asked. "Is Catalina well?"

"No, Suegra, your daughter is well. Señor ha-Rofeh, do not think me brazen, but we must speak at once."

"Might this wait for another time? We are in the middle of dinner."

"I see that, but it will only take a moment."

If the situation was reversed, if Vidal needed an audience with Gabriel, he could not imagine interrupting the boy's prayer at church. He had half a mind to dismiss the interruption and send the boy away. But the trembling in Gabriel's voice and the way sweat trickled down his temples on a cool April night gave Vidal the same feeling in his stomach as when he'd watched the new monarchs' parade.

"Bonita, take the children outside and sing to them."

"Gabriel, what is happening?" Bonadonna asked.

"I'm sorry Señora ha-Rofeh. But if I may speak with your husband?"

Bonadonna detested the practice of forcing a wife outside when company called on a husband. That Gabriel interrupted the Sabbath would give her all the more reason to protest. But she seemed to sense—as Vidal did—that something must be very wrong. Gabriel came from a good Catholic family. He was not raised to intrude without notice.

She instructed the children to follow her into the courtyard. Vidal allowed Eliezer to stay, but when Asher made the same request, Bonadonna dragged him out by the wrist.

"Why, Father?" Asher asked. "With the women?"

"You are not a man yet," Eliezer said.

"Not until Elul," Vidal added.

Bonadonna closed the wooden door to the courtyard behind her. Through the shuttered windows came the sound of her singing "La Prima Vez."

La prima vez ke te vidi
de tuz ojos me 'namori
d'akel momento te ami
fina la tomba te amare…

At the table, Gabriel unfurled the paper, weighing down the four ends with pewter kiddush cups and silver shabbat candlesticks. "There have been rumors in Bib Rambla that the king and queen issued a new decree. I did not wish to alarm you with gossip, but I found this flyer being handed out by nuns at our church steps and could not wait to warn you. Can we have a little light?"

"We cannot."

"Señor ha-Rofeh, please."

"We cannot light the candles."

"I saw light from beneath your doorstep when I knocked."

"They were lit, but we extinguished them. We cannot relight them." Gabriel offered such a bewildered expression that Vidal wondered if the boy ever bothered to learn about his wife's faith before her conversion. The Sabbath not only forbade Vidal from reigniting the candles, but from asking another to light them on his behalf. "You understand, we were doing more than eating our Friday supper?"

"I know what the Sabbath is, and I know it can be broken in the event of an emergency."

"And is this such an occasion?"

"I believe it is."

Vidal reignited the candles with the flame from the hearth. Firelight bathed a decree written in Castilian calligraphy that bore the signatures of King Ferdinand and Queen Isabella and an impression of the seal of the monarchs in fresh black wax. As Vidal's eyesight lacked the ability to see in dim light, he asked his son to read it aloud.

"'King Ferdinand and Queen Isabella,'" Eliezer read, "'by the grace of God, King and Queen of Castile, León, Aragon, Sicily,

Granada—'"

"Yes, we know all that."

"'… to all Jews and all individual Jews of these places… salutations and grace.'"

"They address us?"

"'We have been informed that in these our kingdoms there were some wicked Christians who Judaized and apostatized from our Holy Catholic faith.'" Eliezer continued to read accusations made by the monarchs that Jews circumcised Christian children, fed Christians meat from ritualistic slaughters, and convinced Christians that there was no way but the law of Moses. The words argued that the perversion had caused great harm to the Catholic faith, leaving the monarchs no alternative, but to banish all Jews from their kingdoms. "'We resolve to order the said Jews and Jewesses of our kingdoms to depart and never to return, by the end of the month of July next of the present year. Under pain that if they do not perform and comply with this command, they incur the penalty of death.'"

The threat against his family would have sent Vidal into a fury if the decree did not leave him in disbelief. This could not be the truth; it must be some sort of joke. The Articles of Capitulation swore to protect them against this exact outcome. Passover was less than a month away. Might this be the monarchs' way of fooling their new subjects in honor of the upcoming holiday? A holiday their Christ had once practiced as well? Gabriel said he'd received the decree given out by nuns on the steps of a church. What sort of nun distributed decrees handed down by royalty?

Vidal brought his eyes down to the paper and the heat of the flames danced before his scalp. "What sense am I to make of this decree? Jews have dwelled in the kingdoms of Ferdinand and Isabella for nearly twenty years—centuries longer under their predecessors. Why force us out the moment they acquire Granada?"

"It says right here, Father. Because we circumcise their children."

"Who would believe such a lie?"

"My father knows clerics who work closely with the king,"

34

Gabriel said. "We could arrange for you to stay. All of you. You would only need to—"

"Convert?"

"They do not wish to expel anyone—especially a skilled physician. They only wish for people to cease spreading the law of Moses."

"Who is spreading such a law? When have any of us tried to convert any of you?"

"I am suggesting a possibility—"

"Did I ask you to convert when you married my daughter? Did she? We Jews don't partake in such aggressive tactics. That is why we live in La Judería. We keep to ourselves."

Eliezer acted as a shield to protect Gabriel from Vidal. "Father, please. We could have read this on a signpost on the way to temple tomorrow. Instead, he came to tell us. He wants to help."

Vidal attempted to compose himself, but he could no longer remain naïve to the reality that this decree was as official as the seal it bore. It loitered in his house, rested on his table, and carried the threat of death against his family—a threat made by foreign invaders who had done nothing to learn of the kingdom they'd conquered. The fate of his family made no difference to the monarchs; this threat was merely one step of many in their quest to conquer the peninsula. He remembered his conversation with Catalina the day the monarchs paraded into the city. Even the Catholics of Granada had known nothing of this broken promise, this undisguised hypocrisy, before this decree appeared. He could not fathom the idea of leaving Granada. He'd never gone far beyond the city walls and knew of nobody to go to and nowhere else to live. But to convert sounded equally impossible. God had blessed him with a brilliant mind, skilled hands to perform a respected profession, a grand house, beautiful children. To give up his faith would be the same as turning his back on God and all the fortunes He'd blessed upon him.

Bonadonna called from the other side of the door to ask if they were finished, and Gabriel declared that he needed to be off.

"No, my son is right. I blame you for none of this. Stay. Break bread with us."

"Thank you, Señor ha-Rofeh, but I must be getting back to my family." He requested that Vidal come to his house in the morning. "Perhaps you should bring Catalina the news."

"I will go to you after temple."

"And I will instruct my mother to leave the door open, so your Sabbath is not broken further."

Sabbath had no rules about opening doors, but educating Gabriel in the practices of his faith was the least of Vidal's concerns. Gabriel returned to the dark alleyway outside their door and his clothes blew in the wind tunnel created by the narrow neighborhood streets. The chill of the night air reached into the house, cold and moist when it made contact with the sweat that covered Vidal's neck and armpits. Being a physician made him perturbed by many aspects of life, but living without a home was never one of them. He was born with a roof over his head and expected to die with a roof over his head, that he or his family might live without a home had never before struck him as a possibility.

After he thanked Gabriel and shut the door, Bonadonna returned from the courtyard. "What is going on in here? Why have the candles been re-lit?"

In a most uncommon change of practices, Vidal allowed their children to eat dinner in their bed chambers while he and Bonadonna sat over the decree so that she could read the monarchs' words before the candles thawed into melted wax.

"It cannot be," she said. "We have lived here our whole lives. Our parents are buried here. Sarah—"

"I know. If we leave, we say farewell to her bones forever."

"But if we leave, where do we go?"

"Portugal is the last kingdom in the peninsula not under their rule."

"Portuguese is a difficult language to learn."

"Perhaps Italy? Our tongues are more similar."

"We would need to go through Aragon, Francia... We would never get there by August."

"Perhaps a boat?"

"I hear they are dangerous. All of us on a boat? What if it sinks? Perhaps we should consider the alternative."

"Convert? Bonita, for you to make this suggestion so casually. We have not even explored our options."

"What options, Vidal? All our options are right here in front of us. We cannot leave Granada; we've lived here our whole lives. Our home is here. Your patients are here."

"And what of my Jewish patients? They will be leaving as well."

"Our faith will not protect us in a new country any more than it can here. We'd have nowhere to live and not a coin to our names. We cannot do this to the children."

"We cannot raise them Catholic either."

"It's already worked for one of our daughters. Catalina seems content."

Bonadonna came from a devout Jewish family. Her father, an accountant, had managed the finances of the synagogue. Once she became a mother, she tutored the children in Hebrew after school, kept a kosher home, and always woke earliest on Sabbath morning to prepare the children for service. For her to suggest giving up everything at the first sign of a threat made Vidal question if he knew his wife of nineteen years as well as he'd assumed. If she was not a Jew, who was she?

"My wife, how am I hearing this from you?"

"I don't want to convert any more than you do, but this is the only option that makes sense for our family."

"I disagree. I see many options."

"It is dangerous outside these walls. At least in Granada, we know what threats exist. Our children are safest in our home, not in the wilderness."

Vidal understood her rationale. He'd never ventured far beyond Granada's walls and did not know what sort of landscapes nor bandits might dwell outside civilization to bring harm to a family of traveling Jews. But to convert, to turn away from his faith? It would not only force him to go against everything he believed and stood for, but bring new dangers as well. There had been talk several years ago of the slaughter and drowning of conversos in a river in Toledo, proof to him that it was safer to remain a Jew than convert. He needed to make a choice, but the decree offered no options that would ensure his family's safety. It shamed him that if this were a matter of a patient's ailment, he'd know the solution within moments, but with his family's lives at stake he saw no clear solution. When the other fathers of Granada learned of this decree, would they feel the same? "Tomorrow, we'll go to temple, and there we will find our answer. If the entire community is to leave, then I think it wise to leave with them."

"And if they think it wiser to stay?"

"To suggest we apostatize minutes after learning of the decree? I dare not speak the words."

They finished dinner in silence. As he lay on their straw bed in the dark that night and listened to the belabored snores of a woman who'd eaten too soon before sleeping, he recalled a story his father had once told him. When he was ten years old, he had spent the day exploring Granada with his friends. He looked up at the Nasrid Great Mosque and La Alhambra and envied the Moorish buildings for their extravagant size and architecture, much grander than his school or synagogue. When he came home, he went to his father's table—the same table where the decree still lay—and asked why the Moors' buildings were so much grander than the Jews'. "Because we live in an Islamic nation." "Why don't we live in a Jewish nation?" "No such place has existed for nearly 1,500 years." His father told him the story of the Roman invasion of Jerusalem, the destruction of the Second Temple, and the banishment of the Jews from the city. How a small band of Jews sailed from the easternmost banks of the Mediterranean Sea and settled among the Muslims in the Iberian Peninsula. "The peninsula became our home, and our ancestors have prospered in the city of Granada for more than a millennium."

The sentence echoed in Vidal's mind over the sound of Bonadonna's snores. He looked up at a bedroom ceiling enshrouded in darkness. More than a millennium. And now they would be banished again.

Chapter Four

They misted rose water and lemon juice over the outfits they'd worn the night before, and as Vidal left home with his family, they exited the narrow alleyways of La Judería to walk along a street lined with lemon trees that led to a synagogue nestled along the banks of the Darro River. The sun rose over the peaks of the Sierra Nevadas and the first hint of a warm spring lingered in the brisk air, making the previous night feel no more real than a bad dream. Other men from their neighborhood walked beside Vidal with their families, emerging from the alleyways and side streets like reinforcements accompanying a king into battle. How could they be expected to leave? This was their home; they walked beside their neighbors to prayer, the same as every Sabbath before. Though the decree remained scrolled and pocketed under his gown, Vidal believed that somehow the monarchs would change their minds. Somehow, his community would be allowed to stay.

People congregated at the synagogue doors where their clothes of bright cerulean and vermillion wool contrasted with the modest laid brick of the temple, unpainted but identical to the color of wheat. High windows the shape of horseshoe arches that adorned the second story of the structure made the temple look as Moorish as a mosque at a moment's glance. An iron Star of David adorned the wall above the wooden double doors, doors that were all but unseeable behind a crowd gathered at the entryway. Where men and women usually separated before entering temple to sit in respective sections of the congregation, they instead intermingled at the threshold as if the interior were too crowded to admit additional people.

Vidal pushed his way through the crowd and peered between the shoulders of two men a head taller than himself to witness the lewd act carried out on the door. The ancient oak splintered at its center from an iron nail with a head the size of a man's fist hammered into the wood. The monarchs' decree hung from its shank.

"What does it mean?" people murmured to each other. "Read it again." "It cannot be." "There must be a misunderstanding." The decree had seemed real in his home, like a rat Vidal found scurrying through the kitchen. But now the rat had been set loose to overtake La Judería like a plague. Gabriel had come to warn him. Why had he not gone to warn his neighbors? Why had he waited to let them find out this way?

Asher tugged on the sleeve of Vidal's gown. "Father, what does it mean?"

Vidal became so occupied by the decree that he forgot to share the information with his youngest children. Even if he'd shared the threat posed by the decree, were Asher and Iamila old enough to understand? His son stood beside him a head shorter, looking up with the worry of a child who knows little of the world. Could this boy comprehend what the words handed down by the monarchs meant? "Nothing that concerns you."

"Does it say we don't have to go to temple today?"

"Would that please you?"

He could have screamed fire; nobody broke their eyes from the decree until the synagogue doors opened inward and Rabbi el Barchilon emerged from the atrium. "Enter, enter! I have news to share. All will be explained inside." The rabbi was dressed in the same ceremonial clothes he wore every Sabbath: black robes adorned with a tallit and white cap. The clothes reassured Vidal that things would not seem so dire once they sat to pray.

The crowd soon funneled through the entryway, taking a last look at the decree the way passersby stop to spy on an argument in the street, before entering the synagogue. While Bonadonna and Iamila took their place in the mechitza on the second level of the synagogue, Vidal sat in the congregation of 150 men below beside Eliezer and Asher. He'd come to this synagogue every Sabbath since he was an infant, yet this was the first time he stopped to embrace its beauty. The rabbi approached a wooden bimah placed before a stucco wall with three keyhole-shaped niches that housed the ark. Colonnettes ran along the synagogue walls beneath Hebrew letters branded into wood that served as crown molding. He'd always taken this place for granted. If they left, they would somehow need to bring this synagogue with them. A place of such beauty could not be left behind.

"I know you are all frightened by what you have read on our synagogue doors," the rabbi said. "Times are uncertain and perhaps you are tempted to ignore the threats made by our new monarchs. But I assure you that what we read is real and irreversible." The rabbi recounted a tale he'd overheard the previous day from a wealthy Portuguese man who had come to Granada to stop the expulsion. The man met with King Ferdinand himself and offered a fortune to allow the Jews to remain. The offer tempted the king— "For I do not truly think King Ferdinand to be an enemy of our people," said Rabbi el Barchilon. Yet before an agreement could be reached the Grand Inquisitor, the monarchs' confessor himself, threw a crucifix at the king's feet and cried out: Judas sold our Lord for thirty pieces of silver. His Majesty is about to sell it again for thirty thousand. At that moment, King Ferdinand's mercy left him, and his decision to expel the Jews was determined. "We know now that nothing will change their minds," the rabbi continued. "In the coming weeks, we must all make difficult decisions. Where to go. What to do. For what reason we will choose to leave. If it is God's plan for us to stay, then it will be decided. But I urge you, please, make haste in your decision. As Moses stood up to Pharaoh, as King David faced Goliath, we must all find our courage. We must not hesitate to take action, as the moment now calls upon us."

Asher gave Vidal such a look of betrayal that he imagined the boy might murder him in his sleep. But was it wrong to shelter his son? Or naïve to hope this decree might be overturned? He waited for the rabbi to break into laughter and tell the congregation that this was a great lie, a way for the monarchs to introduce them-selves to La Judería that demonstrated their power while exem-plifying their aptitude for mercy. Why this would happen, Vidal couldn't be sure. He'd known Rabbi el Barchilon since the man was his schoolteacher. The rabbi was not one to carry on with jokes, and Vidal only recalled seeing the man chuckle—often with reluc-tance—when reading from select passages of Genesis or Deuter-onomy. But for the rabbi to simply admit that they leave felt false as well. Jews left their homes throughout history, but the Torah also preached that they resist. It also preached that they negotiate with tyrants, not merely surrender. This was their home. Not the Monarchs'. His!

Vidal could not simply stand up and start asking questions, so he waited with his boot heels tapping on the stone floor, trying to focus on the prayers they recited and sang every Sabbath morning since birth. Two men behind him whispered with impatient hisses in their voices.

"Flee? Sounds more like the rabbi is calling for an uprising." "Don't be a fool. If they can defeat the emir's army, we have no chance." The whispers continued around him. "How do we leave?" "Where do we go?" "They'll have to come to my house and throw me out." "Surely someone else can reason with them. Ferdinand can say no to one man; he cannot say no to us all." "They wouldn't truly kill us, would they? Why not make us convert by force?"

By the time the service concluded, the sun cast spotlights through the high windows onto the hats of the congregation, sig-naling it was already past one. Vidal leaped from his seat to address the rabbi, but even while he stormed down the aisle, the bimah turned into a sea of black gowns as men flooded the rabbi with questions with the fervor of the waves that'd once crashed down on the ark of Noah. Vidal prepared to wait and overhear answers given to others, when his path was barricaded by Shelomo Levin, his oldest friend, father to Eliezer's betrothed, and the only man in Granada who wore his fat with the pride of a nobleman dressed in his finest furs.

"Don't bother talking to the rabbi now. He's swarmed with

questions he doesn't know the answers to." Shelomo was not so large that his girth obstructed the aisle, for other men advanced around them to converse with the rabbi, but because of their relationship, and because Shelomo would provide a substantial dowry on their children's wedding day, Vidal could not simply spurn the most successful merchant in La Judería.

"How long have you known about this?"

"Unimportant. The council of fifteen will meet tonight." Shelomo referred to the eldest and the most influential men of La Judería. Vidal's father had once sat on the council, but since his death—sixteen years ago now—Vidal heard little of what occurred in the meetings, and nearly every member of the council had changed since his father's passing. "We request your presence."

"What do they want with me?"

"If we are to move our entire community, we'll need a physician's opinion. We meet at sundown."

"I no longer even break curfew for my patients—"

"Do you take us for fools? The meeting will be brief."

Vidal assured Shelomo that he would attend and by the time Shelomo cleared the aisle, the rabbi was no longer visible among the men who belabored him with questions. Though Vidal would soon need to address the same interrogations from his family, they could wait for answers until after the council meeting. As Vidal returned to his sons, Eliezer asked, "Aren't you going to find out where he's going?"

"Tonight. I've been summoned by the council of fifteen."

He expected Eliezer to act impressed, but his son only asked, "Do you think we'll follow the emir?"

"What would make you want to live under that coward again?"

"A coward he may be, but he kept us safe."

Vidal pushed his way through the crowd of women in the atrium, who flocked to the threshold of a prayer floor they were forbidden to cross in the hopes that ears which spent a lifetime trained in the art of gossip might pick up on the conversation their fathers, husbands, and sons were having with the rabbi. A blazing sunlight streamed through the exit doors beside where Bonadonna attempted to console Iamila's panicked questions. "Where are we going to go? I don't want to leave Granada. Why didn't you tell me this was happening?"

Bonadonna put her arms around Iamila as Vidal arrived. "What did the rabbi say?"

"I promise you, I will get my answers by this evening." He explained he'd been summoned by the council. "In the meantime, I must speak with Catalina."

"Are you going to tell her as much as you told us?" Asher asked.

"Tell us what?" Iamila asked. "Father never told us anything."

"Speak with Catalina, I'll handle these two," Bonadonna said.

Asher and Iamila looked at him as if they were reevaluating whether this was the man they wanted to call father. "I'm sorry, you shouldn't have learned of this from a rabbi's deresha." He announced he'd be home as soon as possible.

It was rare for a Jew to leave La Judería during the Sabbath and once he crossed the main road, he found himself in a world that looked no different than any other day of the week, yet seemed foreign mid-Sabbath. The people of Granada were working, the Moors selling jewelry, purses, and fruits in the corridor-sized bazaar La Alcaicería, while the Catholics sold armor, satchels, and meat in the open-air Plaza Bib Rambla. As he crossed a bridge over the waters of the Darro River, its cyan ripples glistening in the early afternoon sunlight, his unexpected presence in his traditional prayer robes broke concentration from even the most high-pressure sale.

In an empty plaza, he passed the locked iron doors of the Nasrid Great Mosque. Its towering stucco structure decorated with Moorish arches and painted bricks asserted it as an architectural feat superior to the synagogues and cathedrals of Granada. The monarchs could remove his family; they could demolish his temple. But what about the Moors? Would the monarchs destroy the great mosque as well? It was impossible to think they might destroy a place of such size and beauty. That the monarchs had not touched the mosque could mean they had no plans to convert the kingdom entirely. Perhaps this suggested they might overturn the decree as well.

He passed through the lemon trees to reach Catalina's home. He'd not been to the home since the passing of Señor Aznaro de Zaniçeras a month prior, but knew he would be welcomed for no physician was expected to cure the terminal illnesses brought about by a patriarch's old age. At the front door, he stayed his hand from knocking. Had Gabriel indeed kept it open? Once he pulled on a brass doorknob that held firm, he proceeded to knock.

Catalina's mother-in-law Marquessa de Zaniçeras answered the door, a woman so ordinary, who dressed in clothes so plain and drab, that Vidal had for years mistaken her as a nun before learning she was wife to one of Granada's most successful businessmen. Only the bulge of a second chin hinted at her wealth. When he told Marquessa he'd arrived to call on Catalina, she looked at him as if he'd interrupted her in the middle of a meal.

"Your son did tell you I would come today?"

She instructed him to remove his boots—although her shoes were well-worn with the remnants of dirt and dust—and escorted him through a house that smelled vaguely of pork cooked the previous night out to the courtyard. An abundance of bushes, flower beds, trees, and a fountain inhabited the yard, a personal Eden compared to the stone patio at the center of Vidal's home. At the far end of the courtyard, Catalina chased a brown feathered hen before lifting it into her arms like a newborn. To see her working made the sights of the Granada streets seem normal by comparison. For the first fifteen years of her life, Saturdays had been Catalina's day of rest. Now, they were her day of work.

Catalina wore a simple green dress covered by an apron the color of turmeric. Only two weeks earlier she'd come to him with news that she was expecting a baby, his first grandchild. Though he knew she was too early into her pregnancy, he glanced at her stomach with the expectation that she might show.

"Catalina!" called Marquessa.

"Yes, Mother?"

"You have a visitor."

"Come inside," Vidal said. "We must speak."

Catalina handed the chicken to Marquessa and led Vidal inside to a sitting room where a fireplace was carved from walls made of stone. Cups of gold sat displayed on an oak table—all treasures from her father-in-law's adventures abroad. Vidal pulled open the velvet curtains imported from the Timurid Empire, letting in sunlight that reflected off the white stone of the nearest house and presented her the decree unfurled from within his gown.

"Has your husband shared this with you?"

"No, but he did mention that you'd call on me today."

"Why don't you read this and then we'll speak?"

"I cannot read."

"What sort of lie is that? One does not forget how to read."

"Mi suegra prefers I do not."

He disapproved that the de Zaniçerases forbade his daughter to read, but an argument would need to be saved for another time. He read the decree aloud, and as he read, he tried to ignore the sounds of squawking that came from the kitchen, of bone snapping, and of flesh ripping as Marquessa decapitated the chicken. He concentrated on the decree, trying to imagine how it might sound to her ears, glancing at her face to measure her reaction.

"Who gave you such a horrific letter?"

"It was not given only to me. By now, it covers the city."

"But it must be a lie. Anyone could forge the king and queen's signatures. Can we be certain this is their official sigil?"

"I assure you it's real. The rabbi told us all this morning."

"I promise you, I heard nothing of this in our church. Father, what are you going to do?"

"I haven't yet decided."

"But surely, you will convert." She spoke the words as innocently as if she'd asked him to stay for dinner. Should he say her husband presented the same offer? Judging her reaction, she seemed to know nothing of Gabriel's late hour visit.

"I cannot make such a decision lightly."

"What does the rabbi say?"

Vidal glanced at the kitchen doorway for any sign of

Marquessa. If the woman disapproved of Catalina's reading, he doubted she would approve of Catalina questioning the rabbi. "He did not speak of it as an option."

"What other choice do you have?"

"To leave."

"And go where?"

"I ask myself that same question."

"Father, I know you are proud and that asking you to give up your faith would be like asking you to give up your practice. But if you do not give up Judaism, you'll forfeit everything else."

"In Granada, yes."

"Your Catholic and Muslim patients will need you. They won't miraculously be cured of their ailments in three months' time. There's no reason to make such a sacrifice."

"This is not a decision for you to make."

"Then let me help you. Señor de Zaniçeras has seen the world. He's seen Africa, Asia. Beasts the size of houses. Cities so large they cannot be contained within walls. That is no place for you, Mother, or my siblings. I beg of you to stay here. Stay where it is safe."

The most significant decision he'd ever faced in his life seemed to be no decision for his daughter. He supposed her simple answer to the matter shouldn't surprise him. When she'd married Gabriel, she'd gone willingly into the arms of the Catholic church, leaving Judaism behind as nothing but an afterthought. He had raised her to be a Jew, taught her the Torah. How did she dismiss her old religion so casually? He supposed she did so because her life had always been lived at the service of others. A daughter, an older sister, a nurse, a wife, soon a mother. She had no reason to debate whether her family should convert, for she perceived the king and queen had already made the decision for them. "I assure you, I have everyone's best interests in mind."

"You'll like Catholicism. Our faiths are not so different."

"But those differences are vast. Catholics do not observe the Sabbath, they worship Christ as a false idol, waiting for the second coming of a Messiah when we have never had a first. It's absurd."

"But Christianity has fulfilled a remarkable task father. It has brought people from all over the world to accept God. Adonai will still be your God. I won't lie, it's taken time to adjust to the new laws, the customs, not to mention becoming familiar with Latin at such a late age. But if you can accept Christ into your heart, he will guide you through the process. And if you accept Christ into your heart, you may stay."

The decree gave him three months to either sell his home and pack his possessions or step through a cathedral door with a request to be baptized. Could he see the latter through? It would mean admitting that his entire life, every belief he held was a lie. Every Torah passage he studied, every book he read, mere fiction in the eyes of his new faith. He would not only need to alter his thoughts and beliefs, but those of his family as well.

"I will think on it," Vidal said. He thanked his daughter and announced that he needed to be off, promising he'd speak to her once he learned more. Once he left her, he meant to return home. But all that awaited him would be questions to answers he did not possess. He instead spent the afternoon walking through Granada until the rays of sunlight gave way to a night sky. While the final hours before the Sabbath concluded usually brought him excitement for the week ahead, the sun now seemed like a friend who abandoned him in his moment of need. He was one of the first to arrive at the synagogue, as many members of the council of fifteen stalled the resumption of business until Sabbath concluded, despite it ending concurrently with the beginning of curfew. As they could not be found outside their homes after dark, the men wedged themselves inside the rabbi's windowless study, a room at the back of the synagogue behind the stucco wall that contained the Ark of the Scrolls. A lone candle from the rabbi's desk illuminated the room, its fire so soft that the men's black robes consumed its light, giving the appearance that the council was comprised of fifteen bearded and balding heads floating in the shadows.

Vidal stood at the back shoulder-to-shoulder with Shelomo Levin and listened to the rabbi recite his plan from behind his desk: the rabbi had a brother who lived across the sea in Fez, another rabbi with a synagogue. He'd already dispatched a letter to his brother by way of a messenger and was confident that the Jews of Fez would welcome them. "We have no other choice," the rabbi said. "We must sell our belongings and depart the city at once."

The council replied with all matters of opinions: "They should be the ones to leave. Not us." "Do not be a fool. They will never give up Granada." "We should stay. Fight them off!" "Fight them off with what? Your shovel and hoe?" "The soldiers have fought in this kingdom for a decade. Now they waste away their days in the streets. They are bored. They are hungry. They are tired." "Thus, they would invite an uprising." "Their morale is low. They are weak and we may beat them…"

The rabbi called for quiet and the arguments faded to murmurs. "I know we are all frightened. But that is no reason to be reckless. Presume we were to fight them; we were to convince the Moors to drive the soldiers out of the city. Even if that were possible, we would never breach La Alhambra."

"We could starve them out," said a council member.

"Starve them? I guarantee they have reserves. And in the time it would take to starve them, their armies would cross Las Alpujarras and annihilate us. We have all heard the horrors of the violence against the Jews of Sevilla. I do not wish for anyone of you—or your families—to meet that fate."

"You suggest we flee like cowards?" asked Shelomo Levin. "Give up our homes without a fight?" Vidal could never before recall hearing Shelomo speak with uncertainty in his life.

"Do not think of this in such terms. Did the Hebrews have three months to leave Egypt? Or Jerusalem? We are blessed, for the decree dictates that no Jew can be harmed on our exodus from Granada. God has provided us with three months of safe travel. Let us not spit in the face of His gift." Though an opinion teetered on the tip of each man's tongue, nobody dared speak against the rabbi. "Now, if this matter is settled, I have invited a guest to our meeting. Dr. ha-Rofeh knows the health of this community as well as anyone. How might we prepare ourselves for such a journey across the sea, Vidal?"

Rabbi el Barchilon addressed him by his first name as if Vidal were still his student. He knew the rabbi only meant it as an endearment, yet his name made him feel like a boy who'd wandered into a council of men. He'd treated nearly every council member at one point in his life. They were old and frail, with bad knees, weak hearts, and portly bellies. He would not be performing his physician's duty if he ignored the option in the best interest of their health.

"Rabbi, what if we were to convert?"

Each man looked at him as if he had suggested they sell their daughters to the soldiers. "I cannot believe what I am hearing!" "Surrender our faith?" "Apostatize?" "Has he gone mad?" If he had not made the suggestion under the guise of a physician's treatment, Vidal imagined the men might tear their clothes in rage.

The rabbi called for quiet again. "Is it your plan to convert, Vidal?" He clasped his hands together, the way he always did when listening to a student speak.

"You asked what would be best for the health of the community. Please read no further into my suggestion."

"You are a wise man. No one on this council can pretend to do the work you do. You know texts of medicine as I know the Torah. You can read, so I imagine you know something of politics."

"Politics are for rulers and monarchs—"

"No, but they are for you as well. Aragon and Castile are skeptical of converts. They murder Jews and New Christians alike. Do you remember when I taught you about the massacres in Jáen and Córdoba?"

"I remember."

"The Catholics have developed sophisticated methods to know when we convert falsely, when we continue to practice our beliefs in secret. If you convert, if you choose to stay, I believe they will question the legitimacy of your conversion. And I do not need to tell you what consequences your health will face if the renunciation of our faith is judged false."

A phrase Catalina had spoken earlier echoed in his mind with such force that for a moment his vision went black as if the candle had burned out. *What does the rabbi say?* she'd asked. *Our faiths are not so different.* The de Zaniçerases were a powerful family, but not powerful enough to protect his daughter, not powerful enough to protect the child she'd soon bear. She could meet a fate as deadly as what befell the conversos of Toledo. If they were leaving, would she come with them?

"Forgive me, Rabbi. I have no intention to convert."

"Nothing to forgive. Many of these people will need treatment and care on the road to our new home. I hope you will choose to caravan with us."

Vidal announced that he intended to leave with them and volunteered what supplies were essential to ensure the success and health of the caravan. "Water is obviously the most cumbersome resource to transport, though I'm sure none of you need a doctor to explain why—"

The rabbi called for quiet, sparing Vidal from continuing to ramble, and the conversation turned to what day to leave. Nobody asked him to exit the meeting, making him feel like he'd become a new member of the council. A most prestigious honor, one that would have pleased his father. Yet the pleasure he would have gotten from it now seemed obsolete, for as long as he stayed in this study, he was wasting time. He only wanted to rush out the door, sell his belongings, flee, and deliver his family to safety.

Chapter Five

When Vidal returned home, Bonadonna was preparing a stew, steeping the air with the smell of meat, eggplant, and carrots. "What've you learned?" she asked.

Eliezer looked up from the table where he concentrated on mixing ginger and lemon. In the courtyard, Asher swung a stick through the air like a sword, no doubt dispensing of imaginary foes and committing regicide in his mind, but his sword arm went limp at the arrival of his father. Iamila napped under a wool blanket on the leather chair in the corner of the room. Stretched across her face was the look of a person who slept with the knowledge that unpleasantness awaited them when waking. Her hand twitched under the blanket. Vidal couldn't imagine someone as fragile as her cutting across mountains, sleeping on the ground, or going without food and water. He rocked Iamila gently by the arm and whispered her voice until she awoke, blinking and wiping drool from the corner of her mouth.

"Have I missed dinner?" she asked.

"No, but I would like it if you'd please come to the table."

Vidal's family gathered at the dinner table as if called to supper. He stood over them the way he did when they made the prayer for the candles, then explained in the voice he used to share diagnoses with his patients that the decision was final: once Rabbi el Barchilon's brother sent word, a caravan of Jews would leave Granada for Fez. He expected an outcry of questions and protests, but his family at first only stayed silent and looked at each other seeming to question whether they'd each heard the same story.

"Fez?" Bonadonna asked. "Is there a way to travel by land?"

"Only if God wishes to again part the sea for us."

"I'm not joking, Vidal. You would put our entire family on a ship?"

"We'll be safe. We'll travel with the rabbi."

"Rabbis cannot keep ships from sinking."

"Why would the ship sink?" Iamila asked.

"The ship won't sink," Vidal said. "We'll be very safe. And from what I hear, the passage from Málaga to the Maghreb is less than a day's travel."

"How long do we stay there?" Eliezer asked.

"That I don't know. We may never return."

"Unless the decree is overturned."

"Elie, what is it I say to my patients when I believe the outcome will be grave?"

"That you want to remain hopeful, but need to be honest."

"I doubt we will ever return home. You heard the rabbi, King Ferdinand's decision is final."

"Ferdinand is old," Bonadonna said. "Soon he'll die along with that wife of his and maybe then things will change."

"What about Sarah?" Iamila asked. "Will she come with us?"

"We'll dig her up," Asher said.

"Do not start, Asher," Bonadonna said. "No one's in the mood."

"If we leave, who will place rocks on her grave?" Iamila asked.

Eliezer whispered into Iamila's ear, "It's okay. That's not Sarah lying in the ground. Only a shell she no longer requires. She'll be with us in spirit."

"Maybe I'll stay and watch over Sarah's grave," Bonadonna said.

"We are all leaving together," Vidal said.

"This is too great a decision for you to make alone. You have no right to put your children or me through something so dangerous when we have an effortless alternative."

The children asked what alternative she spoke of.

"She's talking about conversion."

"What would you like to do, children? You should each get to decide. Do you want to risk your lives, pilgrimaging through mountains without food, water, and shelter, embarking on a treacherous journey across a body of water greater than anything we've ever seen? Or do you wish to stay here in our lovely home where it's safe?"

"Please don't burden them with your hesitation."

"You've already burdened them with your cowardice."

"Bonita, you know as well as I that the dangers you've described are nothing compared to the wrath of the Catholic church. I am your husband; I am their father; I say what we do and where we go."

"I will not be responsible for the burial of another child." Bonadonna sprung from the table and bolted down the hallway to close herself in their bedroom. A part of Vidal wanted to follow her, to convince her that even though leaving may sound dangerous in the short term, it was the only way to ensure the future safety of their family. But he could not delay putting his plan into action. Bonadonna would make sense of his decision eventually. Jews fled their homes to preserve their faith all throughout history. His wife would be no different.

Vidal waited for the tension to dissipate following her departure, then continued, "I only sat you down to inform you. I intended to do so with more reassurance than this, but I understand your mother is worried. I promise I will let nothing happen to you."

Iamila and Asher both exclaimed that they did not wish to leave. "I'll convert," Asher said. "I don't care."

"And you?" Vidal asked Eliezer. Would his firstborn, a man who had already been through his bar mitzvah, surrender his faith for the convenience of home as well?

Eliezer gestured to his younger siblings. "I'll speak to them."

"Good. It's late. We've all had a long day. Everybody get ready for bed."

"What about dinner?" Asher asked.

Vidal thought to call Bonadonna to pour the soup, but instead removed the clay bowls from the wooden shelf that hung from the wall out of reach of the cauldron's steam, and poured his children bowls of stew. As he ate with them, he asked that they begin to pack in the morning. They were to separate the family's belongings into three piles: one to take, one to sell, and one to abandon. He asked Asher to look for anything they could use to carry their belongings on the journey to the sea and Eliezer to help the women pack anything too heavy to carry.

"What about our patients?"

"I'll do the rounds on my own tomorrow. I suspect your presence will be more needed at the house."

Eliezer obeyed without hesitation. His son's absence would be ideal, as Vidal could not discuss with Catalina whether she might leave with Eliezer in his presence.

As the children retired to their rooms for the evening, Vidal took paper, ink, and quill from the drawer of a cupboard by the front door and composed letters to the extended members of his family. Both his and Bonadonna's parents were dead, but he had two younger sisters in Madrid and Toledo, and Bonadonna's older brother managed the finances of a synagogue in Córdoba. News of the decree had no doubt reached their cities. He imagined them as worried as he, scrambling to determine what to do and where to go. In his letter he informed them of his intention to journey to Fez and of his rabbi's relationship to the synagogue. He'd not seen their siblings since Eliezer was born. Might they reunite on the other side of the sea?

He left the letters by the front door to deliver to a messenger in the morning. Though the hour grew late, he did not bother to lay in bed beside his wife that evening, and instead reclined in the leather chair where Iamila had napped. It was nearly impossible to fall asleep in the sitting position—a deficiency that would do him no favors on the road to Fez—and as the temperature outside descended closer to freezing and the crisp air seeped through the windows like the long fingers of phantoms stretching to claw at his cheeks, he hugged himself tighter with a blanket that smelled of his daughter's hair. By the time he threw the blanket off himself in the morning, his eyes drooped and his mouth tasted of stomach acid.

He wasted no time gathering the letters, his physician supplies, and leaving to visit his daughter before morning rounds.

The walk through town displayed a Granada that contradicted sights of the day before. People going to set up their shops in the town square or embarking on errands they'd put off during the Sabbath congested the streets of La Judería, but the moment he passed the main road, the city became vacant, as all of Christian Granada packed itself into churches to pray to their Lord. Plaza Bib Rambla was vacant as if curfew had extended into the daytime. Even the fountain's water at the center of the plaza lay still in its basin. A church bell tolled in the distance and its sound traveled lazily through the calm air.

When nobody answered the door at the home of Catalina, Vidal deduced that the family had already left for church. How early did the church hold mass? The sun barely burned a hole through the cloudy morning sky. The church was a short walk further, at the western edge of town, the same church where Catalina and Gabriel had wed. The thought of his patients looking outside their windows and waiting at their doorsteps for his arrival made him hurry.

Halfway down a house-lined street, the road opened to a square that led to a white brick church with a lone bell tower, unremarkable compared to even the most modest mosques and synagogues of Granada. Although he felt the urgency to go inside and call on Catalina, he knew that if people saw a Jew enter with his great big cap and bulging gray beard the scene may cause a scandal—for Catalina if not himself. Catholic masses progressed with the duration of people who believed they'd earn their time back in the afterlife. He imagined he might be stuck waiting outside for hours. He paced in the empty stone square and every time he thought to check on the nearest patient, he imagined the congregation finally streaming out the church doors. That the bell continued to toll each hour only gave him false hope that it was signaling the conclusion of the service.

By the time the congregation poured out the front doors, sunburns marked Vidal's nose and neck, and he searched for a sign of his daughter or the de Zaniçerases in the crowd. He first spotted Gabriel's father, Gabriel Ochoa—or simply Ochoa as he preferred to be called—a man so tall that his head rose over the crowd like a duck that bobs on a lake's surface. The man's head was shaped like a brick and when Vidal imagined the appearances of the emperors of ancient Rome, he imagined they looked like Ochoa.

Ochoa pushed his way through the crowd at the sight of Vidal and as he emerged, Marquessa and Gabriel walked beside him.

"Dr. ha-Rofeh. I don't think I've heard of a doctor calling on a patient at church."

"On the contrary, I'm here to call on Catalina."

"He called on her yesterday," Marquessa said.

"Is everything all right?" Gabriel asked.

Vidal suddenly imagined himself a mad man: someone who sweats in the streets, sunburned, waiting uninvited outside a church for hours when the instrument case in his hand disclosed that he should be seeing patients. Ochoa must've noticed as well, for he requested that Marquessa leave them to speak with a neighbor's wife.

"You never let me hear the good gossip," she complained as she departed.

"Will my daughter be out soon?"

"She's in the middle of confession."

"I thought Catholics gave confession before mass?" Three years of service to Jesus and Catalina still found a way to remind people of her conversion. She fooled nobody.

"She prefers to go after. No competition for the priest's attention, she says. What's troubling you?"

Vidal looked one last time for the sight of Catalina on the church steps, for Ochoa would never entertain the idea of her leaving for Fez. But as the crowd dwindled in anticipation of the lunches that awaited them at home, he knew Ochoa—not Catalina—was the only one who could make this decision. "I believe she may be in danger." He explained what the rabbi had said and recited a brief history of the murders of converted Jews. "Catalina would be safer if she came with us to Fez." A prolonged silence followed his explanation that made his time waiting outside the church feel like seconds by comparison.

"You suggest I give up my wife?" Gabriel asked.

"I know the request is highly unorthodox—"

"Highly unorthodox? It's unspeakable."

Ochoa minded Gabriel to hold his tongue. "Vidal, you and I are both fathers to Catalina, and for that reason I am sympathetic to your cause. Remember that I have married off three daughters, and if I were never to see them again, I would be inconsolable. But I have faith that I married them off to good families who would never see harm befall them. So I ask you, do you have the same faith in me?"

"I mean you no disrespect—"

"Would we let harm befall Catalina?" Ochoa asked his son.

"Never," Gabriel said.

"There you have it. Is there anything else you wish to discuss?"

He recalled the nonchalant manner in which Catalina had spoken about his rabbi and compared their two faiths. Should the monarchs bring her in for questioning, he doubted she would fool anyone. And how would they perceive her child? As the child of a Jewish mother or a Catholic father? Yet he could not risk her life by telling Ochoa and Gabriel more about their conversation either.

"If circumstances for conversos deteriorate in this kingdom, if Catalina's past as a Jew becomes a threat to her, would you send her to live with us in Fez?"

"Have I not been a good husband to your daughter?" Gabriel asked. "Have I not been a good son-in-law? Going to you after curfew to bring news of the decree, I could have been whipped."

"I did not raise you to speak with such disrespect," Ochoa said.

"He is the one who disrespects me."

"Go back inside and wait for your wife."

"But Padre—"

"Do not debate me in public." Gabriel stomped his boot on the ground as he left and a thin cloud of dust rose around the heel. "I apologize for my boy's behavior."

"I did not mean to upset him."

"No apology is necessary. He knows he's not a real man, so he overcompensates with brashness and pride. My father was the same way."

"So was mine."

"Vidal, you have my word that if a soldier or priest so much as looks at Catalina wrong, I will send her to Fez."

"I fear that if someone looks at my daughter wrong, it will already be too late."

"You're frightened because of what they've already done. I understand. This decree is an abomination. You won't hear this from the simple-minded Christians who are indoctrinated by whatever dogma a priest spews at them as long as they can find a half-hearted way to relate it to Christ. But men like me understand."

"And I trust you, Ochoa. I'm most gracious for your sympathies, but if my daughter is in danger, a mere promise is not enough to put my mind at ease."

"What happens if she leaves with you? The legitimacy of her conversion will be forfeited and it may put all other conversos in the city at risk. Trust me when I say that if it comes to it, she will be the most precious cargo I ever shipped across the sea."

It was a surprising confession to come from Ochoa, a man who preferred not to speak except in matters related to business. But as Vidal was the father of his son's wife, and a man who would soon depart, he supposed Ochoa could risk speaking his mind. A mind that Ochoa made clear could not be changed during one conversation at noon.

"I have no doubt." Vidal thanked him, then left the square to deliver the letters to the messenger and begin calling on his patients. He'd need to find a way to call on Catalina another time.

As a new week began, Vidal and his family sorted the clothes, furniture, pots and pans, blankets, rugs, prayer books, and food into one of three piles as they prepared to leave home. The snow melted on the Sierra Nevada mountains and sultry air settled in the Granada valley. The rise of the temperature served as a warning that La Judería could not dally long in their plans to leave, for heat signaled the foreboding arrival of a season where their presence would not be unwelcome, but a crime. La Judería operated under the notion that they would go to Fez, although the rabbi never announced in temple services the reassurance that his brother was prepared to receive their community. Since they had no choice but to leave, Fez sounded as good as Rome, Lisbon, or Constantinople.

Every day, the Catholic and Moorish patients who Vidal called on told him they no longer required his services. "We've cared for your family for years," Vidal replied. He remarked that patients in many families were deathly ill and could not go without treatment. "At least allow me to check on them until I depart. I can educate a new physician of your choosing on their medical history." The families refused, and when he'd turn the conversation to payment for services rendered—a discussion he loathed for he knew it made him sound like the greedy Jew they all imagined him to be—they opened the door and demanded he and his son leave.

"The bastards," Vidal said, as they walked downhill from a house in El Albayzín. "They know we'll be gone soon, so they break their word freely with no consequences to their reputations." They descended an alleyway flanked by stone walls so tall and narrow that the sun could only shine down on them when it peaked at the sky's zenith.

"We should file a dispute."

"Before the monarchs' invasion, I would have gone to the magistrate, but now no such office exists, and if one did, I doubt it'd be designed to settle the financial matters of Jews. This entire town is turning into a city of misers."

"Father, calm your tongue." The bottom of the hill led them out to a stone street that lined the banks of the Darro River. With an hour before their next appointment, Eliezer suggested they go somewhere to collect themselves. As Eliezer was too young for a tavern and both of them too poor, they decided to sit in the grass of the riverbank. The soaring walls of La Alhambra on the far side of the Valley of the Darro concealed the sun and left them in a cold shade that reminded Vidal of autumn. Dew clung to the leaves of trees in the late afternoon hour and the roaring of the river's current drowned out the sounds of the city.

"Father, I find it honorable that you want to care for our patients until the end, but perhaps we should close our business now."

"I've trained you better than to think of our patients as business."

"I would never say this under other circumstances. But there's no reason to stay operational when our most grateful patients turn us away."

"The decree perceives us as monsters. To end my relationship with my sickest and dying patients—what sort of man would I be?"

"What sort of men are they for turning away physicians on the verge of living in the wild? I'd be willing to talk to the patients myself if you prefer not to face them."

"That would be cowardly, indeed. We help our patients until the end, get them the replacement physicians they need."

Eliezer didn't respond, and whether this resolved the matter or Eliezer simply acquiesced made no difference. Vidal heard nothing but the river running along the damp mud banks and the gentle breeze that lightly shook the tree branches. He'd passed this spot countless times in his life, always enjoyed its natural tranquility, but never thought much of it. What could be special about a part of a city he could visit any day of his life? Granada was only becoming special now as he realized that anything he did, whether walking through El Albayzín or sitting on the banks of the Darro, could be for the last time.

"Father, when we get to Fez, will you help me complete my training, so I may be a physician of my own?"

"The qualifications for what make a physician may be different in Fez. But I assure you, you're not meant to be my apprentice forever. Are you excited to leave?"

"Why would I be excited?"

"You more than any of us stand to build a life for yourself in this new land. You'll be a physician; you'll marry Shelomo's daughter—"

"I suppose that will be nice."

"You suppose? What sort of answer is this?"

"Truthfully, nothing excites me more—"

"Then say so. The girl has grown to be beautiful. I see the way she looks at you in temple."

"Father—"

"Don't be embarrassed. She'll be good for you. You'll make each other happy. You'll start a family of your own in Fez and all of this will be behind us."

"Do you think you and Mother will be happy again in Fez?"

"Your mother and I are plenty happy. She doesn't wish to leave Granada is all. She's worried about us on the road, as a mother should be."

"Father, forgive me for prying. I only ask because I'm about to be married myself. But I've noticed—"

"What's on your mind, Eliezer?"

"Ever since Sarah, you and Mother have seemed distant to each other. More like brother and sister than husband and wife. I already have two sisters. How do I make Tsipora happy as my wife?"

Vidal had not expected such a question from Eliezer. His own parents never liked each other, but he never dared address this with his father. The man would not have hesitated to whip him with a belt until certain the discussion was finished for good. But Vidal fancied himself a more tolerant father. He wanted curious children, the trait would make them better physicians.

"Even as I shattered the glass beneath my foot the day of my wedding, I knew little of how to make your mother happy. On our wedding night—"

"I don't want that much information."

"Let me finish." Vidal continued that when they retired to their bedroom the night of the wedding, he could not bring himself to lay a hand on Bonadonna. She offered to let him take her—best to get it over with, she said—but he was a physician apprentice trained to cause no harm. They decided to wait, and only managed to brave the awkwardness of spending the night together when they realized how equally miserable the arrangement made them. They laughed about and mocked their parents, so serious about their daughter's wedding that they'd sold her off like she was a prized horse. Over the years, that humor and laughter brought them closer as husband and wife. When they finally made love, they conceived Goyo. Once Bonadonna became the carrier of his child, true affection blossomed. It had stayed that way until Sarah's death. But unlike their mutual distaste for a wedding, a mutual feeling of guilt could not again bring them together. "There are few greater tests of marriage than the loss of a child. But I don't want you to worry that your marriage will be the same as ours, Eliezer. Your mother and I sought out a girl close to you in age, someone you could grow up knowing and caring for. We didn't want to thrust you into marriage with a stranger like we were. I'm sorry ours has not been a warmer household these past years, but I hope you and Tsipora will do more to bring warmth to your own."

"I hope so as well." Eliezer bit the inside of his cheek.

"Do not be a pig!"

"Apologies, Father."

"Please. I was seventeen not so long ago."

"I suppose that's why you let Catalina marry outside the faith as well? She and her husband seem happy."

Vidal grunted in the affirmative, but said nothing more.

For the rest of the week, as he called on whatever patients would see him, often Jews preparing for the journey to Fez or recent conversos, his wife and Catalina took Iamila and Asher to sell clothes, bedsheets, cooking supplies, and spices on a blanket that covered the floor of a plaza beside the main road. They sold off their finest robes and tunics for a tenth of the price they'd first purchased them, and could often afford to purchase nothing more than bread and carrots for dinner.

"Why are you selling our things at such enormous discounts?" Vidal asked. "Are you trying to make us too poor to leave?"

"Would it work?" Then she said that every one of their neighbors in La Judería sold their belongings in the plaza. "When everything is for sale, even the most precious belongings are worthless. Women sell jewelry to afford a meal, the deed to their house for bread." After she spoke, she'd look at him as if he were a child, a moment away from realizing that leaving and selling off their belongings for scraps was a dreadful idea.

"If everyone else is leaving, then you must realize they all perceive the situation as I."

"I see many frightened and confused neighbors. If some of us bothered to convert, there wouldn't be so much disorder."

"Once we're settled in Fez, things will be better."

"I certainly hope you're right."

After two weeks, the family saved enough reales to acquire a horse and cart. As he walked through La Judería on the eve of the Sabbath, Vidal passed families homeless in the streets who huddled in alcoves carved out of the white walls of alleyways, people who had sold their homes for too little too early and had nowhere to go until the caravan departed from Granada. Though he expected them to beg, they said nothing, looking away when he passed, admiring the sky or talking to each other as if this were a typical spot to loiter, everyone too proud to ask for charity, especially when they knew every family was one poorly negotiated transaction away from living in the streets beside them.

Vidal arrived at a town square at the edge of La Judería, surrounded by a perimeter of tents, and entered the beige canvas tent of Shelomo Levin. The inside of the tent contained every belonging a man could hope to possess: blankets, cauldrons, spices, liquor, swords, wineskins, and uniforms worn by the emir's disgraced soldiers. Items sat in tidy piles on the floor, rested on shelves placed in the tent, or hung from the poles that kept it drawn. Shelomo's daughter Tsipora leaned against a wooden stall cart at the far end of the tent appearing either bored or lost in thought. She had the soft skin of a woman who'd never so much as hung a clothesline or pruned her fingers washing dishes, and a nose, chin, and cheeks so smooth he imagined she would live fifty years without the blemish of a wrinkle creasing them. He did not doubt that she and Eliezer would provide him with beautiful grandchildren. When he greeted her and asked for Shelomo, Tsipora said she'd fetch her father as if she were expecting Vidal and left through a flap in the back of the tent.

Tsipora returned with Shelomo, dressed in a gray tunic soaked with sweat thanks to the heat of the early spring day. With her father present, Tsipora grabbed a rag from behind the cart and dusted the tent's merchandise. She performed the task silently, clearly eavesdropping on their conversation.

"Forgive me for having you wait, Vidal," said Shelomo. "The past two weeks have been absolute madness. What brings you here today?"

"I'm looking to purchase a horse and cart."

"A horse! That will be easy to find. Most men I know want to sell their horse. No need for more than one, especially if we are to leave them stranded at the coast." He asked Tsipora to wait outside the tent. "The doctor and I must talk in private."

"No need, Father, I have not listened to a word."

"Now, Tsipora!"

Tsipora hung her head and exited the tent like a disciplined child being sent to her room. It was Vidal's first clue that something was wrong.

Once alone, Shelomo stated that he had a request for Vidal as well. "Let us move up the wedding. Have it in Granada like we always planned. We'll invite the entire Judería. One last party before we leave this ungracious kingdom, and we'll make it such a party that our reputation will proceed us for generations to come."

At first, his heart fluttered as if Shelomo had offered him a chest of gold. Vidal had waited ten years to receive this dowry and planned to use it to construct a new roof for his home; now he could use it to start a new life in Fez. But with equal immediacy, reality landed on his head as clearly as if one of the cauldrons had slipped off the shelf and struck him. To earn the dowry, he'd need to pay for food and drinks for many guests. He could not ask his family to plan a wedding when they could barely afford food.

"It's a nice thought. But we're caravanning together. Eliezer and Tsipora will marry in the synagogue of the rabbi's brother."

"You would receive many gifts."

"We cannot ask our neighbors for offerings at this time."

"I will be paying you a handsome dowry."

"It's better to wait. A first celebration in our new home."

"Are you too good for my money?"

"I said no such thing."

"Does my daughter not deserve to be married in her homeland?"

"Shelomo, be reasonable. Rabbi el Barchilon may call on us to leave at a moment's notice."

"Then you leave me no choice. I must break the arrangement." Shelomo spoke with such conviction that Vidal felt certain he'd offended him. Was this a salesman's tactic, a way for Shelomo to misbehave while putting all the blame on Vidal's refusal to follow? He tried to think of anything else to change Shelomo's mind. But Shelomo was a businessman. Cutthroat deals and broken promises came with the trade.

"We'll have the wedding in Fez. We gave each other our word that our children would marry—"

"I had your word that Tsipora would marry on her sixteenth birthday."

"Yet she is still fifteen!"

"She will long be sixteen by the time a wedding can be prepared in Fez. If Eliezer will not marry her, I'll find someone else before we leave."

Vidal would have ripped his shirt at the insult if he still had the clothes to spare. He chose his next words carefully. Tsipora was beautiful and many families were in desperate need of a dowry. What sort of suitors would Shelomo attract? "Shelomo, please be reasonable."

"I am reasonable. I made you an offer and you turned it down. So I take my offer elsewhere."

"The rabbi will not allow this."

"The rabbi has greater concerns."

"Our neighbors will be outraged when they hear of this."

"Not as outraged as they'll be at the foolish doctor who turned down a fortune."

"Very well. If that is your decision, I cannot stop you." Vidal left the tent before he could be berated by one of Shelomo's tantrums that he'd been subjected to since the two of them were boys.

"What of the horse and cart?" Shelomo asked.

"I will take my business elsewhere."

"Good riddance to you then."

He found Tsipora leaning against the tent at a section where two poles met. She turned away from him as if avoiding a conversation, but the moment he passed her, she called his name. A silver bracelet dangled from her fingers, which she held as if it were the neck of a dead chicken. Vidal recognized it as a gift Eliezer had given to her on her fourteenth birthday.

"Tell Elie I am sorry."

"It was a gift. Keep it."

"Please. It will only remind me of him." Her voice revealed this was not one of Shelomo's tricks to barter a preferred business deal—she'd known the result of the conversation before he entered the tent. If she revealed to him the name of a man Shelomo had already arranged for her to marry, nothing would surprise him. As the beads of the silver bracelet coiled into his palm, he wondered how he'd explain this to his son.

Tsipora returned to the tent. Should he follow her inside and curse Shelomo for his behavior? Perhaps even damn him the way the Catholics seemed to damn each other—a phrase he always enjoyed though he found it meaningless. Any reaction would only humiliate Tsipora further and Shelomo would make himself out to be the victim if Vidal attacked.

He slipped the bracelet into the pocket of his gown and returned home. At first he tried to tell himself that this was not an issue he should dwell on. Eliezer would soon be a doctor, and every father in La Judería would consider him suitable for their daughters. Once home, Vidal attempted to continue with his afternoon routine, dragging the water bucket into the courtyard to wash up before dinner to begin the Sabbath. But once the bucket was in the center of the yard, he could not bring himself to remove his shirt and dip a washcloth into the cool pond. He stared at his reflection, silhouetted by the blue sky and white clouds behind him, then sat on the stone steps that led up to the roof with the bracelet in his hands. The jewelry weighed heavier than he'd expected. The lingering touch of Tsipora's hands still warmed the silver.

He heard Eliezer come home and greet Bonadonna and Iamila in the kitchen. When Eliezer stepped into the courtyard, the boy pulled his gown over his head to prepare to wash up, and once his black gown was removed, the sleeves still clinging to his arms like the mouths of two great black fish, he noticed Vidal. The bottom of the bracelet swayed where it dangled from the back of Vidal's palm as if taunting Eliezer to discover all he would never possess.

Chapter Six

By the time Vidal finished the story of his encounter with Shelomo, Eliezer stood before him as numb as a patient high on
hemlock. He muttered that he needed air and would return before
dusk, but an hour after sundown, his seat at the dinner table remained vacant. Although Vidal had said the prayers for the candles and wine that now decorated the table, he forbade his family
to eat until his son returned. Asher picked at the bread loaf between them, and Bonadonna continued to feed the fire under the
hearth, even as Vidal reminded her not to use all of their wood.
With the windows closed to conceal their observance of the Sabbath, he could no longer tell how long they'd waited, but he soon
became convinced that the ghost of the prophet Elijah was more
likely to come through the door and take a seat at the dinner table
than Eliezer was to return.

"Did you explain your reasons for why you broke this engagement?" Bonadonna asked.

"Shelomo broke it! He wouldn't listen to me."

"I don't like the idea of Elie being out; it's already past curfew."

"When are we going to eat?" Asher asked. "I'm starving."

"We wait until your brother returns."

Vidal could not ignore this problem as he'd ignored Sarah's
cough. In the courtyard, he looked up at the moon hanging in
the heavens between either side of his roof. The last traces of blue
left the sky giving way to the blackness of space. Although he and
Bonadonna had not married for love, he remembered how it felt

to lust over other girls before their betrothal, the sense of loss from knowing those girls would never be his, that they were destined to marry another man. Curfews and punishments would matter little to a boy who'd just had his heart broken, and every moment Eliezer stayed out made the chances of being captured by the monarchs' soldiers more likely. He removed the black physician's gown from the clothesline, still damp from being washed that afternoon, and wore it over his Sabbath garments.

"Where are you going?" Bonadonna asked.

"I must search for him."

He expected her to order him back to the table, accuse him of madness for going out past curfew, but she only said, "Hurry back."

Asher asked to go with him, but Vidal told his family to start eating and save a plate for Eliezer and himself. "We'll return soon."

Outside, the streets were as quiet as a cemetery and only the faint light of the moon cast a soft glow over the stone pavement. The neighbors' windows were shut so they could observe the Sabbath in secret, and the torches lit at dusk had burnt out hours ago, only the charred remains of the animal fat used to fuel them lingered in their departure. He walked alongside the stone walls of his neighbors' homes, more aware than ever of the few turnoffs and alcoves that lined the streets, assured that if anyone saw him, he'd have no place to hide. He peered around street corners and scurried across barren road crossings, wishing to call out to his son if only it would not attract the wrong attention. Might Eliezer have been captured already?

At the edge of La Judería, soldiers assembled at the cross streets of the north-south and west-east roads, disregarding their duties in favor of sparring with their swords as the white moonlight bathed their polished armor. Vidal strained his eyes for any sign of his son across the street in the empty ascending alleyways of El Albayzín, but when a soldier turned his head, the flash of moonlight reflecting off the helmet, Vidal threw himself back against the jagged stucco of the nearest wall.

He continued to search the shadows of the side streets and alleyways in La Judería, diverging from his path if he so much as heard the murmuring of the guards who patrolled the streets. The moon ascended into the stars—would it make him an easier target in the night? Perhaps he'd been gone so long that Eliezer returned in the interim. He set out on a path toward home, and although he'd spent his life in La Judería and countless hours calling on patients in the night, after so many months of staying home after dark and the general fear of capture, he had trouble discerning which way was home. A fountain trickled in the distance. Might it belong to the Bar Yosefs? If so, home was two streets east and three north. Or could it be the HaLevi's? In that case, three streets west and one north.

He gained his bearings when he happened upon the rabbi's house—two streets east and one north of his home—and as he hurried down a street lined with symmetrical white houses, devoid of turnoffs and alcoves, he found himself on a collision course with another figure walking about in the night. The moonlight fell over the figure's hat and left its face concealed in shadow. Vidal looked side to side, the only way to avoid the person was to retreat back to the last curve in the road. But the figure was small, with none of the armor or helmets of the soldiers. Another Jew braving the night? As they reached each other, Vidal noticed they were wearing the same black gown.

"Father!" The figure stumbled, holding a wineskin in his hand.

"Lower your voice."

"How could you?" Vidal attempted to lead Eliezer in the direction of home, but his son threw off his arm. "How could you do this to me? How could you break my engagement with Tsipora?" Eliezer's mouth reeked of garnacha. His gown was clammy and cold to the touch.

"You refused me the opportunity to explain. Now, please, keep your voice down." Vidal squeezed Eliezer's arm as if holding steady a small child and led him forward. "Where have you been?"

"I went to Shelomo's shop, but he was gone. So I stole the wineskin from his tent."

"You stole from Shelomo?"

"Yes, and I went to his house to change his mind. I banged on that fat man's door and demanded an explanation for why I couldn't marry his daughter. But he wouldn't answer. Such a coward, he would not even ask his servants to come to the door. I could see the candlelight through the drapes and I shouted, 'I know you're in there!'"

"Quiet. Tell me the rest at home."

"Finally he said if I kept it up, he'd call on the soldiers to take me away. Can you believe that?" Vidal shushed him, but Eliezer continued, "I said, 'Can you believe that, Father?'"

"An empty threat. Shelomo wouldn't."

"You take his side?"

"It isn't like that."

"You're both traitors. You betrayed me."

Before Vidal could respond, he pushed his wrist into Eliezer's sternum to make him halt and put a finger to his son's lips. In the distance, the faint shifting and clanging of armor grew louder. The moment Eliezer noticed it, he turned sober as quickly as a wick becomes hot when ignited. Vidal surveyed either direction of the street; an ancient road built before turns, alcoves, and hiding places were essential for evading curfew. Even if they sprinted, the next street crossing was too far. They would never outrun their pursuers.

Eliezer threw the wineskin up the street, far enough that it may not be noticed in the darkness of the late hour. Four soldiers marched down the street dressed in matching uniforms so heavy and massive that they looked like they might trample him and his son if they charged forward. When the soldiers stopped before them, the commander, a man with a deep scar carved into the skin under his right eyelid, approached them. Dried blood and dirt congealed in the scar, revealing he'd withstood the injury recently and suffered poor treatment by a field physician. "State your names and residence."

"I'm a doctor and this is my apprentice. We live only one street east of here."

"For what purpose are you out past curfew?" The commander clutched the hilt of his sword. Did he mean to attack them or was this out of habit?

"It was not our intention to miss curfew. We were out late caring for a very sick patient in El Albayzín. Please understand, it was a matter of life and death."

"If you are physicians, where are your supplies?"

"We left them with the nurse who is staying through the night."

"I could have you whipped for this offense."

"I know. And I hope you will take into consideration that—with this punishment in mind—we chose to put the urgent needs of our patient first."

This answer seemed to satisfy the commander's interrogation, but just as Vidal thought they might be released, Eliezer shouted, "The decree forbids you to touch us!"

"What's wrong with him?"

"I believe he has caught the illness. Do not get too close to him; he has not received treatment."

One of the soldiers lifted the wineskin down the empty road and recoiled at the smell of alcohol under the stopper. "All lies! The boy is drunk."

"You were unaware your colleague was inebriated?" asked the commander.

"The family sent us home with a wineskin. They would have taken offense if we refused."

"Yet your son could not stay his thirst until he returned home? Men, arrest the boy."

"Please, show us mercy." A soldier twisted Vidal's arms behind his back. He felt as if his shoulder might dislocate from its socket, but he pivoted to face the commander. If Sarah could die of a cough, how close would Eliezer's punishment bring him to death? "You cannot do this. We are physicians."

"You are the physician, and you are free to go."

As the soldiers bound Eliezer's wrists behind his back with rope, Vidal asked, "What are you going to do with him?"

"Public intoxication after curfew. What's the punishment for that, men?"

Each soldier responded. "Ten lashes." "Twenty lashes." "Fifty lashes."

"The punishment for this crime is outrageous," said Vidal.

The commander unsheathed the sword far enough for Vidal to see the flawless silver edges of the sharp steel. Continuing with this argument might result in an injury no physician in Granada could remedy. Like his former emir, Vidal resigned his protest to the threat of the sword. Eliezer watched as disheartened as if Vidal had walked off laughing and whistling.

"It is good he is drunk. He will feel the punishment less."

"But he'll bleed more," Vidal said.

"You may claim him in the morning at La Puerta de la Justicia." The commander's sword could be heard slicing through the air that surrounded it as he sheathed the blade and signaled his men to be off. The soldier shoved Vidal into the street, causing him to scramble forward to keep from falling. They surrounded Eliezer like royal escorts protecting a young prince and marched him back the way they'd come. What could he do to save his son? Or let Eliezer know he'd not abandon him completely?

"I love you!" Vidal's declaration caused the soldiers to burst into discordant laughter. Eliezer hung his head in shame, more embarrassed than if he'd simply been taken prisoner. If fate had been different, Vidal imagined he would've been mortified by his father's declaration of love in such a circumstance as well. He waited until the soldiers' laughter faded around the road's bend and made his way back to the rabbi's house.

A beautiful brass mezuzah, subtly painted with flowers, adorned the threshold to the rabbi's door. No light exposed itself from beneath the frame nor any second-story windows. Had they gone to bed? Vidal pounded on the door, knowing it would frighten the rabbi as Gabriel's knocking had frightened him. But let the rabbi be frightened; they should all be frightened.

Vidal saw no reaction but heard the scraping of a window frame from over his head. The rabbi's son Binyamín, a boy as handsome as his father was wise, leaned over the edge of the sill. "It's the Sabbath, good sir. Leave my father to rest."

"I demand you call on your father at once. This is a most urgent matter!"

"My apologies, Doctor. I did not expect to encounter you out here in the night."

Rabbi el Barchilon opened the door, hugging his robes in the cold and looking like a man who'd been pulled back from the threshold of sleep. Vidal explained that his son had been taken by the soldiers, but passed over the situations with Shelomo and the display of public drunkenness. These controversies could be addressed once his son was returned.

The rabbi expressed his deepest sympathies to Vidal. "What would you have me do? I have no power or influence over the monarchs' men."

"They listen to the church. You have tea once a week with Padre Leonardo, no? Ask him to use his influence."

"Oh, Vidal, Padre Leonardo and I have not spoken since the decree."

"Then speak to him now. Rabbi, they have my son and may do God knows what—"

"Do not speak His name in vain."

"This is no time for a sermon, Rabbi. I need your help!" He never could have imagined speaking with such sternness to his rabbi. His attitude would be unthinkable mere months ago, but so was the circumstance in which he found himself.

"I will dress and go to him."

"I'll accompany you."

"No, you'll wait at home. Your tongue is too hot, and I must speak to him with much diplomacy." Though the rabbi expressed this calmly, Vidal heard the subtle warning that if his behavior went unchecked, his rabbi may relinquish aid.

"Very well. What am I to do at home?"

"Wait for me to call on you. Or for Eliezer's return."

"I'll go mad with waiting."

"Then focus your energy on your family. They will need you."

Vidal agreed that this was the best course of action, and although he wished to wait for the rabbi to dress and depart, he knew it would be intrusive to remain in the doorway. "There is one more thing I must tell you, as it may arise in conversation. Eliezer was drunk when they arrested him."

"Your son? Drunk?"

"A long story."

"Does this have anything to do with Señor Levin's daughter?"

So the rabbi had learned of Shelomo's plans before Shelomo had revealed them to Vidal—so assured that Vidal would say no. He could have marched to Shelomo's home, pulled him into the street and beat him. But now was not the time, as he could only bring himself to say, "Yes."

He walked the three streets home, aware that he returned as he'd left: alone. It was his great fortune that the children had eaten and gone to bed before his return. Bonadonna washed the bowls in the courtyard and although work was forbidden on the Sabbath, he knew that to stop her would only exacerbate her anxiety. He had not eaten since midday and could not fathom the idea of asking for food at a time like this. He planned to lie to her the same as the rabbi, for he could not imagine explaining the circumstances concerning Eliezer's arrest, but the moment he found himself before her, he felt as vulnerable as a sickly child and confessed everything.

"Why those monsters! And they dare call us Christ-killers after the sins they partake in on a daily basis? Tell me where he went, I'll get him out myself." He demanded she steady her voice, explaining that the rabbi was negotiating Eliezer's release, and although she seemed ready to flee out into the night, he persuaded her to wait for a knock at the door.

They sat on the leather couch with a wool blanket draped over their legs and faced the door. As his panic dissipated, Vidal's eyes began to droop, but he stayed awake for fear he might miss a knock if it arrived while they dreamed. "Are you going to tell me this might not have happened if we converted?" he asked.

"The curfew is for all Granadinos."

"But I'm sure the punishment is less severe for Christians."

"Christians, yes. But if he were a converso, would it have helped? You're right. It's not safe here."

"So you see now why we have to leave?"

She draped her legs over his lap to create a little more space on the small leather couch. For a time she sat looking at the door without speaking a word. Had she heard someone outside? "There's something I must tell you and I hope you will not become upset. Some of the wives have gone to speak to a priest. They learned if they do not wish to leave Granada with their husbands, they may stay and convert. It would be within their right to divorce. There'd be no shame in it."

Vidal dared not move from where he sat, as if so much as adjusting himself would drive his wife off his lap and into the arms of the church. "Are you going to divorce me, Bonadonna?"

"I thought about it. It wouldn't be difficult to convince the children. Especially Asher, he'll do anything to avoid his bar mitzvah studies. But Eliezer would go with you." Vidal could not find the will to speak. Eliezer could be getting whipped at that very moment. Who knew what his attitude might be toward any of them once he returned? "I couldn't go forward with the idea. I couldn't leave you. I know the journey to Fez may be treacherous, it may even be suicidal, but I know you'll go with or without me. You need me. The children need me. And I do believe that if I'm there to help you, we may all make it safely to Fez together." He could not recall the last time Bonadonna had spoken so plainly of her love and devotion to him. If only it had not followed the threat of divorce. "Please forgive me for my deception."

How could he forgive her? And yet she'd done little wrong. She could have carried this secret to the grave, but he found it admirable she dared tell the truth. Because he could not find the words for this moment, he turned to his understanding of the human body to address this incomprehensible situation. "There's nothing to forgive. People will do anything in an act of self-preservation."

"If you view conversion as an act of self-preservation, why do you resist it?"

"Because without my faith I'd have nothing to preserve."

"You're still a doctor."

"A doctor isn't an identity, it's a profession. Do you think of yourself as only a wife?" Vidal brushed the hair from her eyes. "I'm very humbled that when given the choice between the Vatican or I, you chose me."

"Let us not make this about your pride."

As she grew more tired, the weight of her body melded into his, something they never did although they shared the same bed, an intimacy that'd been absent for almost four years.

"Can you forgive me for breaking Eliezer's betrothal?" Vidal asked.

"I never blamed you. It's Shelomo's doing. You could have just as easily forced me to plan a wedding we have neither time nor coin to afford. You couldn't have known how Eliezer would react. He's not himself."

"Do you think Catalina is in danger? As a converso?"

"She's been a Catholic for many years. I don't think they even recall she's a Jew. I hardly remember."

Should he tell her about his fears for Catalina? He did not think a mother's heart could take any more worry. He'd tell her when the time was right, though given the mystery of the journey that lay ahead, he didn't know when that would be. His wife rested her head against his shoulder and her snores soon filled the blackness of the room. Whether he dozed or merely stared for hours at the sliver of midnight light that rested under the door frame, he could not recall, but when the first hint of sunrise appeared under the door, a knock rattled the hinges and Rabbi el Barchilon called for Vidal. Vidal helped Bonadonna up from the chair and asked her to prepare tea for their return.

In the morning sunlight, the rabbi waited in the street mounted on a horse. The sight of a rabbi dressed in full religious robes seated on a stallion that he'd broken the Sabbath to acquire looked bizarre, like something he might come across at a Purim festival. Tethered to the horse was a wooden carriage the size of a coffin. The rabbi assured him everything would be well and helped Vidal up to take a seat behind him on the horse. Vidal could not recall the last time he'd ridden a horse, but he had no time to marvel at the novelty of towering over the empty street as the rabbi led him through La Judería.

"I've gotten word from my brother in Fez. They'll accept us as soon as we can arrive. I'll get the word out to everyone in service today. We leave in a month's time."

"A month," Vidal repeated, though he was so preoccupied with retrieving his son the concept of leaving Granada felt insignificant by comparison. On the north end of La Judería, where the houses, market squares, and pavement gave way to a grassy tree-lined field, they arrived at an archway gate carved from the finest golden stone, giving the impression that the stonemasons who'd built it meant to imitate the marble columns of ancient Greece. The brick base walls of the Alhambra fortress rose from the ground beside the gate, as ensconced into the earth as the trees that surrounded it. He'd seen this gate once before, when he and Shelomo were boys playing pretend and contemplating the idea of sneaking into the Nasrid Palace, but back then they'd been too afraid to go any further and returned to town to partake in other imaginary adventures. But now a dozen soldiers who guarded the archway waved them through and the horse carried them up a steep hill pockmarked with stones buried in the earth to keep traction for the wheels.

They ascended to La Alhambra. What might he see at the top? The battered body of his tortured son? Or perhaps an officer to greet him and apologize for the theatrics of Eliezer's arrest? It wouldn't hurt if the king or queen themselves came out as a sign of mercy. A father could hope.

Once the hill ascended so that the white roofs of the houses behind him looked no larger than the uneven tiles of a floor, the road doubled back on itself and they arrived at a metal gate within a doorway twice as tall as his family's home, protruding from the palace walls. La Puerta de la Justicia. He'd never before been so close to the palace in his life; he could think of few who had except those who'd worked in service of the emir. But the fear of what awaited him inside outweighed the awe he felt at entering the most forbidden location in Granada.

At their arrival, a tower guard called for the gates to open and a man-sized doorway in the bottom right of the gate unlatched from within. The view behind the door entrance was black as night, but soon a figure limped into the sand that surrounded the walls. He wore a white tunic covered in dark crimson stains. Dirt matted his face and crusted into his hair. A blood vessel had burst in his left eye.

Vidal leaped from the horse and helped Eliezer before he collapsed into the sand. When he laid Eliezer on the back of the cart, a mix of blood and dirt from the boy's shirt painted the palms of Vidal's hands. The entire ride down, Eliezer moaned as if each bump in the road stabbed him like the tip of a sword, and Vidal felt as powerless as when the soldier had twisted his arms behind his back. The moment the horse arrived outside his home, the physician in Vidal took control, and he and the rabbi carried Eliezer through the door where Vidal shouted for Bonadonna to fetch water and blankets.

"We have sold most of our blankets," Bonadonna said.

"Then the cleanest rags you can find."

Vidal led Eliezer to the children's bedroom, which never before seemed less comfortable or inviting with its blank stone walls and twin beds of blanket-covered straw. Asher and Iamila sat cross-legged on one of the beds drawing on paper. Iamila leaped away at the first sight of Eliezer, but Vidal would've knocked Asher onto the floor to lay down his oldest if, at the last moment, Asher hadn't hurdled out of the way as well. The whip marks in Eliezer's shirt allowed Vidal to rip his clothes off with no need for scissors or scalpel. The scars on Eliezer's back seemed as methodically placed as paintbrush strokes and so well grouped that Vidal could not count the number of lashes. If it weren't for the clumps of dirt and linen that clogged the wounds, muscle and bone might have appeared within the gashes that streaked across the skin.

"You don't need to see this," Vidal told his daughter. "Help your mother fetch clean water and rags at once."

Iamila and Bonadonna soon returned with the items and Vidal soaked a rag in the water to clean his son's back.

"What have they done?" Bonadonna screamed as if she could feel the pain of each lash.

"Please, take your mother into the other room. I cannot do my work with you here." Iamila took her mother's hand and led her from the room.

Eliezer moaned and winced, but Vidal hushed him for there was no reason to speak. If he could not prevent infection, his son would die. He had cared for patients for twenty years and realized now that every patient he examined, every remedy he perfected, every hour he studied medical texts, was in preparation for this moment. Eliezer lay in the same bed where Sarah had passed. Vidal would not fail to save another child's life.

"I must be off to prepare for morning service," the rabbi said.

"You have done more than enough to help us. I'll find a way to thank you."

"Will you be attending?"

"No, Rabbi." Though Vidal had broken the Sabbath before, he only did so during the direst of emergencies, usually to nurse a patient to health following a procedure performed by a surgeon. The idea that he should go to service crossed his mind, for he needed God on his side now more than ever, but God would forgive him for staying with his son. "But you will recite the Mi Shebeirach?"

"It will be the most important part of my deresha."

Once the rabbi departed, Asher stood in the corner to gaze at his brother's back with a mix of horror and curiosity. Vidal took his son by the arm. "I have a task for you. Go to Catalina and bring her here at once."

"She's not a nurse anymore."

"She will not have forgotten her training. We need her now. Go."

Though in his heart he knew Catalina would come in great haste, the time between Asher leaving and his oldest daughter arriving felt like months. Was this how patients felt when they awaited his arrival? When she entered, an entourage of the de Zaniçerases accompanied her. The sight of her brother's peeled and tattered back halted her at the threshold of her former bedroom. As a nurse, she'd seen people die, blood pour onto the floor from bloodletting, but she never before saw skin mangled for the purpose of torture. Though he expected her to cry, she behaved as if not a day had elapsed since her last round as her father's nurse, placing fresh linens over Eliezer's back, holding a sponge dusted with opium to his nose, and cleaning away blood on the stone floor.

Once Eliezer fell asleep—or perhaps passed out—Vidal asked his daughter to watch over her brother. He exited their home through the back gate to relieve himself in the outhouse in the alleyway built between his house and his neighbor's. But as he reached the fingerholes to pull the wooden door open, the last of his strength dissipated. He had not whipped his son, he had not caused Eliezer to be out past curfew, but he had allowed the engagement to be broken. In trying to spare his family of the stress and turmoil of planning a wedding, his son had almost died. "Adonai, am I not better at making decisions than this? I've always trusted my instincts to save my patients' lives, but a lifetime of practice could not stop me from committing an error that could scar my son deeper than the wounds in his flesh. Will my wits fail me again on the road to Fez, where I'm responsible for the lives of my family?" Although he received no response, speaking to God lessened his concerns, the way he often realized that his greatest fears sounded insignificant when spoken aloud. This sort of error would not happen again. Next time, God would guide him toward the correct decision.

When he returned to the house, the air carried the faint scent of boiled eggplant and chicken—a meal they'd been preserving for their last days in Granada, but Bonadonna had clearly decided to cook it in the unexpected presence of their in-laws. It didn't surprise him. What else could she do to keep her mind preoccupied?

At the threshold of Eliezer's room, he halted in the shadows at the sound of a woman reciting the Mi Shebeirach. "Mi shebeirach avoteinu. M'kor hab'racha l'imoteinu..." Was it Bonadonna? Iamila? It seemed incomprehensible that they'd be singing in the presence of Ochoa or Marquessa. Yet when he arrived in Eliezer's room, he found Catalina on her knees with her elbows on the mattress. She jumped at the sight of her father, and batted the dust off her dress.

"What is this?"

"Assurance, should God not hear my Christian prayers."

Vidal thought to scold Catalina for speaking Hebrew as a

convert. What Catholic would believe her devotion to Christ if they witnessed such an act? But he could not bring himself to discipline one child while another suffered a punishment that'd brought him to the threshold of death.

He sat at the edge of the bed. He wanted to run his hand through his son's soft, curly hair, but was afraid to rouse him, for sleep suppressed pain better than any medicine. His daughter leaned into the crook of his arm, something she had not done since she was a girl. Would it be wrong to say now what he'd no occasion to ask before?

"The caravan could use a skilled nurse like you."

"Gabriel told me about your conversation outside the church."

"Your husband is livid with me."

"He'd like you to apologize to him, yes."

"I'll worry about that once my son is well."

"Do you truly believe I am at risk if I stay here?"

"Look at your brother's back. And now I catch you singing the prayer for the sick. You tell me."

"My husband and father-in-law would never allow me to leave."

"Perhaps if you told them it was your decision—"

"And I cannot hurt Gabriel that way."

"What do you want to do, Goyo?" Her birth name hung between them like the name of a dead relative who'd gone unmentioned for years. He knew she'd do whatever he or her husband expected of her, but when the decision conflicted between them, a decision was impossible.

"It's not my choice. I can't travel to another nation in my condition." She rubbed her stomach, pulling the cloth tight as a drawn tent. A faint bump protruded beneath her clothes, as smooth and hard as fruit on the verge of ripening.

"I'll take care of you. Monitor you. Half the women in the caravan are midwives. And your mother can help."

"There's no possibility that you would convert instead?"

"None. My mind is made up."

"And you see no possibility that the decree will be overturned?"

"That moment will never come."

"But it could. If that future is a possibility, then you must stay."

"Fifteen hundred years ago, the Romans exiled the Hebrews from Jerusalem, and we have never been welcomed back into the Holy Land. What makes you think Granada will be different?"

Before Catalina could respond, Iamila entered, summoning her sister to eat a bowl of soup their mother prepared. Catalina told her sister she'd be along in a moment and once Iamila left, Vidal added, "It's dangerous for you to stay. The rabbi said so himself."

"I know, Father. We heard enough horror stories in school for me to know how the other kingdoms treat converts."

"Then consider my offer."

"I wouldn't know how to leave even if I wanted to."

"I would help you. If you choose to leave, no one and nothing will stop me from aiding you."

"Give me time to consider your proposal?"

Vidal almost fumbled to speak out the next words. It was the first time his daughter had shown any possibility in leaving, returning to the Jewish faith. Could it happen? "Make it with haste. We have less than a month more."

"A month before what, Father?"

"A month before we must depart." Vidal rested his hand on hers. Even though she belonged to a new family, he could not help but treat her like a daughter again. "No matter what you do," he added, "never speak Hebrew in this city again."

For the next two days, Catalina slept at her family's home, sharing the bed with Iamila while Asher slept between Vidal and Bonadonna. Gabriel arrived in the evenings after work to bring food, but did not speak with Vidal. By the second night, Eliezer's fever broke. The act of standing put too much pressure on his wounds, so he used his elbows to hoist himself into a sitting position on the bed if he wanted to eat. Bonadonna helped him roll off the bedside onto his knees if he wished to relieve himself. Vidal could hear his wife whisper conversations with Eliezer for hours, but when Vidal examined his son, the boy said nothing. Perhaps it hurt his son to talk? Though he suspected Eliezer's silence was meant to show newfound disdain for his father, he assured himself that he should ignore Eliezer's attitude as he did all non-health matters related to his patients. Eliezer was safe and improving each day; nothing else mattered.

One morning, as Vidal departed from home before sunrise, he found a paper envelope slid under the door, resting on the dusty stone floor. He sliced it open with the edge of his calloused finger and read the handwritten note inside. The family ha-Rofeh was formally invited to the wedding of Tsipora Levin to Avraham Mendez, on the 10th of Iyar in the year 5252—or the 7th of May, 1492. A mere week before the caravan was to depart Granada. So Shelomo was marrying off his daughter to a blacksmith's son? A man who would be in urgent need of a dowry and have neither the backbone nor intelligence to reject Shelomo's offer. Vidal pinched either end of the note in preparation to tear it in two. But tearing the message in half would do nothing to rid himself of the situation. He was obliged to go to the wedding of his oldest friend's daughter. All of La Judería would be there and his family's absence would be a noticeable scandal that would do them no favors and make them no friends once they departed Granada. He tucked the letter inside his gown. As Eliezer wouldn't speak to him, he would have Bonadonna share the envelope with him that evening and explain why they would need to attend the wedding, to show solidarity with Shelomo at the precipice of their impending departure.

Chapter Seven

Vidal donned a black gown with blue trim, and adorned his head with his finest golden cap. His wife covered herself in a black dress, wearing around her shoulders a silk scarf to accentuate the outfit, and put her hair in a gold headscarf to match Vidal's headpiece. The only fine clothes they'd chosen not to sell off, and they were wearing them for the wedding of Tsipora Levin to a blacksmith's son.

Asher slumped, waiting in the wooden chair beside the door dressed in his finest Sabbath outfit. Through the doorway, Iamila stood in the courtyard wearing an outfit that matched her mother's. She was feeding carrots to a black Andalusian horse that Ochoa had acquired for them—a favor Bonadonna had asked of Ochoa while Vidal was cleaning their son's wounds, promising the title of their house in exchange for horse and carriage. Vidal called his daughter inside. She stroked the horse's mane and kissed it goodbye. He'd forbidden them from naming the horse as they'd abandon it at the sea. Although Iamila swore she'd give the horse no name, he was certain it was only a matter of time before this promise was broken.

"Why must we go to this wedding?" Asher asked.

"Yes," Iamila said. "I don't want to see Tsipora marry anybody but my brother."

"I'm not answering this question again." Vidal had repeatedly stated to his family that all of the community would be in attendance. To not attend would be scandalous, as their neighbors might view them as disloyal to the community—a suspicion they could not afford leaving Granada in a week's time.

"Don't people have more important things to worry about than us?"

Although he wished to agree with his daughter, he instead opened the front door to let in the daylight. "Out," he said, forcing the matter to be done with. It felt odd leaving for a wedding before sunset, as if they were Catholics who married in the mornings. But the invitation declared that the ceremony start early to conclude before curfew.

At the sound of his mother calling to be off, Eliezer limped from the bedroom down the corridor, taking light steps that suggested his body could not bear the burden of its weight. He was dressed in a simple black gown and cap. Nevertheless, Bonadonna remarked how handsome her boy looked.

"I should inspect the bandages before we depart," Vidal said, but Eliezer walked past his father out the door without a word. "Eliezer ha-Rofeh, you disrespect me."

Eliezer put his forearm on Iamila's shoulder. "If I need to, may I lean on you?"

"If it's all right with you, Father?" Iamila asked.

Did Eliezer need to be reminded that Vidal saved his life? That he brought him back from the brink of death? They would be late for the ceremony and had no time for his son's games. "Only until we reach the synagogue."

"Finally, we've found a use for Iamila," Asher said as he followed.

With the children outside, Vidal asked his wife, "How long should we expect this grudge to last?"

"He knows the importance of attending this wedding. It's noble of him to go. We should expect nothing more."

"We leave in a week. I have every right to expect more."

"Would you have behaved so differently if your father had broken our engagement?"

They'd barely known each other prior to their wedding, she was a child in his eyes, making their interactions at synagogue or school a rarity. He'd loved Viva Alahdab at the time, a girl his age who was now married to Mosse Bar Yosef. If his father had broken his engagement to the little girl named Bonadonna at the time, he doubted he would've minded. But if that'd been the case, none of their children would be born, and that was enough for him to understand his son. Could Eliezer be dwelling on children he might've had with Tsipora who were now wiped from existence? Did seventeen-year-old boys think such thoughts?

Nearly 200 members of La Judería packed inside the temple, more eager to see this wedding than they were to read the decree that'd vandalized the now mended doors two months prior. Their outfits were as colorful and diverse as the many hues of stained glass that decorated the Ottoman lamps that hung in El Albayzín. Afternoon sunlight streamed in through the stained glass windows, bathing the bimah and congregation in a cascade of azure, gold, and scarlet. Rumors around La Judería confirmed that the rabbi had sold the synagogue to a captain in the Castilian army to acquire the coin needed to purchase the caravan's passage across the Mediterranean Sea. How might the captain transform such a place? Would he turn it into his house, a ballroom, a museum for the Kingdom of Castile to gaze upon artifacts of an exiled faith? To think, in a week, this place would be abandoned, with no Jew left to gaze upon the ark, nor the stonecutting craftmanship, nor the honeycomb tiles that adorned the columns that supported the synagogue's roof.

He stood beside his sons in the congregation and watched over the caps of the men in the rows before them the marriage of Tsipora Levin to Avraham Mendez. The bride and groom stood at the bimah with their heads covered by a white wedding tallit with black stitching. Rabbi el Barchilon recited the seven blessings of the Sheva B'Rachot as Shelomo bounced where he stood in the front row like a man who'd like the affair to be over with so the party could begin.

That the rabbi had allowed Shelomo to break the betrothal and marry off his daughter to a blacksmith's son no longer surprised Vidal, once he'd learned that Shelomo spun Vidal's refusal of an ultimatum into a breaking of the marriage agreement. This might not have happened in another time, but the departure preparations preoccupied the rabbi from further investigating the matter. Shelomo had wronged him, yet somehow Vidal found himself to be the fool, as he'd overheard people talking about him in the synagogue or the market over the past weeks. Who was this man that turned down a generous dowry from Señor Levin while so many others went without food? Vidal ha-Rofeh may be the doctor, but Señor Mendez was unquestionably the wiser father.

Eliezer gave a soft whimper and at first Vidal suspected his son may cry at the occasion, but Eliezer only wore the grimace of a wounded man forced to stand. "It's fine to sit," Vidal whispered and his voice gave Eliezer the strength to stop hobbling and bear the pain. Why had he forced his son to attend? Couldn't he have simply lied that Eliezer was still too wounded to leave the house? A broken engagement, a whipped son, and now that same son forced to endure the wedding of his love to another. In Vidal's attempt to protect his family, it seemed he'd only caused more suffering. He longed to set things right, dash up the aisle and convince Shelomo to reconsider. He didn't care if people saw him as a fool—it was too late for that—but a futile bartering session with Shelomo before the congregation would certainly humiliate his son further. The apprentice whose betrothed left him for a blacksmith's son, who was whipped for public drunkenness. The congregation pitied Eliezer, for the Talmud ordained that any man who has no wife is not a man. Yet they loved his exploits. He was something to talk about besides leaving home, someone to laugh at besides themselves.

From under the tallit, Avraham stomped on the glass wrapped in cloth. The congregation shouted "Mazel tov" as Eliezer lost Tsipora forever.

The guests migrated to an open courtyard behind the synagogue. The ground was laid with oven-baked brick the color of copper, which stretched to the banks of the Darro River that ran opposite the temple. A net tethered as tightly as a man on a rack ran the length of the courtyard to separate the men from the women and the tables surrounded the perimeter to make room for a dance floor at the center. As Vidal ushered his sons to be seated, Eliezer walked past him to join Binyamín, the rabbi's son, at a table near the water. Asher stood obediently by his father, but started humming in an apparent effort to be obnoxious.

"Go. Join him," Vidal said. Once alone, Vidal claimed his seat at a table devoid of people, but adorned with plates of cheese, olives, and clay pitchers of red wine. His sitting alone would be enough to cause the people of La Judería to talk. Vidal's sons are not sitting with him? A scandal! He poured a cup of red wine, nursing it at first, then gulping down the tart drink so it might quell his anxiety.

As the festivities began, and Vidal drank and ate, the dance floor came alive with the sound of a drummer and tambourine player performing a song to entertain the bride and groom, seated next to each other on the men's side of the net. Tsipora watched the performance with polite attentiveness, yet never seemed to crack a smile, looking more like a woman posing for a painting than a bride celebrating her wedding. Eliezer appeared concentrated on the music, though his eyes kept glancing at the bride. She looked beautiful in her white lace dress, as beautiful as Catalina had looked at her wedding.

When the dance commenced, the men lifted the bride and groom in their chairs. They revolved in a circle around the couple while the women danced in place on the far side of the gate. Vidal finished his cup of wine and rose from his chair to ask Eliezer to join him in the circle, but his son watched the celebration from the seat as if his father were speaking to him from beyond the grave.

"Don't be so dour. There's no reason not to have a good time."

"It's okay, Doctor," Binyamín said on Eliezer's behalf. "Leave him be."

"Asher?"

"I'm not going to dance with a bunch of old men!"

"It's okay, Asher," Eliezer whispered. "You can go."

"No, Brother, I wouldn't betray you like that."

So now he'd indoctrinated Asher? Vidal abandoned them and wedged his way into the circle, wrapping his arms around the men on either side of him to expand the chain with his presence.

The force of the dancing men flung him around the circle and he became overzealous with showing that he was having a good time, but after two revolutions the novelty wore off. People would note that he danced at the wedding. Nobody could say with certainty that he was angry with Shelomo now. But how did celebrating Tsipora's marriage to another help his son?

He returned to his table where Rabbi el Barchilon now sat picking at olives and discarding their pits onto an empty plate.

"Not sitting with your son, Rabbi?"

"The youth have overtaken his table." Vidal offered to pour the rabbi a cup of wine, but the rabbi abstained. "It's not uncommon for a member of our congregation to wait until the end of the party to speak with me. I cannot be intoxicated in this situation."

"Half of my patients have left me, and the other half are here, so I think another cup of wine is in order. Rabbi, since you are sober, may I ask your advice?"

"I think I can guess what troubles you. And I guess it has something to do with your son not sharing your table."

"What am I to do, Rabbi? I know what Shelomo says, that it was I who broke the engagement, but it was only because he made an impossible offer. I did so to protect my family and as a result my son is punished? How could I have expected such a consequence? Now it's less than a week until we depart and the boy pretends I don't exist. How am I to protect him in the mountains? Or once we cross the sea?"

"Your problems are more common than you perceive."

"Forgive me, Rabbi, but I see no one else here whose son was whipped at the hands of the monarchs' men."

"In that aspect, your situation is the exception. But genuinely, do you think you are the only father filled with dread at the journey to come? Many have never ventured outside the city walls, and the concept of an ocean—a pond so vast that one cannot see the other side—is incomprehensible to them. It pays us no favors that the youth are apt to convert. They talk to Binyamín about it more than they do I."

"And what do you tell them?"

"Our community, our families, our religion—we've held together since the beginning of time; since we were enslaved in Egypt, since we wandered in the desert in search of the Promised Land. In the coming months, we'll hold together as we've always done. This will not be the moment that breaks us. Keep moving forward, Vidal, and forgive yourself for past errors. There's nothing else you can do."

Before Vidal could ask another word, Avraham's father approached the rabbi and conversed about saying a blessing for the food before the meal was served. In an instant, the rabbi was off with the father of the groom. But perhaps Vidal needed to hear no more. Although the rabbi frequently used Biblical examples—usually from Exodus—his words always had a way of helping Vidal see order in life. His son had been whipped and there was nothing he could do. Why should he not forgive himself for his past errors? Who could say he was not capable of doing better?

Not a moment passed before a tremendous hand landed on his shoulder. "Vidal! How is Eliezer? How's our boy?" Shelomo swayed where he stood with a wineskin in his hand.

"He'll be fine, Shelomo. His back is doing much better."

"He wouldn't speak to me when I approached him. Haven't seen someone look at me with such anger since I stopped doing business with the Moors."

"Did you apologize to him?"

"Why would I apologize? He was the one who showed up at my door on the Sabbath to cause a scene."

"He was upset when he heard the news. You know how boys can be. You have two yourself."

"But everything is well between you and me?" Shelomo extended a hand and Vidal rose intending to shake it. Some wedding guests watched them, while others feigned that they were looking at the river when they only wanted to see if the doctor and businessman would make peace. For the first time in three weeks, Eliezer gave his father attention as well, looking at Vidal with a face that betrayed no emotion.

Vidal kept his hand at his side. "Regretfully, Shelomo, all is not well with you and I."

"First, you break the engagement—"

"You broke the engagement. You forced my hand."

"I don't know what you're talking about."

"We could've held this wedding in Fez, at the same time our children were always meant to be married, but you saw an opportunity to unload your daughter from your family and seized it."

"I don't need to listen to this."

"What was it all for, then? The rest of us starve or are on the brink of losing our homes, while you have so much coin that you can afford a dowry and a wedding? So why did you need to be rid of her? One less mouth to feed?"

"Are you drunk? Is that it? Have you had too much to drink?"

"Perhaps enough to loosen my tongue, but not so much to fabricate my memory."

"Be off with you. You're no longer welcome at this wedding."

"If only I'd spoken to you this way when you were younger, you might not have grown up to be such an ass."

"I said be off!"

The fury of the debate had made Vidal nearsighted, so much so that he could see every detail of Shelomo's face, the pores of his nose, the first milky signs of glaucoma in his eyes, while the rest of the world was none other than a blur behind the sides of his scalp. But beyond Shelomo, all the wedding guests looked at him save for the musicians, who continued their job in an earnest attempt to distract from the scene. The amused expression on Eliezer's face seemed to say, 'This little performance fixes nothing.'

Vidal made his leave, and as all of La Judería had assembled at the reception, the street in front of the synagogue was abandoned. Two soldiers stood at a nearby crossing, bored and kicking back and forth a rock fallen from a nearby wall. As Bonadonna arrived with both Asher and Iamila, Vidal braced himself for a lecture about his behavior, but his wife only asked, "What on Earth has gotten into you?"

"Go back and enjoy the reception. Who knows when we'll

feast again. Don't worry about me; eat a good meal."

"You're a good man, Father," Iamila said. "Señor Levin deserved every word."

"Yes. He betrayed our brother," Asher added.

"No, I betrayed your brother," Vidal said. "And I betrayed you all by forcing you to come here today."

"I don't want to go back to the party," Iamila said.

"Me neither," said Asher.

Had his children taken his side? Did they prefer his company, and his principles, over a celebration and one last meal? He was ashamed to admit that if his father had made the same outburst, he would not have been so keen to depart with him. "It would be inappropriate for us all to leave," Vidal said. "It could send the wrong impression that we're not devoted to the community."

"I think you've already set that precedent," Bonadonna said.

"You're right. What difference will it make? Let's be off. Where do you wish to go? We have all afternoon—no house calls, no chores, anywhere in Granada. Perhaps the mirador?" he asked Iamila. "Or the city walls to look at the soldiers' armor?" he asked Asher.

"I want to visit Sarah," Iamila said.

As Eliezer refused to leave, preferring the company of Binyamín to that of his family, Vidal walked with his wife and two youngest children to the cemetery at the eastern end of La Judería. The streets were empty and the plaster walls that lined the alleyways painted the color of clouds made the neighborhood seem as if it might stretch to the heavens. The only sounds came from the faint purrs of stray cats who leaped from one house to the next, heard but otherwise invisible among the rooftops. Vidal collected loose rocks he found in the street along the way, as he'd done before the invasion, before the decree, when it'd been more common to find time to visit Sarah.

The cemetery waited on the far side of the building that housed the children's school, behind two opened iron gates adorned with metalwork of the Star of David, one star for either gate that swung inward. The graveyard was no larger than a market square and so overflowed with centuries of gravestones that there was no room to walk over the plots without stepping on ground that contained the dead beneath. Vidal carried Iamila so she would not slip and fall on the jagged edges of the eroded grave markers.

On the way to Sarah's grave, they stopped at the tombstones of Vidal's and Bonadonna's parents. Everyone placed stones on the graves to mark symbols of their final visit. Vidal laid down extra stones on behalf of his two sisters and Bonadonna's brother. Letters had arrived from each sibling in reply to his offer to meet in Fez. Though no siblings spoke to one another, they each responded that they were going to Portugal to escape the decree. Vidal thought to alter his plans and follow them, but after all that Rabbi el Barchilon had done to free Eliezer from La Alhambra, he resolved to stay at the rabbi's side on the journey to Fez.

Vidal gave his final goodbyes to his parents and led his family to where Sarah's headstone waited on the north end of the cemetery, chiseled with Hebrew letters that marked her birth and death dates. 5 Tishri 5246 – 3 Tishri 5249. 14 September 1485 – 8 September 1488. Less than three years old, dead now longer than she'd been alive, such a brief part of his life that every year his memories of her diminished, crowded out by the ever-accumulating moments with his living children. How long before he'd forget the shape of her face or the sound of her voice?

He placed the rocks he'd collected at the base of her grave marker. He never knew what to say in these moments. When other people in the cemetery visited the graves, they often spoke to their loved ones as if they were still alive, as if they were dozing under the earth, lying in wait for a visit from their family to learn the latest gossip and news. For the first year after her death, he'd tried speaking to Sarah. He'd begged for her forgiveness, as she laid there because of an illness he could not cure, but no response or sign was ever given and now her soul had long since departed Earth to rest in the company of God. Could another one of his children meet her fate as they departed on this uncertain journey? Or Catalina, if she stayed behind?

"Will we come back here again?" Iamila asked.

"I can't imagine so," Bonadonna said. "Too much left to do."

For months he'd thought of nothing save their preparations to leave Granada, but now he wanted nothing more than to stay. How could he bring himself to say farewell to the last physical remnants of his daughter?

When it was time to be off, Bonadonna kissed the ground. "Goodbye, my sweet girl. Goodbye, my love." Vidal helped her to her feet. She took a last look at the headstone, a look that would need to last a lifetime, and Vidal held his wife's hand as they left the cemetery.

Chapter Eight

With two days before departure, and a day lost yesterday due to the conclusion of the Sabbath, the family rushed to clean and sort through the final possessions of a house that'd been in Vidal's family for five generations—and had accumulated the amount of both belongings and dust to prove it. Vidal hauled leather cases and wooden crates filled with blankets, clothes, food, pots, water, and firewood to the front door. Bonadonna swept the floors and Iamila fed the horse. Eliezer sat on the floor sewing coins into the insides of their pants pockets, leaning to the right so as not to inflame the month-old whip marks on his back.

"Why must we kill ourselves cleaning this house when we're about to abandon it?" Asher asked, doing nothing but complaining to his mother.

"We may be moving, but that doesn't mean we need to leave this place in filth," Bonadonna said. "It should be clean for your sister once we've gone."

"Then why doesn't she clean it?"

"You turn thirteen in two months," Vidal said. "I expect you to start acting like a man."

"Why? I do not have a bar mitzvah."

Before their argument could escalate, Catalina arrived at the open front door, announcing herself as politely as if she were only visiting for a cup of tea. "Is everything well? I could hear shouting from down the street."

"Goyo! Thank goodness you're here." In her frantic mood to

finish with the house, Bonadonna diverted back to calling Catalina by her old name. "Take Asher out for a walk. The boy's driving us all mad."

"No, there's too much to do," Vidal said. "Catalina, would you please help your brother pack?"

Catalina held out a hand and asked Asher to follow her to their old bedroom and Asher went with her as obediently as a pet follows its favorite owner. She'd married and moved to the de Zaniçeras' house when Asher turned nine. Before she left, Asher had been a sweet boy who would follow around his mother and only ever wanted to be held by his older sister. But as he transformed into an irascible adolescent in her absence, she remained the only one in the family who could pull the boy's old manners from him, making Vidal wonder if Asher's entire demeanor was only an act he could perform as he pleased.

Vidal soon found himself moving the leather bags he'd placed by the door to a new spot on the floor, so Bonadonna could sweep where they'd been initially. As they worked, he regretted that they treated Catalina more like a volunteer in their household than a daughter. It'd been nearly a month since Eliezer's whipping and any time Vidal asked about her decision to leave, she gave him a non-committal response. "I'm not sure if it's right for the baby." "How would Gabriel react?" "I need to pray over it." He'd given her space—this was an impossible decision for anyone to make—but now time was up and if she intended to leave with them, a plan was necessary.

In the children's bedroom, he found Catalina and Asher seated on the bed beside each other, with an old wooden box opened on Catalina's lap—an item from her childhood she'd never taken to Gabriel's. From the box, she pulled two articles of clothing she'd knitted as a child in the hopes of dressing them on mice, and now showed Asher how to stitch together the two shirts with needle and thread. She instructed him to pull tightly after each incision and stitch a surgical knot to ensure the wound stayed shut.

"Has Father taught you anything about being a physician? The journey may be dangerous. Should someone become injured—"

"How dangerous will it be?"

"I'm only being cautious. But it will be to everybody's benefit if you can suture a wound."

"But this is wool. I'll need to suture flesh."

"You'll do fine. It is easier with practice."

Vidal cleared his throat and asked Catalina if he might speak with her in private. Once Asher left, he found himself standing over her old bed as if she were still a child having a talk with her father. Conversations had once been about her studies, or why she had not eaten supper, but he now asked a question that reminded him how much of an adult she'd become. "What is your decision? I need to know." She stuttered as if trying to concoct an answer that would satisfy them. "If you stay here, the church may not accept your conversion as legitimate."

"But I have been baptized—"

"You spoke Hebrew when Elie was wounded."

"The prayer you trained me to sing when we care for a patient."

"You need to come with us. I cannot help you after we're gone."

"I cannot go on this journey with child."

"You won't be the only pregnant woman in the caravan."

"My husband will never let me leave."

"Have you asked him?"

"How can I ask him when he's still upset with your asking? Why haven't you apologized to him?"

"He'll need to forgive me; I've been preoccupied these past few months. Now let us not change the subject. Gabriel is a good man. If he understands the lives of you and his child are threatened, I'm sure he'll let you go. He may even come with us if he pleases."

"I'll go to church. I'll pray and tomorrow morning, you will have your answer."

"You've done that already."

"Then I'll do it again. It's supposed to work, isn't it? It seems to work for everybody else."

When she said things like this, it made him doubt how devoted or attuned she was to the Catholic faith. She could voice her misunderstandings of Catholicism aloud to him, but would

Gabriel and his family protect her if she said something that rang false to the ears of the church? He doubted Gabriel understood the dedication required to be a converso, for her piousness would be held up to a level of scrutiny he'd never need to face. If she could not fool him, how could she fool an inquisitor? "Promise me you'll talk to him. Promise you'll express the concerns I've raised. If it's to be the last thing I ask of you, do not deny me this request."

"Father, I don't know how to confront him."

"Be direct. Honest. Talk to him the way I talk to a patient's family."

"A dying patient or a healthy patient?"

"Be truthful, Catalina. You will be fine."

She looked like a frightened child being ordered to admit a wrongdoing to her rabbi. He knew she did not want to confront Gabriel, but how could he let her say nothing with so much at risk? She hugged him and he held the delicate body of his oldest daughter in his arms. Could it be for the last time?

Cleaning and chores filled the remaining hours of the day, and as he prepared for bed that night with his feet numb, his legs singing and his elbows on fire, Bonadonna remarked that they'd forgotten to clean the roof. "Remember to clean it tomorrow."

"Are you crazy, woman? Tomorrow I have to assemble the wagon, hitch it to the horse, load our belongings—"

"How long will that take?"

"With your constant dusting and cleaning? Up until the commencement of the decree."

As his mind had stayed occupied throughout the day with what Catalina would say, he ascended the stone steps of the courtyard with a bucket of water in each hand and a mop tucked under his armpit. Night made the roof as dark as a black pool so that he would not know how well of a job he'd done. As long as Bonadonna stayed downstairs, would it matter? The only glimmer of light came from the moon and stars, and the torches that burned throughout the night on the perimeter of the golden bricks of La Alhambra's walls, a sight he'd found majestic all his life, but now reviled as if the palace itself were built centuries ago for the pure purpose of torturing his son. Faint moonlight reflected off the white roofs of the houses around him, making them look like a fleet of ships on a black sea.

Careful to avoid being garroted by the clotheslines that remained hung and bobbed in the summer breeze, he tossed the bucket of water over the roof and began to mop. As no person was around, he turned to God. "Adonai, won't You please watch over my daughter? Won't You please make sure she is set on the path that will keep her protected? She, as well as the baby. Oh, I know You may think she turned away from You because of her conversion. But she loves You still and prays to You in her way. That much is clear. Perhaps You are angrier with me for allowing this conversion? Please, Adonai, You must understand that was a different time. With all of those who worship You living together. I wanted her to be happy, to marry who she wanted, rather than who I selected for her. We did not realize how different we were until our new king and queen told us. Do not punish her because I allowed her to convert. It was done for love. I know I do not talk to You often; my practice keeps me busy—is that not what You want from me?—but please keep her safe. Please help her do what is right. Amen."

Catalina returned the following day with Gabriel as Vidal and Asher loaded the leather cases and wooden crates onto the wagon. Neighbors' wagons of all lengths and girths clogged the street in preparation for tomorrow's departure at dawn, forcing Catalina to wedge her way between the sides of wagons and walls of houses, while avoiding people who hurried to load their belongings as if the rabbi himself was exclaiming they were late. As she drew closer, he noticed her empty hands. Did any hope remain that she might still leave? If he asked to speak to her, his family would certainly find his behavior suspicious. He could not bring himself to greet her, instead returning inside for the next bags to hoist onto the wagon bed. If Gabriel was upset with him, his demeanor betrayed no ill feelings. He helped them pack the cart while Catalina helped Eliezer and Iamila dust the rooms and floors inside.

Though so much of the furniture had been sold off, Gabriel

requested that the table of ancient chestnut and the chairs that accompanied it remain in the house. That evening, the adults sat around the table for the last time, while Asher and Iamila squeezed together on the leather chair by the door to eat. Bonadonna prepared a stew of two boiled chickens—a parting gift from Gabriel's father.

"Please tell your father nothing of our meal this evening," Vidal said. "He intended for us to eat this on the road, but to bring a live chicken on the caravan? It could be stolen or spawn jealousy."

Vidal expected Gabriel's contempt to keep him silent, but Gabriel said, "I will say nothing. How long will it take to reach Fez?"

"Two weeks to reach the port at Málaga," Vidal said. From there, he continued, they would have one month to find a ferry across the Mediterranean Sea before the monarchs' decree took effect. After they landed at a seaport in the Maghreb, they'd make their way inland to Fez. As he shared the itinerary, he tried to imagine traversing the mountains and sea with his family at his side, including Catalina. If she stayed behind, how would he go on this great journey with the knowledge that he'd never see her again? "We hope to settle in Fez by winter."

Bonadonna changed the subject to Catalina's pregnancy, how many months until she was due, how they would arrange for a messenger to deliver letters back and forth once they settled in Fez. Questions Vidal asked himself drowned out the conversation. Would she leave with them? If so, why hadn't she told him? Perhaps she could not make this known in the presence of Gabriel. But if she planned to leave without telling her husband, Gabriel would catch her. It was a guarantee that Gabriel would pursue them on horseback while the caravan moved at a slug's pace. Or would Gabriel realize this conundrum, and that would be the ultimate excuse to let her go? No answer seemed likely or certain.

The moment dinner ended, Catalina volunteered to wash the plates in the courtyard and Vidal lit a candle on a tray to accompany her. She set the unwashed dishes by the door and stood at the center of the murky enclosure.

"Father, I'm sorry, but I cannot leave."

"You went to prayer as you promised? You spoke with Gabriel?"

"Gabriel assures me I'll be safe. He says my conversion is legitimate, and even if someone were to accuse me otherwise, his family and Padre Leonardo would all swear that I am a Catholic now and for the rest of my life. Please do not hate me, Father."

"I don't hate you. But I worry for you. I worry that, should this city, or the crown, or the church bring your conversion into question, no amount of well-intentioned Catholics can save you. The rabbi has convinced me as much."

"Then I think the rabbi's wrong."

"You know the stories of what this kingdom has done to conversos as well as I do."

"Yes, but even Queen Isabella and King Ferdinand are subjects of Christ. I have made my decision, Father. Please do not make this any more difficult than it already is by attempting to sway that decision." The way she spoke reminded him of their conversation after Gabriel asked for her hand. She'd fallen in love with Gabriel while acting as nurse for his sick grandmother. While Vidal had returned home to sleep each evening, Catalina stayed at the grandmother's bedside and spent many evenings talking with Gabriel—far more time than she'd ever spent speaking with a boy in any other circumstance. This led to the natural conclusion that they fall in love and wish to marry. Catalina was usually passive and did as she was told. He never expected her to come to him and ask for permission to marry outside the faith. But the memory was enough to remind him that she was an adult, more mature than a father could see. If she could advocate for her own betrothal, she could find a way to care for herself after he left.

"I understand. I hope you will not blame me for wishing things were different." He held her with the same tenderness that he'd held her the day she was born. A way he'd held her too few times in her life. When each child was born, he never imagined he'd need to say goodbye to any of them—only that one day he would be an old man and they'd bid farewell to him. Though this goodbye was not related to death, that did not make the reality of their impending separation any less painful.

"Allow us to accompany you to the city gates?" Catalina asked. "Your siblings would like that."

That night, Vidal lay in bed beside his wife, confined within the safety of their four walls and roof for the last time. Bonadonna fretted about their departure all day, but when bedtime arrived, she fell asleep without a moment's hesitation, filling their bedroom with a cacophony of snores as if this were any other night. But Vidal could not sleep with such a momentous period of his life beginning at dawn. As he did not want to return to the roof to pray aloud, he spoke to God through his thoughts. "Please keep Catalina safe. Please do not punish or test me for giving in to my daughter's decision to stay. Give her a long, happy life with a beautiful new baby—and more. Never let her suffer through an exile like that which my family and I must now endure. Amen."

At dawn, tarps stood erected over wagons in the street like the canopies of trees that'd grown overnight, and neighbors exited and entered their houses like worker ants marching to and from their anthill. Catalina hugged Iamila while she shivered in the morning air and Asher yawned as he strapped the horse to the wagon. As Eliezer could still not lift his arms above his head, Gabriel helped him raise a satchel strap over his shoulder. How were they supposed to make it across the sea when they already looked so weak?

After they covered the wagon supplies with a woven tapestry that'd once hung on their wall, Vidal circled the center of the empty sitting room, committing the stone walls and floors to memory, running his hand along the chestnut table where he'd eaten nearly every meal of his life, but would never sit or eat at again. He smelled the dust that lingered in the room with the leftover fragrances of his wife's cooking. Each of his children had been born in this house, and Sarah had died here. Might the decree be overturned? He dreamed that one day, even as an old man with mere weeks of life left in him, he'd see the inside of this home one more time. But this was not the end of the ha-Rofeh's residency in La Judería. Catalina and Gabriel would live here; his grandchild would grow here. Though the name and religion differed, the blood remained the same. Would his grandchild know of them or would the ha-Rofeh name pass out of existence like the names of his ancestors he had never bothered to learn? Such questions were irrelevant now, as he stepped into the street. He used a pocketknife to pry the wooden mezuzah off the doorframe and closed the door for the last time.

With his hand around the horse's reins, he led the cart and his family forward. They walked beside the wagon like mourners escorting a body to the graveside. Vidal knew the wagon would need to last many days and many leagues, and he wished to avoid weighing it down with humans unless necessary. The wagons around them moved forward in single file, as if heading to a parade route rather than banishment.

The sun stayed below the buildings when they traveled west down the main road. It was still too dark to see his neighbors' faces, and at first he only heard the sounds of children whimpering, couples bickering, old men yawning, and the amalgamation of voices of so many people he'd known growing up. Then the song of a woman's voice from down the line cut through the noise the way rainwater breaks through leaves fallen in the street. She sang "Avre Tu Puerta Cerrada" and the music spread as infectious as the plague, up the caravan until his family found themselves singing as well.

Avre tu puerta cerrada,
qu´en tu balcòn luz no hay
el amor a ti te vela,
partemos Rosa, partemos de aqui.

The soldiers who lined either side of the exit road acted passive and deaf as the caravan turned onto the street that divided the Catholic part of town from El Albayzín. At the base of the hill, families who wore turbans and aljubas watched from their darkened windows or along the roadside as the caravan funneled toward the city gate. Half seemed to look upon the exodus with the weary eyes of those who knew they were next, while others watched with indifference at this sight that would feel like a dream once they returned to sleep. The chanting continued and although Vidal knew his community would have liked nothing more than to return to their homes and the unmatched comfort of their beds, they sang as if they were praying in the synagogue, loud enough so that God would hear the cries of His people sent once again into banishment, even louder so that the song might resound from the city walls to the highest towers of La Alhambra and into the ears of Ferdinand and Isabella.

Yo demandi por la tu hermozura,
como te la dio el Dio
la hermozura tuya es pura,
la meresco solo yo.

At La Puerta de Elvira, the horseshoe-shaped western gate built into the city wall, the caravan clogged and Vidal pulled on the horse's reins. Over the caps and wagon tarps was the first glimpse of the dead grass that waited in the field beyond the city. He'd only been outside five times before, once to nurse Bonadonna's mourning, but otherwise when called to see a patient in Alfacar or Zujaira, but always on horseback or in a carriage provided by the patient's family, and never so far that he could not look back and see Granada or La Alhambra from a distance. The world beyond seemed as immeasurable and mysterious as the Catholic's description of Heaven; he could barely comprehend how far beyond the horizon his family would need to travel.

"Say goodbye to Gabriel and your sister."

"We'll go beyond the wall with you," Catalina said.

He could no longer steel himself to prolong their farewell. "You're pregnant. You should go home and rest."

"Father, I'm fine—"

"It's time for you to go home."

While Catalina kissed Iamila's forehead, and embraced Eliezer so as not to upset his scars, Vidal offered his hand to Gabriel. "I have put you through an uncomfortable situation. I hope you will not hold a father's lack of control against him."

"I forgive you, Dr. ha-Rofeh. Any disagreements between us are finished."

As he hugged his son-in-law, he heard Catalina offer advice to Asher. "Be brave on this journey. And remember what I taught you should Father and Eliezer need an assistant."

106

"You'll come to visit us in Fez one day, right?"

Catalina seemed on the cusp of lying, but Vidal interrupted so that their last words to each other would not be an empty promise. "We'll write Catalina when we get to Fez. For now, that's how we'll correspond."

Bonadonna had not cried in three years, but when she hugged Catalina, tears streamed down her cheeks with the unexpected force of a monsoon. "Why has God chosen to punish me so that I must again look upon a daughter's face for the last time?"

"It's not the last time. I will be right here."

"Ignore my tears. I am so relieved you're not a part of this."

"It's wrong that I stand by while you go."

"You have no reason to feel ashamed. Because of you, a part of us stays in Granada." She put a palm on Catalina's stomach. "Promise me you'll watch over Sarah's grave."

"I promise, Mother."

With that, there was only Vidal and Catalina left to say their farewells. He pulled her close and she whispered, "Do not hate me for my decision."

"I would never hate you. You're my daughter." He walked her to the side of the road with Gabriel in tow, and then, as a bird chases off its young when they are of age, he left her at the edge of the road beside the spectators of El Albayzín, never to look back or speak to her again.

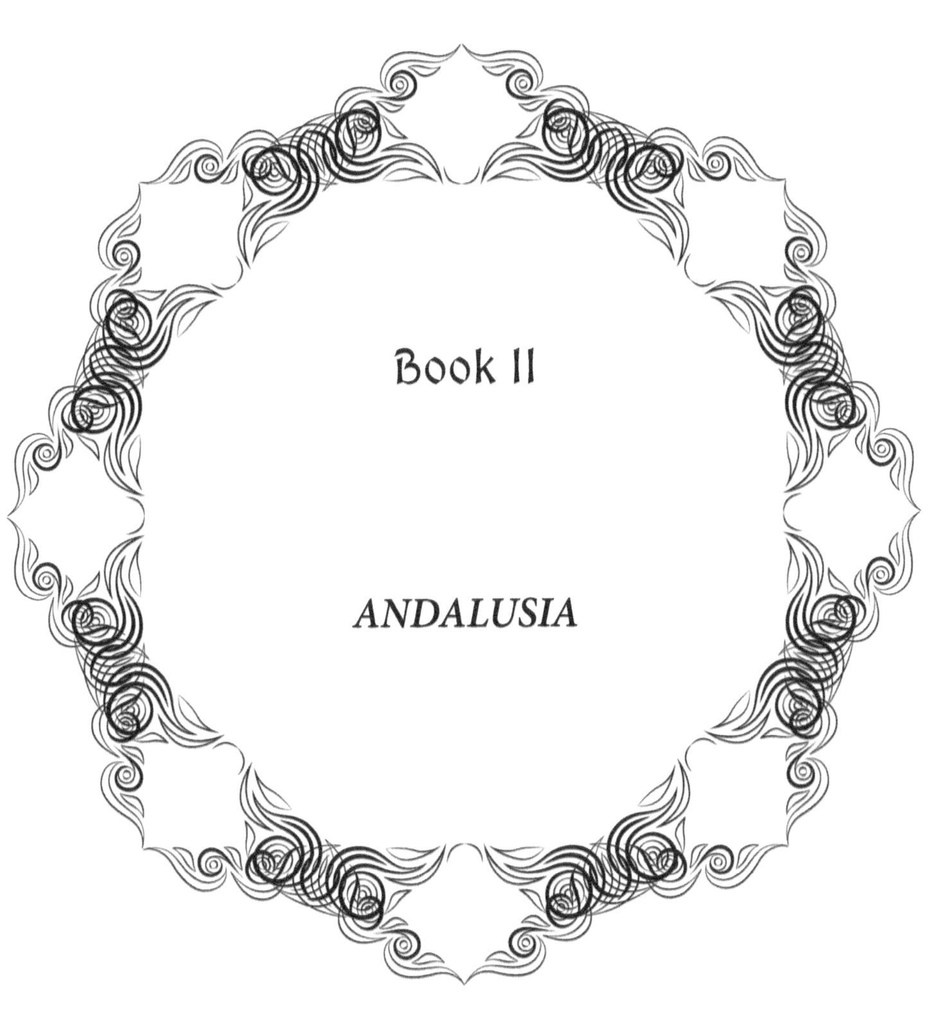

Book II

ANDALUSIA

Chapter Nine

The singing continued throughout the night, but the next morning people awoke with hoarse voices, and while at first the humming of the most dedicated singers could be heard down the line, all songs ended by the time the sun crested the sky on the second day. Two hundred people hauled seventy wagons in a single-file caravan through meadows and forests of treeless branches, over dirt roads and narrow wooden bridges built on dry riverbeds. At first, the world with its endless horizons seemed vast in every direction, yet Vidal quickly discovered this vastness was not something to behold but despise, as the only land he could reach with each step was monotonous grass or dirt, and the western Sierra Nevada mountains ahead grew no closer no matter how many hours they marched forward. If Vidal wished to take another look back at Granada, he needed only to turn around and look past the forty-odd wagons behind him to see the vague impression of the city walls and the architecture of La Alhambra perched atop the city like a watchful guardian. Only now that he'd left did the view of the city tempt him to return, for every step away from Granada was a step away from Catalina and Sarah.

For the first two days, Vidal stayed with the wagon and the company of his family, attempting to rouse their spirits with the hypothesis of what life would be like in Fez. "We will have a bigger house," he said. "A farm. A few chickens and some horses." Since he knew nothing of cooking, he gathered wood from the nearby gray and spindly pine trees and kindled a fire for Bonadonna to cook a supper of boiled carrots and eggplant. On the third day, as the June weather grew hotter and people drank through their water rations, members of the caravan sought Vidal for medical assistance and he left his family to pull the horse and wagon while he tended to ill patients down the line. He made no effort to beseech Eliezer to serve as his apprentice, as the boy's vow of silence remained devout.

Vidal examined limbs and tongues; listened to breathing and heartbeats. He diagnosed ailments quickly thanks to his decades-long relationships with many patients, but afflictions that'd once seemed manageable in Granada were becoming exacerbated by the heat and the twelve-hour days of walking. Arthritic joints flared, ankles twisted, and sciaticas inflamed in the never-ending march. The old and sick grew confused in the unfamiliar wilderness and when they asked for relatives who were long dead, they became frightened and inconsolable when their families reminded them of their reality. When the patients' families offered coin, he declined, knowing no one could spare the reales needed to rebuild their lives across the sea.

At the end of the third day, Vidal treated the broken nose of a man who'd been caught trying to steal a live chicken from one of the wagons. Once Vidal reset the nose bone, causing the man's nostrils to gush with blood like a clogged fountain finally released, two men from the council of fifteen banished the man and his family to the rear of the caravan to deter further thievery. Did Vidal's family own any valuables someone might steal? Although La Judería had become a mobile community, the lack of walls and soldiers, along with the surplus of hunger and desperation, tempted to dissolve the moral contracts of their society. Would anyone steal from a doctor?

That evening, when the caravan rested for the night on the outskirts of Láchar in a field of dried weeds that rose to the height of a man's chest, news spread of an unexpected sermon to be given by the rabbi. Without a mechitza to separate the men from the women, only the men attended. With no bimah or synagogue, Rabbi el Barchilon stood in full ceremonial robes on a wooden crate. Some fifty men gathered around him. Vidal counted not one member of the council of fifteen present.

"The council has made a decision. From now until we reach Fez, all observance of the Sabbath is hereby suspended. Tomorrow evening, we will stop the caravan like we always have and you may say what prayers and eat what meals you like, but at dawn, we will continue forward."

An eruption of groans emitted from the men, and indeed in the grass, he felt like they were a collection of woodland creatures receiving orders from their alpha. He could not fault the others for being displeased by the decision. After two days of intense preparation to leave and another three on the road, he was as ready for a day of rest as anyone, but if fleeing their home before they were all forced to convert or be executed wasn't an emergency required to break the Sabbath, what was?

"But my family has been desperate to rest all week," the men said. "For what purpose are we fleeing the monarchs' decree if we are giving up our beliefs on our own volition?" "If we do not practice until we reach Fez, does that not put our devotedness to our religion into question?" He'd never heard his neighbors challenge their rabbi in this manner, when they were usually so willing to follow him as if he were the mouth of God. But it seemed odd that traditions and customs that were so necessary for all of their lives could be halted for the sake of convenience, no matter how well-intended the suspension.

"Trust me when I say this is how things must be done. What if we must wait until the final days before the decree to find passage from these shores? If we observe the Sabbath, we will have lost precious days unnecessarily."

As Vidal returned to the wagon, the sun glowed on the grass and made the billowing of the blades look like waves on a lake of gold. Despite nearly 200 people among them, conversations down the line fell to a murmur as husbands and fathers returned to their families to share news of the Sabbath. He discussed with Bonadonna first, as she portioned out a ladle of eggplant soup into the clay bowl that Vidal used to eat every one of his meals on the journey. The meal looked as drab as day-old oatmeal, but his hunger convinced him it would taste as rich as lamb.

"I assume this means you'll be off with your patients tomorrow," she said.

"Without the Sabbath I have no reason to neglect them."

"While you've been away, I've been dragging your horse and feeding your children. Asher is driving me mad with his constant complaining and it seems he cannot take a moment's rest without ridiculing Iamila."

"I'll speak with him."

"Vidal, I know many patients are sick. We've been on the road for three days and I haven't complained once—I understand their health is more urgent than my needs, but I could use your help around the wagon."

"What would you like me to do? I'm here now."

"I don't need you now. I need you when you're away. I need you to wrangle the horse and, at times, Asher as well."

"Then when we set off tomorrow I'll do just that."

"And if someone pulls you away to inspect another ailment?"

"Bonita, if someone comes to me for medical assistance, I cannot deny them."

"Refer them, then. There are other doctors on the caravan."

"I assure you they're as busy as I."

"Please. I need you to help me. I shouldn't have to beg."

"I'll arrange a way to be at the wagon more."

"What will you arrange?"

Truthfully, he had no idea. His thighs ached, his stomach grumbled for food, and his throat burned from lack of water. The soup might help give him the stamina to concoct a solution to Bonadonna's request—although his head was so preoccupied with the diagnoses and ailments of the other caravanners, he doubted an idea would come with haste. "I'll think of something."

"And how long will this take?"

"By tomorrow. You have my word."

"God will know if you lie to your wife."

"Even if He didn't, I have no doubt you'd get His attention."

Bonadonna called forth the children for their servings of soup. They ate in different sections of the grass; none seemed interested in speaking with one another. He could not recall seeing such low morale since viewing the emir's soldiers stationed throughout Granada; exhausted, hungry, dirty and with their heads hung, waiting for the inevitable surrender. If he were a general, he'd thought at the time, he'd find a way to lift their spirits. And so, as the patriarch of the family, he must find a way to raise his family's spirits now.

He approached Eliezer, whose back was now strong enough to sit cross-legged as he ate from a clay bowl nestled in his lap. "Talk to me," Vidal said. "I want you to come back and be my apprentice again." Eliezer ignored him, as he did at the wedding, concentrating on the broth as if he were reading a book submerged inside. "Please, you're going to have to speak to me at some point. Stop this behavior. We're both men. We can have a conversation."

Although the scars usually made him slow to rise, Eliezer hoisted himself to his feet while hiding the grimace of someone who irritated their wounds by accident. The tips of the tall grass plummeted around Eliezer's feet as he stomped away from his father.

"You are my son and I demand you speak to me. You refuse to show me respect, you neglect all of your duties as an apprentice, and from the sound of it, you barely help your mother at the wagon. This must stop at once."

"Please leave me alone." His voice sounded wilted as if his vocal cords had been whipped as well.

"You will come back here and start acting like a proper son and physician's apprentice."

"Is that all I am to you, an apprentice?"

"I did not raise you to behave this way."

"You didn't raise me at all." An object sailed through the air at Vidal's head, the liquid discharging from its basin like a great wet tongue sticking out of an animal's mouth. Before Vidal could react, lukewarm eggplant soup splashed across his face and the clay bowl struck his collarbone. The pot somersaulted in the air before landing face down in the ground, its fall cushioned by the grass. Thick, mucous-like broth dripped down Vidal's face and sent a chill through his body as it dripped down the inside of his gown. Every member of the caravan, ten wagons in either direction, ceased their bickering about the Sabbath to look at the broth-covered doctor. If news of the fight traveled down the line to the rabbi's tent at the head of the caravan, Vidal would not be surprised.

The bowl was Eliezer's only eating platter and Vidal lifted his boot over the upturned dome with the nerve to stomp it into a dozen pieces. The rage in Eliezer's face soon gave way to concern over whether to call his father's bluff.

"Vidal!" Bonadonna's scream pierced the afternoon air and, as it did, he saw clearly what might happen if he crushed the bowl. His wife would not speak to him until they reached Fez; the action would splinter his family like the shards of broken clay. He retracted his boot, picked up the bowl, and handed it to his son without a word. The moment Eliezer took the bowl, Vidal returned to finish his soup in silence, and neither Bonadonna nor the family of sick patients bothered him the rest of the evening.

Vidal awoke at dawn to find his tongue and head had cooled along with the refreshing surprise of cloudy weather. If they could not rest for God, perhaps God would allow the sun to rest on their behalf. His wife had not bothered to rouse him and already he heard families down the line preparing to move forward at first light. From the head of his wagon came the sound of Asher and Iamila feeding the horse. He abandoned the blissful support of the tall grass, as forgiving on his back as a featherbed, and found Asher teasing the horse by dangling a carrot over its muzzle while Iamila offered the animal carrots like a doting mother feeding her child.

"Very good, eat up, María, we have a long day ahead."

"What did I tell you about naming the horse?" Vidal asked.

"See," Asher said to Iamila. "I warned you. Now Father's going to smash your bowl too."

Was that all he was to them? A father who disciplined and kept them in line? Was there no sense of joy for these two young ones after he'd given them a pleasurable life as the son of a physician? After he allowed them to devote their young lives to studies of the Torah? Rather than reacting, he listened to his youngest children bicker.

"But she deserves a name. Look at how much she's done for us."

"Father told us not to name the horse. He doesn't want us to grow attached."

"That would be the first time you followed Father's orders."

"It's okay, Asher," Vidal said. "In truth, I was surprised you didn't name her the moment Ochoa delivered her to our home." Vidal plucked the carrot from Asher's hand and offered it to the horse, who grabbed the vegetable with its teeth and sucked it into its mouth. "But we will have to leave her at the coast. Don't fall in love with her; there's no future with her."

"But if we leave her, how will we get from the African coast to Fez?"

"The rabbi's brother will greet us at the port and escort us to our new homes."

"Do you think it'll be much farther when we get to Africa?"

"I don't know. I suppose it depends on which port city we make berth. Don't fuss over it. This travel is only for a few weeks, then we'll be settled in our new home and never have to move again."

"Until Father marries you off," Asher said. Iamila went quiet, as if Asher had insensitively reminded her that one day she would die.

"Asher! Don't worry, Iamila, we're in no rush to marry you out of the family. Besides, I am in no position to afford a dowry."

"Please let me stay with you and Mother. I'll take care of you when you grow old."

"That's kind of you, but trust me when I say one day you'll feel differently."

"That would be perfect," Asher said. "And after Mother and Father croak, you can care for my family and me."

"Oh shut up, Asher!" Iamila said. "You're almost thirteen. Start acting like a man."

"I'll act like a man when I have my bar mitzvah."

"That's not how it works. It's the age that makes you the man, not the ceremony."

"Your sister is right, you know?" A new solution dawned on Vidal. If Eliezer had resigned as an apprentice, he had another son on the cusp of manhood equipped to inherit the duties. One Bonadonna was eager to have taken off her hands. "Asher, how would you like to help me see patients tomorrow?"

"Won't that upset my brother?"

"He's already upset, and I could use the help."

"I'll help you, Father," Iamila said.

"I'm sorry, Mila, but I was only asking your brother."

"But you let Catalina be your nurse."

"And one day, you'll be my nurse as well. But there's an order to these things and right now I'm asking your brother for his help. Your mother needs yours."

"And it'd be best if you helped mother so you learn how to cook and clean for whatever old, fat man they marry you off to," Asher said.

Vidal was tempted to slap his son, but after yesterday's scene, the last thing his family needed was another demonstration of his discipline for the caravan to gossip over. "Enough! Now help your mother with the wagon, then follow me."

"Will I see blood? Or dead people?"

"God willing, no."

"Doesn't sound all too exciting."

"It'll be good for you." He ruffled Asher's hair and kissed Iamila on the cheek, which he meant out of affection, but because he did it so rarely, she acted as if the kiss had turned her to stone. As he walked away, he caught her wiping the wetness of his lips off her face. He took a bread loaf from under the tapestry that covered their wagon and sliced pieces for his family. She'd be happier with Asher away from her, and Vidal would be gone fewer hours if he had a helper. Like a general building his soldiers' morale, Vidal thought this would begin to improve things.

As the caravan marched forward and the surroundings turned to a lowland at the base of the western Sierra Nevada range, Vidal led Asher down the line. Conducting rounds with a son by his side made him feel normal again—no difference, save they were calling on patients in nature rather than the congested alleyways of a stench-filled city. One day he may even feel nostalgic for his time doing rounds along the caravan, especially if the experience was brief.

When they arrived at different wagons, the sight of Asher seemed to perk up the spirits of the sick who either walked slowly with a family member holding their hand, or lay in a nook of a wagon bed carved from their family's many belongings. This young boy, who did not look haggard and dragged down by age like his father, enchanted the patients. It soon grew difficult for Vidal to tell how sick some were when they asked Asher if he was excited to follow in his father's footsteps as a physician. To Vidal's surprise, Asher nodded in agreement with the patients or asked them how they were feeling. He even asked questions about their lives back in Granada—although Asher knew them from the synagogue, he seemed to recall little of their trades or the histories of their families.

When Vidal examined a sprained ankle, or in one patient's case a crushed toe from where a wagon wheel had rolled over his foot, Asher's eyes sparkled with excitement as if he was being invited to inspect a cadaver. When a young mother of three complained of chest pain, and Vidal examined her in one of the tent-covered wagons, asking her to disrobe so he could assess her breasts for lumps and listen to her heartbeat, Asher made no protest about being left outside. When Vidal completed the examination, he birthed himself from the tent flaps to find his son standing guard with his back turned to the wagon.

Asher's old mannerisms disappeared until the evening when he was served another bowl of eggplant soup by his mother. He tossed the serving onto the ground and handed back a bowl that dripped with the creamy remnants of discarded soup. "Eggplant again? I'm a physician now, Mother. Cook me something else!"

"Speak to me that way again and you'll see what happens."

Bonadonna had never struck their children before, but Vidal was quick to layaway his hard-earned soup on the ground and separate her from his youngest son before a medical examination was necessary at his own wagon. Where at first he expected to take Asher away to discipline him, Bonadonna seemed the one more in need of being calmed.

"Is this the kind of behavior you condone?" she asked him. "Who fills him with these delusions?"

"I don't know, Bonita. It's a mystery to me."

"You see now why I need you here? I've done everything you've asked. I've given up my entire life to follow you. All I want is your help with the wagon. I don't understand why you can't give me that."

He shushed her and ordered Asher to calm his temper at the front of the wagon.

"What about my dinner?"

"Scoop it off the ground if you're hungry," Vidal said.

He walked his wife away from the caravan and brought her under a nearby tree to speak with her. Beyond the tree were groves of what appeared to be a winery, though he saw no people who owned it nor farmhouse where those people might dwell.

"I've been trying to help you, Bonita. I've gotten Asher away from you for several hours a day—"

"But you're gone as well. No other women are keeping their wagons and families together while their husbands carry on with business. I cannot continue to do all this while you're off playing hero to the rest of the caravan. Do you see Señor Bar Yosef practicing astronomy while his wife works? Or Señor Levin selling goods? Even the rabbi doesn't pray when he knows he must help his family. Nobody can expect you to be the only man in the caravan who continues his practice on this journey. You cannot be gone for so many hours."

Although he was reluctant to lose the argument, his wife was right. He couldn't refuse a sick patient, but he needed to do better to help Bonadonna. Could he truly be the only husband and father who was working on this caravan? There were other doctors. And men who foraged for food and chopped down trees for kindling. Although the rabbi had skipped the Sabbath, that did not mean he was not constantly working with the council of fifteen to determine how to get the caravan to Málaga day by day.

"You're right. I'm sorry, I don't know what to do. It's not in my nature to refuse a patient. The very thought fills me with loathing."

"Why don't you speak with the rabbi? At dawn, you go to his tent."

"You think prayer will fix this?"

"Not to pray. Ask for his guidance. Maybe his family can help us."

The next morning, Vidal rose before sunrise to a horizon the color of radish skin. He made his way up the line to reach the rabbi at the head of the caravan. As he walked, he passed nearly thirty wagons. Some families slept in circles on the ground with their backs to each other like animals prepared to wake at the sign of predators. Other families rose early, ripping bread off loaves and hanging buckets of water over open flames to boil tea in anticipation of the movement forward of the caravan.

The rabbi's octagonal tent was made of emerald velvet with golden fringes, large enough to shelter the man, his wife, son, and two daughters. Binyamín sat on an apple crate turned upside down, asleep with his head hung over his chest, like a guard who stood watch through the night outside a king's chambers. When Vidal whispered, Binyamín lurched awake at the sound of his name.

"Is your father up?"

"Come back at sunrise, Dr. ha-Rofeh."

"The sun will rise within minutes."

"My family needs the morning to pack our tent. Come back this evening."

"This cannot wait."

"Dr. ha-Rofeh, I mean you no disrespect, but many people come to my father with troubles and he, too, needs his rest on this long journey."

"I am a doctor for this caravan and my physician duties have not been suspended since we left Granada, so please understand, Binyamín, that I need to speak with the rabbi this morning."

At that moment, Rabbi el Barchilon emerged from the tent opening into the morning air. The curly hairs of his beard were messy and unkempt and the few wisps of wavy hair over his head stood with the volume of a younger man's hairline. The rabbi's appearance reminded Vidal of when he'd come to ask for help to save Eliezer in the middle of the night.

"Binyamín, what noise is this?" The rabbi looked up to find Vidal standing there. "Doctor, is something wrong? Is someone unwell?"

Binyamín began to apologize to his father for the disturbance, but Vidal spoke over him. "I do not mean to disturb you, but I must speak with you."

"No disturbance." The rabbi tucked the tent partition shut as if it were enough to block the sound of their conversation from reaching the inside. Vidal heard the people of the caravan rouse behind him and felt the sun rising in the east by the second.

"Father, you need your rest," Binyamín said.

"We rest when we reach Fez." Rabbi el Barchilon brought Vidal to the far end of the tent to a crater of ash, the remnants of a late-night campfire. The two men sat on stones likely carried and placed there by Binyamín. The two aurochs the rabbi had acquired to pull his wagon rested on each other, tied to the trunk of a nearby oak tree, with the first auroch's neck supported by the great scimitar-like horns of the second's. The grassy lowland and mountains that waited ahead made Vidal's legs ache at the sight of the journey to come. "You will not believe the sorts of questions our people have come to ask me this week. First, they ask for the blessing for travel. Now they want the blessing for tents, the blessing for good weather, every blessing they can think of. What sort of idea is that, the blessing for weather?"

"There are the prayers for rain and dew in the Amidah."

"Please, there's hardly a pagan left these days who thinks that prayer may actually control the weather."

"You will be happy to know I do not come asking for words to a prayer."

Rabbi el Barchilon clasped his hands together. "How can I help you, Doctor?"

"Most of the men in this caravan aren't working. Their only occupation now is to deliver their families to Fez. But it appears I am like you, neither of our duties relieved. My wife asks me to see fewer patients, but I cannot do that, Rabbi. I was hoping perhaps your family could help my family? I ask you not to cook and clean for us, merely for your wife to help my wife, your children to assist my children, and we will do the same in trade. Or perhaps you can help me find a family interested in the opportunity?"

"You have many friends and neighbors, Vidal. You're a beloved member of our community. I cannot imagine anyone saying no."

"I wish I shared your optimism. But I fear to ask for favors." He recalled the thief who had his nose broken, but spoke none of this to the rabbi. "People are desperate now and I cannot be certain who to trust."

"You trust me."

"More than anyone."

"I have only one son, and he's taken on the burden of being my mouth and ears for the people I haven't the time to speak with. I need my wife to help with our wagon and my daughters are too young for me to lend them out for help. But perhaps your family could move your wagon farther up the line? Just behind my family. That way we can check on each other and help each other throughout the day."

"You would allow me that honor? Even ahead of the council members?"

"Oh, the council is useless now that we've departed Granada. You should have seen the uproar they raised over suspending our practice of the Sabbath."

"I thought that was their idea."

"It wasn't their idea until I convinced them, then they took credit for it. Look at where we are. This is no place for bureaucrats. We need men who have solutions, men who do not stop their work simply because we're in transition. If a man with solutions makes a request as simple as support for his family, he deserves a place up the line more than anyone."

The rabbi's offer was so moving that Vidal felt the pressure of hot tears convening behind his retinas. Any doubts for why he'd chosen to go on this journey, why he'd left Granada rather than convert, vanished. He thanked the rabbi and told him he'd bring their wagon up the line at once. As he returned to his family, the sun rose ahead of him dead center over the plains they'd crossed. Strokes of azure, gold, and scarlet spilled across the grass and reminded him of the stained glass light that'd once streamed through the synagogue windows. What colors would those light streaks be when they reached Fez?

Chapter Ten

For three days the caravan did nothing but ascend the first mountain. All day and night, life existed on an incline. Everything grew heavier, from the pull of the wagon to the step in each foot to the air in their empty bellies. Sweat poured down brows and necks the way rain streams down the side of a house and people took each breath as if the humidity in the air might drown them. But they kept pushing forward. No one turned back. Unlike their emir, they would not surrender.

On the third day, Vidal treated the wounds of two families whose wagons had smashed together, as one rolled backward down the hill, tugging its horse with it and the weight of the wagon crushing the horse behind it. As Vidal relocated the shoulders and wrapped the sprained wrists of the family who'd attempted to catch the plummeting wagon, the owners examined their broken horses' legs then slit the horses' throats with the coolness one beheads a chicken. News of the tragic accident slipped out of memory the moment the two families debated the implications of whether to eat the horses. The animals' lack of split hooves made it forbidden under kosher law, one family argued, but if they could suspend the Sabbath, argued the other family, why not break their dietary restrictions as well? Before the horses could be carved up and distributed to anyone whose hunger outweighed their faith, Rabbi el Barchilon arrived to settle the matter and said they would offer the horses in trade to the next travelers they encountered on the road. Vidal ascertained that this was the right thing to do, though the thought of juicy meat and a full belly tempted him to break Jewish law more than any royal decree.

Vidal and the rabbi's family instead ate a supper of boiled lentils, sitting in a circle around a fire pit dug by Binyamín. Their horses were stopped on an incline, wooden planks wedged under wheels so no more wagons could roll backward. The sun hung low in the sky and the high overhead clouds turned a delicate lavender.

Within the circle of two families that surrounded the fire pit, tighter groups formed. Bonadonna laughed with Señora el Barchilon, a woman her age and twenty years the rabbi's junior, who'd married the rabbi and birthed his three children after his first wife died when Vidal was still his student. The promotion to the deputy location of the caravan had changed Bonadonna's attitude as drastically as soup can mend a cold. Asher listened to Binyamín and Eliezer reminisce about their school days, and Iamila bickered with the rabbi's two young daughters, who stole glances at Asher and teased about what they'd like to do with the curls of his hair.

"Are your daughters promised to anybody, Rabbi?" Vidal asked, knowing full well that they'd been betrothed to council families since birth. "I think they're developing a little affection for my Asher."

"You'd marry off your youngest before Eliezer? Vidal, I'm insulted." The rabbi laughed as if he'd quoted Genesis 25:30.

"No insult implied, Rabbi. It's quite an age difference between my Eliezer and your girls. Besides, I doubt he'd honor another betrothal arranged by me."

"He's quite guarded around you."

"Guarded would be an improvement."

"I've seen many grudges held in my life, but his determination is exceptional."

"Has he spoken to you?"

"I don't think he's much pleased with me either, Vidal. I'm the one who married them."

"But he respects you. Would you speak to him?"

"There's no need. Binyamín tells me everything. Your son is

in great distress. Binyamín doesn't know if he'll ever recover from what he went through."

"The scars on his back will heal."

"You're meticulous with the process necessary to heal the flesh, but overzealous to mend wounds of the heart. Give him time. He lost his bride, he lost his house, he lost his dignity—"

"I'm sure he wishes he could lose me too."

"Let him blame you. Imagine the despair that might befall him if he blamed himself."

All Vidal wanted was to sit with Eliezer, talk with him and Binyamín, laugh with the boys, share stories of his own, but Eliezer felt no more accessible to him than Sarah or Catalina. "Thank you, Rabbi. You are most wise."

When the caravan crested the mountain the following day, the peak offered a view of the endless expanse of the Sierra Nevadas. The mountains continued one after the other into the distance until they met the horizon, emerging from the westward earth like the dorsal fins of great fish that momentarily breached the water's surface. On either side of the dirt road, the slopes of their mountain plummeted 100 leagues downward into valleys untouched since before the days of Abraham. A plethora of trees, bushes, and grass covered the mountains on the other side of the valley, making it seem as if every mountain offered shade and vegetation save the one they now traversed. Though reaching the top of the mountain felt like a great coup, the isolation from civilization and the proximity to the sun forewarned new tests that awaited.

After a week on the road, in a June month with heat that reminded Vidal of standing beside a baker's oven, people finished their water supplies with no rivers or streams on the path to replenish them. As Vidal could not give to patients the paltry amount of water meant for his own family—even he did not need Bonadonna to remind him of that—he began to use sage and rosemary to revive caravanners who fainted. At each wagon that called upon him, Vidal asked Asher to reach for the proper concoction from his instrument case and the boy did nothing but obey. Yet when Vidal checked the bag himself, he realized that only thistles of sage and rosemary remained in the glass vials where he stored his supplies.

To prolong his rations, Vidal told Asher to use the medicinal herbs for only their frailest patients and improvised remedies with the lemon and honey he still carried in abundant supply. When they moved down the caravan line to the next patient, they passed men with their shirts around their heads to block the sun, and women who fanned themselves with paper torn from books, for they were forbidden to reveal their skin to strangers even in the oppressive heat.

Asher tugged on his father's shirt sleeve. "Do we have more medicine in our wagon?"

"I'm afraid what I'm carrying is all that remains."

"How long will it last us?"

"Three days. Maybe four."

"And how many more days to Fez?"

"Too many." Somehow, he'd need to acquire new supplies. He'd need to spirit himself away from the caravan and find a small town in the mountains to provide him with any herbs and remedies they could spare. He'd pay for supplies if he had to, though it'd be better to beg. Would Bonadonna support his plan? His leaving the caravan would not be welcome news. But they were in desperate need of supplies. Patients would die without medicine—water was even more urgent. She would need to understand.

"Then how do you decide who gets what medicine?" Asher asked.

"I must be selective. We can't give precious medication to one person who may need it less than another."

"How do you decide who needs it more?"

"I've never had to decide before. And once we reach Fez, I pray I'll never have to again."

"Did you have the right medicine for Sarah?"

Asher's question startled him as if a snake had risen from the grass. "Why do you want to know this?"

"I'm curious. You don't speak about it."

"Perhaps I have a reason for not speaking of it."

"Yes, but there's no one else around and I've always wanted to know."

It would be simple to tell Asher to leave the subject alone; this was none of his business. But the boy worked for free, and if Asher stopped helping, there was nothing Vidal could do to change his mind. Was his son ready for such details? "I assumed your sister had a simple cough and administrated the right medicine. But she was young and her lungs were weak. It's obvious now, the nights were cold and she was phlegmatic. I didn't have the skill nor knowledge to save her. Neither then nor now."

"Is there anyone you feel that way about here?"

"If we don't get some water soon, I'll feel that way about everyone." He put a hand on the boy's shoulder. "Don't dwell on these things, Asher. You're too young."

"I'll be thirteen soon."

"Now you wish to be an adult! These are concerns of older men. Simply because you're thirteen doesn't mean we'll burden you with all of life's problems at once."

"What do we do when a patient is past help, Father?"

"We try to make them comfortable. Give them a little opium to ease their pain and fears. Better to do that than risk any drastic procedures to keep them alive, which rarely work and only prolong their suffering."

"You wouldn't try to save them?"

"Not if they're past saving."

"Even if they're part of the family?"

"Enough of these questions."

By the end of the day, Vidal and Asher's lips were dried and cracked, their cheeks and noses as red as the shells of pomegranates. He began asking patients when they last drank water. People passed out with more frequency as the caravan traveled over the shallow slopes of the mountain's ridge, and when they collapsed on the dirt ground, both their families and the families of the nearest wagons lifted them to their feet and waved air over their earth-covered faces to resuscitate them. Families who'd drunk the last of their supply asked for the smallest sips from their neighbors whose larger wagons accommodated more abundant rations. Vidal witnessed the scenes and checked on the patients as helpless as he'd been when Granada had been under siege in the previous year. He recalled how scarce the water had been, how in the late summer, several elderly died from heatstroke and dehydration, the skin of their corpses as dry as shriveled grapes and their mouths frozen in the air as if, in their final moments, they attempted to raise their mouths to drink from fountainheads that existed only in their dying minds.

He returned to the front of the caravan that evening to speak with Rabbi el Barchilon about his plan to acquire water. The rabbi stood outside his tent surrounded by the council of fifteen when Vidal arrived. These wise men who'd once worn their grandest robes for council meetings now crowded beside each other with bare chests, their large pale bellies splaying over their waists like growths of great trees. Vidal entered the circle, recalling what the rabbi had confided in him about the council the previous week. Nobody bothered to expel him, as they were too busy debating whether to stop to gather supplies. The rabbi insisted now was not the time; they needed to move forward to the coast. But the council exclaimed there'd be no one to reach the coast without water.

"You worry too much," the rabbi said. "This route is the major artery between Granada and Málaga. We should come along a stream any day now."

"Rabbi, these people may not have that long," Vidal said. To disagree with the rabbi felt like a great insult, but with his patients in dire condition, he dwelled little on the manners of his words.

"We told them to bring a month's worth of water."

"To follow those orders, each family would need an additional wagon simply to store the rations. I agree we stop. I'm low on medical supplies as well."

"You said you had enough remedies to last a year."

"I'm sure he only told you that to make his way up the wagon," said a council member.

"I did have the remedies," Vidal said. "But I underestimated the amount of illness and injury that would occur on such a short journey. I thought perhaps my supplies would be depleted at the sea or once we reached the Maghreb, but these people are too weak and fragile to make it to their own shores."

Shelomo stood at the rabbi's right hand and addressed Vidal for the first time since Tsipora's wedding. "Do remedies not come from plants? Is there nothing in these mountains you may use to create the medicines you need?"

"Everything here is grass. Many of my herbs come from Las Alpujarras or were imported by the de Zaniçerases. I won't find what I need here. We need to do something, Rabbi, or our people will begin to die in a way that is both torturous and prolonged. The old and sick will be the first to go."

Though the council of fifteen were wealthy enough to afford wagons capable of carrying the prescribed amounts of water, each looked at one another as if Vidal's words were a diagnosis that their age would sentence them to a fate from which no amount of coin could spare them.

"We can afford to waste no time," the rabbi said. "You see how slowly these people move. You expect them to detour to collect supplies?"

"Not everyone needs to go. A small party could be dispatched to a village or town, anywhere nearby to acquire supplies."

"No Catholic city will give an entire caravan access to its water," a council member said.

"They will if we have the coin—coin the decree forbids us from taking across the sea anyway."

"I favor Vidal's idea," Shelomo said. Shelomo's support surprised Vidal until he remembered that every decision in his old friend's life involved money. "I've traveled this road before with my father when we imported goods from Egypt. If my geography serves me well, I imagine we're near Periana. A small town, but developed enough to have the supplies we need." The rabbi asked Shelomo how far Periana was by horseback. "I imagine less than a day's ride. But it's difficult to tell; the caravan alters the landscape it passes. I see only mere fragments of the road I recognize."

"How does this benefit you?"

"Vidal, I'm insulted."

"We'd be going to Periana to gather supplies to give to the caravan, not sell them. I hope that doesn't alter your interest?"

"Of course not. I wouldn't dream of taking advantage of my neighbors in their time of need."

"He only takes advantage when we are well," said a council member.

Rabbi el Barchilon called for the council to silence their laughter and for a moment Vidal felt as if they were all children again ordered to settle in the rabbi's classroom. "All of you stop before I change my mind. Shelomo, you have a spare horse. Will you go to Periana and find someone to accompany you?"

"My new son-in-law will be eager to accept the opportunity." For the first time, Vidal was pleased that Shelomo had not become his in-law, for he could not imagine the man ordering Eliezer to embark on such missions.

When Shelomo and Avraham returned from their reconnaissance to Periana the following day, the council of fifteen reconvened at the far end of the rabbi's tent pitched beside a ravine of boulders. To assert his authority, the rabbi stood elevated on a rock to look down at the council. Although Vidal had never been sworn in as a council member, that hardly mattered as he picked a spot beside the rabbi. It was the council of sixteen now, he decided, in practice if not in name.

Shelomo explained that the city's council agreed to allow ten men to enter their walls, and another twenty to wait outside to help carry back supplies. The city wanted the caravan nowhere near the gate, as other travelers from Loreto and Valenzuela had camped outside in weeks prior, and left a disarray of droppings, both human and horse, as well as animal bones and rubbish.

"I detest this arrangement," the rabbi said. "Our caravan has every right to enter their city to purchase goods. They enforce these restrictions because we're Jews, and I imagine they'll take every coin they can from us." Despite his outburst, the rabbi declared that the council send out a call for their thirty most abled men to embark on the journey back to Periana at dawn. "I'll volunteer my son to accompany them."

Vidal had scribbled a list of supplies onto paper that could be given to any town physician or pharmacist. With it, he'd prepared a drawstring sack of 100 reales—the most he could spare without risking coin they'd need to leave the peninsula. After the meeting concluded and the council dispersed to call upon their sons and son-in-laws for the mission, Vidal handed both items to Shelomo. "This is very important. Promise me you won't lose it." Even as he spoke, he imagined Shelomo or one of the boys who accompanied him coming back with nothing but bottles of honey and lavender, none of the rarer items required.

"I have a better idea." Shelomo passed the paper back to him. "You go to Periana and get the supplies yourself."

"I'd be a burden; I'm too old."

"And I am too fat, yet I made it there and back. You know as well as I that we can't have only our youngest enter Periana. If we send them with every real we can spare, they're as likely to be wooed by a whorehouse as a chance to convert. We need a respected member of the community to lead the party."

"Now that you need something, I am a respected member of the community?"

"What are you going on about? Of course you are. You're a doctor. You save lives!"

"I garner little respect, especially from the likes of you."

"Is this about our children?"

"What else would it be about?"

"Vidal, I'm sorry. I did what I thought was right in a moment of urgency. That was in Granada. All those events are behind us now; they're irrelevant. Please consider leading the party. It'll be our youth who are going and they need a man like you to keep them on their mission and return them safely."

Could Shelomo be sorry? Did the man understand the meaning of the word remorse? Or was this simply the salesman speaking, knowing precisely what to say to convince someone to buy into the shit they didn't need? Nevertheless, Vidal knew his old friend was right. No one else could be trusted to return with the supplies he needed, and if only young men went on this mission, they were as likely to return with nothing at all.

"Put out a word for thirty young men to meet me here at dawn."

"Where will you be going?"

"To speak with my wife."

He found Bonadonna beside their wagon, washing clothes in a wooden bucket with Iamila. As they could not spare fresh water, the clothes were being rewashed in the same tub as last time, and specks of dirt and an oily film covered the surface of the black bath. He took a soiled tunic of his from the pile beside Bonadonna, slathered it in soap, and rubbed it together as he spoke to her about what would happen.

"What about your patients?"

"I'll have to trust Asher to do morning rounds alone. He'll report on those I need to see when I return."

"Why do you have to do this? They should send businessmen and traders. You're no negotiator. You couldn't convince your patients to pay us before we left Granada."

"But if I entrust my list of remedies to someone else, they may return with the wrong supplies."

"Do you really think so little of our neighbors?"

"Of course not. I'd trust them with many things. But no one is going to know the difference between wormwood and abrotanum. No one's going to know that they're paying for salve when they think they're buying sumac. They could get fooled and cheated and never realize it. But I'd know. That's why I need to go myself."

Bonadonna held out her arms, letting one of Asher's shirts wade on the water's surface. "I wish it wasn't the case, but I understand. Be safe. Do your business and get out. If you come across a local with a broken leg, I don't want you stopping to mend them."

"I won't even tell them I'm a doctor." Vidal washed several more shirts by his wife's side, eager to earn her affection before the plan he'd need to present next. "Another thing. I'd like Eliezer to come with me."

"No. Others can volunteer for this mission. Find somebody else."

"I can go, Father," Iamila said.

Vidal and Bonadonna responded with a united, "No."

"You haven't been down the line like I have," Vidal told Bonadonna. "Men between the ages of thirteen and thirty are few in our ranks. Eliezer is the perfect age. You told me yourself his back is healing well. We need him to carry supplies." Before she said anything, he added, "If you truly refuse, I won't press the conversation."

"How considerate of you." Bonadonna pulled a tunic from the water and rung it dry. "Other mothers are volunteering their sons?"

"Other mothers have no say. I hope you'll take into consideration that I chose to ask you first. I'll be with him the entire time."

"If Eliezer wants to go, I won't stop him."

"So you'll talk to him?"

"No. You'll talk to him. If you can get him to go, you have my blessing."

"But he only talks to you."

"Good luck."

With no nearby trees to string a clothesline, Bonadonna began to lay clothes on the edge of the wagon. Vidal knew he'd gain no further approval from his wife, and went in search of Eliezer. He was seated on a boulder at the entrance to the ravine, hunched over a book of poetry Catalina had gifted him on his last birthday. Although Vidal had cautioned his children from taking any leisurely possessions, Eliezer protested every time he turned to the last totem of his relationship with his sister. Vidal had seen him read it cover to cover nearly every day since their journey began. When his son noticed him approaching, he flipped the book shut and began to rise, but the pain in his back made him too slow to flee.

"Please sit. I'll only disturb you for a moment." Vidal used the precious few seconds Eliezer attempted to stand to explain the expedition. "I need you to come with me. Binyamín will be in the party too; I'm sure it would warm his heart if you joined."

"This idea is dangerous and stupid."

"If they harm us, they'd be defying the monarchs' orders."

"No orders stopped them from harming me."

"If you prefer to call on the patients and report back to me, I'd consider taking Asher instead." It was a bluff, but might it convince his son? Eliezer could do something for his brother without betraying the hateful vow of silence he'd taken against his father. Although he found the conversation unpleasant, Vidal had to admit that hearing his son speak to him again was as pleasurable to his ears as listening to a song from a musician's lute.

"I'll go." Eliezer opened his book to signal the conversation was over. Vidal returned to the wagon, his thoughts filled with the possibility that tomorrow might bring him medicines, supplies, and a chance to repair the relationship with his oldest son.

When he sat alone with his back resting against the wagon wheel that evening, he closed his eyes and whispered, "Adonai, please provide us safe passage, as You did the twelve spies who entered Canaan. Please make our mission successful and allow us to return with a bounty of goods to nourish our people. But of most importance, please allow our brave volunteers to return home safely to their families. Bless you, Adonai. Amen."

Chapter Eleven

Past the rabbi's tent, the fog lingered and obscured the country beyond like a whiteout. Though Eliezer accompanied him, Vidal was forced to carry the stubborn boy's instrument case with his free shoulder. He dropped both cases into the weeds of dry grass beside Binyamín, who stood in the mist, shivering in the tunic and trousers he'd worn in anticipation of the day's heat. Binyamín clung to the reins of an Andalusian horse tied to a wagon that held six wooden barrels the height of a man's torso. Four barrels lay on the bottom, fit snuggly together in the wagon bed so as not to roll. Two other barrels were placed on top between them, fastened down with rope.

After they greeted each other, Vidal asked Binyamín how many men had volunteered.

"Seven more to enter the city. Another ten to carry back supplies."

"I thought more would volunteer."

"I didn't."

"But they have a chance to acquire extra goods for their families—"

"With what money?"

"Whatever money they have left, I suppose."

"I doubt they have any. We are not all so lucky to have professions where the funds continue to flow."

Though tempted to make an outburst about how he charged nobody for his medical care, Vidal kept his thoughts to himself. As the mist cleared, more young men arrived at the front. Despite the sunburns on their cheeks and necks, the dirt-encrusted in their hair and eyebrows from sleeping on the ground, and the bloody cracks at the centers of their lips, their faces remained unblemished with age. He must be the oldest man to enter Periana by ten years.

Avraham Mendez arrived atop an Arabian horse. Its earth-colored coat was so vibrant, it challenged even the rabbi's tent for the most beautiful possession in the caravan. Once Avraham realized that no one else rode their horses, he dismounted. Vidal expected to find a quiet rage adorning his son's face. Nothing could make Eliezer hate him more than an afternoon with Tsipora's new husband. However, Eliezer looked as disinterested in Avraham as he appeared when Vidal offered him his ten-thousandth apology.

Vidal called for the men to gather around him. With no luck, he found himself standing downhill, the smallest of the group. He looked into the eyes of weary boys who'd received neither enough sleep, food, nor drink in the past week, who had given up the only chance for a day's rest to haul supplies up a steep hill. Who was he to think of himself as their leader? He was a doctor. He worked with but one patient at a time and only addressed a crowd to announce whether their family member was healing or dying. Instructing anyone other than an apprentice felt false to him. How could he lead men into a city he'd never seen—never heard of—before yesterday?

"They expect us at the gates within the hour, so I will be brief." Vidal reiterated the plan provided by Shelomo the day before. "Do you have any questions?"

The boys said nothing, which concerned him more than if they'd protested that they'd not understood a word. People should have questions for their leader.

Vidal led the nineteen boys down the hill in the direction of Periana. With each step, dirt poured into his ripped leather boots. His inner thighs were chaffed from yesterday's sweat. A sunrise cut through the fog ahead, signaling the heat of the day that awaited. A vast valley soon appeared below the mountain. From where he walked, Vidal could see the clusters of trees, meadows, and jagged rock formations beneath them. His tongue rolled along the insides of his dry cheeks. All this land and no pond or stream? Hills on all sides of the horizon surrounded the valley and the sight made him believe that a great lake had once existed here. But it had dried up eons ago and left behind nothing but a dehydrated seafloor.

As he turned a bend on the mountain trail, Periana appeared. The city was built onto the side of the mountain. Its labyrinthine streets and hill dwelling houses reminded Vidal of El Albayzín, where a short house could be closer to the heavens than a tall one by pure virtue of where its original builders settled on the hillside. Was this what El Albayzín might have looked like if the rest of Granada had never been developed around it? The question made him yearn to look upon Granada again.

The gate to Periana was on the lowest elevation of the hill. Like the wall that surrounded the city, it was made of timber cut from the nearby olive trees. Hardly a fortification should the city be under siege. But Granada's walls were made of brick and the city had fallen to the monarchs all the same.

A guard on the wall announced that the party from Granada had arrived. From a man-door in the lower-left corner of the gate, a boy no older than Asher emerged. He wore a metal helmet and white tunic emblazoned with a crimson crucifix.

Vidal approached the boy with caution. Why would Periana send a child to greet him? It may be a prank. He prepared to hear the guards along the wall howl with laughter. "Is Señor Torres here?" he asked, recalling the name of the council member Shelomo had mentioned the day before. "He agreed yesterday to escort us into the city."

"It is Señor Torres' day off." The helmet looked heavy on the boy's head and he kept pushing up the side to set it level. But his voice boomed with the authority of a wartime general. "We cannot keep these gates open all day. Which of these ten are to enter?"

Vidal looked to Binyamín. Would the rabbi's son humor this insult? Binyamín stood at attention before the boy with the same respect he might show a council member or magistrate. Vidal called for the others to enter and Eliezer, Binyamín, Avraham, and six others approached the gate. The boy guard counted ten heads, then waved them through with urgency, as if keeping the gates open for too long would spell peril for those who lived inside. Should he stay back, request that the boy bring Señor Torres to the entrance to ensure their agreement remained unaltered?

The gates parted down the middle, the grunting of men pulling them open could be heard from within. Eliezer followed Binyamín as he escorted the horse and wagon into the city. Vidal had no time to debate. If he asked about Señor Torres again, he imagined the boy might bar him from the city, leaving him separated from his son and the needed medicine.

Within the city walls, stone roads split in two directions, both straight ahead and up the hill. After walking over coarse earth for a week, the paved road felt smooth as ice. Smoke-colored houses lined the streets, but not a single civilian stood outside to meet them. Only guards dressed identical to the boy waited for them in the street. Vidal reminded himself to relax. Ten men braver than him waited outside the gates. The road was empty because it was still early in the morning.

"What is it you wish to acquire?" the boy guard asked.

"Did our messenger not explain this to Señor Torres yesterday?" Vidal asked, delighting in the idea of demoting Shelomo to the rank of messenger.

"Señor Torres is an oaf who fancies himself the magistrate of this town, when he is little more than a drunk and a womanizer. My men and I will escort you. Where do you want to go?"

If he wasn't Asher's father, Vidal might have asked where the boy learned such words. He explained that they needed a well or stream where they might gather water for their barrels, a market to purchase clothes, grains, vegetables, and livestock, as well as any medicinal herbs the town physician would be willing to sell.

"My men and I will escort you in groups."

"There is no way we might travel together?"

"You are to be gone from this town in one hour."

"So you did speak with Señor Torres—?"

"I did not speak with Señor Torres. If you are not gone within one hour's time, my men and I will have trouble keeping the peace. Even he would know that."

From the corners of his eyes, Vidal noticed a window slam shut down the street. It sounded violent and unwelcoming, as if the town were hiding from Vidal.

Now was no time to quarrel. He assigned each man to go with a pair of guards to collect particular supplies. "And Eliezer, you will come with me." Eliezer stood beside the horse and wagon with Binyamín and Avraham. "Eliezer—"

"You don't need my help carrying herbs and glass vials," Eliezer said with such a clenched mouth that Vidal wondered if he'd only imagined the boy's words. His son would rather fetch water—the most laborious of all the tasks—and with Avraham? Perhaps that was how deep Eliezer's hatred burrowed, that he would rather stay with Tsipora's husband than his father. He wanted to shout at his son to follow him, but knew he was powerless to raise his voice in this strange town. His son knew it as well.

Despite the boy guard's demeanor, he tugged on Vidal's sleeve to get his attention, announcing that he would escort him to the town doctor.

"I will meet you back at the wagon," Vidal told Eliezer's backside.

Vidal followed the boy guard up the incline beside the eastern wall. The sounds of families stirring could be heard from the houses they passed on his left. The fatty smell of eggs wafted from a cracked window. What it would feel like to wake up from a good night's sleep on a feather bed. To leisurely prepare for the day rather than pack the wagon before sunrise each morning, to eat a meal other than eggplant soup. He would never take such pleasantries for granted again.

The guard took two steps for every one of Vidal's. They said nothing as they walked, and Vidal pondered how a boy who looked to be no older than nine had managed to command guards twice his age. Perhaps the boy was a dwarf—though, like Asher, none of his features resembled traits mentioned in medical texts. Or he was Señor Torres' son and had been given special treatment? He was certain this may be a prank, a way for the town to remind Vidal that although they would help him, they refused to take him seriously.

After traversing two narrow side streets west of the wall, the boy guard stopped in front of a three-story house. Unlike the other homes they'd passed, paint did not chip from a single section of the residence. This doctor must be wealthy indeed. Stone steps were carved from the outside wall that ascended to a blue door on the second story. Through the open windows above, he could hear the faint sound of plates being set out and children talking.

"Our doctor lives here. I will wait for you outside and escort you back to the gate."

Vidal glanced at the sun. It wasted no time kissing the back of his neck with its heat. "Do you think he's awake?"

"Of course he is awake. He has already had morning prayer."

Morning prayer? He'd heard of no such Catholic practice. Vidal ascended the steps and at first only tapped on the door. Nobody answered and Vidal waited another minute before knocking again. At the bottom of the steps, the boy guard—now alone on the street—kicked around a loose rock. Vidal imagined that soon the boy would grow impatient and order him back to the gate. He knocked louder and waited. What if the town doctor could hear him but refused to answer? The town was undoubtedly aware that Jews had entered. Perhaps they'd chosen to ignore his presence until he and his party left. What had happened to the Jews of Periana? He imagined they'd departed long ago and the eerie absence of people in the streets following their banishment disturbed him. Was Granada like this now? A ghost town after his people had been expelled? How was Catalina faring? He would only ever know through her letters.

Footsteps approached the door from inside and a man answered. His white beard concealed his neck and matched the color of his turban, which wrapped around his head and ran down the side of his face with the smoothness of fountain water. He looked at Vidal as if he had been expecting him, yet said nothing.

"I am sorry to disturb you so early in the morning." Vidal introduced himself and explained that he would pay for any medicine the man could spare.

The man introduced himself as Dr. Ubayd Zamorar and held open the door. Vidal entered a dark house where the sun's morning light did not yet stream through the windows. The room smelled of cinnamon. Pots and pans sat on the ground scattered and unwashed beside ruffled blankets and a wooden toy horse—the sort of disarray he only saw in houses when company was unexpected. Dr. Zamorar's wife stood over an oak table at the opposite end of the room and served bowls of porridge to two girls. She wore a red hijab, the curls of her black hair falling down the front of her face. When she noticed Vidal, she tucked in her hair. "May I offer you something to eat?"

As hungry as Vidal was, he could not fathom the idea of eating breakfast while his family rationed their portions back at the caravan and his son ate nothing. He held up his hand to decline.

Dr. Zamorar led him to a room at the back of the house. Dust danced in sunlight that streamed through a small window, landing on a sanded workbench at the center of the room. Jars of different herbs lined a shelf that covered the entirety of the far wall. The room smelled of poppies, though he could not find the flowers among the jars. What a dream study for a doctor. He'd had too many children and too small a house to devote such space to his work.

Dr. Zamorar asked what Vidal required and Vidal recited a list of herbs he'd committed to memory. Salve, sumac, seeds of the white poppy, peony, badaward, abrotanum, wormwood. Dr. Zamorar brought the plants from his shelf to the workbench. "You are on your way to the Maghreb?"

"To Fez. Yes."

"I hope you are not thinking of leaving from Málaga."

"Málaga is precisely where we are headed."

"From what I've heard, the city has descended into madness." Dr. Zamorar explained that his brother had just returned from Málaga. Thousands lined the beaches, all trying to barter passage to the Maghreb before the decree went into effect. Though sailors were eager to service them—even more eager to charge a family every real they had—there were not enough ships to carry so many on the crossing. "I hope this news does not upset you."

"Do not worry. This has been the year for upsetting news."

Vidal recalled his first instinct upon learning that he must leave the Iberian Peninsula. Not to cross the sea, but journey to Portugal or Italy instead. Now he was standing in a Moorish doctor's house halfway between his home and the sea wondering why he had decided to follow the rabbi to Fez. He knew Dr. Zamorar was telling the truth. For what reason would he lie? Vidal tried to recall the date—it was difficult to do now that his community had postponed observing the Sabbath. It was mid-June; they'd been on the road for over a week. The decree that would banish them from the monarchs' kingdoms would go into effect in six weeks and he and his family would face death if they remained on Iberian shores. It was too late to turn east. He had no choice but to proceed to the southern coast.

Dr. Zamorar extracted a map from a drawer and unrolled it across the workstation, placing jars on the four corners of the map to weigh it down. The map illustrated the Kingdom of Granada along Iberia's southern coast colored in a shade of light green that greatly exaggerated how much vegetation existed in this part of the world. The doctor suggested that Vidal proceed to Marbella, a dot on the coast as far west of Málaga as Málaga was west of Granada. "Málaga is at the bottom of a valley. Once you enter, your caravan will never be able to climb its way back out."

"May I have this map? I must show it to the man who leads our caravan."

"This is my only map."

"Were you planning on going somewhere? Is it your family the monarchs are ordering to leave?" Vidal explained that they'd been on the road for nine days. They had 200 people in their caravan and could travel no farther than Málaga.

Without a word, Dr. Zamorar rolled the map shut and brought it back to his drawer. He instructed Vidal to take the herbs and leave. Vidal regretted his behavior immediately. He worked swiftly to remove the dried wormwood and wilted abrotanum from their jars. As the glass vials Vidal had brought were less than a sixth of the size of Dr. Zamorar's jars, with bottlenecks too tight to squeeze the herbs through, he removed a scalpel from his bag and cut the herbs in half. "Forgive my outburst. You're kind to allow me into your home. I should not have spoken to you that way."

"They will make us leave next."

"Don't say such things."

"This is to be a Christian kingdom, no? How can a Christian kingdom have Muslims?"

"God willing, the same way a Muslim kingdom once had Jews." Vidal removed his leather coin purse from the satchel and produced the reales he'd collected to purchase the medicine.

"I would give you this for free if I could."

"Don't feel shameful for accepting the money. The decree forbids us to take it with us."

Once Vidal left the home of Dr. Zamorar, the boy guard stood at the bottom step of the house and shouted that they must return to the gates. "You've taken too long!"

"I was told I had an hour." As he hurried down the steps, he wondered why he allowed himself to take commands from a child.

The stone streets were slick with morning dew and Vidal chose his steps carefully to keep from slipping as he followed the boy guard in the direction of the city gates. The boy marched ahead of him the way Asher walked when someone in the family irritated him and forced him to leave the room in a huff. Who was this child who sauntered through the world with the irritation of a person infested with ticks, yet garnered the respect of soldiers twice his age?

As they descended the street beside the east wall, Vidal noticed a crowd of twenty men gathered at the city gates with their backs turned to him. They carried no weapons—as far as he could tell—and wore loose-fitting clothes as if they'd only recently awakened. Were they surrounding someone? Was somebody hurt? Vidal felt the urge to dash forward and investigate the situation, but knew better than to run into a mob of locals. Perhaps this was only some kind of outside mass or city ritual, nothing to fear.

Once they reached the perimeter of the crowd, the boy guard shouted for the men to make way. That the boy cut his way through a gathering of grown men as easily as Vidal's sharpest scalpel cut through flesh no longer astonished Vidal, though he was surprised that nobody bothered to antagonize the Jewish doctor passing through their ranks. He expected to find someone addressing the crowd or—God forbid—a wounded boy lying on the floor at the center of the circle. But the men only looked out at the open gate of the city, where all the boys from his party waited beyond the threshold where the stone of the city floor turned to the dried grass of the mountainside. The boys loaded blankets, baskets, and satchels onto the back of Binyamín's cart while glancing over their shoulders to see if the men of Periana might break this demarcation line. The look in the Perianenses' eyes suggested no threat, merely a satisfaction that they'd never need to look on such visitors again.

Once Vidal rejoined his party, the boy guard ordered for the gate to be shut and Vidal shouted a thank you as the two doors came together like two hands covering a person's eyes. Vidal looked up and down his ranks at the goods that'd been acquired: the boots, the flint rocks, the apples, and the meat. The bed of the cart sagged at the center from the weight of the newly filled water barrels. They'd return to the caravan with supplies and morale. He felt as successful as a general who'd led his men to victory.

"Good work, men! What do you say to a drink of water before the long walk back? You've earned it."

Binyamín stood on top of the wagon, fastening down the barrels with rope. "We haven't any water to spare."

"I know we need to ration, but I think you're each entitled to a drink."

"We didn't get enough water."

"I can't believe you thanked them," Eliezer muttered under his breath. Before Vidal could ask what he was implying, Eliezer left for the far side of the wagon.

"What are you talking about?" he asked Binyamín. "I see clothes, boots, food, and the wagon sits heavy with the weight of water."

"It sags because it's old. We barely filled a barrel."

"Was there no well? There were three of you. How is this possible?"

"We were chased off."

"You were chased off," Avraham corrected him. He stood on the ground beside the wagon, eye level with the boot of the rabbi's son. "I tried to ignore them for as long as I could, Dr. ha-Rofeh. But too many people from the town gathered and demanded we leave."

"But you had every right to be there. You and your father-in-law arranged it that way, did you not?"

"I tried to remind them. It only made them angrier."

Even as he thought to inquire further, he pictured the mob of townspeople he'd passed. If they had turned to him with any sort of threat he would've been powerless to stand in defiance. "It doesn't matter. What's important is that you're okay."

"We won't be okay for long without water," Binyamín said.

"We'll determine another solution. We have everything else?" The boys responded in the affirmative. "Good. Let's get these supplies back to the caravan."

Vidal led them up the hill as confidentially as if he knew another place to gather water. But he could not think of any other place between Granada and Málaga where they could acquire the rations they needed. Thirst that he'd ignored all morning swelled in his throat at the realization that he might go the rest of the day without the liquid caressing his lips. He looked up with a desperate hope that it might rain but was greeted by a cloudless blue sky.

Chapter Twelve

As the men returned from Periana, sweat slathered Vidal's neck and brow and soaked his pit-stained shirt. His satchel bags hung heavy on his back and the sun beamed down as if all the world's heat were meant only for him. What had it been like to be cold? To shiver on a winter's night? A wisp of air brushed past his face, tantalizing him with the possibility of a breeze, but carried no more promise than a kiss blown by a whore in a Granada alley. He swallowed hard and the shallow drop of saliva only made him yearn more for a drink. He scanned the sand-covered ground for any sign of water, a plant that may store liquid inside it, a flower that could provide nectar. Could such a thing exist out here? In a blade of grass? The thistle of a flower?

The men behind him spat, heaved, and coughed; air hissed out of their nostrils. They put their hands over their brows and the shadows concealed their eyes. Linen and leather satchels that contained grains, vegetables, salts, breads, and fabric hung from their shoulders. The satchels hit their knees with each step. One man carried the carcass of a slaughtered calf over his shoulders. The cow's body was wrapped in cloth, but its stiff black hooves stuck out and pointed into the air. The salty smell of warm meat wafted off its carcass and mixed with the scent of the men's bodies and sweat. Vidal could gag, if only to flood his mouth with saliva. His son grunted with each step, his tongue flicking from his mouth to wet his lips. As Eliezer stomped across the ground, he kicked up a mist of dirt and sand. Grains twisted and danced in the light of the sun before landing on the men's clothes.

At the mountain's crest, a single file line of wagons and tents extended along the hillside. The caravan stretched so far back that the rear merged into a distant blur of wood, people, and tents. Dead grass grew from the ground as unevenly as the last hint of thinning hair that remained on Vidal's head beneath his cap. Families sat against their wagons in the shade of the quickly shrinking shadows and boys scattered along the hillside to find relief under the leafless trees. An Andalusian horse covered in mud whipped its head back and forth. Its hooves dug into the ground in an effort to lurch forward the wagon to which it was strapped. Was it normal for a horse to behave this way? No doubt it craved shade as much as he. But the wooden blocks under the wheels confined the horse to where it stood. It whinnied, causing more horses down the line to cry out in response. An Arabian horse bucked back and forth as if trying to knock its wagon over and its master sacrificed his refuge in the shade to stroke the horse's forelock and calm it.

Women dressed in qamis and headscarves laid out blankets and quilts at the sight of the return of Vidal and the boys. Blankets, some centuries-old, lost their whiteness at the touch of the dirt floor. The women stepped on quilts, digging the corners into the earth, their boots leaving inklike marks. Lighter sheets blew into the air, though Vidal could not feel the wind that carried them. Two girls sprinted down the hillside to chase after the sheets and jumped to catch them. Such energy. He could not imagine having that kind of spirit again. The mothers shouted for the girls to slow down, then laughed at each other. Was it a laugh of joy? Or had they grown delirious?

A line of thirty women came forth to help them carry the supplies to the quilts. His wife and daughter were among them, and the relative lightness in their steps, thanks to a good night's rest and a calm morning on the hillside, was enough to make him forget his thirst momentarily. There would be no complaining about Eliezer to Bonadonna, as she would only remind him to be gentler on their son. Look what being gentler on Eliezer had done. One barrel for 200 people.

148

Up close, the women's faces were sunburnt, their lips bloody and cracked. Water would have solved it all. What had they done to deserve this?

Binyamín told his mother to take the barrel from the rear of the wagon. "We return with less water than anticipated, so be mindful of how you distribute the rations."

Vidal whispered in Binyamín's ear. "No person is to taste a drop before we bring that water to our sick."

"We will set aside a quarter of the barrel."

"You underestimate how many are ill."

Bonadonna arrived beside Vidal. "What's this about?"

"If we set aside a quarter of the barrel, there will not be enough for the others," Binyamín said.

"Set aside less and we'll have more dead to bury beside the road."

Bonadonna tried to interject before the argument escalated, but Binyamín spoke over her. "How much water do you need, Doctor?"

"Half."

Both the boys who returned from Periana and the women who'd come to aid them now congregated around the conversation. They all wanted water, and he half expected the group to haul the barrel away before the argument could continue. But they remained silent, glancing at one another to see who was willing to second either side of the argument. Many had a parent with a bad leg, a grandparent who was ill, a brother or sister bedridden from eating wild mushrooms or an undercooked hare caught on the road. Would they sacrifice members of the caravan for a drink of water?

"And who is to decide who will drink from that half, Doctor? My sisters have had no water all day."

"Then we will give that half to our youngest."

"The failure of our mission to acquire water rests not on my shoulders alone. Eliezer failed us as well."

Eliezer stood at the rear of the men as if he wished to go unnoticed. Vidal expected him to speak—Eliezer had spoken earlier;

why not now? But his son remained mute. "If that is the case, then I will not have a drop."

Vidal called for Eliezer to pour half of the water into another barrel, but his son grabbed a satchel of leather from one of the boys, brushed past Vidal and met Iamila up the hill, where he placed an arm around her shoulder and walked with her to the quilts.

Bonadonna appeared in front of him with her finger in the air. "One barrel of water, Vidal?"

"There was a quarrel of some kind. I have not yet learned the full story."

"Yet you must know if Binyamín is blaming our son."

Vidal remained silent. The truth of his separation from Eliezer at the Periana gates suggested he'd broken his promise to his wife. He could rationalize what'd happened by blaming Eliezer for leaving him, but knew that passing off fault to his son would do nothing to win the boy's forgiveness.

"I'm sorry," Vidal said.

Bonadonna ignored him, wrenching a basketful of eggplants from one of the boys and returning up the hill. He turned to the business of pouring half the amount of water from the full barrel into an empty barrel. Even as several boys stood around, enticed by the sight of the rushing water glistening under the hot sun, nobody begged for a drink.

He carried half a barrel of water back to the caravan. At the rabbi's tent, he set down the barrel and caught his breath. He saw not a speck of dirt, not a single stray thread on the pristine tent. Did the rabbi's family clean it? Perhaps he had blessed it in such a way that made it impervious to the elements. Nonsense, blessings could not do such things. He listened for the sound of the rabbi inside, but heard nothing. What was it like inside this beautiful tent? So many days pilgrimaging behind them and he'd not seen it. Might there be water? He imagined a bucket filled with cool black liquid, its surface as still as glass.

A boy who wore only a tunic knocked into Vidal as he raced past and Vidal yanked the boy back by his bony shoulder. The boy's face was so thick with mud and dirt that he looked like he'd slathered it on himself. He offered a smile of apology that only bore two bottom teeth. Vidal released him and the boy bounded away, his bare feet crushing the sharp, dried grass. The cycling motion of the boy's legs dizzied Vidal and acidic juices wailed in his stomach. Might he vomit? He'd had nothing to eat. His kneecaps cracked as he crouched into a sliver of shade beside the tent that cast too short a shadow to cover his head. His scent, musty and sour as the dead calf, made him wince. He craned his neck back and sucked in the mountain air, so crisp it felt like it might cut a gash in his city lungs. Looking up at God with his eyes closed, he imagined a passerby would think he'd gone mad. Had this new life broken him already?

The ground ahead ascended from a meadow of weeds to a flat ridge that marked the mountain's peak. Above that, only cloudless sky. He imagined a battalion of soldiers appearing along the ridge, each of their helmets reflecting the hot sun. Their faces silhouetted by the blue sky behind them. But the space around him was quieter than a city before sunrise. An animal skittered through the weeds. Could it be a rabbit? Something to eat? He had no strength left to hunt. Though his father had been dead sixteen long years, he lamented that the man had never taught him how to string an arrow.

At Vidal's wagon, the horse stood tied to the front, its tail whipping flies off its ass, its expression indifferent to the surroundings and heat. For the first time, Vidal envied an animal. The bucket of water meant for the horse rested in the shade under the wagon. He pulled it out to find flies dancing and circling above the bucket. An oil-like film coated the surface. A sip wouldn't hurt. But a faint cramp persisted in his side. He shoved the bucket back under the wagon with his foot. A drop flung out and splashed onto the dirt and the earth absorbed the liquid. Had someone seen him waste the water?

He found Asher hidden in the shade with his back pressed against the spokes of the wagon's wooden wheel. His son rubbed together two pieces of shirt stained with blood. "What sort of mischief have you gotten into?"

"A patient had a wart on his foot. I used the blade to let it."

"What have I told you about interacting with our patients?"

"You were gone all morning. He was in a great deal of pain."

"You are to evaluate them only."

"The wart looked ready to explode."

Vidal grabbed Asher's shirt as evidence. "Appears it did explode."

"I was only trying to help."

"Now his foot may become infected."

Now that his son had performed a procedure, no matter how unskillful, Vidal wondered why he hadn't anticipated this. Asher used to catch mice around the house and cut open their bellies to see what was inside. Once an opportunity to perform bloodletting presented itself, Asher had seized the moment.

"I'm sorry, Father."

"Bring me to the patient at once." Vidal balanced the barrel of water on his hip and put his free hand on the back of his son's soft neck to push Asher down the caravan line. Splinters stuck out of Asher's back through his shirt. Could the boy not feel them? Vidal picked the splinters out with his fingernails and tossed them onto the ground. Asher jerked his shoulders with each motion, but said nothing. They passed a family who slept under their wagon, a girl who bounced a crying infant on her lap, a boy who threw clothes off the top of a wagon as he screamed for an apple he had saved, and a woman who begged for food as flakes of skin peeled from her pink face. How long before the heat would drive him mad as well?

As they arrived at the wagon, leather chests and wooden crates covered in a white muslin sheet blocked their path. The patient lay inside on the wagon bed. He whimpered, took sharp breaths, and spoke through clenched teeth. It was wrong to judge the patient, but Vidal saw him like a wounded animal that attempted to conceal its injury to avoid being identified as prey.

The man's foot rested on its heel. Linen ripped from a tunic wrapped around the foot soaked through with pus and blood. The edge of the linen bobbed on the verge of unpeeling itself. Vidal had trained his son to dress a wound better than this. He unraveled the wrapping, each rotation bloodier and more soaked than the last, until the foot was free and the linen rested in his hand like a wet shawl.

A hasty and uneven suture zigzagged through a gash that ran from the ball to the center of the foot. Skin that bloomed open from the lack of precise stitches parted on either side of the wound like an orifice. Dried blood surrounded the dirty, blackened skin. The blood inside the wound was so dark that Vidal could see no sign of muscle nor bone. The patient's wife handed him a cup, its clay exterior greasy from previous use. The water looked as tempting and forbidden as an apple from the tree of knowledge of good and evil. He poured water down the patient's foot. Drops of dirt and blood streaked down the pale skin and pooled into a muddy swamp on the wagon bed before soaking into the wood.

Vidal cut loose the sutures with scissors, cleaned the wound with a fresh rag given to him by Dr. Zamorar, then slathered the slick skin of the patient's foot with black salve the texture of honey. As he worked, he apologized on behalf of his son and demanded Asher fill a cup of water for the patient.

"I heard there was no water," the patient said.

Vidal paused to consider this. If only the caravan could travel as fast as the news it spread. "Only enough for the sick."

"Give my ration to my wife."

"You should drink first, Señor Uziel. You have lost blood today."

"I will not drink a drop before my wife."

If anyone saw the patient's wife drink, the caravan would accuse Vidal of hypocrisy. But without water the patient might faint. Perhaps Binyamín knew what he was doing when he so stubbornly dismissed the idea of giving the water to the sick. He needed to speak with the rabbi, for he felt lost without the man's advice.

"If I pour your wife a cup, will you drink?" Vidal asked. The patient nodded in compliance and Vidal whispered for Asher to pour a cup of water for the patient's wife.

"May I pour some for myself?"

"I cannot give you special treatment."

"But I'm your son."

"Exactly."

Asher dipped the cup into the bucket and handed it to the wife. She crouched behind the far side of the wagon and poured the water into her mouth as if it were the most potent liquor.

The crunching of dried leaves behind him alerted Vidal, and he urged the wife to finish drinking before someone saw her. When he turned around, Iamila arrived at the wagon. Fresh sunburns covered her forehead and neck.

"Could you use my help, Father?"

"No. We don't know the next time we will spend a day at rest. I suggest you enjoy it."

"It is wrong that I rest while you slave away."

Although Iamila knew nothing of patient care, he imagined that with her around, she could stop Asher from doing anything foolish while he went to the rabbi. "Go with your brother. Help him distribute the water and keep him out of trouble."

"I won't let him out of my sight."

"Good. If you do, who knows what might happen." Vidal lifted the barrel and handed it to his son. "Iamila is going to help you distribute water—"

"I don't need her help."

"I don't care."

"She'll only slow me down. Caring for the patients and babies, it's too much."

Iamila grabbed one end of the barrel. "I think I'm the one who'll be caring for the baby."

"Father!"

Vidal was already leaving them, as he hurried to the rabbi's tent. "I'll return to check on you."

"This isn't fair."

"I'll be inspecting every wart, blister, and bunion when I return and I expect them to be intact."

As Vidal returned up the line, he noticed that the satchels and baskets from Periana had been laid out on blankets and sheets on the mountain incline. An ever-growing line of people hoping to get rations for their families extended along the hillside, challenging the caravan for its length. They would not find the bounty of supplies they anticipated. Once they learned there were too few resources for too many people, might the orderliness of the line descend into a fray where adults and children alike brawled for scraps? That they did not already behave this way gave him hope. Even in the wilderness, the caravan appeared more civil than the water hoarders of Periana. La Judería was not a location in Granada, but a community that now existed only in the mountains of Andalusia, and that meant it could exist again in Fez.

When he reached the rabbi's tent, he called for Rabbi el Barchilon from outside the flaps and was invited to enter. Turkish oil lamps hung from the hooks of golden stands that lit the tent from within, the light passing through cardinal and jade stained glass. Rumpled blankets on the ground marked where the family had slept and Vidal stepped over feather pillows as bulging as a portly man's belly after a Rosh Hashanah dinner to stand before the rabbi.

At the far center of the room, Rabbi el Barchilon sat hunched over his oak desk scanning a Torah scroll over an unrolled passage of the Five Books of Moses. What could Leviticus teach the rabbi about their predicament? For the first time in his life, Vidal questioned how the rabbi could be at study with all that was going on. The morning at Periana had been a failure, his family was working themselves to death, yet the rabbi was reading? Though his thoughts were sinful, he could not help but look upon the rabbi's activity—in a tent the size of his family's kitchen back home—as a luxury, one he could not see himself partaking in for many years.

When the rabbi took his eyes off the Torah and offered for Vidal to sit in the empty chair opposite him, Vidal repeated what Dr. Zamorar had told him. "He says Málaga is a lost cause. We should proceed to Marbella."

"Everything will be fine, Dr. ha-Rofeh."

"I do not mean to question your strategy, but if what the doctor says is true, we will be trapped. It will be impossible to lead the caravan out of the city back into the mountains. The sick and the old will have no chance." Vidal recalled his siblings' intentions to journey to Portugal and for a moment every destination seemed a wiser option than Fez.

The rabbi reclined in his chair and seemed to consider Vidal's claim. "Do you know how far Marbella is from Málaga?"

"I've seen it on a map."

"You are our community's most trusted physician. You know the health of the people better than I. Do you believe they can make it to Marbella?"

The young and healthy would survive. As long as they could find drinking water, that was obvious. But the ones fighting to see the port at Málaga would never live to view Marbella. "Many would perish. But many will also perish if Málaga is as the Muslim doctor has foretold."

"Then I offer to ease your worries. I will send a rider ahead to report back the situation at Málaga. Perhaps Eliezer—"

"My family has done enough. I beg you send someone else."

"I will send my son. He's anxious to lead. The story he has told me of his encounters with the locals today assures me that he can keep his wits about him in a tense situation." The rabbi laid his soft hand atop Vidal's. "Now, since we are not to travel today, let us enjoy the blessing of rest."

Chapter Thirteen

As the first light of morning peaked over the eastern hills, Vidal and Bonadonna fastened down the family's possessions in the wagon. His wife tucked the edges of the tapestry that covered their belongings under the sides of the wagon bed while he tightened the rope that held down their leather bags and box crates. Down the hill, Binyamín hugged goodbye the rabbi, his mother, and two sisters, then mounted the horse with the heroic posture of a young man sent off on a mission to save his community. He rode away with a speed that made Vidal envious after so many days trudging alongside the caravan. The rabbi held his wife while she cried. Should Vidal have volunteered Eliezer? Rabbi el Barchilon was already doing so much for the community, and Vidal saw little justice in the decision to send Binyamín ahead. He took solace in the knowledge that, if Bonadonna knew that he'd turned down the opportunity to volunteer Eliezer for the mission, she'd be grateful.

On his knees, he removed the wooden blocks from beneath the wheels that held the wagon in place. The horse pulled the wagon forward with the same stiffness in its legs as his own and he held the horse's reins and walked alongside it as they descended the mountain.

Their wagon was both too small to fit all the possessions they'd wanted to take and too heavy to maneuver easily. Its weight pushed it forward against the horse's behind, and Vidal brushed its forelock and whispered to it so it would not be spooked. Behind him, he heard people shouting for someone to slow down. A woman screamed and he looked back. Could a runaway wagon plummet down the mountain? If a sequence of wagons collided again, he'd spend all day tending to the wounded. Although he had patients to call on, he felt he should stay at the wagon and help in the morning after his absence in Periana. Besides, it was difficult to treat patients while the caravan moved downhill—he would check on them later.

By midmorning, the sun had returned to test them once more. He breathed heavier and waved the hot air in front of his face. Bonadonna walked beside him, her clothes covering all of her but her face and hands. Sweat trickled down the inside of her dress and seeped through the wool like droplets of a light rain. The men were allowed to roll up their sleeves; the fatter ones even pulled off their shirts to let their stomachs tan in the sun. Yet his wife's body must remain concealed. Perhaps in the Maghreb, women did not need to cover themselves? He'd heard tales from Ochoa of women who danced with their bellies exposed, women who wore face paint, women who lived together with no need for a man's protection. If that was allowed, perhaps she could walk outside with her skin feeling the sun. He doubted it and knew God would disapprove no matter what part of the world they lived in, but the concept was enough to keep him occupied.

The land leveled out halfway down the mountain, where the dried weeds and dead grass turned a shade greener until the grass did not crunch beneath his feet but bent and silently lay flat. Trees soon covered them, shielding them from the heat of the sun. He heard the trickle of water first. Ahead, a stream as powerful as the thrust of a storm cut across the caravan's path. The water sparkled in the sun like diamonds, and the rushing current sounded more beautiful than any music he'd heard. The stream looked so precious in the wilderness, so sacred that he would have believed it if the rabbi said they had stumbled upon Eden.

The rabbi's two daughters ran from their wagon back down the line, shouting and announcing that water had been discovered. The rabbi's wife touched Bonadonna on the shoulder and told her to drink from the stream first. Eliezer climbed onto the wagon bed, threw off the tapestry and found their water bucket, now bone dry from lack of use. He handed it down to Asher along with the horse's drinking bucket—half the size of their own—where the remaining water turned brown from a mix of dirt and saliva. Asher kicked the bucket over into the grass and Bonadonna ordered her children to hurry to the stream.

With the river rushing around his knees, Vidal cupped the water into his hands and brought the first drink to his lips. The iciness of the water belayed the temperature that surrounded it. Could it be a miracle? Could God have made the temperature of the water so? Perhaps this was a sign. His way of telling them that the worst was over. That their fortunes would soon improve. The silky liquid washed out the rancid taste in his mouth. He splashed the water onto his face and although he wore the same filthy gown he'd worn for three days, standing in the water, with his bare feet over the soft pebble floor, he felt clean again.

Eliezer plunged their buckets into the stream and the force of the water filled the buckets itself. Iamila took a rock from the stream floor and scraped the grime off the insides of the horse's bucket. By the time she was finished, the rock looked covered in filth. Placing the bucket aside, Iamila knelt in the stream and stuck her mouth into the water to drink it like a horse.

"Not too much, Iamila. You'll get a pain in your stomach," Vidal said.

Eliezer thrust his hands through the water to create a wave that splashed across the side of his sister's body. Iamila shivered with delight and kicked the water back at him.

As Bonadonna and Eliezer bathed in the water, and Asher and Iamila compared the sizes of pebbles they each found on the stream bed, other families ran down the caravan line toward the river. Mothers brought their empty buckets on top of their heads or held at their sides. Children raced each other. A boy threw off his clothes with every step, his mother hurrying after him to pick the filthy garments off the ground while shouting for him to stop. They reached the river and spread out from the center like the opening of a gypsy's fan. Each family tried to claim a section farther upriver, everyone wanting the water they used for bathing to be free of the filth that eroded off the person upstream. It could mean more injured, more illnesses, but before he could dwell on this, his wife splashed him with a wave of water. He cupped the water in his hands and dropped it over her back as well. He imagined they could've stayed at the stream all day.

Iamila helped Bonadonna wash their clothes in the river bucket as Vidal carried the clothes back to the wagon to string the garments from a rope tied to the nearest tree. After the clothes had been scrubbed with lye and water, they hung dripping from the rope. Looking at the clothesline, Vidal almost felt like he was back home, where they hung the clothes between two wooden poles on their roof. Asher beat the clothes with a washing paddle and once Vidal squatted to take a break, he realized he needed to pee. When was the last time he had gone? He imagined almost two days had passed.

He could barely see the rushing current, as it had been absorbed by the bodies of the people who now stood in its place. Children splashed in the stream. They threw their hands up to let the droplets soar through the air. Women spoke to each other, soaking their bare feet in the cold water. An old man sat naked downstream, the water mercifully obscuring him as he scrubbed himself with a rag. Vidal felt as if they were not on their way to start a new life, but enjoying an afternoon at a stream no further from Granada than the far side of a mountain.

He told Bonadonna to watch the wagon while he went to find a place to relieve himself, but she said she needed to go as well and preferred they go together so he could keep watch. On the left-hand side of the wagon, the earth sloped downward at the tree line. They walked downhill among trees that were as tall as the home they had left behind and searched for a place where nobody would see them. The sounds of laughter, conversation, and the thwacking of Asher hitting the clothes faded. Soon, he could only hear the gentle hum of a breeze coasting through the tree leaves. A bird sang a tune he'd never heard in Granada. He looked up to the canopy. Did the birds look different here than back home? He saw no sign of the creatures, only the green leaves and the gray-brown tree bark.

Vidal stood guard as his wife pressed her back against the rough bark of an elm tree and pulled up her skirt to relieve herself.

"Thank you for staying with us today. I think it makes the children happy."

"I hoped it might make you happy as well."

"Not as happy as I am to have water."

"A difficult thing to compete with." Vidal urinated on the stone pine tree beside her.

"What happened yesterday with our son in Periana?"

"I have no idea. I hoped he might discuss it with you. He won't address me unless it's to do away with me—which I will say is an improvement from several weeks ago."

"He won't speak to me about it either."

"I assumed you spoke all the time at the wagon."

"We do. But not about matters relating to you."

"Bonita, I'm crestfallen."

"He speaks about where to acquire firewood, what to eat. He's being a good brother to Iamila." As he heard this, Vidal wished he could spend more time with them. Bonadonna was speaking about a family he saw every day, yet the routines of their wagon were more mysterious to him than the day-to-day habits of the patients he visited. "She does too much around the wagon. I think Asher's put it in her head that we're going to marry her off, so she's trying to make herself indispensable."

"No one's marrying her off. I've told her as such."

"You have?"

"Yes. I do speak to my daughter." He glanced over his shoulder to where his wife looked at him as if he insisted he'd completed a chore she assumed he forgot. "What's that face for?"

"Nothing. I'm surprised. And pleased if I must say so."

As Vidal and Bonadonna hiked back up the hill, something black moved across his view. He startled. Was someone watching them? A short sprint up the hill, two men stood turned away from them looking up to the people at the stream. They wore identical red tunics and green undershirts.

Vidal and Bonadonna hid behind a tree to spy on the men. The backs of the men's heads told him nothing as to whether they were a threat. He strained his ears to make out what they discussed, but the bird sang again and he could not hear a word over its melody. If they ran, the men would hear their boots crushing one of the branches that covered the ground. Perhaps they were nothing to worry about. They were hunters or trappers working in the wild. The sight of a city on wheels intrigued them. If the men's lives were anything like his, they had seen nothing like it before.

He gestured for Bonadonna to step backward over the fallen leaves. Once out of earshot, they crept back up the hill toward the caravan. As they reached the next tree, another black mark appeared in the corner of his eye. He looked downhill, where a boy stood behind a bush. Because he was lower than them, with his legs hidden, Vidal could not tell how tall the boy was. A small dagger rested in a sheath around his belt. Vidal could do nothing but freeze. If he cried out for help, would anyone hear them? Even if the caravan did, would anyone reach them in time? They could not outrun this boy, nor could they outrun the dagger should he be skilled enough to throw it.

The boy only waved to them. Vidal and Bonadonna backed away up the hill. The other men remained looking at the stream with their arms crossed. One turned his head and said something Vidal could not hear. As he gestured for Bonadonna to make a run for it, they startled at the sight of a woman standing on the incline above them. The woman wore a white apron over her dress. Her blonde hair peeked out from under her green shawl. No dirt or sunburns marked her face. Vidal did not recognize her as one from their community.

Before Vidal or Bonadonna could address her, the boy and two men flanked them. If they ran, they'd be chased. If they screamed, their sounds might draw others into this trap. All he could do was greet them.

One of the men planted a walking stick into the ground to keep his balance. "Dr. ha-Rofeh, no?"

"And who are you?"

The man introduced himself as Hernando Castillo. "Do not be frightened. I know you entered Periana yesterday and we only wish to have an audience."

The woman groveled at Vidal's knees. "My daughter is dying. Please, Doctor, won't you return to Periana to treat her?"

"What about Dr. Zamorar? Can he not treat her?"

"Ubayd Zamorar only treats the nobles. We haven't the title nor coin to afford him."

Vidal always despised physicians who treated only the royal and wealthy while ignoring the sick most in need. No great physician throughout history forsook the sick in favor of riches, yet the practice was continued by lesser doctors.

"What are her symptoms?" He tried to ignore the sound of Bonadonna clearing her throat, the feel of her eyes on the back of his head. Why should he learn anything more about this girl? As far as Bonadonna was concerned, returning to Periana was not an option. Hernando explained that the girl was bedridden, and she vomited if she drank so much as a sip of water. Her symptoms had lasted for three days. "That could be any numbers of diseases. Often an illness like this resolves itself, but if she's been unable to drink water, that makes her condition urgent." How could he help them without returning to Periana? Even if he provided them with all his medical knowledge, he could not guarantee they'd know how to treat the girl themselves. "Are you certain you cannot ask Dr. Zamorar to make an exception? He seemed like a very sensible man."

"Please, Doctor," said the woman. "We've already gone to beg him and he's refused. We need your help."

"Our caravan leaves at dawn and it is already a day's walk back to your town. I'm sorry, I cannot risk separation from my family."

"You cannot take your horse?" asked Hernando.

"The horse is for the wagon. Not I."

"We could gift you a horse when you arrive," the boy said. He glanced between the adults to determine whether they found the idea as brilliant as he. "That way, once you treat Elena you can return to your wagon with haste."

Before Vidal could reply, Bonadonna interjected, "He'll need to discuss with the others."

He glanced at his wife. Never before had she involved herself in his business.

Hernando addressed Vidal. "Discuss with them. We'll wait here for you and we can return together."

"He knows the way back, you should be with your daughter."

"Are you sure?" he asked Vidal.

If an answer existed that would satisfy both the Castillos and his wife, he couldn't find it. Bonadonna had supported his decision to enter Periana to acquire medications, but as long as she perceived another doctor available to the Castillos, he saw no way to convince her to let him leave the caravan again. But he could not allow himself to leave this little girl to die. He knew what happened to families who lost their daughters. "I insist. Depart now and tell the men who guard your walls to expect me."

He shook hands with the men and the family returned to the tree line. Why hadn't they kept to the road? Perhaps they were too ashamed to walk beside the people who lined the caravan.

"Tell me you're not going back there," Bonadonna said.

"I know this may be hard to understand—"

"Vidal, you cannot do this."

"Their child is sick. I'm the only one who can help them."

"Their doctor can help them. They only ask you because you do it for free. You have patients here. What about them? They're to be neglected for two days?"

"They have water now. And a day's absence will not make a difference for even the most ill. Bonita, I cannot let this little girl die."

"Is this about the little girl or is this about Sarah?" Bonadonna never before used Sarah as a pawn in their disagreements. But her rebuttal convinced him all the more that God had brought the Periana family to him for a reason. Whatever ailment the girl suffered, he would be thorough enough to find the cure.

"I wish you would not scold me for trying to help people."

"That's the thing, Vidal. You're so preoccupied with what

happened to Sarah, you forget your responsibility to our other children." She let out an exasperated sigh as sharp as any blade and trudged up the hill alone.

Chapter Fourteen

As night fell, the men built the evening bonfire on the far bank of the stream. They removed their boots and waded through the water to congregate in the formation of a crescent moon around the embers, while the women assembled on the shore beside the fire. The flames reflected in the running water, bathing the faces, trees, and surrounding rocks in warm orange light. Vidal could see his wife and daughter going to the bonfire as he and Asher returned to the wagon from evening rounds. Would Bonadonna want him to say goodbye? He'd spent the afternoon explaining to the families of his patients how they should treat their sick in his absence. After answering so many questions, he felt as exhausted as if he'd faced a tribunal. Despite deep breaths of fatigue, he threw back the tapestry covering the wagon bed to gather clothes and fruit into a leather bag for the journey to Periana.

"Are you leaving tonight?" Eliezer asked from the head of the wagon.

Had Eliezer finally broken his silence? Vidal tried to contain the hope in his eyes as he turned to his son. "At first light."

"May I have a word?"

"You may."

"Away from…" Eliezer nodded to Asher.

Asher looked up from plucking blades of grass. "What makes you think I want to listen to your boring conversation?"

Vidal took Eliezer by the arm and suggested they walk. Finding privacy on the hillside proved a futile effort. Although they

166

had all of nature to speak in confidence, Vidal noticed that families stopped their conversations mid-sentence as he and his son passed. Women cleaned plates with bucket water far longer than necessary to eavesdrop. Even the tree line was occupied with young men whom the rabbi had appointed to guard the caravan overnight. They rocked back and forth, determining whether it was better to lean on the left or right foot for hours on end. Overhearing a conversation between father and son would certainly break up the monotony of guarding a seventy-wagon caravan and Vidal wanted no distractions to keep Eliezer from speaking his mind.

They stopped beside a wagon left unwatched by a family who'd gone to the bonfire. The wagon leaned on a back-left wheel that was smaller than the others. The weight of whatever the family had hidden under the blanket that covered the wagon put pressure on the wheel's splintering wood. Eliezer faced him. Perhaps it was the glow of the fire, but his son's face looked warm in a way his otherwise sickly and pasty appearance had not looked in many weeks.

"Do not return to Periana."

"Where's this coming from?"

"Father, it's dangerous." Eliezer shared the story of what'd happened at the well with Binyamín and Avraham. When they'd arrived at the plaza that contained the well, two women were using a bucket to pull water. The guards forced the women away so that Eliezer could fill the barrels before a curfew was imposed on their hour-long presence in the city. But before they could fill one barrel, a gathering of men—the same gathering Vidal had seen at the gate—arrived to intimidate and force them out. When they refused and announced they had the right to the water, the men kicked Avraham in the stomach and held him in a headlock until they agreed to leave. They were lucky to escape the square with even their empty barrels, fleeing like soldiers retreating from a battle.

As Eliezer spoke, a man stepped out from the wagon behind Vidal and urinated on the roadside. He swayed back and forth, no doubt inebriated with wine.

"Would you have any reason to suspect that Señor Castillo and his family were part of that mob?" Vidal asked.

"I have no way of knowing. No one gave their names, and I never saw the face of the man you spoke with today."

"Thus, I cannot hold him accountable for the actions of his neighbors."

"Father, you cannot go. You'd be gone for two days, maybe more."

"There is a very sick little girl back there who may die if I do not treat her."

"There are people here who will die if you leave."

"I already gave them my word; I cannot forsake them. I am compelled to treat all who seek my care—or have you forgotten what I taught you already?"

"I know, Father. I remember. But things are different now. This isn't Granada."

"You forsook the privilege of telling me what to do when you renounced your position as my apprentice."

"I want to be your apprentice again."

"I am too tired for false promises."

"I mean it, Father. I've been searching to find a way to ask you."

"Yet you ask me so I will not go to Periana. Do you take me for a fool? Your mother persuaded you to do this."

"Father, please take me back. Stay here where you are needed most. We will care for the people together. Let this go on no longer. I am sorry for the way I have behaved."

Vidal steadied his tongue from making one more accusatory remark. Could these be Eliezer's true intentions? His son's forgiveness felt at the brink of becoming a reality. "You're not saying this simply so I will not go to Periana?"

"I am saying we all need you. And because I think you're acting a little mad."

Vidal threw his arms around his son. The embrace was rare; he could not recall holding his son since Eliezer's bar mitzvah. He realized the boy was taller than him by nearly a head. How had he not noticed before? He put his head against Eliezer's chest and emitted a soft wail. He'd only cried once before in front of his children, when he discovered Sarah's corpse. He'd not cried at her funeral, at the gates of Granada, at the moment he bid farewell to Catalina. Why would he cry now, where his son, the men keeping guard, and the man drunkenly urinating might hear? Eliezer rubbed his hands against the coarse linen that covered Vidal's back, then pushed him away. Vidal sniffed and turned to hide his tears. In his peripheral view, his wet cheeks reflected the dance of the bonfire's light.

As they returned to the wagon, the rectification of their relationship overpowered the guilt he felt for breaking his word to the Perianenses. Was it wrong to forsake the town? Certainly. But the Castillos would need to find another doctor. He could not let their misfortune distract him when he had enough misfortune of his own. The girl was not Sarah. She was young and would have the strength to recover on her own. But Eliezer was back! He would train under him again! Life had become a little easier, and that was worth God's praise.

While Eliezer stayed at the wagon to share the good news with Asher, Vidal felt in the spirit to join the others at the bonfire. As he cut through the darkness and blackened grass, an energy that he earlier that day believed might never return now enveloped him as if he'd drunk a potent elixir. He wanted to share this change of plans with his wife, but could not enter the side of the river where the women sat along the water's edge. He caught his wife's eye as he passed. He should not have burdened her with the idea of leaving for Periana. For all the time he'd spent caring for others, he had not done enough to care for his family.

He removed his boots and waded across a stream no wider than the size of his bed in Granada. The water rose to his ankles, and although he was hot from the summer night, the water was so piercing that it sent a shiver through his body.

In the middle of the crescent, Shelomo Levin stood and rotated in the direction of a sundial's shadow as he regaled the people with a story. "Since I was a boy, anytime I would look up at La Alhambra; I would ask myself what I believed to be inside the palace walls. This was back when it belonged to the emir, before the monarchs no doubt plundered the palace for its riches." He shared a story that Vidal recalled from childhood. When they were seven or eight years old, he, Shelomo, and two other boys—Mosse the tailor and Natan the baker, if he recalled correctly—met outside Temple and discussed the idea of sneaking into La Alhambra to steal the emir's treasures.

"My father is short of money," Shelomo had said. "If I cannot help him, he will sell my favorite horse. I say we go to La Alhambra and steal the gold we need to help him save his business."

"If they see us approaching, the guards on the walls will shoot us," Vidal said. He pictured them dead on the hill below the palace, their bodies riddled with arrows. Though he would not be a doctor for many years, he knew that if even a single arrow punctured the body, it likely meant death.

"That is why we must be clever about it. We're small. We will sneak in. They will never expect it." Vidal looked to Moshe and Natan for reason, but when they agreed to help Shelomo, he said he would follow. This was back during the part of his life where he would do anything for his friends, before his loyalties turned to vocation and family. He left his home after sundown that night. The torches that lined the alleyway outside their door were already lit. He moved through the narrow stone streets to meet his friends at the edge of La Judería. His parents rarely allowed him to go out after nightfall, but he'd said he was going to Shelomo's house because Shelomo's father had promised a pail of fresh milk. How to get the milk, he did not know. He assumed he would either return wealthy enough to render the original story obsolete or that he'd be killed at the palace walls, proving a punishment for his earlier lie to be superfluous.

He met Shelomo and his friends at the street corner where La Judería met Bib Rambla. The boys were dressed all in black, with black shawls wrapped over their heads. In his reluctance to go along with the plan, Vidal had worn white without a thought.

"What are you wearing? They'll see us from a league away."

"You never told me to wear black."

"And you want to be a doctor? You have no sense at all."

"If you want me to go home, I will."

"It's too late now. Keep to the shadows."

Vidal reached the far side of the shore and shook off the water by kicking his feet into the air. As Shelomo recited the conversation by the stream, he, of course, remembered every embarrassing word verbatim. Even he was curious to hear Shelomo recount the story. Shelomo was a businessman, his life revolved around payments and debts, and Vidal was surprised that his old friend had kept enough room in his brain to recall such an old tale.

At the campfire, Vidal sat at the edge of the crescent in the grass beside the river. The blades were so wet that he cursed when he sat in them. These trousers would be ruined, a green swatch running across his behind as if he'd sat in paint. He looked around at the others, their clothes encrusted with dried mud, permeant yellow stains under the armpits of their tunics, filth no amount of river water would wash away. His body felt cold for the first time in days.

Shelomo recited that their path took them northwest through Granada. They passed mosques and empty plazas in the Moorish section of town. Deep shadows engulfed the far corners of the courtyards and a breeze blew fallen leaves from one side of the squares to the other. Tree branches bounded up and down in the wind, like phantoms that might come to life and give chase. Vidal tried to ignore the encroaching paranoia as he listened to Shelomo and his friends discuss what they'd do with the treasure. Shelomo would pay his father, Natan would buy the wood needed for a new roof for his family, and Moshe would put it toward a dowry to sell off his wretched sister.

"And what did your Dr. ha-Rofeh say?" Shelomo asked the crowd. "He told us to turn back. But I knew better than to listen. We soldiered forth to the bottom of La Alhambra. And when we arrived, two guards—the most enormous men we'd ever seen— stood waiting for us." Shelomo described the hill's base, where horses and carriages passed through a guarded stone archway to ascend the road to the palace. But what he said next rang false for Vidal: as they approached the archway, the guards crossed their staffs and forbade them to enter. Shelomo exclaimed to the other boys that he had no fear. He confronted the guards and explained that the emir had commissioned his father to weave a beautiful rug for the palace. Shelomo's father had sent him to measure the dimensions of a room where the carpet would cover all four corners. The guards fell for his trickery and escorted the four of them up the hill to the palace. Inside, a servant of the emir guided them from room to room. They saw chambers packed floor to ceiling with rare exotic treasures, indoor bathroom pools, bowls filled with pomegranates, apples, and olives. The tour concluded in the harem, where the most beautiful women throughout the Kingdom of Granada lay in waiting for their emir. The servant instructed Shelomo to measure the room.

"And we did just that," Shelomo told his audience. "I stood on one end of the room and counted my steps, one foot in front of the other, to acquire the measurements."

Vidal put his hand over his mouth to stifle his laughter. Shelomo's father was a businessman, not a carpet-weaver. The man never made a rug in his life. Did anyone believe this nonsense? How was it that Shelomo, Granada's best salesman, managed to be its worst storyteller? He'd not thought of the real story in over a decade, but now, he could remember the events. They'd hiked up the sloping paved road that led to the entrance archway. When the archway appeared, they noticed a handful of guards waiting with their staffs and sheathed swords. The four boys quarreled in the shadows for the next ten minutes about who was brave enough to approach the guards, until finally Shelomo accused them each of cowardice and was the first to turn back down the hill.

"Did you get the treasure?" asked a professor who Vidal thought too wise to fall for such a tale.

"The treasure proved to be unnecessary. My story got back to the emir and he was so taken that he commissioned my father to weave the rug."

"Tell us more about the harem," shouted a boy who had not yet had his bar mitzvah. The men laughed in approval.

"You are too young to hear such details—especially in the presence of women."

Vidal searched for his wife's face across the stream to see if she had fallen for the story. If she believed he'd gone to a harem, he'd never hear the end of it. He could already picture his future. Anytime she wanted him to clean their home, attend to the children, fetch the ingredients for a meal, she would remind him of the time he'd once come upon Shelomo's imaginary harem. He found her face among the women across the river. She shook her head with her eyes closed the way she did when he told a joke she found more repulsive than humorous. Vidal recounted Shelomo's version of the story in his mind and cackled like an animal.

"What is so amusing, Dr. ha-Rofeh?" Vidal opened his eyes to find Shelomo addressing him, and the entirety of the bonfire looking his way. "Have I forgotten a part of the story?"

Would it be wrong to call out Shelomo on his fiction? To expose him as a liar before the caravan would be fitting, revenge for all the pain Shelomo had caused his family. Pain Shelomo had barely apologized for causing. But Shelomo's story was not meant to be the truth; it was a tale, like something out of the New Testament. Merely meant to entertain their weary caravan. What good would it do if people knew the truth?

"No. You have told the story well."

As the men continued to press Shelomo for information about the palace and the patterns woven into the rug, exhaustion overcame Vidal. His head ached, his cheeks weighed down the sides of his face. He pushed himself up and began the tedious task of crossing the stream back to his wagon. By the time he had his boots on, Bonadonna was waiting under the crown shyness of two tree branches.

"I didn't realize our doctor had time for Shelomo's story."

"I'm staying. Eliezer convinced me."

"He spoke to you?"

"I thought you put him up to it."

"Not at all."

"I'm sorry, Bonita. You were right, I should've refused them. I shouldn't have made you worry."

"I forgive you. But next time a stranger asks for you to leave your family—"

"I will refuse."

Bonadonna touched his arm. "The girl will be okay," she reassured him, although they'd never know the fate of the little girl from Periana.

"I can't keep my eyes open. Will you come back to the wagon with me?"

"I think I've spent enough time at the wagon. I rather enjoy listening to your old friend make a fool of himself."

"Don't believe a word Shelomo says."

"Trust me, if you'd gone to a harem as a boy, I'd know about it."

"I have no doubt of that."

"Good night, Vidal."

"Good night, Bonita." Vidal leaned in and kissed his wife, something he could not remember doing in many months. He did not care that the public act may be considered indecent by the caravanners to his back. The touch of her lips made him feel like he had made the right decision to stay, and for only a moment, being out in the wilderness, leagues away from the house they'd left or the city they journeyed to, he felt at home. She held him close as if her embrace might make his presence at the wagon permanent.

Over the next eleven days, marked by two unobserved Sabbaths, the view of the mountains remained monotonous. Hills, valleys, bushes, trees. The caravan greeted every ascent with a sigh, and every descent with a blessing, for those were the days that God eased their journey. The caravan rounded mountain after mountain, and although the rabbi assured everyone they were moving in the right direction, Vidal imagined they would never find their way out. Could the map be incorrect? Were they walking in a circle? He only believed they continued forward because they never encountered another stream, river, nor lake. Where he'd first greeted the breadth of the world with admiration and wonder, he now resented its vastness, for that immensity kept his family in the wild day after day with no refuge in sight. He became certain that if they could not reach the coast by the date of the decree's effect, they would be stranded and need to hide in the mountains when the monarchs' army came to annihilate them.

Yet Vidal also observed the fortunes afforded to him. For the first time in his life, he had two apprentices. While Vidal continued rounds with Asher, Eliezer called on new patients—specifically those at the rear of the caravan—and brought back the diagnoses. If Vidal believed his son was capable of treating these patients himself, he allowed Eliezer to administer remedies and offer recommendations for how families could treat their sick, anything short of permitting his son to perform a bloodletting. With the number of patients he needed to see divided in half, Vidal spent time at the wagon helping Bonadonna. On rounds, he mentored Asher on the most serious cases, such as patients who'd acquired gangrene, who'd sprained their ankles, or who developed hernias from the endless pulling of the wagons. When time allowed, Vidal sutured gashes and cuts slowly enough to demonstrate the technique to his son.

On the twelfth day, he guided the wagon along a dirt trail that cut through the olive-colored grass of the mountainside. At first the land to his left sloped downward, but as he pulled the wagon around the bend, the cliff made a vertical drop. Vertigo forced him close to the wagon's side and he dared not look at the cavernous valley below. Where were the children? He called for them to stay by the wagon. Then a chill that blew through the air carried the vague smell of salt. Were they near a city?

As he rounded the mountainside, his first glimpse of Málaga appeared in the valley beneath. The city was farther away than one end of Granada from the other and many leagues below. From where he stood, the entirety of the city looked no more extensive in circumference than his palm. Its walls parted from the mountains' base to meet the coast at either end of the city. He could see no walls on the shore itself, save for what appeared to be a stone-built fortress by the water. This was the largest port city in the Kingdom of Granada, yet it seemed insignificant beside the sea. Nothing could have prepared him for this first view of the Mediterranean. A pool of blue water stretched away from the coast toward infinity. What little marine layer that covered the point where the horizon met the sky was powerless against the rising sun. Were they supposed to cross that? Where did the sea end? To navigate it, he felt they were as likely to plummet off the edge of the map as drown.

But he needed to have faith. They'd survived the mountains. He halted the horse and stood on the cliffside to look down at the city. Bonadonna ushered Iamila to the side of the wagon farthest from the cliff and told her husband not to stand so close to the edge as she arrived beside him. "It is beautiful, no?" he asked.

"I can only hope the hardest part of our journey is behind us."

He doubted the idea. Though he'd never seen a map of the Maghreb, nobody had spoken of Fez as if it were on the coast. Once they reached African shores, they'd have a long journey yet. "Who can say? We've made it this far. We will make it to the end. Thank you for taking care of our family. I'm sorry I have been so busy with the patients."

"I'm glad we have each other on this journey."

He rarely heard her speak this way. After Sarah's death, he'd grown uncertain whether he and Bonadonna were capable of loving each other again the way they'd once loved each other. Yet standing beside his wife on a cliffside overlooking the sea, he felt a warmth in his stomach, and an instinctual reassurance that there was nobody better suited for him than Bonadonna. He rubbed his hand on her back and together they gazed at the ripples of the sea.

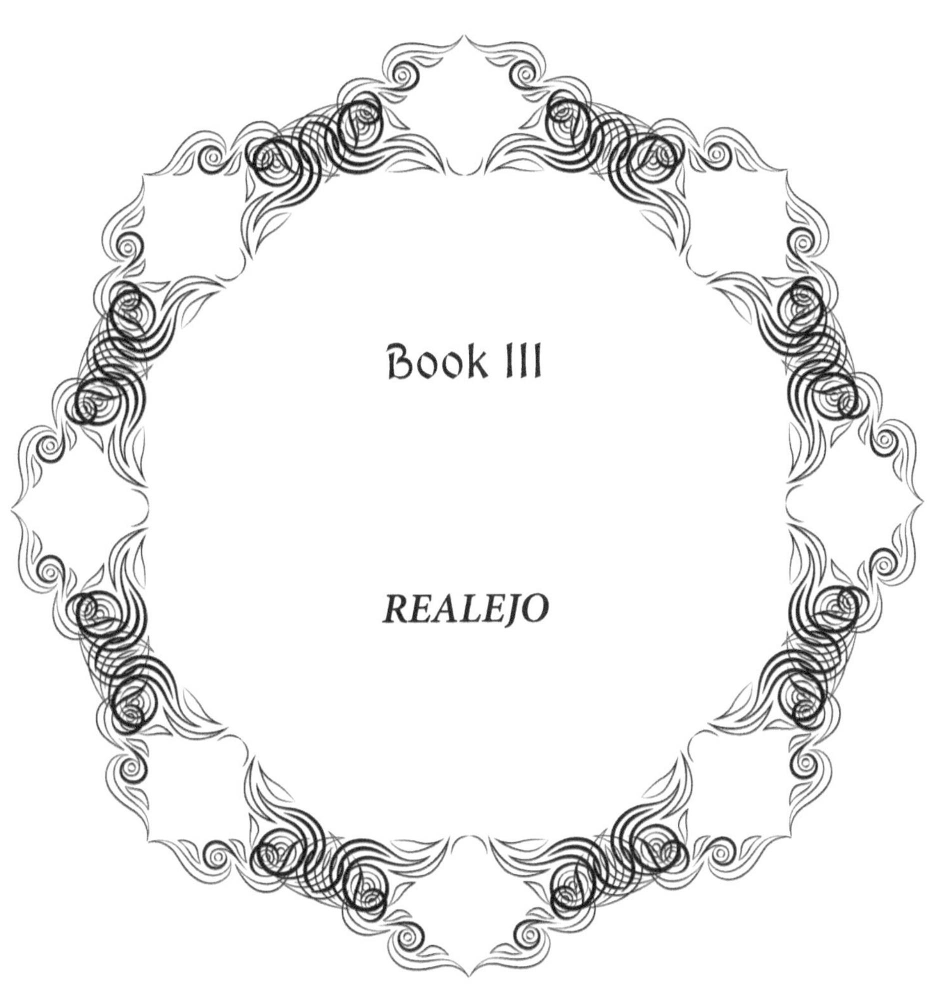

Book III

REALEJO

Chapter Fifteen

Every day that Catalina walked through La Judería to her parents' old home, she saw Granada transform. Workers broke off the clay Stars of David from the fronts of the temples and schoolhouses and erected tall crucifixes on the lawns in their place. New families moved into the abandoned houses. The Ibn Ezras became the Zamoras, the Hagornis became the Machados, and the Yudahs became the Guerreros. At first, the changes made her want to weep. The monarchs had already committed an evil enough act by exiling her family. Now they were going to erase any evidence of their existence? She attempted to convince herself that the altered neighborhood shouldn't disturb her. What did she expect would happen—that everything Jewish would be preserved in spite of the banishment? She reminded herself not to be bothered and prayed to Christ that the Jews of Granada never learn of the fate of their old Judería.

Ochoa had purchased her family's home to give her father money to buy the horse and cart, and Catalina checked the house every day to make sure no squatters occupied it. The air inside felt stale without the five bodies of her family passing through. The rooms smelled of mildew and dust, no matter how much she cleaned them. Sometimes the sound of her father's voice, a cough, or a sneeze emanated from the wall, a reminder that this was the closest she'd come to hearing her father again. How soon until all sound that remained in the walls escaped? She counted the days until her family's first letter arrived from Fez.

Gabriel suggested they move into the home, but Catalina could not imagine raising a family of her own, laughing, and growing old in a place that her family was forced to abandon. She told Gabriel she was not comfortable living in a neighborhood now inhabited by the monarchs' soldiers and their families, and that she did not want to go into labor in the house alone while he was away at work. They compromised that they would live with his parents until the baby was born. "But we cannot leave it vacant forever," he said. "It was a gift from Father. It will insult him if we neglect it."

After tending to her family's home, she continued down the vacant serpentine alleyways of La Judería to the east end of town to honor a promise she'd made to her mother. The cemetery was small and hidden behind a newly converted Catholic school, where a crucifix mounted to the wall above the entryway covered the sun-damaged tan line of where a Star of David once stood. In the cemetery, Catalina traversed obstacles of gravestones to reach her sister's headstone at the northeast end of the cemetery. At Sarah's grave, she placed a bouquet of pomegranate flowers. It was not a Jewish custom, and she considered picking up rocks scattered throughout the cemetery grass to lay on the grave instead, for stones were a more permanent memento to leave on a grave than terminal flowers, but if anyone who tended to the graveyard noticed the stones, they'd suspect a Jew had stayed behind in the city.

In church, the priest never mentioned the absence of the Jewish community. Catalina looked around at the faces of the congregation and could tell that if she brought up the topic, they would wonder why she was gossiping about old news. Her father once told her that the Jews left Jerusalem for the Kingdom of Granada 1,500 years ago. One thousand five hundred years in Granada and it had taken the city mere weeks to forget.

A month after the caravan had left, as Catalina finished visiting her family's house and sister's grave for the day, she noticed two men at the far end of the cemetery, beside the barrier that doubled as the eastern wall of Granada. Two men surveyed the land; three others dug a hole. Had a Jew stayed behind and died? She noticed the men were digging below a grave marker. A burial shroud, half-eaten away by insects, and stained the color of earth, lay on the grass beside the pit. Something milk-white within the soiled linen reflected off the sunlight: human bone.

A surveyor who stood beside the pit seemed to sense her presence. He called out to her. She looked away and walked toward the exit.

"You!" the surveyor said. "Stop there. I am speaking to you."

She hurried to the gate. If she could make it out of the cemetery, she doubted he would follow her. His boots stomped over the dirt behind her. A hand wrapped around her arm and yanked her back. She startled as if she had not expected him. The surveyor wore brown linens. He had tartar in his teeth, dirt under his fingernails, and the same head of blond hair as Gabriel. "What business have you here?"

"Sir, unhand me immediately."

He squeezed her arm tighter. "I asked you a question. Why are you here?"

"This is a public place. Does a lady need a reason to enjoy an afternoon walk?"

"A public place? This is a Jew cemetery."

"I have already explained myself. Now, if you are a gentleman, then I ask you please to unhand me."

He squinted as if trying to place her. She feared her nose looked enormous to him, her hair frizzy and unkempt. She had changed her faith, but the distinct Jewish features of her face remained. Her father's warnings began to carry weight. "Have we met?" he asked.

"Granada is a small town. Perhaps we attend the same church."

"You are employed, are you not?"

"I am a married woman. I do not work."

"No, I recognize you. You were a nurse. You worked for Dr. ha-Rofeh?"

If he could place her as her father's nurse, then he could place her as his daughter as well. She reminded herself that being a convert was no crime, but she did not need him drawing this conclusion in a Jewish cemetery.

"I worked for Dr. ha-Rofeh before marriage."

The surveyor let go of her arm. "He saved my brother's life."

She tried to place his face. She had aided her father's work in many houses and could not recall the face of this man or his brother. "I hope your brother is well."

"His wounds healed. He has gone to be a monk in León. How is El Doctor?"

"He left with the caravan. That was the last I heard of him."

"A shame he did not convert."

For a moment, Catalina imagined an alternative life where her family stayed in Granada with her. She pictured them beside her in the cemetery. How would they react to the sight of a body pulled from the ground? What would they think of her for fleeing such an upsetting scene at the first sign of trouble? "Am I free to leave, Señor?"

He bowed. "Yes, forgive me." He looked back to the open pit. "Señora, it is best that you do not return here. Find another place for your afternoon walks."

She glanced towards Sarah's grave. "Why?"

"That is none of your concern." He chucked her chin and turned away. She thought to call out to him, demand an answer, enough with these cryptic warnings, but she knew a different man from the graveside might follow her next. She left the cemetery.

On the walk home, she tried to predict what the men were doing there. Did they only plan to dig up one grave? And if so, why? To look for treasures the Jews had left buried in their tombs? Jews would never engage in such a practice. Or did they mean to desecrate the bodies? Dig up all the graves to use the land for something else? The baby kicked in her womb and she feared that must be the case. What would become of Sarah's grave? The graves of her grandparents?

In the afternoon, the temperature rose to an unbearable level. Catalina finished her chores at home and waited for Gabriel and Ochoa to return. She tied her hair in a bun to escape the humidity and fanned her stomach, fearing the heat would harm the baby inside of her.

Gabriel found her at the kitchen table where she rubbed salt into an uncooked rack of pork ribs. The heat caused the smell of blood to fill the air.

"Has the pork gone bad?" Gabriel asked.

She flipped the rack over. "I passed by Sarah's grave today." She told him about the men who had dug up the body at the cemetery.

"Are you certain they were robbing the grave?"

"For what other purpose would they pull it from the ground?"

"Perhaps there is a logical explanation."

"Or perhaps Sarah's grave will be next."

"Why would they raze an entire cemetery?"

"It's a Jewish cemetery. Why would they keep it?"

"I'll ask Father if he knows anything."

That night, while Gabriel and Ochoa ate at the dining table, Catalina and Marquessa waited in the kitchen. Her stomach rumbled, but she was too anxious to hear from Ochoa. If he believed the grave might be robbed, she imagined they might have to excavate Sarah's remains and move her elsewhere. The image of Sarah's body through holes in the crypt, the smell of her flesh that had not seen fresh air in almost four years, made Catalina feel like she might faint.

"One of Ochoa's men returned from Málaga today," Marquessa said. "I asked if a letter had arrived from your family, but he said he received nothing."

Catalina had trouble thinking of her family on some incredible journey, going to start their lives over in a world she would never be part of. "I imagine they must be crossing the sea by now."

"They have only several more days before the decree goes into effect."

"Already?" Catalina knew the end of July was eight days away, but she needed to act aloof when her mother-in-law brought up Jewish news. If she acted too excited, it would appease Marquessa's never-ending suspicion that she still held onto some aspect of the faith. Marquessa was the only person in Granada unconvinced by a baptism and communion.

Ochoa called for more wine and Marquessa grabbed a clay

pitcher off the counter and went to the dining room to refill his cup. Alone, Catalina wondered if Ochoa's worker had delivered letters from the caravan to anyone else in Granada. Several families had chosen to convert to Catholicism rather than leave. She considered asking them about the caravan or the cemetery, but knew both situations were dangerous. They were Catholic now. Their ties to the Jewish community were finished.

Gabriel and Ochoa soon called them to the table to eat. They discussed a demanding customer who had purchased silk shirts from them, only to argue for his money back every day for a week, and Gabriel theorized ways to stop the customer from returning. Nobody spoke of the cemetery and Catalina knew better than to bring it up. Once Ochoa stood to smoke his pipe, Catalina asked Gabriel to accompany her behind the house to wash the plates. The alley was pitch-black, save for the faint white glow of the moon shining down from between the houses. She knelt over a bucket of water and scrubbed the plates. Gabriel stood over her, holding the other dishes.

"What did your father say?" she asked.

"He knew nothing."

"But he will ask on my behalf?"

"He promised he would. He also asks that you not return to the cemetery until he has his answer."

She handed him a clean plate and took the next dirty one. "How long does he expect that will take?"

"He will ask as soon as he can. But he wants you to understand; this inquiry does not come without risk."

"What risk?"

"Father wants to help you; do not think me false. But he must be stealth with his inquiries. He has already earned a reputation among his colleagues as a Jew sympathizer."

"Those are your mother's words."

"You do not know the ridicule Father faced so we could marry."

Catalina feared the questions she was asking were more dangerous than she realized. Nobody had brought up her Jewish heritage as a negative before, but now that the caravan had left it seemed to have returned as one of her defining traits.

"It is my sister I worry about. Not the faith of those interred at the cemetery." The statement felt wretched coming from her mouth, but she feared that saying otherwise would give Gabriel the wrong idea. If the monarchs had plans to raze the cemetery, she could only protect Sarah. There was nothing she could do for the other bodies, except to never send a letter to her family with news of the cemetery that would spread anguish throughout the caravan.

"I'm aware of that," Gabriel said. "But others may not understand the difference."

Catalina slid the plate into the bucket of water. She imagined the men digging up her sister's grave, raising the tiny body from its resting place, making theories and jokes about how such a young girl had died. "How long does your father need?"

"He was not certain. But you must be patient—"

"What if they are digging up her grave this instant?"

"Be calm. Father will learn the situation in a day or two."

"I feel wrong waiting that long."

"You have no choice. What if the men you encountered in the cemetery had harmed you?"

"One of them knew my father."

Because Gabriel's hands were full, he nodded to her stomach. "This is what you need to watch over now, what you need to protect. This is your only concern."

"I promised my mother I would watch over Sarah's body. Now my family is out there facing God-knows-what. What kind of daughter will I be if something happens to her?"

"Your mother may have said that, but not at the expense of harm befalling you or our child," Gabriel said. "You are protecting Sarah by telling us what you saw. Now, Father will look into the matter, and neither you nor any of us will return to the cemetery before then. Those are Father's orders, not mine."

She wanted to argue more. She knew she could go to the cemetery in the morning while they were out of the house. But she reminded herself she had learned nothing from the surveyor. She'd learn more by waiting for Ochoa then sneaking off to spy in the cemetery.

"I understand." She rubbed her hand against her cheek. "And I apologize. My body has gotten the better of me since this pregnancy began."

"That is all right." He kissed her forehead. "Now finish cleaning. I will help you."

She knelt over the bucket and returned to the dishes.

The next day, she stayed away from the cemetery. She remained in the house, washing the bedsheets, clearing space in her room for the baby, dusting the shelves, anything to keep herself distracted. Every day, Gabriel and Ochoa returned home together. Catalina would meet her husband in their room before dinner and ask if he'd heard any word about the cemetery. "Nothing," Gabriel said as he changed his clothes. "Father is cautious about who he asks and the people he feels comfortable asking know nothing." After their conversations, she wanted to go back to the cemetery and investigate, but every day she convinced herself that tomorrow Ochoa would come home with an answer.

Catalina reconsidered her initial refusal to seek out conversos in the city. Perhaps the Abrozes, who had become the Francos, or the Govons, who had become the Garcias. She'd not spoken to the families since her conversion, but was now tempted to stop them when she passed them in the streets, speak to them about the situation she imagined all of them were going through as well. She could learn if they knew anything about the cemetery. But she could not bring herself to approach them. Perhaps the Abrozes were committed to forgetting their faith. Perhaps the Govons would turn her over to the soldiers if they heard her speak about the fate of the cemetery. In attempting to confide in them, she would put herself and her baby in danger.

That Sunday she sat on Our Ladies side of the church aisle beside Marquessa. After mass, she accompanied her mother-in-law to the church steps outside and waited while Marquessa spoke to other women who came to her with the latest gossip. Women spoke to her about feuds with their husbands, sons who slept with strange women, brothers who fathered bastard children during the war. Every woman in Granada seemed capable of speaking with Marquessa about their most personal secrets, but because Marquessa had never truly accepted her as a daughter-in-law, Catalina felt unable to do the same.

As she waited for Marquessa to conclude her conversations, a finger tapped her on the shoulder. Catalina turned to see Linda Alfandari, now Beatriz Calderón, the family's oldest daughter who was one year her junior. They had gone to school together and sat next to each other often at the synagogue. But ever since her marriage to Gabriel, they had barely spoken, not even when Beatriz's family converted in response to the decree. Seeing a familiar face made her realize how much she'd missed Beatriz and lamented the years they had spent apart.

"I never had the opportunity to congratulate you on becoming a mother," Beatriz said.

"Thank you." She held her stomach. "Gabriel and I are truly blessed."

"How many months more?"

"Four. Perhaps a little longer."

"So you are to have a baby in November?"

"I imagine so."

"A good month to be born. I was born in December. It is so close to La Nochebuena, everyone is always so preoccupied."

Catalina wasn't certain, but she saw Beatriz's announcement as a subtle hint. Before her family converted, they would have paid no mind to La Nochebuena or La Navidad. The nearest Jewish holiday, Chanukah, was a minor one. A candle lighting ceremony would not have gotten in the way of a birthday.

"A December birthday does not sound so terrible," Catalina said. "It lengthens the celebrations."

"I will have to start thinking of it that way."

Catalina had so much she wanted to ask, but before she could say anything, Beatriz gave an awkward courtesy and turned to go back into the church. Catalina could not help but watch her go. She believed that Beatriz was trying to tell her something. She knew better than to follow her, that she should stay beside Marquessa, but she craved the possibility that Beatriz or her family might have information about the caravan.

She followed Beatriz up the steps and called for her to wait. Beatriz looked back at her with surprise. Standing in front of Beatriz, Catalina glanced side to side. The church steps were filled with people, mostly men talking business and wives bribing their children to keep quiet. It was crowded, but she doubted anyone was listening. "Did anyone from your family leave with the caravan?" she whispered.

Beatriz looked at her, as if she'd mentioned a scandalous story shared among Marquessa's friends. "Not a one." She leaned in. "Catalina, would you like to join me for tea tomorrow?"

Catalina hadn't imagined it, Beatriz did want to talk. "I would love to. You live on the south end of the city?"

"We moved back to our old home. In Realejo."

Catalina pursed her lips, searching for the name. "Come again?"

"Realejo. The neighborhood where we grew up?"

Catalina began to say La Judería, but Beatriz held up her hand for Catalina to stop. Beatriz closed her eyes and nodded her head. At first the very idea of referring to La Judería by another name seemed absurd. She'd seen no pamphlets nor decrees. How had the word slipped into usage? But almost immediately, she accepted it. It did not surprise her. Why did she think the monarchs would keep the name of a people who no longer existed?

"Realejo. Of course," Catalina said. "My apologizes. I will meet you at your house tomorrow."

Catalina returned to Marquessa's side and spent the remainder of the day fantasizing about how tea with Beatriz would go. She hoped to speak openly about news from the caravan and their situation as conversos in Granada. God willing, this would be a chance to connect with people going through the same situation as her, and if she felt she could truly trust them, she might ask about the cemetery too.

The next day, Catalina completed her morning chores with haste—no easy task with child—and left the house at two in the afternoon, telling Marquessa that she was going to check on her family's home. Once she crossed the main road into La Judería—now Realejo, she reminded herself—she did not go down the street that led to the house. Instead she walked down a wider street farther north. All the houses shared walls and she needed to look for a number beside the door to be sure she'd found the Calderón's. She arrived at a house three doors from the end—where the city wall cut off the street, found house number thirty-three and knocked on the blue door.

Beatriz's mother—Catalina could not recall learning her new Christian name—answered the door and welcomed her inside. Couches and tables filled the large interior of the house, which belayed its snug exterior. The sounds of Beatriz's younger sisters shouting and running upstairs came through the ceiling. Crucifixes adorned the walls, as if overcompensating. Beatriz was waiting for Catalina at a table in the middle of the room when she arrived. Two chairs faced each other, and Señora Calderón offered for them to sit and announced she would bring tea. Catalina could not imagine Marquessa, nor her own mother, waiting on her this way.

"Your mother is too kind," Catalina said, sitting across from Beatriz.

"It is not often we have company these days. So many of our old friends have moved away."

"Have they written you?"

"I know not. Perhaps they have written my father."

Señora Calderón returned with the tea and poured them each a cup. Catalina felt selfish for hoping that the mother would leave them. She believed she could speak to Beatriz with honesty and would not want that to be jeopardized by Señora Calderón's presence. However, Señora Calderón brought a nearby chair and joined them.

"Are you not going to have a cup of tea as well?" Catalina asked.

"I never developed a taste for the drink," Señora Calderón said. She then dominated the conversation, asking Catalina when she was due, what gender she hoped the baby would be, and if she had found godparents for the child.

"One of Señor de Zaniçeras' business partners will be godfather, most likely."

"Has the agreement been made?"

"I am uncertain. I have little say in those matters."

"If you were looking for godparents, my husband and I would be happy to take on the task," Señora Calderón said.

Catalina realized why she had been invited. It was not to make a friend or out of a camaraderie for their shared identity, but because the Calderóns wanted to further legitimize themselves. They wanted to take credit for being godparents, so that they could use it as proof of their devotion to their new faith. "That is very kind of you to offer."

"Will your family consider it?"

Catalina only wanted to leave. This family had not invited her for the reasons she'd hoped and whatever hints she had read from Beatriz the day before were her own imagination. They did not care about the people who the city had banished, they did not care what was happening at the cemetery, they only cared about using her baby to prove their dedication to the crown.

"Señora Calderón," Catalina said. "I feel a bit faint. Could I trouble you for a cup of water?"

"Of course." Señora Calderón went to the kitchen.

"I hope you do not think our request forward," Beatriz said. "I told my mother this was not the way. We brought you here under false assumptions."

"No, you brought me here as a friend and your offer is very generous. Is your family only asking for this because we are both converts?"

The base of Beatriz's teacup chattered like teeth on a snowy morning as she placed it back on the saucer. "We are asking because you and I grew up together. Your father made my grandparents comfortable in their final days. Honestly, my father wanted to ask your father-in-law, but he was too nervous. We do not know the de Zaniçerases like we know you."

Señora Calderón returned with a cup of water. Catalina thanked her and drank. They continued to talk about Bible verses and church throughout the next five cups of tea. The moment darkness fell outside, Catalina thanked them for their hospitality and departed.

Chapter Sixteen

Another week passed. July ended. Catalina expected some sort of occasion to mark the first day of the decree, but no parade occurred in the street and no announcement came from the palace. She knew that in staying, she had passed the point of no return. She counted the days that had transpired since the caravan left the city and wondered if her family had made it the Maghreb. Every day, Marquessa returned home from the city center and Catalina asked if she had received a letter from her parents, but Marquessa shook her head. If her family had missed the boat, if Jews had remained trapped in Málaga after the decree, she knew Ochoa and Gabriel would have heard. News traveled fast along Ochoa's shipping routes, but word from her family remained silent.

As she slipped into the sixth month of her pregnancy, her stomach popped out as if she carried a melon under her dress. One day, she sat on her bed knitting clothes for the baby, when the front door opened. Marquessa came up the stairs to hand her a letter. The paper bore her full name in her father's handwriting.

Catalina opened the letter. Though her father usually corresponded in Ladino, the letter was written in Castilian and ran the length of the page. Catalina's excitement overtook her and she began to read, forgetting that Marquessa detested the ability.

"You understand it?" Marquessa asked.

Catalina pressed the paper to her chest. "Not a word."

"You seem as if you do."

"I was only admiring the familiarity of my father's handwriting."

"You must miss him."

"I miss all of them."

"A shame they did not convert."

"I asked him many times."

Marquessa took the letter back. "I will have Gabriel read it to us after dinner." She told Catalina to follow her downstairs to help prepare the meal.

After dinner, the family lounged in the sitting room. Ochoa smoked from an opium pipe and Marquessa and Gabriel drank from cups of wine. Catalina sat beside Gabriel as he read the letter. Her father wrote that it had taken nearly a month to cross the mountains to arrive in Málaga, but everyone in her family was in good health. In a few days, they planned to board a ship for Africa. He would write her again after they settled in Fez.

"Is that all?" Catalina asked.

Gabriel flipped the paper over in search of additional correspondence. "I doubt the journey gives him much time to write."

Her father never addressed her as his daughter, nor did he say he loved her. The vagueness of the letter both frustrated her and gave her the impression that he'd written it out of obligation. After months of waiting, she expected more. But perhaps he omitted additional details to protect her, so that if someone intercepted the letter, it would give them no reason to think that a person of Jewish heritage remained in Granada.

"It is all good news," Ochoa said. "The less eventful your father's letter, the better."

"Unless, of course, he is lying," Marquessa said.

"Why would he lie?" Catalina asked.

Ochoa looked to his wife. "Marquessa, the girl is worried enough. Do not put such nonsense in her head."

"Your father is no liar," Gabriel said. "If there was a problem, he would've been forthcoming."

Catalina never thought of her father as a liar. But did Marquessa feel otherwise? How many more times would her mother-in-law make such an accusation before Catalina suspected it could be true? How long until others' opinions of her father overtook her true memories of the man, as had happened with Sarah?

"May I have the letter?" Catalina asked.

Gabriel folded the letter and handed it to her.

"What does she need the letter for?" Marquessa asked.

"It's her letter," Gabriel said.

"She cannot read it. What is the purpose?"

"She recognizes his handwriting." Gabriel knew she could read, and she always loved that he had never asked her to give up this ability, as long as she never read around his parents.

"If anyone were to catch her with that letter, they may question her," Ochoa said.

"Who's going to question her?"

"Please let me keep it," Catalina said. "Our child may want to read his grandfather's words one day."

Marquessa opened her mouth with force, but Ochoa interrupted her. "Do not let those words leave your mouth."

"What is it?" Catalina asked.

"Nothing. That letter is not to leave this house. Understood?"

Catalina nodded and Gabriel handed her the letter. As the room descended into an awkward silence, she realized what her mother-in-law was going to say. Her family was gone, her parents were gone, and she was not to defy the decree by reminding her child that part of it was a descendant of the people who'd been banished.

The next morning, as she walked through Realejo toward her parents' house, she could not stop thinking of Ochoa's words. She had already lost her family, now she was supposed to lose her memory of them, and never pass along that memory to her child? It was the same as when Ochoa told her not to visit her sister's grave. How was she supposed to never visit Sarah, the only blood she had left in the kingdom? Catalina hadn't gone to the cemetery in a month. Ochoa had learned nothing. She stopped at the street where she would turn if she wanted to visit the cemetery. Why not pass by? Was she truly never supposed to visit again? What would be the harm? The cemetery was wide enough, the graves low enough to the ground. If anyone saw her, she could sneak away.

She turned down the street in the direction of the cemetery. She'd committed the letter to memory and believed Sarah deserved to have their father's brief message recited to her.

At the entrance to the cemetery, she halted. The stone gate that surrounded the graveyard remained standing, but inside, the countless headstones that once stacked crooked and cramped beside each other were absent; the grass ripped out with them. Only a large plot of dirt remained. Catalina looked back at the street behind her. Perhaps she had ventured down the wrong road? Maybe the cemetery was the next street over. But the familiar houses and new Catholic school that lined either side of the entrance assured her this was the place.

She walked through the gate over the clods of loose dirt to the rear of the cemetery and tried to recall the exact location of Sarah's grave. She had visited her a million times, but had only remembered Sarah's resting place by the stone that marked it. Catalina knelt where she guessed her sister might be. The shock of seeing the cemetery removed prevented her from reacting. Should she scream? Cry? Dig to see if Sarah was still underground?

The faint sound of laughter came from the cemetery entrance and Catalina turned to see five men. Among them, she recognized the surveyor who had stopped her a month earlier and a man who wore a robe emblazoned with the Castilian coat of arms draped over his left shoulder. She knew she should hide, but rage overtook her. She marched to them, her nerves burning inside her body with the heat of a fever.

"What have you done?" She met them at the entrance and they looked at her as if she were a madwoman they needed to pass in the street. "Where have you put the bodies? How could you have committed such a heinous act?"

"Do not be upset," said one of the men. "Hardly a person remembers there was a cemetery here."

"You are monsters."

The man with the robe glared at her. "Did you know someone who was buried here?"

"My sister. And my grandparents and my neighbors."

"You are a Jew?"

Catalina trembled. She wanted to scratch their eyes out. But the man's question pushed through her rage. She stepped back and took labored breaths.

The surveyor stepped between them. "She is no Jew. She nursed my brother when he returned from the war."

The man with the robe kept his eyes on Catalina. "I asked you a question, Señora. What is your name?"

"Catalina de Zaniçeras." She spoke in a hush to control her words.

"That was the name given to you at birth?"

The baby's foot ran down the inside of her stomach. She startled and held her belly. "My father is Ochoa de Zaniçeras. He supplies imported goods to your army. Perhaps you have heard of him?"

"I am familiar with Ochoa. He has a weakness for Jews. Even gave one to his son." Catalina averted her eyes. She had played a dangerous game, defying her father-in-law's orders, and she was on the brink of losing.

The man grabbed her chin and forced her to look him in the eye. The way he moved, pivoting the right side of his body toward her, she realized he only had one arm and was using the cloak to conceal the other. "We did not raze the cemetery. We are not pagans. We removed a handful of crypts to make way for the foundation, but otherwise left the other bodies undisturbed."

"Of course," she said. "Forgive me, Señor." Her head went limp in his hand. She had never before loathed herself for such cowardice.

The man looked to her stomach, then turned to the surveyor. "Andrés, take her to the constable. Have him hold her until Ochoa de Zaniçeras claims her."

Andrés held Catalina's arms behind her back. She tried to imagine what clever words her father had used to escape a whipping for staying out past curfew. If only she were as smart as him. The soldiers had whipped her brother. What would they do to her?

She forced herself to look at the man with the robe. "Señor, I have done nothing wrong."

"You are trespassing and disturbing the peace on the property of the monarchs. Be grateful that is all I am charging you with." The man with the robe passed her, and the others followed him into the cemetery. Andrés grabbed her arms and pushed her out of the gates. They walked down the road past the Catholic school.

"I told you not to come back here," Andrés said.

Catalina uttered no reply as they walked and tried to prepare herself for what would come next.

Andrés escorted her to the constable's office on the main road, north of the hulking Nasrid Mosque. The inside of the office was a small room with wooden walls and a desk. A guard who wore a vest, chainmail, and brown leather pants received Catalina. "We found her wandering around the Realejo cemetery," Andrés said, making no mention of her outburst.

The guard grabbed her arm, opened a wooden door in the floor, and led her down a flight of stone stairs to the dungeon. She looked back to Andrés who turned away to leave the office. As she descended the steps, she tried to remember how she'd gotten here. Why had she let things go this far? Was there any moment where she could have avoided this fate?

The dungeon had four cells lined side-by-side. Crisscrossing steel beams stretched from stone wall to stone wall. In the far-left cell, a drunk slept on his back and snored. The guard locked her inside the second cell from the right and returned upstairs without a word. None of the torches were lit and she feared he would close the trap door and plunge her into darkness, but he seemed to pay her a kindness by keeping the door open to allow the faintest diffusion of sunlight to descend down the steps.

Catalina looked at her surroundings. There was nowhere to sit, sawdust scattered the floor, and a large pile of hay bunched up in the corner smelled of shit. She held the beams, lowered herself onto the ground, and leaned with her side against the cell door.

For what felt like an eternity, she looked at the sliver of light hitting the stairs and followed its path as it shrank to nothing. The baby kicked at sunset, no doubt calling for its meal. Thirst and hunger seeped into her throat and stomach. The guard would feed her, would he not? Even prisoners received meals. At sundown, the dungeon went momentarily dark, until a bright orange light reflected off the steps, a sign that the guard had lit a torch in the office. The baby's kicking grew softer and less frequent. How much longer were they going to leave her down here? How long could her baby go in the womb without nutrients?

"Hello! Señor?" she continued to call out to the guard. Her shouts woke the drunk and he screamed at her in a language she did not understand—perhaps French or Portuguese. He took off his shoe and threw it at the beams, rattling the steel. She ignored him and continued to call out to the guard until she heard his footsteps above. He walked halfway down the stairs, used flint to ignite the tinder on a torch lamp that clung to the wall, and kept his back to her as he returned up the stairs and slammed the trap door shut.

The drunk yelled at her, gesturing to where the sunlight had been. He spat at her and the phlegm landed on the floor at the cell between them. Though he couldn't hurt her, she retreated to the farthest corner of her cell. He made a fist, slapped his other hand on his bicep, then turned away.

She didn't dare breathe until his snores returned. Her thoughts returned to her baby. Could the child die? A saying her father once told her soothed her. "It takes humans a very long time to pass away. Time is in our favor." But that was for humans. How long did an unborn child have?

She looked at the sawdust and pictured the dirt covered boots that'd walked over it, the filthy bodies that had laid on it, the people who had defecated on it. Perhaps there was no food because the constable wanted her to eat this. She decided to wait longer. Her family no doubt wondered where she was. Soon they would go looking for her.

Sitting on the floor made her back ache, her neck strain, her stomach weigh heavier than she could remember. She changed position to keep the pressure off any part of her body for too long. As the hours passed—or perhaps they were only moments—she thought of her behavior in the cemetery. Why had she yelled at those men? Did she think Sarah was watching her from Heaven, judging her reaction? Sarah didn't believe in Heaven. And if she was watching, she would judge her not for defending her grave, but for being so reckless while with child.

Gabriel was right. She needed to care for nobody but the baby, not even Sarah's body. She had been playing a dangerous game since the decree was announced. She had thought to leave with her father, abandoning Gabriel. She had asked Gabriel to learn why men were desecrating the cemetery, revealed to Marquessa that she could read, rekindled a relationship with Beatriz only to ask about the caravan, and defied Ochoa's order to avoid her sister's grave. These did not sound like the actions of a Christian, but of a Jew doing a poor job of hiding. As much as she had been accepted as a Catholic by Gabriel's family, strangers could still see the Jewishness in her. She could not rid herself of these features any more than she could change the color of her eyes. She could no longer take these risks. She needed to embrace her future as a Catholic entirely and forget about anything that had to do with her old faith—even if that meant forgetting about her sister's grave and the caravan.

She looked up to speak with Christ, for He must be anywhere but in her cell and asked for His forgiveness, and for Him to accept her again. "Please, free me from this dungeon. Let me go home to my family, the only family I have left. Let my child be healthy. Do not punish my baby for my errors. Do not let my child's life be briefer on this earth than my sister's. Please do this and I will follow You the way I promised the day of my baptism. No more hesitance. I will be honest."

Time passed at an unknowable rate. She never slept, only closed her eyes and leaned her heavy head against the beams. The other prisoner woke on occasion and slumped against the wall, but never spoke.

At some point in the night, the trap door opened. A man ran down the stairs and she recognized him by the way he walked before she saw his face. She threw her herself against the cell door and curled her fingers around the steel beams. "Gabriel!"

He dropped to his knees. "I'm here to get you out. Did they hurt you?"

She smiled and shook her head. Gabriel stood and waited for the guard to lumber down the stairs holding keys on a metal ring the size of a fist. She looked up at the ceiling and whispered a thank you. The guard unlocked the door, and she fell into Gabriel's arms.

Her body was sore and stiff from hours of sitting. Gabriel put his arm around her back and helped her up the stairs. In the front office, Ochoa signed a letter on the guard's wooden desk. The soft blue hue of dawn fell over the mosque outside the doorway.

"Forgive us for not coming sooner," Gabriel said. "We knew nothing of your arrest until evening and by that time it was difficult to secure your release."

Ochoa handed the letter to the guard and met Catalina's eye with a stern look. She had defied them, Ochoa knew it, perhaps Gabriel as well. Escaping the dungeon would not be the end of her punishment. Ochoa motioned for them to leave without uttering a word.

When they returned home, Marquessa cooked Catalina breakfast, a kindness Catalina could not recall her mother-in-law affording to her before. Catalina imagined that her mother-in-law showed genuine concern for her at first, though Marquessa only asked how the baby was feeling. The baby kicked with every new bite of fried egg. Catalina no longer resented Marquessa's words from the other night; her mother-in-law was only instructing her to move forward, not hold onto letters that would remind everyone of her old life.

While Ochoa and Gabriel went to work, Catalina bathed in the courtyard and slept in her room. She woke to the sound of someone knocking on the doorway and looked up to see Ochoa standing at the threshold.

"How are you feeling?" he asked.

Sleep made her groggy and flushed her body with the sticky warmth of post-nap heat. Outside the window, the sun was out. Ochoa must have returned for lunch. "Tired. But recovering. Thank you."

"You had a difficult night."

"If you call sitting on the floor difficult." She laughed, trying to make light of the situation, as she remembered the look Ochoa had given her at the constable's office. "Did Gabriel return for lunch?"

"Only me. I wanted to speak with you."

For what other purpose could he be here? She sat up in bed and waited for him to continue. What would her father have said to her, done to her, if he'd learned of the trouble she caused? Extreme disappointment, silence, but otherwise nothing more than a command to never make such a mistake again. She decided she needed to receive whatever punishment Ochoa gave her. It would be part of her penance, a spiritual cleansing to set her back on the right path.

"The constable told me why you were brought in," he said.

"I imagined he would."

"Gabriel told you not to return to that cemetery."

"Gabriel knows?"

"No. I thought to tell him and have him deal with you. I should have, but I chose not to."

The way he stood over her made her feel vulnerable, sitting in bed in the middle of the day, wearing only a nightgown. "May I ask why?"

"Because I do not want him to lie to you again." He sat at the foot of the bed. "Gabriel asked me to inquire about the cemetery. He told you I learned nothing?" She nodded. "I never even asked."

The news would have disappointed her the day before. But after last night, she was relieved Ochoa had not involved his colleagues in the situation. "Is that because you knew it was too dangerous?"

"I knew it could lead to danger." Ochoa took her hand. "Did Gabriel ever tell you of my time in Constantinople?"

She shook her head.

"When I was about your age, I was a second mate on a ship that imported spices from the Ottomans. I was close friends with the first mate. The man was impossibly handsome. Women would turn to swoon at him as he passed them in the streets." Ochoa told Catalina of one night when the first mate returned to their ship and woke him. The first mate bragged of sleeping with the harbormaster's wife, the most beautiful woman in the city. The following evening, Ochoa got drunk with the captain. The captain complained about the outrageous docking fees and Ochoa cheered him up by gossiping about the affair. The night they set sail home, the first mate missed the ship. Ochoa thought maybe he had run off with the wife. He did not discover what happened until he returned to Constantinople two years later. The harbormaster had learned of the affair. He murdered them both and hung himself.

It was a strange story for Ochoa to tell. Catalina had always heard of his life as a sailor. She imagined a youth full of adventures, bordering on the mythical and awe-inspiring. She'd never before heard a true story of his time abroad. "Perhaps the harbormaster discovered the affair himself."

"Or perhaps the captain told him what I had learned." He squeezed her hand. "We are all irrational creatures. We sleep with other men's wives though we know it can cost us our lives. We gossip about secrets that we know can make their way back to the ones we speak of. I understand that what happened to your parents, what is happening in La Judería, must be a gaping wound for you. I know the crown is more interested in building a new plaza than honoring the resting place of your sister. You are trying to do what you think is best, but do not think that your actions do not have consequences. Once you understand that, you will be better for it."

At first, Catalina could not find the words to respond. A part of her was not ready to accept the cemetery's fate. But she remembered the promise she'd made in her cell. She owed this promise to Gabriel's family as well. What was more, she believed Ochoa could see the concerns she tried to keep guarded, and he was hesitant over whether her actions had betrayed her identity as a converso. "I do understand—"

"It will take you time—"

"The way I behaved in the cemetery yesterday, it was a terrible mistake made without a moment's thought."

"I imagine if the crown had desecrated my father's grave, I would have acted the same." He let go of her hand. "Promise me that I do not need to worry about you more?"

"I promise."

As he was about to leave, his attention turned to the dresser stand. He picked up her father's letter. "Was this on your person when they arrested you?"

"No, I left it here"

"That is the truth?"

Catalina nodded. Ochoa read the letter again and folded it on his way out the door.

"Where are taking that?"

"To burn it." He left the room.

She wanted to protest but knew this was another sacrifice that she must make to distance herself from her past. For the rest of the week, Catalina held to the oath she'd made in the dungeon. At first, she caught herself slipping into old routines, a temptation to feel guilt over her sister. When she read the cover of Gabriel's book on the dresser out of habit, she whipped her head away from it and told herself to no longer read. But with each day that passed, her mindset felt more natural. Her conscience cleared and it brought a lightness to her body she could not recall having—even before learning of the decree.

In church, she concentrated during mass, believing that every word of Latin the priest spoke would lead her toward becoming a better person. As the congregation filed out of the church after service, she entered the confessional box and recounted every detail of the cemetery. It was painful to bring up the experience again. How could she have behaved so stupidly less than a week ago? She wanted to make up excuses for why she had gone to the cemetery, but Padre Leonardo had baptized her and she believed he would understand her attachment to her sister. But when she arrived at the story of the dungeon, she said she believed that Christ was testing her. He put her in that dungeon and the moment she opened her heart to Him, He secured her release. She wished she believed her words with the amount of sincerity hinted in her voice, but she convinced herself that if she spoke this way from now on, she would find the right path.

"Did you question your faith before?" Padre Leonardo asked.

"No, Padre. But I fear that in my concern for my late sister, my actions gave people the wrong perception of me."

"Why did you not come to me with this problem before?"

"I thought I could solve the problem myself. Is it wrong for me to love my sister, even if she was Jewish?"

"Of course, not. She was your sister. Her passing was a tragedy."

"Then is she not regarded as dangerous like the others?"

"She was only a small child. But the Jews held powers over us. You have a strong spirit, my daughter. I have no doubt that Jewishness was the burden the Lord place upon you to test your virtue. You are powerful beyond your years for breaking its spell." She wanted to ask what spell he spoke of. Her parents knew no magic. But she told herself not to question Padre Leonardo, to instead accept his answers as the truth. She would need to believe his every word if she hoped to become closer to Christ.

Padre Leonardo instructed her to say five Hail Marys and Our Fathers, then recited the prayer of absolution. She had once found the prayer bizarre, a few words to atone for one's sins, when the Jews would spend every Sabbath reflecting on their week and an entire day of atonement for Yom Kippur. But now it made more sense. People sinned often, which meant they needed to be absolved often, so that they might reflect on their mistakes often. "Go, and sin no more."

After he dismissed her, she met Gabriel at the entrance. She held her stomach and smiled down at her unborn child. She would soon be on the right course, and not a moment too late, on her journey to motherhood.

Chapter Seventeen

Every week, more people from Ferdinand and Isabella's king-doms arrived in Granada. They purchased homes in Realejo and every time Catalina walked through the old neighborhood, she encountered new faces. People from the north had skin as light as a dove's feathers. They arrived with new fashions: doublets worn a size too small that allowed their shirts to protrude from underneath for the men; bodices held together by laces to expose the white chemises below for the women. The Catalonians spoke of literature, art, and fashion with a knowledge that matched no person she'd ever met, not even her father. The Galicians shared stories of their homeland: beautiful beaches, lush valleys, and a cathedral so majestic it rivaled La Alhambra in comparison. The Madrilenians pronounced Castilian with such succinct articulation that their every word made them sound like actors in the theater.

At first, she wanted to speak with each of them, ones who came from Aragon, Murcia, and Sevilla. Gabriel would introduce himself to them at church, wanting to know their business and make connections to expand his shipping routes. But the more stories Catalina heard, the more everyone sounded the same. They moved here because there was an entire neighborhood of empty homes for sale, they wanted to be in the presence of the monarchs, word had spread across the peninsula that Granada was the queen's favorite of her kingdoms. Soon, Catalina and Gabriel stopped speaking to new people. She heard no new stories, unless Marquessa gossiped of a scandal that had brought a family there. Thus, when Catalina first heard of the inquisitors, she paid the news no mind.

"They traveled here from Compostela," one of Marquessa's friends remarked on the church steps. "They came with nothing but their horses and the clothes on their backs."

"I heard they are from Rome," said one of Ochoa and Gabriel's business partners, when he came for dinner. "Sent here by the new pope."

Rumors circulated about the inquisitors' appearances. Marquessa had seen one in the town square and described him as hulking in stature with flesh that seemed to droop down his face like soft clay. Women in church spoke of them as if they were giants who had come from the countryside. But Catalina trusted Ochoa's description most, that the inquisitors shaved their heads, wore black habits, and tied ropes around their waists.

She saw them for the first time in front of the Nasrid Mosque. Six of them faced each other and prayed in a circle. Their clothes were as Ochoa described, but while the tops of their heads were shaved, hair circled their brows like haloes. A man her father's age interrupted their prayer. His entire body shook with nerves as if he were about to address the pope. Catalina had never seen anyone interact with the inquisitors before and she pretended to examine spices and teas at a nearby stall to eavesdrop on the conversation.

The man wept as he spoke to the inquisitors. When Castile laid siege to Granada, he confessed to them, his family exhausted their food supplies. To feed his children, he stole grains from a neighbor's stable. The neighbor's horse died from starvation as a result. Could Christ forgive him?

Catalina could not hear the inquisitors' replies over the sound of a mother with three children bartering for saffron with the stall vendor. She only saw one of the inquisitors put their hand on the man's shoulder and lean in to speak to him the way a father imparts life wisdom to a son. The man left the inquisitors, clutching his heart in relief, and sat at the stone edge of a nearby fountain to recite Hail Marys and Our Fathers while he wept tears of joy. She continued to hear his recitation as she left the plaza to attend to errands in other parts of town. She could not help but feel a sting of envy. Why had she not thought to approach the inquisitors?

A week later, she noticed one of them walking alone through the market square with his hands folded together. The inquisitor seemed to have no interest in shopping, only in observing people. Despite the crowd in the market, a circle of empty space surrounded him. She had nothing to confess, but entered the space where others kept away. What better way to prove her Christian values than by welcoming a new resident to the city?

"You must be new to Granada."

He looked at her as if she'd hugged him without permission. "May I help you?" His voice had a higher pitch than she'd expected. She found his age impossible to place.

"Is this your first time in the market?"

He looked at her as if judging her, then accepted that she was genuine. "I came here to purchase pomegranates. I hear this city grows the best in the world."

She waved for him to follow her through the crowded square to a cart that sold pomegranates. Without asking, she paid a real for a pomegranate and handed it to him.

He squeezed the fruit's hard exterior. "I was not expecting such a protective shell."

"You'll have to cut it open. But I assure you, it is worth the trouble." She wanted him to thank her, offer some kind of approval. His presence had an intoxicating effect, a yearning for validation she'd only felt before from Gabriel's parents. She wanted him to invite her to study under him, request an invitation to her house for dinner. But he only tossed the fruit in the air and caught it. "Buen día," he said, and left, disappearing into the crowd.

The next Sunday during mass, Padre Leonardo stood at the altar and spoke of the inquisitors. "I met with them and they have provided me with a message they wish for me to communicate with you." The inquisitors had set up a court for inquisition to ensure Granada's successful transition to a Catholic kingdom. For the next thirty days, the inquisitors offered a grace period for residents to come forward and make voluntary confessions of past wrongdoings. After that time, they would conduct further investigations.

Catalina watched as the men on the opposite aisle stood to address the priest. "What sort of wrongdoings?" "Granada is already Catholic. Why the theatrics?" Other members of the congregation voiced their support. "The inquisitors work in service of the monarchs. Let them do whatever is necessary to ensure Granada is a pure kingdom."

Catalina thought of her own wrongdoings. Those were months ago now. Besides, she'd paid for her crimes with a night in the dungeon. But Ochoa had bartered her freedom. Did that absolve her of all accountability? Surely an inquisition was only a formality. A way for people to admit to petty theft, public drunkenness. If they could forgive the thief in front of the cathedral, she doubted they'd take issue with her past. They were searching for more dishonest people than an expectant mother.

From across the aisle, Gabriel looked at Catalina and all reassuring thoughts left her.

That night, she lay in bed beside her husband. A candle sat on the desk beside him, silhouetting his face. He turned the pages of the Bible, searching for names that would be good for their child.

"When I spent that night in the constable's dungeon," she said, "I paid for my crime, no?"

"Paid for it? The punishment was excessive."

"Might it have been worse had your father not secured my release?"

"Why do you talk about this now?"

"I think I should confess to the inquisitors."

"Because of what happened at the cemetery? The men who turned you in should confess. Throwing a pregnant woman into that hole, they should be ashamed."

"That may be. But I think it would be better to come forth with my own story, less I allow others to misconstrue it later."

Gabriel closed the Book and stared at the dark wall beyond the candlelight's reach. "They may not appreciate your actions."

"You just said I did nothing wrong."

"These men are radicals brought here to instill fear. First your family has three months to leave. Now we have thirty days to confess? When does it end?"

"Are those the words of a Catholic?"

"I care not what they represent or why they are here. Things were better under the emir and now I fear the monarchs may go too far."

"What do you expect they will do?"

"I have no idea. This is why I don't want you to speak with them. Understood?"

Gabriel was Catholic born. She always looked to him to teach her about the faith. He was her husband and she needed to honor his request. But to agree with him felt false. As a converso, she needed to behave twice as Catholic as him to be accepted. One inquisitor had already appreciated her help in the market. If the inquisitors posed any sort of threat, she needed to ingratiate herself to them as she did the first. If that meant defying Gabriel, it was only to fortify her position with her new faith. To earn not only the inquisitors' approval of her, but of their child.

"I will not go," she said. She leaned her head on his shoulder and looked down at the Bible cover. "Did you find any names you like?"

The following afternoon, she left home and walked to Plaza Bib Rambla where she followed the shores of the Darro River through the neighborhood until it brought her to the main road. From there she walked along the cobblestone streets and followed the river north in the direction of La Alhambra. In the shadow of the mountain where La Alhambra stood, she arrived at a three-story house between the banks of the river and the base of El Albayzín. A line of four people waited on the road outside a closed green door and a nun dressed in a white wimple and black veil led them in one at a time. The nun soon brought Catalina inside the house, so clean that no dust danced in the beam of sunlight coming through the window, to an outdoor courtyard with orange trees planted in the ground and a water fountain running at the center. An inquisitor, stockier than the one she'd met in the marketplace, sat under the sun at a wooden desk and wrote with a quill and paper. She was surprised they had so much space to themselves and looked for signs of the other confessors.

"Sister Ana," he said. "Bring a chair, please. This woman is with child."

The nun brought a chair from the corner of the courtyard and placed it opposite the inquisitor. Catalina thanked her and sat.

"I am Brother Eduardo Domínguez. State your name." The inquisitor exhaled as if he had asked the question for the hundredth time.

"Catalina de Zaniçeras."

He kept his eyes on the paper. "No."

"That is my Christian name, Señor."

"If you came here to confess, start telling the truth."

Was it so obvious? He had barely looked at her and it was as if God had whispered the correct answer in his ear. Or perhaps someone had already told him of her? Even saying her birth name in the presence of the inquisitor made her squirm. "My birth name was Goyo ha-Rofeh."

"You are a converso."

"Yes, but I have not gone by that name in almost four years."

He smiled and placed his hand over his heart. "I, too, am a converso. The Grand Inquisitor is descended from converts, as well. Did you know?"

"No, Señor." The reality that these men anointed by the crown, the pope, or God—depending on who she asked—shared her ancestry made her smile. The twelve apostles had been conversos as well, she recalled. Perhaps conversos were the most special of all, born to the wrong faith in a test by the Lord to discover the true one.

"For what reason did you convert?"

"Marriage."

"You could not have married a Jew?"

"My family worked closely with the Catholic community."

"This was a business decision?"

"I chose to convert to marry a good man. My father only gave me his blessing."

He made note on his paper. "Why did you come here?"

"I exchanged words with a man—I am not sure who, perhaps

an officer of the king—several months ago in the Realejo cemetery." She explained what had caused the argument and her night in the dungeon, that she had already confessed to the priest, but wished to tell the inquisitor as well to help his mission. Once she finished her story, he looked at his paper. A prolonged silence tempted her to apologize further, but she waited.

"Your forthcoming will not go unappreciated," he said. "Are there many conversos in Granada?"

"Several. Not many."

"Their names, please."

Her lips wobbled. She could think of names to give, the identities of the other converted families were no secret, but why did he want them? Could the reasons be as sinister as Gabriel suggested? The act felt as wicked as Judas' admission of Christ's whereabouts in the garden of Gethsemane. "You know as well as I that it is unbecoming of a lady to gossip of her neighbors."

"You think this is gossip?" He set down his quill. "Señora, my brothers and I have been tasked with a mission by God. The most difficult any of us have ever faced."

"Yes, and I can think of at least thirty passages from the Bible that discourage gossip."

"What is your age?"

"Twenty."

"Are you so naïve to believe that each of your neighbors apostatized with the same sincerity as yourself? Many have converted falsely, for no other reason than to keep their homes and businesses. If we are to save the soul of Granada, we must find these heretics."

She tried to imagine how her father would respond. If only he were here to help her. "You have given them thirty days. They will come to you."

"It is my instructions to tell you that should you not provide evidence, you will be held under suspicion of heresy. Do you know what the punishment is for that crime?"

She remembered the stories of the killings her father had told her about when he urged her to not take her conversion lightly. Of the attacks on the conversos of Segovia and Valladolid the year she was born. "Yes, Brother Eduardo."

"Then provide me with names."

She looked at the orange trees and listened to the running water. It had all sounded so relaxing when she'd arrived. Now it felt like a trick and she could not regain her cleverness quickly enough to outwit her inquisitor. "Surely the church could provide you with these names."

"I am not asking the church, I am asking you. And I grow tired of asking again."

"Please, Brother Eduardo, I do not want to make trouble for anyone."

"Do you believe any have apostatized falsely?"

"No—"

"Then you have no reason to withhold their names." His voice stayed measured and he gave her the warm, trusting face that a good priest gives a child. "You will be hastening our investigation in service of Christ. No harm will come to good people. You have my word."

She imagined she'd know exactly what to say the moment she went back to the street. But if everyone in Granada had converted honestly, then she had nothing to lose by providing their names, only the trust of the inquisitors. She took a breath and gave him the names. The Francos, the Garcias, the Calderóns, and more. He copied each name onto the paper and the moment she was done, he gestured for her to show herself out.

When she reemerged onto the street, she expected to feel elated for helping the inquisitor, but only saw herself as a traitor. The air felt heavier, her body could barely walk under its own weight. She wanted to throw herself into the Darro. What if someone had done this to her? How would she react? She thought again of the violence against Jews in other cities and wondered if something like that could happen in Granada. She stumbled home with no idea of what consequences her actions would have on the other conversos or what she should do next to warn them.

Chapter Eighteen

That night, Catalina sat in silence at the dinner table with Gabriel and his parents. They spoke about buying a bed for the baby, no one noticing the self-loathing in her face in the soft candlelight. Why had she provided real names of conversos? Why had she named all the families, rather than some? She had no other choice but to tell them the truth. The inquisitor had seen through her lies the moment she said her name, and if she lied to his face it would be the same as telling him nothing. She would be held under suspicion of heresy.

She wished the meal would end. She wanted nothing more than to go to bed and never wake again. She felt she did not even deserve sleep; she did not deserve the meal in front of her nor the beautiful bed they would buy for her child. She looked at Gabriel sitting across from her. Why hadn't she listened to him? She'd betrayed his trust again and now she could not even tell him what she'd done. He never responded in anger. Certainly, this would be the story that sent him into a rage. As she cleared the table and washed the dishes in the alleyway alone, she realized there was only one thing she could do: warn the people she'd named.

The next morning, she told Marquessa she needed to leave to check on her parents' old house. She felt cramps in her stomach and groin, pain she had not felt since before her pregnancy. Nevertheless, she hurried through the streets of Realejo, passed the street where her family once lived, and knocked on the blue door of the Calderón's home. Hushed but hurried whispers came from inside. A minute passed before Beatriz's mother, Señora Calderón, opened the door wide enough to fit her head through.

"Catalina!" She spoke loud enough for her family inside to hear. "We were not expecting you."

"Is Beatriz home? May I speak with her?"

Señora Calderón glanced behind the door, as if checking to see if the house were presentable, then opened it wide. "We just finished breakfast. Had we known you were coming—"

"I only need a moment of your daughter's time." Catalina entered the house. Beatriz and her four younger sisters sat at the table inside the house in their sleeping gowns. Brass candle holders stood on the table covered in hardened melted wax.

"Beatriz, brew some tea," Señora Calderón said.

Without a word, Beatriz went through a door into the kitchen. Catalina wanted to follow her, but a man who descended the stairway beyond the table came to greet her. At first she did not identify the cleanshaven man with the cherublike face, but as he stood before her she recognized his blue eyes, the sole person in La Judería with the distinct Catholic feature. Beatriz's father had sported a beard the same shade of gray as her father's all her life, but it appeared he'd now shaven the beard to assimilate into the Catholic faith. Although an architect by trade, his face was so smooth and untouched by sun damage that it made him look like a noble who'd never performed a day's work. "Catalina, you must be due at any moment," he said, adjusting his glasses. His words reminded her of her cramps, which grew tighter now that she was resting.

"Less than a month." She smiled, sick with herself for gloating in the house of a family she had named.

"If only your father had stayed. He would be filled with pride at the arrival of a grandchild." Señora Calderón shushed him and he became alert like he realized he had spilled a secret. He put his hand on Catalina's back. "Take my daughter's seat, she will return in a moment."

Catalina hated to wait a moment longer. She wanted to tell the family what she'd done at once, but felt Beatriz needed to know first. "I do not wish to intrude. Let me help Beatriz with the tea."

Before Señor Calderón could object, Catalina hurried past the table through the door where Beatriz had gone. Inside the kitchen, Beatriz hung a tin bucket of water over the hearth.

"I met with the inquisitors," Catalina said. Beatriz attempted to ignite the hearth's kindling as Catalina spoke to Beatriz's back. "It will be fine though. You need only go to them and let them know your conversion is true."

Beatriz faced her without igniting the hearth. "Our conversion is true."

"Then you will have no problem."

"Perhaps when I go, I will tell them about our conversation on the church steps."

An unbearable feeling, a cramp so tight she thought her stomach might burst from the pressure, came over her. She knelt to one side and tried not to fall over in pain. "What about it?"

"You are obsessed with the caravan."

"My family is on that caravan."

"You act suspicious and you ask too many questions. Questions that are going to get us all into trouble." Beatriz grabbed a bucket off the floor. She motioned for Catalina to wait and walked outside to the well in their courtyard. The moment she was gone, Catalina fell onto a countertop and took labored breaths to bear the pain.

Señor Calderón entered the kitchen. "Is everything all right in here?"

Catalina tried to say yes. She didn't care anymore, she needed to leave the house, but she could barely get her words to screech out through the pain. Her legs buckled and Señor Calderón ran to catch her.

Beatriz reentered with the water bucket. "What is this? What is she doing?"

The Calderóns laid Catalina down in Beatriz's new featherbed upstairs and Señor Calderón went to find Gabriel at his work. By the time Gabriel arrived, Catalina's body was sweaty with fever and her clothes soaked through. Gabriel put his hand to her forehead. "You're burning."

She brought his hands to her chest. The pain in her body had faded and only the traumatic memory of the contraction lingered. "The baby is coming," she said, smiling through a dull pain.

"We need to get you home."

Señor Calderón entered from the doorway. "It is all right. Let her rest here today."

"I do not mean to inconvenience you."

"It is no inconvenience. We have known Catalina her whole life."

"But the baby could come here."

"Dr. ha-Rofeh cared for my family for many years. It would be a kindness to welcome his first grandchild into our home." Catalina realized that Señor Calderón had substituted the word kindness for mitzvah and it sounded odd to her ears.

"Then I shall call on the midwife." Gabriel kissed Catalina's forehead and said he would return.

Her condition made her weak, and although the pain disappeared, she remained in bed all day. Señora Calderón sat on a chair beside her and knitted in silence. The girls checked on her and offered to bring her water, but Beatriz never passed through the hallway outside. Catalina feared Beatriz had gone to the inquisitors but was in no condition to chase her. Even if Beatriz told the inquisitors about their conversation on the church steps, Catalina had done nothing wrong beyond seeking out information about her family. Thank God she had never brought up the cemetery to Beatriz. But warning Beatriz of her conversation with the inquisitors could be the greatest offense. "You made that great uproar about gossip and now I learn you indulge in the practice yourself," she could hear Brother Eduardo Domínguez say. Even if they planned to punish her, she needed to trust that they would show her mercy once they learned she was in labor. They were men of God, not a mob.

When the sun set outside the window, Gabriel returned with the midwife, an old woman who Catalina recognized from church. Gabriel waited outside as the midwife instructed Catalina to sit up with her legs over the bed and ran a hand up Catalina's dress. Her fingers were cold from the chilly October air.

"How many months?" the midwife asked.

"Eight."

"As I suspected." The midwife took her hand back. "It is not time yet."

"How could it not be time?"

Catalina had seen her mother go into labor four times. The births seemed as painful as what she'd experienced this morning. But Catalina's water had not broken on the floor—not that she could recall—and her pain subsided while her mother's returned over many hours; nearly three days for Asher.

"Soon." The midwife cleaned her hands with a bucket of water Señor Calderón had set out for her. "I recommend bedrest until the baby is born."

"No, that will not be necessary." She could not spend the next month lying in bed. She needed to warn the others. "Bedrest can cause sores and infections."

The midwife held up her hand for Catalina to stop and went into the hallway to speak with Gabriel. Catalina noticed Beatriz standing beside him. She tried to push herself off the bed, but her breath grew heavy and her clothes felt like rags soaked in ice water. She sat back on the bed and rested. There would be a chance to fix things later.

Gabriel told Catalina he would walk the midwife home. "I will come for you in the morning."

"I am well enough to walk home."

"It is too cold outside and the midwife says you cannot walk. I'll come before work tomorrow." He left the room without touching or kissing her, and she stared out into the dark corridor of the empty hallway after he left.

The next morning, she changed into a clean gown borrowed from Señora Calderón. Gabriel arrived and put his arm under hers to walk her into the sitting room. She thanked the family for their hospitality, and they shared their excitement for the baby to be born, but she saw no sign of Beatriz.

Gabriel lifted Catalina into his arms and carried her out of the Calderón's house in the direction of Bib Rambla. She felt awkward being carried through the streets like a child. Strangers glanced at them as they passed. Normally, Gabriel would make light of an awkward situation with a joke, but he walked forward not even wincing at her weight. "You are going to make a great father," she said. He grunted in response.

After getting Catalina into bed at home, Gabriel brought her a tray of bread and tea.

"While I appreciate this," she said, "I feel foolish being waited on."

"This is what the midwife told us to do." He thrusted the tray onto her legs and left the room. She wanted to call after him but could tell he was in no mood to talk. Gabriel did not return the rest of the day. Though she heard the front door open in the evening, Gabriel never came upstairs. At dusk, Marquessa brought her a tray of eggs and bread for dinner. The room grew dark while Marquessa lit candles on the leather trunk and beside the bed.

"Is Gabriel downstairs?" Catalina asked.

"He is still at work."

"I heard him come home earlier."

"That was Ochoa."

It was unlike Gabriel to work late, especially since the monarchs conquered the kingdom. "He will be out past curfew."

"That is less of an issue these days." Marquessa told Catalina she'd return for the tray and walked to the door.

"Mother?" Catalina asked. Marquessa looked back at her. "Have you heard from my family or the caravan?" The last and only letter that had arrived came three months ago.

"Nothing. I am sure their next letter is finding its way here as we speak."

Catalina finished dinner and sat in bed, more bored than she could recall. She would have preferred chores to this. Her thoughts wandered to the other families she had named. How could she warn them now, if she was confined to her bed for nearly a month? She'd send them a letter, if only she were not forbidden to write. If

Beatriz had told Gabriel, Catalina hoped she would tell the other families too. Better the others hate her than find themselves in harm's way.

She tried to sleep, rest her worries until dawn, but in the middle of the night, she woke to the sound of the front door creaking open downstairs. The mattress beside her laid empty. Boots stomped loudly over the stone floor below. She got up, cradled her stomach and went downstairs. To hell with the midwife's advice, her father knew better.

The candles were extinguished. Moonlight shone through the velvet curtains in the sitting room, but she saw no sign of a person. She lit a candlestick on the bureau by the stairs and carried the light into the sitting room. Gabriel laid on the couch balancing a bottle of wine on his stomach. He looked at her as she entered, pressed a finger to his lips, and shushed her. She could not recall the last time she saw him drunk. As she stood over him, she no longer worried if yesterday's action upset him.

"Are you choleric? You are about to be a father. Wash up and go to bed this instant."

He placed the empty wine bottle on the ground. "Why did you tell my mother that you were going to your parents' house yesterday?"

"I did go."

"Then how did you come to be at the house of the Calderóns?"

"I visited Beatriz. She is an old friend."

"She spoke as no friend of yours. You are a liar. You have lied to me at every turn."

"Calm your voice. You will wake your parents."

He jumped to his feet and stood over her. She leapt back and tried to hold up her hand in case he might strike her, but could do nothing without dropping the candlestick.

"You were going to leave me, take my child from me. I know your father talked to you, I could see it in your eyes. You were arrested in the cemetery. But that is not the worst of it. Can you explain to me why you went to the inquisitors, especially after I asked you not to?"

Despite her intentions, Catalina knew she betrayed him. Even after she promised God she would be a better person. Tears filled her eyes and her voice caught. She realized she was not going to be able to speak, so she turned away from him. He grabbed her arm and for a moment she feared he would strike her, but he pulled her into an embrace. He held her tight and she sobbed into his shoulder. Even with her husband before her and a baby between them, she never felt so alone. She missed her family as badly as the day they'd left. She remembered how it felt to be a child, waiting by the door for her father to come home from attending to a patient. When he would not return before bedtime, her mother would hold her back from running out and sprinting through the streets to find him. Now she wanted nothing more than to flee this house, run through town, beyond the city walls and not stop until she reached Fez. But this was impossible with a child on the way. A child to be born into what situation?

She lifted her head from Gabriel's shoulder. "I am sorry. I promise I will never go behind your back again."

"Why should I trust you?"

She tried to gather all of her thoughts to avoid saying anything that would make matters worse. "I am afraid that no matter how good of a Catholic I am, no matter how close I become with Christ, there will always be people who see me for what I once was. I do not want them to see Goyo. I defied you because I want them to see me."

"Did you tell the inquisitors that Beatriz's family converted falsely?"

"No. But I fear the inquisitors will see what they want to see."

"And what do you think they will do?"

"I fear my actions may lead to the murder of conversos. Please tell me I am mad. I would rather be mad than right."

"I believe that if the monarchs are capable of sending away an entire people, they are capable of doing anything. But they also want to establish order; killing conversos would create chaos. That is why we must keep to ourselves and not give them more information than they require."

"Do you believe I have endangered the others?"

"If their faith is true, I believe they will be safe. If it is not, they should have left with the caravan." This thought disturbed her. Who were they to judge who was faithful enough? Where would the line be drawn between someone who was trying to be faithful and someone who was masquerading? "I promise I will never let anything happen to you or our child. But as long as you engage in this reckless behavior, I fear trouble will follow."

"I see that now. From now on I will only do as you say. I promise."

He locked eyes with her for another moment, then held her again. With his embrace, she felt ready for the past year, for everything she'd gone through, to leave her body. Finally, she felt ready to move forward.

Chapter Nineteen

The feeling of 100 knives ran down her body, threatening to rip her in half. She clutched the edges of the bed frame as blood poured onto the sheets beneath her. She screamed, panted, and tried to focus on the dark ceiling where one panel of wood met the next. The midwife shouted to push again. She had neither the bravery nor energy to force out the child. The next push would surely kill her, break her in two. But she sucked in what little air her lungs could hold, shut her eyes like a prisoner awaiting execution and pushed one final time. Pain rushed through her body, tempting her to tear off her own skin in an attempt to escape, but then a great weight slipped out from inside her. Below her feet, somebody smacked a soft piece of flesh. A child's cry pierced the air. She looked beyond her stomach for a first glimpse of the baby. The midwife announced that it was a boy and Catalina had enough energy again to sit up in search of her son. She saw only the backs of the midwife and Marquessa as they swaddled the baby in a blanket, then handed it to her.

She brought the baby to her face, whose wails sounded loud enough to awaken the entire neighborhood in the late hours of the night, and looked at him for the first time. He was the size of her forearm. His skin was red and the texture of eczema, his eyes shut tight, his brows furrowed like an old man deep in concentration. He looked like her father, and for a moment she sensed her father's presence in the room. She kissed his forehead.

After the baby settled into his first sleep and the midwife

changed the bedsheets with Catalina still in them, Gabriel entered the room to hold his son. "He has a wise face. Perhaps he will be a doctor."

"Better a shrewd businessman like his father," Catalina said. "What shall we name him?"

"He looks like a Vidal."

"We cannot name him Vidal."

"Why not Vidal? It would be a great honor to your father."

If the boy looked like her father and had her father's name, people might think the boy was Jewish. The name Vidal was not exclusive to Jews. Vidal was derived from the Castilian word Vida. Life. But it might remind people of his grandfather's identity. "If we cannot keep my father's letter, I doubt your parents will allow us to keep his name."

"We could name him Aznaro." It was the name of his grandfather, who passed at the beginning of the year.

"Aznaro. Of course." She brought the baby into her arms. "We will name you Aznaro."

Catalina spent the next week in bed, caring for and nursing the baby. The first snow fell on the streets outside. She remembered her father's only letter. Had they left Málaga? Had they reached Fez? She imagined a city like El Albayzín, except massive and sprawling. Too large to be contained within walls. She pictured a small house on a hill where her family was rebuilding their lives, the inside of the house filled with the belongings they'd brought from Granada. She pictured them praying at the temple that belonged to the brother of her former rabbi.

By La Nochebuena, Catalina returned to performing chores around the house. They feasted before La Misa Del Gallo with Gabriel's sister Ana and her husband and children, who had come to visit the baby from Alfacar. La Nochevieja passed and two days later came the first anniversary of La Reconquista. Catalina attended the parade that went through the main street of town as it had one year prior, and watched the procession of soldiers in armor, followed by residents of Granada dressed in their warmest coats. This year, the civilians carried the banner of the new monarchs, a flag stitched with the patterned images of castles, lions, and black eagles. She could not help but reminisce how one year prior her father had first expressed fears of what would happen to the Jews of Granada, a conversation that seemed like nothing to her but a paranoid worry at the time.

Once the endless celebrations of winter concluded, they baptized Aznaro in the church, and the quiet month of January allowed her to fall into the routine of caring for her new son: wake throughout the night to feed him, clean the house while Marquessa played with him, bathe him in the courtyard in the afternoon, attempt to nap when he napped. Gabriel took Aznaro during dinner, when the men ate first, and although he said to lay Aznaro to sleep in the crib at night, he often let their son fall asleep between them. On Sundays, they carried Aznaro to her family's house in Realejo, preparing to move as soon as she no longer needed his mother's help.

On the last Friday of January, Aznaro missed his nap. He cried through dinner and Catalina brought him upstairs to put him to bed. After carrying him around the room, rocking him to sleep, and lowering him into his crib, a knock came at the door. She couldn't remember if they were expecting guests, but people still arrived unannounced to meet the baby.

She blew out the bedroom candle and walked to the top of the stairs, prepared to tell whoever had arrived that her son had gone to bed for the night. But when she turned the corner to the stairs, Ochoa was standing at the top step. "Is he asleep?"

"Yes."

"Dress warm. There are two soldiers here. They have orders to escort you to the inquisitors."

When her father would be summoned to a patient's bedside at night, it was always to treat the most severe illnesses. She'd grown up with the belief that nothing good came from a caller after dark.

Catalina put on her warmest black wool coat and kissed her son in his cradle. "I will be home before you wake." She walked downstairs, where Gabriel stood speaking with two soldiers who carried torches and were dressed in full armor.

"Please," Gabriel said. "It is very late. We have a newborn. She cannot go out now."

"Our sympathies," a soldier said. "But our orders come from the Commissioner of the Holy Inquisition himself."

Through the threshold that led to the sitting room, Ochoa and Marquessa spoke softly to each other. "Did I not tell you this would happen?" Marquessa whispered. "I begged you not to bring her into this family. You did not listen."

"Ease your tongue. They could be calling on her for any number of reasons."

"What are the orders?" Catalina asked. "What do they want with me?"

"Our orders are to bring you to the inquisitors," one soldier said. "That is all we know."

Gabriel extended his arm to block the threshold of the doorway. "Please, it is too late. I will escort her to them at dawn."

A soldier put a hand on the hilt of his sword. "We grow tired of repeating ourselves, Granadino."

"Who are you to threaten my son?" asked Ochoa.

"Step aside, the both of you."

An altercation seemed inevitable and Catalina would not allow anyone to be harmed on her account. The best she could hope was that the inquisitors liked her. She was a good converso; someone they could trust. Perhaps they only wanted information.

"It is all right." She put her hand on Gabriel's outstretched arm.

"I will say whether it is all right."

"It is only an audience with me they want. Let us not argue over such a simple request." She looked to the eyes of Gabriel, Ochoa, and the men, pleading for them to stand down.

Finally, Gabriel turned to the men. "Allow me to accompany her."

"Only the girl," said a soldier. "Those are our orders."

Gabriel looked to Catalina as if asking for her guidance. She knew he wanted to fight for her, but was powerless to raise a finger. "We trust you will return her to us with great haste?" he asked the men. They said nothing, no doubt tired of his resistance.

"If Aznaro awakes," Catalina asked Gabriel, "you will put him to bed?"

"Yes. Yes, of course."

"If he is hungry—"

"Marquessa will mash some fruit into paste," Ochoa said.

"We raised four children," Marquessa said. "Aznaro will be fine."

"I will be home by the time you wake," Catalina said.

"I will stay up in anticipation of your return."

She kissed him and went to the men. A soldier took her arm and guided her outside. The front door remained open as her family came out onto the street to watch her go.

The soldiers' torches lit their way through the dark, narrow streets. She could tell they were passing Plaza Bib Rambla by the sound of the Darro's running water, but could see nothing beyond the torch's reach in the moonless night. A chill ran through the air, so cold that Catalina looked up for signs of snow.

They lead her to the inquisitors' home on the riverbank. When they arrived, the wooden door of the grand entryway swung inward as if pushed open by a powerful phantom in expectation of their arrival. A nun who waited in the house's candlelit atrium took Catalina behind a dressing screen made of silk and handed her a maroon monk's habit without instruction. Fearing any sign of resistance would only complicate the situation, Catalina slipped the habit over her clothes, then the steel jaws of chain shackles, cold as a block of ice on this January night, locked around her ankles. The nun put the shackles on Catalina's wrists with the routine of a doctor taking a patient's temperature.

The soldiers brought her around the courtyard of oranges to the far wing of the house. Over the noise of their footsteps and the jangling of her chains, she strained to hear what sounded like a man weeping. At the far wing of the house, they stopped at two doors twice her height. Faint candlelight danced under the doorframe along with the even fainter murmuring of men's voices. She listened for the weeping she no longer heard. She wanted to keep calm, this was only a meeting, but it was impossible to rationalize the habit and chains as a formality. She closed her eyes and told herself she would get through this. She would answer their questions and return home.

"Pasarle," a voice called from beyond the door.

The soldiers pushed open the heavy door. Inside a room large enough to receive a wedding celebration, three inquisitors dressed in black habits who bore matching crown-shaped haircuts sat behind a singular oak table that ran the width of the far end of the space. Their walnut chairs were upholstered with velvet the color of the tree line behind La Alhambra. Torches hung from the ceiling and candelabras were placed beside each inquisitor. Draped behind them, a flag the size of a house ran the length of the wall adorned with a design she'd never seen before. The flag depicted a crucifix that looked as if it'd been carved from two tree trunks and painted a green as deep as the first leaves of spring. An olive branch and a sword flanked either side of the cross and the text of Psalm 73 encircled the image in Latin. "Exurge Domine et Judica Causam Taum." Her years of devotion to Christ allowed her to translate. "Arise, O God, and defend your cause."

The soldiers placed her on a stool at the center of the room, and the moment they bowed to the inquisitors and moved into the shadows of the ballroom, she missed their presence, not realizing how reassuring their grips on her arm were until they were gone.

"Señora Catalina de Zaniçeras," said the inquisitor seated to the left of the center. He had a thin face, as if he survived on nothing but a diet of berries and nuts.

"Yes, Brother?" The moment she spoke, the sound of something like the scurrying of a rat startled her. In the corner of the room, a notary sat at an unremarkable wooden desk, copying down their meeting onto paper.

The inquisitor gestured to the crucifix on the flag. "Do you swear by the Father, the Son, and the Holy Ghost, and by this sacred cross, to tell the truth?"

"Yes, Brother."

"You were born Goyo ha-Rofeh?"

"I was, Brother."

"Which name do you prefer we address you?"

"Catalina. Please." She managed to curtsy where she sat.

"Señora de Zaniçeras, you confessed to Brother Eduardo Domínguez on the seventh of October in the year of our lord 1492 that you were a converso and that you had an altercation with a knight of King Ferdinand's court at the former site of La Judería Cemetery, no?"

She tried to steady her nerves and reminded herself they could be asking the question for any number of reasons. "Yes, but Brother Eduardo and I discussed—"

"You were momentarily imprisoned for this offense?"

"Yes, but—"

"Then we have no reason to suspect that any information you shared with Brother Eduardo was false?"

"I would not lie during confession."

The thin inquisitor looked at the paper on the table before him. "In your confession you named several conversos who you believe apostatized falsely, no?" She scanned the faces of the three men in search of the inquisitor she'd confessed to, but recognized none of them. "Señora de Zaniçeras, yes, or no?"

"I provided the names of converso families, but I never made the accusation that they converted falsely." The notary scribbled the transcript with the fury of a man with tremors. The thin inquisitor whispered with the commissioner at the center, while the inquisitor to her right yawned. "I want to make it clear—"

"Do not speak unless questioned." The command came from the commissioner at the center. He had a large nose that pushed flat against his face like it'd once been broken.

What was she supposed to do? She'd made no accusation, but as she'd feared, they were hearing what they wanted to hear. "Brothers, if I may explain."

The thin inquisitor huffed. "Speak."

"The families I named, it was only at Brother Eduardo's request. They are good faithful Christians and nothing if not followers of Christ."

"You are sympathetic to them?" All the questions seemed like tricks, only this one was the most obvious. She searched for her next words and regretted that this conversation hadn't taken place during the day when she would be sharper.

"They are good Christians and they are my neighbors."

"Yes or no."

"Yes, I am sympathetic—"

"Silence," the thin inquisitor said. She bit her lips shut. "Señora de Zaniçeras, you yourself have been accused of apostatizing falsely and continuing to reside in this kingdom as an imposter. Is this the truth as well?"

The question came with such abruptness that the change in subject bewildered her. She looked around at the inquisitors, at the soldiers in the shadows who stood against the wall, waiting for someone to tell her this was a joke, that they only wanted to test her and now she could go home.

"What are you saying?"

"Answer the question."

"I will not answer that question. It is a lie."

"Why would a person invent such a serious allegation if it were not true?"

"I know not, for I am innocent. I am a faithful servant of Christ. Who is my accuser?"

The inquisitor to her right leapt from his seat. "You lie. Repent!"

"I am no liar. Who has made such an accusation against me?"

The thin inquisitor signaled to the soldiers with a wave of his hand. The soldiers grabbed her arm before she could react and pulled her from of the room.

"Please, stop. Stop! This a mistake." She dragged the heels of her boots.

The commissioner stood. "Repent and your interrogation will be swift."

She fought against the soldiers and slipped from their grasp, only for them to wrap their arms around her waist and lift her into the air. "Where are you taking me?" she called to the inquisitors.

"To ascertain the truth." The soldiers led her out of the room and the ghostly force that'd welcomed her into the house returned to shut the door behind them. The soldiers blindfolded her at the atrium and she could tell that they were leading her outside by the kiss of the cold night air. She screamed for help, in the hope that men from El Albayzín might come to her aid, but a soldier shoved something warm and leathery into her mouth. They made her crawl into what she imagined must be a wagon and sat her on a bench between them. The wagon jolted forward. A horse whinnied.

"Are you going to scream again?" the soldier asked. "Or may I take back my glove?"

She wanted nothing more than to call out again, but knew she would need to find another solution. She gestured toward him and he took the glove from her mouth. She remained silent and tried to determine where the wagon was taking her. Would it be a whipping, like what Eliezer had experienced? If so, then she would take it. She'd gone through the pain of childbirth and she'd go through this, too, to get home to her son.

As the cart ascended a hill, she leaned to one side. So they were taking her to where Eliezer had been punished. "I know where La Alhambra is."

"We're not going to La Alhambra."

She tried to predict what this interrogation would be. She knew little of torture, beyond what she'd read in the Bible or the stories Asher would concoct to frighten Iamila. No good would come of guessing her worst fears, so she tried to determine who was instead her accuser. Was it Andrés, the guard from the cemetery? Or the man who had sent her to the dungeon—the knight, as the inquisitors had referred to him. Could it be her priest, Padre Leonardo? Or one of the inquisitors? Brother Eduardo himself? Her own mother-in-law, who had never approved of her marriage to Gabriel? Or one of the conversos she'd named, naming her in turn to save themselves. Beatriz. Yes, it had to be Beatriz. That traitor! That coward. Beatriz had gone to the inquisitors and told them about Catalina's inquiries regarding the caravan. How dare she. Catalina had named the Calderón family as conversos, nothing more. She even went to their home to warn them. And Beatriz had sold her out at the first sign of trouble.

The wagon stopped. All was silent except for the wind. The air smelled fresher, far from the pungent scents of markets and bodies in the city below. The wagon door opened and the familiar touch of the soldiers' grasp wrapped around her arm. They exited the wagon and walked over gravel. Her body clenched up at the thought that the punishment may begin without warning.

The faint sounds of rattling chains grew louder. Yelling and the familiar sound of weeping came from the distance. The stench of filth and excrement soon arrived, far worse than what she'd smelled in the constable's dungeon. A soldier told her to watch her step and helped her walk down a flight of circular stairs. The stairs felt hard like brick, but were caked in loose sand that wafted under her ankles with each step. Where had they brought her? She could think of one hundred staircases in Granada built like this, yet could not determine this as any particular one.

At the bottom of the stairs, they led her down a hallway. Screaming, howling, and crying came from all sides. It was hot and muggy, the stench of sweat filled the air and the room smelled like meat left out in the sun. She hugged the soldiers' arms tighter. Suddenly, they'd become her only friends in the world. Had they brought her to a madhouse? Or were these the noises of the other accused?

The soldier pulled the blindfold down around her neck. She found herself at the end of a hallway carved out of the earth, facing a chair made of spikes. Spikes no larger than needles—too many to count—lined the seat, arm, and leg rests of the chair. It was an iron chair, something she'd only heard about from Asher's stories. She tried to move back, but the soldier held her still.

She took small breaths to keep the space from spinning. They would use threat of torture to elicit a confession, but she could not let them. She shut her eyes and prayed. "Please, Christ, give me strength. You know I am devout in spite of my past. If I must, I will do this to show You that my love for You is strongest. I am ready, but please let this punishment be brief."

The jangling of chains approached from behind. She tried to turn, but the soldier held her head forward. The inquisitor from the market appeared before her, followed by a man in a hooded mask, and a prisoner. The prisoner was her father's age; shirtless, with bruises and burns covering his torso, and an arm that hung dislocated from its socket. He looked at her with shock and recognition, and she recognized the cleanshaven face and blue eyes of Señor Calderón—Beatriz's father.

Catalina screamed. Was he here because of her? She regretted all of her resentful thoughts toward his daughter.

The inquisitor stepped in front of her. "My brothers tell me I am to draw a confession from you." His high-pitched voice made him appear friendly even in this situation. She felt an urge to seek his approval.

Catalina trembled to speak. "I have already confessed. I am innocent. I have committed no crime. Neither has he."

"That man has already confessed to his crime."

What crime? Was he a heretic? Guilty of false conversion? Perhaps this was a trick, they had only brought him here to get her to say what they wanted. "Please, Brother, have mercy."

The inquisitor nodded to the man in the hood. The man grabbed Señor Calderón, who cried out in fear, and pushed him into the chair. Señor Calderón only winced and shut his mouth tight. Tears streamed down his hot red face.

Catalina tried to advance on the inquisitor, but the soldier held her back. "Stop this. Stop this at once."

The inquisitor looked back at her. "You can end this."

"Tell me what to do."

"Repent."

Blood trickled over the edges of the chair. She needed to protect Señor Calderón, she had no other choice. But what would they do to her if she confessed? What would they do to Aznaro, the son of a woman branded a heretic? Señor Calderón had confessed. He'd made his decision and her playing this game would not save him. He held back his cries to keep her from meeting the same fate, she was sure of it. She needed to be strong, like Queen Isabella.

"Repent," the inquisitor whispered in her ear. "Repent."

Señor Calderón could no longer hold in his pain. He opened his mouth and wailed. She tried to stay passive, but the man's screams, devoid of all personality, sounded no different than the cries of her father the night Sarah died. What if her father had stayed, like she had asked? What if he were the one sitting in this chair? Would she not confess to save him? She would have confessed before he ever sat down. She could not let her father, nor Señor Calderón, die so she could pretend she was a most loyal Catholic. To love her family, to love her neighbors, she would always need to keep part of her old faith. She could not eviscerate the Jewish part of her, no matter how hard she convinced herself to believe in Christ. She was the daughter of a Jew, the mother of a Jew, and no number of prayers, holy water, and absolution would change that. She could hide behind her faith, she could hide behind the new identity she had built to marry Gabriel, she could hide behind the new name she had given herself, but deep down a part of her was still Goyo ha-Rofeh. If she did not confess now, she would be haunted by Señor Calderón's fate for the rest of her life.

"I am a Jew," she said. "I repent. I am a Jew."

Within the hour, Goyo faced the three inquisitors in the ballroom again. Her hands were shackled and a chain crisscrossed in front of her chest, wrapping around her waist and neck. Nearly an hour had passed since the interrogation, and the inquisitor who she'd once gifted a pomegranate recited her confessions to the others. She knew she would face severe consequences and the only option left was to beg for mercy.

"Señora de Zaniçeras," the thin inquisitor said. "Was your husband aware of your deceit?"

"No. He had not the slightest idea. I beg of you not to tell him. It would be his greatest shame." The thought of Gabriel or their family being brought into this situation frightened her more than whatever fate awaited her.

"I am afraid he is going to learn of this."

"Is that to be my punishment?" she asked, aware of her naïveté.

"Is that what you think this is? A punishment? My dear, we are here to rescue you."

"I am most gracious for your mercy." She no longer believed a moment of her act. It was all a performance to save her son. Would it fool them? "I believe deep down that I am capable of being a Christian, that I can live as a member of our community. Am I to be re-educated?"

"That is beyond our power."

"Please. Who could help me better than you?"

"He who sent us here. And He will be the one who shows you mercy."

Goyo held her breath, uncertain of what they were implying. "What do you mean?"

"Your physical form is beyond saving. But that does not relieve us of our responsibility to rescue your soul. We will absolve you of your sins and you are to be relaxed in an Act of Faith."

Though she'd never heard such an expression, the sternness of his tone made her so lightheaded she might faint. She thought of her son, who she might never see again. She could remind the inquisitors she was a new mother, pray for the opportunity to raise him, but she feared to even evoke Aznaro's name to these men.

"Brothers, I beg you for mercy. I am but twenty years old. In my love for my husband, I foolishly chose to stay beyond the decree. If I am no longer welcome in this kingdom, then exile me. Throw me out beyond the city walls. Banish me to the sea—"

The commissioner slammed his fist on the table. "Your king and queen were exceedingly generous, giving you and your people three months to depart this kingdom. Yet you defied a royal decree." He looked to the soldiers. "Take her away."

She continued to beg for her life, but the soldiers pulled her from the room. They brought her to the dungeon below the inquisitors' home, unlocked her from the shackles, and pushed her into a cell carved out of the hill it dwelled inside. Goyo threw her weight into the iron door as they locked it shut. She called out for help and asked to speak to her husband, but nobody listened. On the far side of the cell, she found a small grate in the ceiling that looked up at the dark sky. She screamed upwards for help, but nobody came to her aid.

Her voice grew hoarse and she slumped against the wall. How long was she meant to stay down here? Her only hope was for the events to move slowly, so that her husband and Ochoa could rescue her. She breathed to calm her nerves. Ochoa was an influential man, well-liked by the soldiers and workers in La Alhambra. He would have the right connections to secure her release.

The first hint of a hazy blue dawn brightened the overhead sky. She imagined her son waking up, crying for his mother, refusing Marquessa's fruit paste when he only wanted milk. She should never have done anything to put her future as a mother in jeopardy. She was already pregnant when the decree was announced, why had she not thought more like a mother? If released, she would think of nobody but Aznaro again, not even herself. But she would need to get him out of Granada, both of them. She would take him to Fez, what she should have done from the beginning.

Once sunlight came through the grate, a loud clank came from the door. Goyo rose with a start and brushed off the dust clinging to her dress. A woman's voice told someone standing outside that they had five minutes, and Gabriel rushed through the door to embrace her. Tears streaked down his face, and he sobbed into her arm before saying a word. "I am sorry. I am so sorry."

"No, I am sorry." She brushed her finger down his cheek. "I should never have gotten myself into this impossible situation."

"Father and I have tried everything to secure your release. We offered the inquisitors gold, our possessions, our business, your family's house and ours. They said none of it could purchase your freedom."

Her vision grew sharper and the room smelled more pungent as dread filled her body. She wasn't getting out of this. She would never grow old, never raise her son, and never say goodbye to her family. "Please, is there nothing we can do?"

"I have tried everything. I would take your place if they let me."

"I would never allow that—"

"You confessed to heresy. Why?"

"They were torturing Alfonso Calderón. They strapped him to a chair made of spikes."

"But, is it true?"

She wanted to tell him that in the end she had been honest about her faith. She did not want her last conversation with Gabriel to be a lie. But if this could be their last moments together, she did not want him to realize she had been a heretic all along. It was better that he know nothing, that he remember her the way he imagined her. "Of course not. I lied in the hope I might spare him. Have you spoken with his family? Was he freed?"

"Nobody has heard from him."

Her arms went limp. She wanted to ask more, but the guard had only given them five minutes. She only had enough time left for the most urgent questions. "Where is our son?"

"At home, with Mother."

"Gabriel, he is not safe."

"But he has been baptized. What did they say?"

"Nothing. The inquisitors made no threat against our son. But he was bore from a Jewish womb. That makes him Jewish whether he is baptized or not. If the inquisitors were to recognize this, I fear they will come for him next." Gabriel let go of her hands. He turned away from her and let out a labored breath. "Take him to Fez. My family will care for him."

"They have not written us. I would not know how to find them."

"Their caravan was being taken in by the brother of Rabbi el Barchilon. If you go, I doubt they will be hard to find."

He stared at the wall, his lips trembling. "I should have let you leave with them."

"This is not your fault."

"A part of me always agreed with your father. I could sense the danger. Why did I ignore my instincts?"

Everyone had felt the same. Why did she ignore this instinct to flee? Out of convenience? A desire to stay with Gabriel? She could no longer recall. No reason to fear a life outside Granada sounded worse than the situation she found herself in now.

A nun opened the door. "Time to go."

Gabriel turned to Goyo and put his hands behind her head. "I will take Aznaro. After your burial."

"I beg of you to leave tonight. Do not attend my execution." If she was to be relaxed in an Act of Faith, did that mean there would be any part of her left to bury? She dared not ask.

He stared at her, seeming to commit her face to memory. She had looked at her family the same way on the day of their departure. An image that would need to last a lifetime. He leaned in to kiss her, but she turned her head away. "No. They may suspect you."

Gabriel pulled her into him and kissed her. Although she stood rigid as a staff, she did not push him away, taking in his touch for as long as the nun would allow, for she knew she would never feel her husband's lips again.

The nun took Gabriel's hand and pulled him back. "I will protect him," Gabriel whispered.

"Tell him I love him."

The nun led Gabriel out and shut the door behind them. The sound of the steel shutting echoed through the small cell, and all went quiet. Goyo looked up at the clouds in the sky beyond the grate and tried to soothe herself. Soon this would be over. Soon she would be in Heaven with her sister. But Sarah did not believe in Heaven. Do people go to a place they do not believe in? She was unsure whether she still believed. She pictured a black void, sleeping without the ability to wake, a sleep that would go on not for one night, but forever. She tried to push the thoughts away. It would be like before she was born—except without the possibility of birth. She told herself to be brave. Her little sister had gone four years before her and soon she would rest as well.

Hours passed. No guard fed her or offered her water, but she longed for neither. She repeated her Our Fathers and Hail Marys like a woman who had gone mad. She gave herself the prayer of absolution, a prayer she'd heard Padre Leonardo recite every week, but now struggled to remember it in its entirety. She looked up through the grate and asked God for forgiveness. What was a window in the ceiling for if not a way for her words to travel undisturbed from the cell to God's ears?

But none of the prayers comforted her. Nobody was listening. Clouds passed over the sun to cast Granada in shade. To anyone outside the cell, the day must have felt ordinary. It was a Tuesday. Women across Granada were cleaning clothes, stitching pants, making beds, preparing lunch. A day so normal that they would live it only to forget it. She envied the normalcy of their lives, the boredom. Her thoughts turned to her family. She pictured them, not in a new home, nor in Fez, only together, sitting in a circle, eating lunch. Perhaps Eliezer was a doctor by now, Asher finally had his bar mitzvah, and Iamila was preparing for hers. Her father and mother were wondering whether their latest letter had reached Granada and when she would write back. They were all curious about their new grandchild, their new nephew. They did not yet know Aznaro's name, not even if she had birthed a boy or girl. For only a moment, she imagined Gabriel showing up at their home with Aznaro, telling them the news of her end, her mother's cries, but she forced the images from her mind. She had little strength left for such thoughts.

She focused on her son instead. He would never know her, not her appearance, the sound of her voice, her scent. He would know of her only through the stories Gabriel told: how they first met when she and her father had cared for Gabriel's dying grandmother, how she had consoled Gabriel upon his grandmother's passing, and how—despite different religions—their parents had allowed them to marry for love. She hoped Gabriel would never speak of her end or the reasons for it, only that in her last moments, her worries were not for herself, but for her son's safety. She prayed to God, or whoever was listening, that Gabriel not witness her execution, and slipped into reciting the Kaddish as one obsesses over recounting a memory they'd long determined forgotten.

"Yitgadal, v'yitkadash, sh'meih raba—" What if no family awaited Gabriel's arrival in Fez? "—b'alma divra chiruteih—" What if her family had only written once, not because of the difficulty of delivering a letter to Granada, but because they'd died on the road or drowned at sea? "—v'yamlich malchuteih—" If that was the case, who in Granada would pray for their souls? "—b'chayeichon uv'yomeichon—" And who in Granada would pray for hers? "—uv'chayei d'chol beit—"

She halted her prayer at the sound of a voice that cut through the air as sharp as a needle. The acoustics of the cell fell as quiet as the leveled Judería cemetery. At first, she convinced herself that she'd only heard the nun murmuring in the hallway. But she could not stop herself from believing that she'd heard the sound of a small child singing back to her.

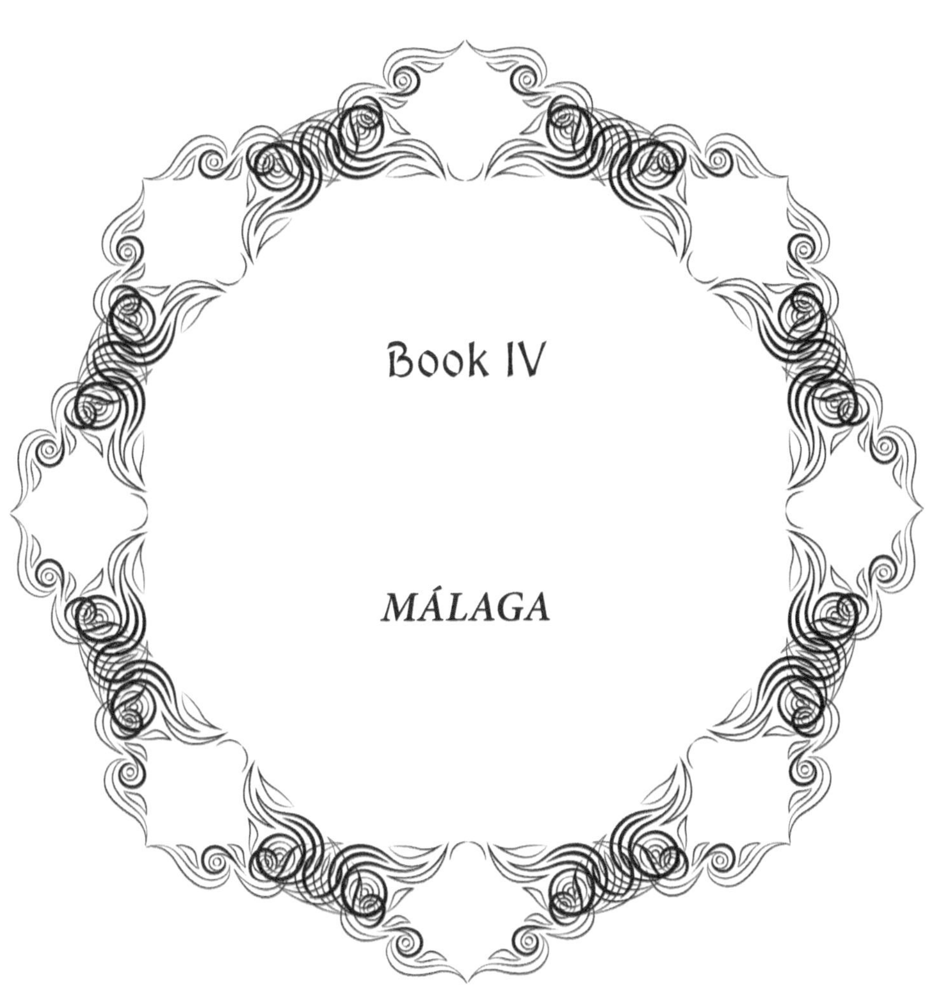

Book IV

MÁLAGA

Chapter Twenty

The earth beneath their feet shook, and the rocks that surrounded the wall rattled atop the earth as the wooden gates of Málaga parted inward. The gates, carved from the trunks of chestnut trees, were painted bronze to match the color of the surrounding brick wall. They looked as grand as if they'd been built to welcome the caravan into the Kingdom of Heaven itself. Beyond the gates, rows of white houses with crimson roofs lined the stone-paved street. The day grew late and the setting sun cast elongated shadows from the houses onto the stones. The road grew smaller and narrower until it disappeared at a vanishing point in the distance. Vidal felt a cold breeze pass from the ocean through the gate to kiss his face. He let the sharp air fill his lungs.

A guard who stood on the wall that overlooked the gate shouted down to them. "All Jews who seek passage across the sea are hereby ordered to take quarter on the beach." He repeated the command over and over. Vidal could not see who was talking, as the men's helmets appeared black against the bright afternoon sky. The guards looked like a flock of birds perched on a roof above them.

Vidal tugged on the horse's reins and his family followed the rabbi's wagon through the mouth of the gate. The first thing Vidal noticed upon crossing the threshold was that the city smelled differently. Whereas Granada had smelled of mountain air, peach trees, pomegranates, and the countless spices of El Albayzín, this place carried the rich smells of salt, fat, and honey. The stench of roasting pork felt like an affront, as it had when he smelled the fatty meat every time he visited the home of Catalina's in-laws. It reminded him of the smell of human flesh when a surgeon cauterized a gaping wound.

He noticed not a single civilian walking along the main road, only lines of soldiers who guarded the thoroughfare. They wore full armor, their sheathed swords weighing down their leather belts as they stalked alongside Vidal's wagon. The setting sun haloed their helmets and cast their eyes in the shadows of their visors.

What if this was all a trick? Binyamín had never returned to the caravan from this city and only now Vidal entertained the direst of possibilities. If his family, the caravan, were indeed a real threat to the kingdoms of Ferdinand and Isabella, why not lure them into the city walls, hungry, tired, and sick, and execute them once trapped on the road? They'd have no option but to escape to the sea. He supposed the monarchs had offered the opportunity for them to flee without harm as a kindness. They had delayed the beginnings of their ideal Catholic kingdom so that it could be founded in peace rather than bloodshed. Of course, that was what the monarchs must have wanted him to think. They were doing him and his family a favor by letting them leave in peace. The king and queen must have seen themselves as merciful, especially as they considered Vidal the descendant of a people who killed their savior.

Behind him, the city walls looked no larger than the door of his house in Granada. The rearmost wagon of the caravan must have passed through in a single file by now. A church tower appeared on his left. It was the highest spire he had ever seen, as grand as La Alhambra. A greater elevation than some of the hills they had encountered on their journey. Wooden construction rafters encircled the tower; their planks wrapped around it like a cocoon. No man worked on the rafters. Was today Sunday? How he looked forward to getting back to a life where the days of the week mattered, where he could rebuild his routine, the Sabbath.

At the tower base, he could see horseshoe arches, arabesques, and muqarnas that decorated the entrance—remnants of a Moorish mosque. So the rumors were true. Though the monarchs had allowed the Moors to stay, they forced the Muslims to watch their houses of worship desecrated and reincarnated into churches. The Nasrid Great Mosque in Granada would be next—as the rumors had anticipated.

The journey down the main road continued for nearly an hour. The sun sat on the cusp of setting behind the mountains at the west end of the valley that surrounded Málaga. Apart from the soldiers, they had barely encountered a soul. If the city were genuinely overrun with Jews—as the doctor in Periana had predicted—wouldn't Vidal have seen them by now? Heard them? Smelled them? Perhaps the Muslim doctor had not known what he was talking about, or the idea of anyone going to Málaga after what the monarchs had done to its Moors distressed him. What the doctor had expected to gain by telling Vidal to proceed to Marbella, he could not know.

At sundown, the road opened up into a square. Moorish workers dressed in ripped tunics and damp trousers pulled a rope that hauled stone blocks as large as war horses into the plaza from the west entrance. Merchants stood behind their wooden carts and shouted for people to buy fruits and fish. Past the square, through an archway carved out of the wall, he saw the port, a bay populated with an archipelago of boats, ships, and carracks. Enough vessels to invade Italy, never mind deliver their caravan to Africa. The smaller boats bobbed in the choppy water, tied to wooden docks that rose and fell with the waves like water snakes slithering across the surface. The carracks, some of them as large as a synagogue, sat anchored at sea, so heavy that they stayed still and erect despite the motion of the tide. The smell of saltwater and driftwood overpowered the lingering of pork.

The cold black waves rippled with gold when they came in contact with the setting sun. The marine layer he had seen on the mountainside that morning had evaporated, and he now looked out into the bottomless blackness of the horizon. He had expected to see torches burning in the distance, beacons of light that marked the African shore, the same as standing on one side of a lake and looking to the opposite, but the world beyond was swallowed in darkness. He'd never seen such a sight. None of them had, and whether it was his sons at the rear of the wagon, or his wife and daughter atop the wagon bed, they looked out at the water as if they had been offered a glimpse into the most sacred and luxurious room of the Nasrid Palace.

"You see that?" The rabbi himself addressed them from the back of his wagon. "And you worried there would be not enough ships to have us cross."

The soldiers who flanked the caravan now closed in on them and ordered them to continue their march to the beach. Beyond the square, the road turned west and funneled through a narrow stone archway corroded from its proximity to the sea, leading out to a strip of beach that stretched to the water. The sand was barely visible beneath the hordes of wagons, tents, and people that crowded the shore. They appeared like a garden of gravel placed over dirt, so populous they hid the earth beneath. What were the chances these were not Jews attempting to leave the Iberian Peninsula for the Maghreb? Could it be possible that these were simply Malagueños enjoying a summer night by the water? Perhaps taking one's tent, wagon, and family was merely a custom of the city.

A sandstone pathway no wider than the distance between the wagons' wheels protruded from the wall like a trail in the mountains and the caravan journeyed in single file down the pathway in search of untouched beach. A figure—silhouetted against the light of a bonfire behind him—pushed his way off the crowded beach to confront the rabbi's wagon. Vidal noticed that the soldiers no longer flanked their path. He stepped forward, preparing to shout and warn the rabbi, but the rabbi emerged from the front of his caravan and conversed with the figure before taking the figure into his arms.

"Thank God, you are all safe," the figure said. Vidal recognized the voice of the rabbi's son. Binyamín looked taller now, the handsome face of his youth gone, replaced by the emaciated body of a feral creature that had survived on its own in the wilderness. The rabbi's wife and two daughters embraced Binyamín. What would it be like to hold Catalina in his arms again? Or Sarah? He blocked the thoughts from his mind with the simplicity of a blink.

Binyamín waved for his family to follow him down the road. Vidal extended his ear in the hope of learning more. Since Binyamín's departure, had he managed to acquire a section of coastline wide enough to quarter seventy wagons worth of Granadinos? Had he reserved passage on one of the ships at the port? The carrack, he hoped. It rocked the least in the water.

As they continued down the road, Vidal looked out at the community they passed on the beach. With the sun now set, it was difficult to make out their faces. He heard people speaking Castilian and Ladino. Children splashed and shouted in the ocean as their parents called for them to stay near the coast. Families cooked eggplants and onions impaled on sticks over open fires. Other families prayed in Hebrew over the meal they were about to consume. A rabbi stood on a wooden crate and led a congregation of a dozen people in prayer. A group of young men tossed back and forth a bottle of wine as they stumbled drunkenly into a tent. From another tent came the soft moans of lovemaking, where a couple unaware of the thinness of the wool walls annunciated their passion. Though they overran the beach, the people appeared peaceful. Everyone had come to this place for the same reason, and it seemed they had suffered enough misadventures to not bother arguing or fighting among themselves.

The farther they journeyed down the road, the sights and sounds of people dissipated, replaced by only the crashing of the waves on the sand. The moon rose over the water. Suspended and spherical in the sky, even it looked closer than the shores of Africa.

Once the beach's population dwindled to no more than a small encirclement of tents, Rabbi el Barchilon halted his wagon ahead of them. The rabbi took Binyamín's hand and pulled himself up onto the wagon bed to face those farther down the caravan line. The wagon buckled and adjusted under the rabbi's weight.

"My fellow Granadinos." The rabbi addressed them with the booming voice he projected in the synagogue and told those at the front of the caravan to send a message down the line that they would sleep here tonight as his son made the final preparations for them to cross the sea. "Do not yet abandon your horses. We may need them to pull the wagons back to the docks."

"We have to walk back to the docks?" Asher asked.

"Quiet," Vidal said.

"Why did we waste time walking here when we must return to the ships?"

"Did you see those people waiting along the coast?"

"Yes."

"So, you have two eyes?"

"I do have two eyes, Father."

"Then, use them." The thought of making the walk back exhausted Vidal. Perhaps now that they had reached the coast, he could ride the horse. He hadn't wanted to exhaust it before, but what did it matter now? At least once they set sail, they would leave behind horses to wander around and defecate all over the city. Hardly a finger of defiance raised to the monarchs as they fled into exile, but better than nothing. He helped Bonadonna and Iamila onto the ground so they could push the wagon off the road into the sand.

The horse whinnied in protest as he tugged it forward by its reins. He called for everyone to push the rear of the wagon and the wheels rotated as much as dragged through the sand as they shoved it toward the smooth wet earth by the coast.

Binyamín chased after them, sprays of sand kicking up in the wake of his heels. He greeted Eliezer with a hug, then implored Vidal not to set up camp so close to the water.

"Why?" Iamila asked. "Is there something in the water?"

Bonadonna laughed. "Only fish. Nothing to worry about." She looked to Binyamín, curious for an explanation.

"Now the tide is low," Binyamín said. "Later, it will rise."

"What do you mean?"

"The water will come forward to there." He pointed to a spot on the beach where the dry and wet sand met. Down the coast, the wagons that had camped before them halted behind the line. "It rises no higher than our knees, but you would be wise to be behind that point when it arrives, less the wheels of your wagon become waterlogged."

Vidal had seen many fountains and pools in Granada. Lakes he had visited the few times he had been outside the city walls. Had he ever seen water behave like this? "How is this possible?"

"Locals believe it is caused by the moon. When overhead, its rays evaporate the water and cause the tide to recede until it is replenished at dawn."

"But if the sun is hotter, would not the very opposite be true?"

"I asked the same thing. The man who told me simply shrugged and said, 'That's what the Britons told us.'"

Asher crawled his fingers up Iamila's back. "And then the tide carries in the monsters."

Iamila swatted away her brother's hand. "Stop that, Asher!"

"Leave your sister be," Vidal said. "We're all tired. Not only from walking, but from your silly games as well." Vidal ordered Eliezer to help him push the wagon back up the beach out of the damp sand. As Binyamín turned to leave, Vidal asked, "When do we board the ships?"

The look on Binyamín's face was one Vidal knew all too well. The look his children made when they failed to complete their chores, when they forgot to return home to help their mother prepare dinner, when they neglected to study their Torah portions. It was enough to break Vidal's heart. They had arrived, they had delivered La Judería to the sea, but Binyamín had not completed his end of the mission.

"My father will address everyone in the morning." Binyamín turned toward the rabbi's wagon, but Vidal grabbed his arm.

"It is the twenty-ninth of June."

"I am aware of the date."

"The decree will go into effect in a month."

"And we will be far from here when it does." Binyamín attempted to take back his arm, but Vidal held tight. Bonadonna called for Vidal to release his arm, yet Vidal dug his fingers deeper into Binyamín's flesh.

"Do not speak to me as if my confidence cannot be trusted."

"Dr. ha-Rofeh, release me at once."

"Father, release him," Eliezer said.

Binyamín pulled his arm free and shook off the pain. "Need I remind you I am your rabbi's son?"

"And I am the doctor responsible for the health and wellbeing of this caravan."

"Your father has gone too long without rest," Binyamín told Eliezer.

"That may be, but my father is right. Why do you remain tight-lipped with the plans?"

"I am not tight-lipped. We will tell the plan to all at once. That way, we have no need to repeat ourselves. That way, false rumors and gossip do not spread throughout the caravan." Binyamín turned to Vidal once more with a feral look in his eye. The time on the beach had altered his physical appearance and perhaps mental state as well. What had happened to him while he had been alone out here? Binyamín returned to his father's wagon stationed up the shore.

Bonadonna faced Vidal. "Calm yourself. Binyamín wouldn't lie to us."

"Look at him. He has no plan."

"You're being paranoid. Help me build a fire." She took blankets off the wagon bed and rolled them out over the sand. Vidal looked around at the sand and surf. Build a fire with what? Now that they had arrived, did she expect him to break down the wagon for kindling? They would need to take it aboard the ship. Once they reached the shores of Africa, they would have farther yet to journey to Fez.

"There is no wood."

Bonadonna pulled sticks and branches from the wagon bed and dropped them in a pile on the ground. She must've gathered them on the road. "I told you, you wouldn't survive without me."

Though he only wanted to bathe in the sea and go to sleep, he knew that food came first. As he dug a hole in the sand, dropped the sticks inside, and used the flint rock he kept in his instrument case to strike a flame, he tried to forget the conversation with

Binyamín. Perhaps the rabbi's son was right, and he had gone too long without rest. Binyamín had been in Málaga for weeks. There was no reason to believe that he had not arranged for passage. The number of people who lined the beach should not affect their plans. But why did he have that feeling in his stomach that things were not as they seemed? It was the same way he felt when families rushed him from their homes and exclaimed, "Thank you for your time, we are sure he will recover shortly," or when he watched the parade that signaled the arrival of the monarchs.

As the ocean breeze fattened the fire, Vidal watched Bonadonna and Asher weigh down the blankets with their leather bags and wooden crates. Iamila fed the horse, and Eliezer inventoried the amount of medicine that remained in his leather satchel. The beach was orderly but overwhelmed. There were many ships in the port, but how many people could they fit? How many were even destined for the Maghreb? What if Dr. Zamorar had told him the truth, and now Vidal had led his family into a corner and forsaken the opportunity to sojourn to Marbella where they could find safe passage? He could ignore this fear no longer. The sea was right beside him, yet he felt no closer to Fez than when he had walked out his front door in Granada.

Eliezer tied shut the leather straps of his satchel. "Are you ready for evening rounds?"

"Start without me. I'll meet you before you reach the Levis."

"Where will you be?"

"Asher! Watch the fire."

"I thought I was not allowed."

"As long as you do not set the wagon ablaze, I see little damage you can do." Vidal marched toward the rabbi's wagon. Eliezer walked beside him, struggling to face his father without tripping over the sand.

"Father, I forbid you to disturb the rabbi."

Vidal imagined speaking to his father this way. The beating he would've gotten. "And I forbid you to follow me."

"In this instance, it is not impossible that I know better than you."

"Yes, it is. You would not understand. You are not a father."

"An experience you robbed me of for who knows how many more years."

"We agreed we would not speak of that again."

"You are tired, you are hungry, and you are afraid. We all are. Stop now. Listen to reason."

"Look at where we are. The beach is teeming with Jews from across the peninsula, just as I was warned. I had the chance to listen to reason in Periana, and I ignored it."

"If Binyamín says he has booked passage to Africa, then I believe him. He has never lied to me before."

"Would you wager your life and that of your siblings on this belief?"

Eliezer hesitated and stuttered out an answer. Vidal moved past him and arrived at the rabbi's tent. The emerald octagonal tent had already been fully erected, pulled tight from the top center peak down to the nails driven into the sand. A fire crackled in front of the tent, heating a steel cauldron that boiled water that smelled of tomato and garlic. Eliezer continued behind Vidal, exclaiming that his father should wait until morning, but gave up when the rabbi emerged from the tent in a clean gown the scent of lavender. The rabbi opened his arms at the sight of Vidal. "Dr. ha-Rofeh, is your family settled?"

"When do we set sail?"

Binyamín rose from behind the fire and ran to his father. "That is no way to talk to your rabbi."

"And that is no way to talk to your doctor," the rabbi said. Binyamín looked between Vidal and the rabbi, no doubt desperate to concoct a reason to nullify this impending conversation. But he only put his hands behind the back of his head and shut his eyes in resignation. "What concerns you, Vidal?"

"Is this not what the Muslim doctor had forewarned?" Vidal explained his concerns, and the rabbi listened with his hands clasped together as he always did when a member of his congregation came to him to express concern. Binyamín's eyes shifted between them, seeming in search of a way back into the conversation, and Eliezer let out an exasperated sigh every few seconds to remind his father he was overreacting. When Vidal finished his speech, the rabbi pondered it in silence as if having a deep conversation with his mind.

"Come, sit with me. We have much to discuss and important decisions to make."

As the rabbi invited them into the tent, he requested that his wife and daughters wait outside for the duration of the conversation. His wife protested that the children were exhausted as the girls struggled to spread out their white sheets over the beach sand. But Señora el Barchilon required no more than a glance from her husband to gather the girls and hurry them into the night. As Vidal watched them pass, hesitation momentarily overtook trepidation and he wondered if perhaps his neuroticism was doing nothing more than denying young girls their rest.

Once the women left and the entrance flap swayed with no more force than the gentle ocean breeze, the rabbi explained how circumstances had changed. Binyamín had informed him that all ships in port asked exorbitant sums to ferry passengers across the Mediterranean. Some ships, as many as 1,000 reales a person. An impossible sum, as much as Vidal made in two months when his practice was in highest demand. With these costs, the funds the rabbi managed to raise by selling the synagogue would pay for the crossing of no more than twenty people. "We sail for Tétouan tomorrow. I have decided to take my family, Shelomo's, and yours."

The decision sounded poorly thought out, planned in haste, but perhaps this was because the rabbi stood in the center of the tent with only a gown, looking no more confident in Vidal's eyes than a sick, convalescent patient. Nothing like the man who dressed in robes and tallits, who sat behind an oak desk when Vidal spoke with him.

"What of the others?"

The rabbi offered the kind of smile a houseguest gives when they accidentally break a plate with no ability to reconcile the problem. "They will need to find their own way across. We've done as much as we can for them. We have led them to the coast. God will deliver them across the sea."

"Deliver them? God will not even provide them with the coin they need to secure passage." Vidal was aware his words were blasphemous, but such fury overcame him that if God Himself appeared in the tent, Vidal would not ask for forgiveness.

"Do not lecture me on the workings of God."

"If this is your plan, then you have no understanding of how God works."

"And you do? A man of science? How dare you speak this way to me after all I've done for you. After I saved your son from La Alhambra."

"You cannot bring our people all this way only to abandon them on the shore."

"Our people? You speak as if you were Moses. Very good, do as Moses did and part the sea so our people may walk across."

Binyamín asked his father for permission to speak. "We are not abandoning them," Binyamín told Vidal. "I have been here two weeks, Doctor. I have attempted to barter every deal that exists in this nightmare of a city. If we don't leave tomorrow, we'll never afford passage again. We'd stay for what? To keep company with the people we cannot save? In the end, we'll spend the money all the same, only we'd rescue even less than twenty. We will never have this opportunity again. Please try to look to the positive."

Vidal had admired Rabbi el Barchilon all his life, yet now this great man chose to flee at the first opportunity, for no thought of those left behind. How could they leave so many to their fates? And if those people did manage to reach Fez, how would they ever trust the families that abandoned them? Eliezer whispered in Vidal's ear that they leave, but Vidal only addressed the rabbi.

"They followed you here. The only reason they left Granada was because of you."

"They followed me because the monarchs ordered them from their homes. They followed me because they had nowhere else to go. The same as you."

For the first time in Vidal's life, he felt an eagerness to inflict harm, to strike a man he'd once looked upon with devotion but now saw as nothing more than an old coward, who forsook a community willing to follow him to a land beyond any map they owned. "If you had any honor you'd put the youngest children on that ship and remain behind with us."

"Again you act as if I have not considered these options. Our community will need a leader in this new land, as it will need a cunning negotiator like Señor Levin and a skilled physician like yourself."

"Give my place on your ship to others. I refuse to leave."

"The rabbi is bestowing on you a great honor," Eliezer said. "What about Asher and Iamila?"

Vidal wanted to secure passage for his children even more than he wanted to show the rabbi the error of his decision, but to admit this might allow the rabbi to use Asher and Iamila against him. "I will not go. If you leave, you leave without a physician."

"You think there're no doctors where they're going?"

"Listen to your boy, Vidal," said the rabbi.

"Doctor, forgive me," Binyamín said, "but I must remind you that you turned down a great offer once already this year and as a consequence, Eliezer was whipped."

"How dare you compare my son's punishment to your cowardice."

"I say this only with love. Do not repeat past mistakes."

The suggestion that Vidal's decision to stay was the equivalent of breaking his son's nuptials made him hate both el Barchilons as he hated children who refused to say goodbye to their fathers on their deathbeds and husbands who insisted Vidal prolong the lives of their wives who teetered at the precipice of death. "We have already been forced to leave La Judería, but I will not abandon its people. I hope you reach the same decision."

Vidal departed the tent with Eliezer behind him. The holes in his boots kicked sand in the air and in making such haste to return to his wagon he was careful not to lose his footing with the rabbi watching him. Vidal's face felt as hot as the fire that Asher had succeeded in building when he arrived. They roasted carrots for dinner again, and Vidal was so livid from his conversation that he would not have tasted the meal if it were made of sugar and the sweetest bread. Bonadonna pressed him for information, but he refused to speak, certain that if he opened his mouth, he would spew such vile expletives that the Malagueño soldiers would drag him to the church to perform an exorcism.

"Fine, keep it to yourself. Just promise me there's nothing wrong with the boat?" To get her to stop asking questions, he promised. "I don't know what's put you in such a mood. Sometimes you're more dramatic than all our children combined."

Vidal did not expect sleep, but even his rage could not withstand the effects of a day's journey under the punishing sun. He soon lay on his back beside the wavering smoke and crackling embers of the night's fire and rested his heavy head on a mound gathered up from the sand. As the snores of his wife and children rose from nearby, he looked up the beach at the rabbi's tent. The candlelight within was extinguished, the entrance flap strung shut. No movement along the tent's walls signaled that people moved about inside.

He did not remember falling asleep, but when he awoke the next morning, only sand and powder blue sky occupied the space of the rabbi's tent. As he went to investigate, he found no evidence that a tent had marked this oddly vacant spot on the otherwise crowded beach. The el Barchilons had departed so many hours ago that the wind had swept away any sign of their presence in Málaga.

Chapter Twenty-One

The moment Vidal realized the rabbi had fled the beach, he dressed and left his wagon in pursuit. He hurried down the narrow sandstone that stretched along the path where the beach met the outside of the city walls and weaved around travelers, families, and food peddlers who sold cheeses, meats, and fish no one he knew could afford. As he reached the archway that brought people from the beach into the city, he feared that soldiers who loitered on box crates with their gloved hands held up to block the sun would bar him from entering the town square, but he hurried past them with the vigor of a man determined to go forward. If the soldiers gave notice to him, they did not stop him.

White clay buildings flanked a street that led back into the city, through a gate in the brick wall, to the port. Single file lines fifty men deep waited to exit to the coast. Young men stood in line, likely sailors to be rowed out from the shore to the carracks that idled in the water. The smell of waterlogged wood and unwashed mariners assaulted Vidal's nostrils. He jumped and stood on his toes to catch sight of either the rabbi, Binyamín, their family, or wagon. A hat on the rabbi's head should have been obvious to spot among the gentiles. Yet, Vidal saw no sign of them, as if the rabbi's family had not merely fled but evaporated from the city. He wanted to call out—*Rabbi! Binyamín!*—but it would only draw the attention of the dour and cheerless sailors. Soldiers would likely escort him away, back to the beach if he was lucky, to the gallows if he was not.

Vidal continued searching the columns of men, even as sailors stole glances at him, likely eager to start a fight if he tried to cut in line. The rabbi could not leave. Vidal would not let him. But the longer he continued his search, the less quiet and calm he could muster. When he looked again at the ships in the water, his heart told him that the rabbi already sailed for the Maghreb.

As Vidal trudged back down the stone pathway in the direction of his wagon, the full brunt of the day's heat pushing away the faint breeze from the coast, he hoped that perhaps the rabbi had spoken to someone in their caravan before he departed. Maybe the rabbi had offered a solution for how the rest of them could cross the sea. The moment Vidal stepped off the pathway and onto the beach, men from the Pardo family and women from the Salomon family leaped up from where they sat beside their wagons to accost him.

"Thank God, you've come back," they said. "Is it true, Dr. ha-Rofeh? Did the rabbi leave without us?"

How had they learned of this? Had Eliezer told others about the conversation? Or had they merely noticed the absence of the rabbi's wagon and deduced what had happened? As Vidal kept walking, the circle of families grew around him as if he were a spindle gathering yarn. "Quiet, quiet. Where did you hear such a story?"

One of the Pardos grabbed his arm. "Señor Levin woke me. Bragged he was leaving with the rabbi in the middle of the night."

Vidal felt the urge to spit venom. So Shelomo had accepted the rabbi's offer. And they'd likely taken a family in place of Vidal's or no others at all. Was this indeed a surprise? The news made Vidal dizzier than the circle gathering around him. His refusal to leave was meant to make the rabbi reconsider, but it had accomplished nothing. The rabbi had left and taken the one businessman savvy enough to get them out of this situation with him. Shelomo was smart enough to save his family, and Vidal stupid enough to keep his stranded in Málaga after turning down the offer of salvation. He had no money left, nothing of value that would serve as a bargaining chip for passage. To what fate had he sentenced his family? He could not see what options he had left; a concern never felt when caring for even the most medically complex patient.

"What do we do, Doctor?" they continued to ask. "We cannot afford passage of our own."

"Neither can I."

"Maybe the rabbi has gone to acquire more funds? Or charter ships from the Maghreb back to us? He'll return and save us all."

"Doubtful."

"The Bernals and the Uziels have already gone to convert. Do we go with them?"

Vidal held out his hands and asked everyone to step back so he might breathe. "Do nothing rash. Let me think and I will gather you tonight." He pushed his way out of the circle with less grace than was becoming of a doctor. Though he did not look over his shoulder—that would only invite company—he heard their chatter grow more distant. He weaved through tents packed so close it was difficult to find footing on the sand. A mother and daughter folded together the linen of their tent as the father and son prepared to pull their wagon out of the sand. Were they going to convert? To plea for passage?

He knew he needed to begin morning rounds, his patients were likely asking for him, but he could not treat anyone in this state of mind. What had he done to deserve this? He'd tried to be honorable by turning down the rabbi's offer, yet he doomed his family. What was God's plan? Might this be punishment for not going back to Periana to treat that young girl?

He went to the water's edge to think. With the tide come in, he stood on a sliver of beach unoccupied by the multitude of wagons and tents that bordered the surrounding shoreline. To his surprise, the wet sand did not stick to his boots like mud, but was as soft and forgiving as dew-covered grass, where each step left an imprint of his boot in its wake. Water poured into the open holes of his boots, and despite the day's heat, the liquid felt cold as snow. As he faced the ocean, calm and flat in the morning, he squinted at the horizon for a sign of the African coast. He was facing south; he knew it was straight ahead, and yet no landmass disturbed the line where the ocean met the sky. Were his eyes too weak? The African coast too far away? Perhaps he could swim. If he swam to the other side, he could find a boat, hire someone not overwhelmed with Jews attempting to seek passage, and return to ferry all across. People had done wilder things and succeeded. If Jericho's walls could fall, if water could come to Jehoshaphat's army, if Moses could part the Sea of Reeds, he could get the people to Africa. It would be less of a miracle than raising the money to charter a ship out of Málaga.

Before he could act, the sound of his wife calling his name cut through the soft sound of the surf. He turned, ready to share their predicament with her. Maybe she might help concoct a solution he could not see? But Bonadonna marched toward him down the coast with the furor of a general leading 10,000 men into battle. Before he could ask what she wanted, she attacked him and scratched at his cheeks and eyelids with her fingernails. "You liar!"

He held out his hands to keep her at bay as he backed into the frigid water. "Bonita, what is the matter?"

"I should have converted when we were still in Granada."

Vidal's steps grew heavy in the underwater sand, which sucked on the torn soles of his shoes like a bottom-feeder. "Stop with these theatrics."

"The rabbi offers you the opportunity to leave, to rescue us from this Godforsaken beach, and you say no?" He thought to ask how she learned of this, but the answer came immediately. Eliezer had confessed all while he'd been away. Bonadonna waded into the water, her feet splashing like two fish caught on a line. As he held her back by the wrists, she kneed him in the testicles. The air left his body and his stomach churned as if begging him to defecate. "I trusted you to deliver us to Fez. To keep our family safe. You've sentenced us to death. Did you give any consideration to our children when you made this decision? To me?"

He pulled her close to his body to soften the blows, and Bonadonna put her leg behind his calf to send them tripping over each other into the surf. A splash of water soared over them and although the ocean was no deeper than his ankles, he lay soaked on his back. As Bonadonna scrambled to get up, Vidal only lay with the surf brushing him side to side in the sand. If he mentioned his plan to swim to Africa, he imagined she'd drown him for his delusion.

"I will find a way to get us out of here."

She wrung out the water from her dress. "I see no more use in empty promises. Since you've failed to protect us, now it's my turn. We will go into the city, find the first church we can, and we will convert." Vidal pushed himself out of the water, eager to protest, but she spoke over him. "Once we are Catholics, we will return to Granada. If we hurry, Ochoa may even sell us our house back."

She stood over him with water dripping down the front strands of her hair, and Vidal admitted, in the deepest part of his soul, that the offer tempted him. The chance to return to Granada, to enter his old house, to sleep in his bed, to breathe the crisp mountain air, to take in the smell of the mandarin trees, to hold Catalina again, and one day soon, meet his grandchild. Catholics worshiped the same God; this opportunity would cost no more than swearing an oath to Christ. He had no evidence to suggest their fortunes might improve before the commencement of the decree. But what kind of man would give up his beliefs, the beliefs of his ancestors, for comfort and security?

"We have four weeks more. How can you see conversion as anything but a last resort?"

"If I must choose between reciting Hail Marys the rest of my days or watching our children be dragged to the gallows, it is no choice at all."

"Give me more time. One week to find another way to Africa and if I fail, we carry forth with your idea."

"The most devout follower of our faith abandoned us this morning, yet you continue to follow it blindly."

"You know I will not put us in a position where any harm will come to our family."

"No more than you already have?" Bonadonna stepped over him to return to shore without the slightest offer to help him stand. "I'll give you one week. Then I take the children to convert. I assure you, I could not be more eager to be finished with our defeated religion." She left the water with sand clinging to her boots and dress.

Though Vidal longed to change into clean clothes, to drink water and find something to eat, his circumstances offered no time to rest at the wagon. With the sailors departed, Vidal journeyed back beyond the city wall to the small stretch of shore that served as the port. He walked dock to dock, beached boat to beached boat, speaking to any captain, sailor, or harbormaster who offered acknowledgment. Binyamín had called the prices exorbitant, yet Vidal needed to hear these quotes himself, to ensure Binyamín had not lied to him as his father had lied about delivering all of La Judería to Fez. But Binyamín proved himself no liar. The captains and harbormasters demanded 300 reales, 500 reales, 1,000 reales a soul. Only the richest of Jews could afford such prices and Vidal knew the captains had learned this so they could focus on ferrying across only the most profitable of passengers.

The most affordable sum he received was 250 a soul, yet it came from a man with no boat to speak of, who stood beside a dark strip of sand that marked where a rowboat had been pushed into the water. He introduced himself as a former captain in King Ferdinand's fleet. Whether he was a successful businessman with his ship out at sea or a charlatan posed beside somebody else's landing, Vidal could not be certain. Perhaps he charged less out of pity for the role he'd played in the war. The captain assured Vidal that if he gathered the money, and if he were in port when Vidal returned, they would sail to Tétouan.

"Is that near Fez?" Vidal asked. The former captain only shrugged. He was not the most intelligent, perhaps the more likely reason for why he charged so little. "I will return with the funds as soon as I can." He shook hands with the captain, a gesture of agreement he hoped the man would honor.

Doubting a better deal would be found, Vidal began the journey back to the wagon. At the center of the town square, the men he'd seen pulling a stone slab the evening before were using ropes and wooden scaffolding to hoist a slab the size of a house onto its side. Their tattered and moth-eaten rags made even Vidal's clothes look luxurious by comparison. Sweat dripped off their dark skin and black beards. They moved with crooked backs as if they'd never had the opportunity to stand up straight in their lives. A soldier stood nearby with a whip curled into his belt.

The men were slaves, no different than the Israelites who suffered in Egypt, but had they been brought to Málaga from some other land? Their features looked so familiar, they could be from El Albayzín. He'd heard rumors after the fall of Málaga of the monarchs putting a percentage of the Moorish population into bondage. In the final days before the emir's surrender, he'd feared Granada would meet a similar fate. That he and his family had been allowed to leave with their lives seemed like a great mercy by comparison. Without a doubt, the monarchs felt the same. Yet that mercy expired in four weeks. Why put everyone to death if they could be used as labor to build statues and buildings to honor their conquerors? If he could not come up with the money needed or the former captain was absent upon his return, conversion was his final solution.

When he summoned a meeting of the families of La Judería that evening, he was surprised to find only the families of Benvenuto Pardo, a fishmonger, and Yitzhak Salomon, a spice trader, in attendance. Although the fathers, sons, and brothers who accompanied them numbered into the twenties, the pitiful number made Vidal doubt that anyone beyond the most desperate saw him as their savior. Had they witnessed his duel with Bonadonna on the beach and realized he was no man to lead them? The families stood in a circle along the water's edge, the vermillion sun setting over the bay behind them. With Eliezer at his side, Vidal shared what he'd learned from the sailor at the port and that the only way to acquire the coin needed to cross was to beg for it, offer work, and do anything necessary.

"But I have no fish to sell," said Benvenuto Pardo.

"What are you saying?" asked Yitzhak Salomon. "You have a whole ocean of fish behind you to catch."

"I know how to catch fish in a lake with a boat, but not on the shore of the sea."

"And I have no spice to trade. We must rely on whatever skills they'll pay us for."

"You're both gifted traders," Vidal said. "Perhaps if we gathered what valuables remain in our wagons, you could barter a fair price for them in the town square." Even as he spoke the idea aloud, he knew it was destined for failure. Going back to Periana to fetch water seemed a more optimistic outcome. But the Pardos and Salomons agreed with his plan.

"And what will you do, Dr. ha-Rofeh?" asked Señor Pardo.

"I will tend to my patients, then go to the streets to beg."

After the circle disbanded, agreeing they'd meet tomorrow to exchange what supplies could fetch a price, Eliezer and Vidal walked along the soft forgiving sand of the coastline in the direction of their wagon—a wagon he'd avoided since his fight with Bonadonna.

"Do you really believe it's possible to raise these funds?" Eliezer asked.

"I'm trying to stay hopeful, Elie. I'd appreciate it if you didn't allow me to reckon with how cursed we are."

"You always know the likelihood of a successful procedure. If this situation were a patient—?"

"All we'd do is make it comfortable."

Down the shoreline, he noticed a woman in a clearing between four crimson-colored tents. Her black hair shined in the reflection of the setting sun and he could make out her figure through her apricot-colored dress and tan waist belt. It couldn't be her; she'd left with her father for Africa that morning. Yet when she turned her head at the sound of a child calling out from a nearby wagon, she looked exactly like Shelomo's daughter. Indeed, she was Tsipora. But why was she here?

Vidal knew better than to address Tsipora in his son's presence, but his natural physician concern brought him to her. "Tsipora?"

She looked at him as if he'd spoken in tongues. "Hello, Dr. ha-Rofeh. Eliezer." Addressing his son by proper name sounded oddly formal. Even as children, she'd called him Elie. His son seemed to notice this, as he offered her a smile but no words of greeting.

"Why are you not on the boat to Africa with your family?"

"Do you truly need to ask?"

What he was missing dawned on him. Though her family had left for Africa, she was no longer part of the Levins, but of Avraham's family. Shelomo had left without her—something Vidal might've anticipated in Shelomo's anxiousness to marry her off. "I'm sorry. I didn't mean to offend. When my family refused to leave, I naturally thought yours would take our place." He hoped his recovery sounded genuine, rather than as a reminder that her father had chosen to save his own skin without a thought to hers.

"I suppose that's an honest mistake to make."

Eliezer took his father's arm. "We should be off."

"In a moment," Vidal said. "Why was Señor Mendez absent at our meeting? Has he had any luck securing passage to Africa?"

"Quite the opposite. We've decided to convert."

Avraham's father was a blacksmith, and as such, Vidal imagined a man of his profession spent only so many hours in a day thinking about God. But Tsipora had been raised in a devotedly Jewish household. Now she'd be forced into another arrangement before God's eyes without say. "But you've already come all this way."

"Unless a Catholic lord will pay him to smith his metals, he sees no other choice."

"I'm sorry to hear that's his decision."

He knew he'd played a role in her unfortunate circumstances, but before she allowed him to feel guilty, she asked, "Would you happen to have any food to spare?"

"You have nothing to eat?" Eliezer asked.

"Not unless Avraham succeeds in catching a fish. But they don't swim so close to the shore."

Before Vidal could apologize for her misfortunate, Eliezer offered her the silver bracelet from his pocket. The sight of the bracelet caused Vidal as much alarm as if Eliezer had proposed Tsipora run away with him. He'd not once seen the bracelet since the night of Eliezer's whipping and figured it lost or sold off in the hurry to move. Scratches, dents, scuffs, and fingerprints covered the jewelry; a sign Tsipora had worn it often, and when she'd looked at it, given thought to the idea of their marriage. Despite its wear, the silver might fetch a small meal.

"No, please. I told your father, I don't want it."

"I'm not asking you to have it, I'm asking you to sell it."

Tsipora looked to Vidal as if asking his permission. Vidal could tell she wanted to refuse. A lady should not accept such an offer from a man who is not her husband—especially one who'd at one point been groomed for the opportunity. But her stomach growled over the crashing of the waves. What harm was there? Vidal saw no future between her and Eliezer, as she would soon be a Catholic and his fate left to be determined.

She accepted the bracelet with as much care as if he'd written her a love note, but Vidal sensed a hint of melancholy in her thank you to his son. This bracelet was the last evidence of their former betrothal and tomorrow it'd be sold off for a loaf of bread.

Vidal and Eliezer said nothing more of the bracelet as they returned to the wagon and prepared for bed that evening. Bonadonna adopted Eliezer's previous vow of silence, saying nothing to Vidal when he returned. That night they slept on opposite sides of the wagon. When he awoke, sunrise cast a bold stroke of scarlet and bronze over the calm blue sea. Vidal rose and made his way through the caravan tents and wagons to check on his patients. The health of some was improving, while others now refused to eat or drink water. Family members remarked their sick relatives were speaking to parents and grandparents who'd been dead for years, a clear indication to Vidal that these people were past saving. In his experience, the dead often returned from the beyond to help the sick into the afterlife, a belief he held no matter how little validity Rabbi el Barchilon gave to the claim. Many would die on this beach and Vidal dreaded the idea of determining how or where to bury the bodies. Would their funerals be allowed to follow the Jewish customs? Would they have funerals at all? Vidal could do nothing for his patients save bring them the comfort of his attention and—in the rabbi's absence—recite the Mi Shebeirach.

Once morning rounds were complete, he returned to town to

do whatever necessary to acquire coin, leaving Eliezer and Asher to call on any patient who needed them. In the shade of a white stucco building, Vidal stood in the town square and looked out at the stone slabs that sat undisturbed. Locals strolled through the square, parents let their children chase each other, families entered a church on the opposite end for morning mass. Hadn't Sunday occurred only two days prior? He approached people in the square dressed in their finest jewelry and clothes and begged. "Please. I am trying to pay for passage to Africa..." They kept their distance as if he were a leper.

How could he go from a doctor one hour to a beggar the next? How many other doctors in the world, nay throughout history, needed to involve themselves in such opposing activities?

As the sun rose above the buildings, stealing away what little shade Vidal could call his own, hunger and thirst overcame him. He wanted to rob these people, follow them to their homes, tie them up, and wound them if necessary, to secure the funds to get his family to Fez. If he knew how to heal a body, he knew how to inflict harm on one without causing death. Was anyone assessing the progress of the stone slabs in the center of the square? Slabs no doubt commissioned by a lord who'd grown wealthy in the aftermath of the war. If only he knew how to find this man, he'd hold the sharpest scalpel to his throat and demand the 1,250 reales needed to ferry his family to Africa. Even more coin for the others.

Once the shadows retreated from the ground and walls, the church bells at the opposite end of the square tolled twelve times. Wooden doors, twice the size of a man, opened and families came streaming out into the summer day. People laughed, neighbors hugged one another, fathers lifted their daughters into the air to kiss their cheeks. Though they benefitted from his misery, Vidal remembered that these were people; families, fathers, the same as him. He did not have the heart to pull one of them aside and threaten their life in exchange for coin. To do so would make him no better than them or their rulers. He was a doctor, put on this earth to heal. To act in any other way would oppose God's plan, and if he had no other options, he would rather convert.

He journeyed across the square, through the church doors and the narthex. After hours in the sun, Vidal found the church's nave dim and cavernous, lit only by racks of glowing votive candles and the muted light of the high northeast windows. Voices dropped to a whisper as men made conversation in the narthex while women bowed on their knees in the empty nave and muttered prayers while running rosary beads through their fingers. On the inside wall above the entrance hung a life-sized statue of Jesus on the cross. Dried blood dripped from the nails driven into his palms down the meaty sides of his hands. So many nerves met at that exact spot, and Vidal could not fathom the endless pain crucifixion produced. Through the anguish, Jesus' face looked up with hope, as if communicating directly with God. Vidal had not entered a church since Catalina's marriage, and although that church certainly had a statue like this, he had paid it no mind. So this was the image that had caused so much anger toward his community, for who had driven those nails into the palms of Jesus' hands and the bridges of his feet but Vidal's ancestors? Jesus could not save himself, yet served as the savior for an entire religion of people. Nobody else could protect Vidal's family, but could Jesus?

"May I help you?" A voice spoke behind Vidal, and he turned to see a young priest with black robes, a belt made of rope, and wooden eyeglasses standing in the aisle. Vidal regretted setting foot inside the church with his tattered rags and sunburnt skin.

"Forgive my appearance. I only wished to see the church."

"Your accent is Granadino."

To Vidal, the priest spoke with an accent, formally pronouncing the syllables of every word. It seemed odd, like a wise man speaking through the body of a boy. "I was not aware I had an accent."

"My brother recently returned from your city. He told me of the drawl in which your people speak. Hard to understand, even to a native Castilian."

"You have a good ear. I come from Granada."

"What brings you to our church, Señor…?"

"Doctor. Ha-Rofeh."

"Doctor." He repeated the word as if it were an insightful answer to a difficult question. Where did this flattery come from? Likely a trick priests used to lure people into their faith.

"Can you tell me what it might take to convert to Catholicism?"

The priest smiled like he'd been waiting for this question, then asked Vidal to follow him to the rearrest row of seats. The priest sat beside Vidal and introduced himself as Padre Morales. To convert, Vidal would only need to recite several prayers, swear on the Bible, be baptized, and take a Catholic name. "Many like you have come through these doors ready to make this change in their lives, and I have prepared our church to make the process most accommodating. We can perform the ceremony tomorrow if you like. Once you come into our faith, you may do as you please. Return to Granada even."

Though the routine sounded simple—he was familiar with the rituals from watching Catalina do the same—could he take this step? He supposed he could practice Judaism in private, pray in Hebrew every night for the forgiveness of both God and his ancestors. God would understand he had taken this step to save his family. Would He not?

"I have no money."

"We do not charge."

"I will need to speak to my wife about this."

"Take the time you need. It is essential you are prepared to accept Christ into your heart." The priest spoke as if Jesus would come down from the cross and possess Vidal's body. Perhaps this explained why Padre Morales spoke with such eloquence? As they rose to conclude their conversation, the priest requested a favor. "My brother I spoke of, the one who returned from Granada, he is very ill and could use the examination of a good doctor. Might I trouble you to visit him this evening?"

"With the utmost respect, are there not Catholic doctors who can treat him?"

"They only recommend amputation, and from what I hear, Jewish doctors have more sophisticated methods."

"But I will not be a Jewish doctor for long."

266

"I'm sure once you have converted, you will be the most sought-after physician in the kingdom."

"What are his ailments?"

"He was wounded near Granada. A Muslim arrow through his left shoulder, seemingly piercing the joint. The field doctors bandaged him, but he complains of pain and cannot move his arm since he has returned home. He has been burning with a fever that has not broken for six days."

Padre Morales' brother had laid siege to Granada, had played a role—no matter how small—in the overthrowing of the emir and the installation of the monarchs who had ordered Vidal's banishment. Vidal wanted to spit on the church floor and leave, but he saw no good excuse to refuse this request as he'd refused to treat the sick girl in Periana. Perhaps helping this priest's brother might improve his fortunes. Vidal agreed to pay a house call that evening and asked directions for where to meet.

Chapter Twenty-Two

At dusk, Vidal and Eliezer walked along the streets of Málaga in the direction of the priest's home. The sun fell below the white-roofed buildings and, after months of living under curfew in Granada, Vidal found it discomforting to be out in a city after nightfall. The last time the two of them had been out after dark, Eliezer had been arrested and flogged. Vidal clutched a letter from Padre Morales composed on stationary from the Holy Office of the Inquisition, explaining their business in the city if stopped by soldiers.

A sign on a wooden post marked that they'd reached Calle de los Labrodores, where the priest said he lived. Three whitewashed houses surrounded an old oak tree in the communal courtyard at the street corner, as the priest had described. As Vidal held his knuckles an inch from the door of the easternmost house, he thought to tell Eliezer the reason they were here, not simply that a priest had enlisted his medical services, but that he was arranging to apostatize. He'd avoided the conversation for fear Eliezer would refuse to come, and now only hoped that Padre Morales would not bring up the topic while they examined his brother.

Vidal's knocks were answered by a man so enormous that his chest, neck, forehead, and jawline bulged outwards, as if he were a descendant of giants. Eliezer stepped back and looked the man over like they were old acquaintances. Whose door had Vidal knocked on? Before Vidal could speak, Padre Morales held open the door behind the giant and ushered them inside. Eliezer stayed back, but Vidal whispered for his son to follow him and Eliezer stepped around the giant as they entered.

Inside, eleven more men loitered in the atrium. They were all of similar age and build to the giant and looked Vidal and Eliezer up and down as if two homeless people had wandered off the street uninvited into their household. He knew they bore no relation, for they looked nothing alike, save for the hardened jaws and sad eyes of men who'd gone to war together and lived to carry those memories home. They stood on a neglected Persian rug, sat on chairs made of feather blankets, and lay on pillows the size of men. It looked as if they had moved into a Moorish family's home but never bothered to redecorate. The houses of La Judería likely looked the same by now.

Padre Morales introduced Vidal and Eliezer as "the doctors come to call on Marcos," and the twelve men examined them like an amateur tribunal waiting to interrogate them.

Padre Morales guided them through a door into a windowless bedchamber. Flames from a dozen candles placed on the floor and bureau illuminated the beige walls of a square room with a featherbed at the center. A boy lay shirtless in bed shuddering and moaning with a damp cloth over his forehead.

Padre Morales kneeled at the bedside. "Marcos! The physicians are here."

Marcos turned his head on the pillow and met Vidal with the same look of exhaustion and defeat that Sarah's deceased face held when he returned home the night of her death. He refused to let the expression trouble him; he'd treated thousands of patients since Sarah's last night—some this very morning. He instructed Eliezer to prepare some chamomile from their instrument case, but Eliezer was preoccupied looking over his shoulder at the giant standing in the open door.

Vidal shut the door without meeting the twelve men's eyes. "What's gotten into you?"

"Nothing."

"Bring me the chamomile. Everything will be fine."

While Padre Morales assisted by bringing water for the

chamomile, Vidal brought a wooden chair from the wall to place beside Marcos. The boy looked younger than his priest brother, no older than Eliezer or Avraham. Although Vidal would not dare admit it, the wound gave him satisfaction. Look at the part—no matter how small—that this boy had played in his family's misery and community's banishment. Let him squirm with fever. So many of Vidal's neighbors suffered on the beach with the same ailments as Marcos, yet they had no feather pillow beneath their head nor shelter to keep them warm. Perhaps he should leave, forsake this stupid boy to have his arm sawed off. But it was not Vidal's place to play God and decide the fate of the ill. He brought the back of his hand to Marcos' forehead to feel the heat of fever.

"You were wounded before the fall of Granada?"

"Yes, Señor." The boy didn't even have the courtesy to address him as a doctor.

"It is most uncommon for a wound to lay dormant for half a year only to bring on a fever."

Through shallow breaths, Marcos explained that field doctors had treated him during the siege. They'd broken off the arrowhead inside of him, believing it was too close to the heart to attempt an operation, sutured the wound, and because his arm would never be strong enough to raise a sword or string an arrow again, sent him home with the next caravan of wounded.

Vidal pulled down the blanket to see the wound.

"Don't touch it," Marcos said.

Vidal shushed him and examined the wound in the soft spot below the collarbone. It was a simple running suture, only three stitches across a cut that looked about as straight as the tilde of an eñe. Puss seeped from the wound over surrounding skin as purple as a grape that smelled like a dead animal found under his old house. Vidal had seen worse, save for the sign of green threads protruding through the scar tissue. "What color tunic were you wearing the day of your wound?"

"Green. The color of our uniform."

"Did the field doctors remove your shirt before they treated you?"

"I cannot remember."

Once Padre Morales returned with an iron kettle and poured hot water into a clay cup filled with dehydrated flowers, Vidal brought the cup to Marcos' lips and pressed his fingers against the back of Marcos' head to help him sit up to drink. He announced that this would calm the fever, but it was not enough to cure the infection. "The field doctors did a negligent job on your brother," he explained to Padre Morales. "I cannot tell if the infection is being caused by the arrowhead, the cloth sewed into the wound, the general lack of cleanliness, or all three. The only chance to save the arm is to call on a surgeon immediately to reopen the wound and clean it out."

"Then begin your work, Doctor," Padre Morales said.

"My good priest, this kind of procedure is beyond my skill level."

"But you are a physician."

"Physicians and surgeons are not the same. I diagnose and provide remedies where possible. That does not qualify me to open a man's body."

"But all others have suggested amputation."

"Before the infection spreads, certainly. But what threat do they see in surgery? This wound is near no vital organs."

"No, but it is directly beside the heart." Padre Morales put his hand on his brother's bare chest to demonstrate and Vidal could only snicker at the comment.

He laid his hand over Marcos' sternum. "The heart is here."

"You accuse our most trusted doctors of lying?"

"No, Padre. To call them liars would be to claim that they intentionally deceived you. I imagine they generally believe the heart is over the left breast."

"If they are so unlearned, then it would be negligent for you not to operate on him."

"I cannot take such a gamble with your brother's life."

"You diagnosed the problem and offered a solution faster than any doctor of my parish. Look at him. He is eighteen years old. Do not let him go through life with one arm, not after the sacrifices he has made for Castile. If it is a matter of money to persuade you, name your price."

Vidal knew better than to accept such an offer. The art of surgery had as much in common with butchery as it did with medicine and he understood enough regarding patient care to recognize how little he knew about executing such an invasive procedure. A surgery required cauterizers and clamps to hold the wound open, devices he did not own and would barely know how to operate if he did. But if the priest's brother needed an operation and he needed passage across the sea, money could solve everyone's problems. In Granada, he'd observed surgeries performed by other physicians when he apprenticed under his father, but the ordeal itself never seemed as complicated as they led him to believe. He could make an incision in Marcos' shoulder, extract the cloth and arrowhead—only muscle and fat would've grown over it and if he encountered tendon or nerve, he'd work around them—clean the wound on his way out and stitch it closed. The bleeding worried him most. He was no stranger to bloodletting or treating injuries, but how was he supposed to clean anything with an overflowing pool of blood pouring out around him? The solution would be in his medical books. Yes, the books in his wagon would tell him everything he needed to know!

"For me to perform this surgery?" If he only named a price to save his own family, he would forever label himself a hypocrite. One thousand two hundred and fifty reales was too little for such a risky procedure. He needed enough coin to save others. "Ten thousand reales."

From the corner of the room, Eliezer put his palm to his chest in disbelief. Padre Morales looked at Vidal as if he'd made a joke about Christ's death. "An insulting price."

"This procedure requires highly specialized training."

"Training you admit you do not possess."

"Neither do your surgeons. Not if they don't know where a heart is."

"I would rather you have refused."

"I am reluctant to go through with this, yes. But you need a good physician who understands anatomy. My work will cost him neither his life nor his arm. You asked me to name a price, and you believed in me until I named that price, so pay me for my work or let me be on my way. I have patients to call on other than him."

Padre Morales opened the door to the atrium and called the twelve men inside. Eliezer backed away from them to stand beside his father. "These are all soldiers from Marcos' battalion," Padre Morales said. "Tell them what you told me."

As Vidal repeated himself, explaining why he should perform the procedure even as he barely believed his abilities, he wished he had more time to consider all of his options, to talk to Eliezer more about this idea, to speak with his wife. But an opportunity to make 10,000 reales would never happen again. The money would rescue his family and more. The Pardos and the Salomons would have no more success than he'd had in the town square that morning; he could not take this risk for any less reward. After Vidal's speech, the priest asked if the men were willing to contribute to give the money requested.

"Padre Morales tells us you plan to join our parish," said the giant.

"What did you tell them?" Eliezer whispered, but Vidal hushed him.

"You're a new member of our community. Do you truly find this to be a fair price?"

Vidal gestured to his tattered outfit. "If I charged more than a fair price, do you think I would come to you dressed like this? The money is for more than my salary. It is for supplies, medications. Not to mention costs that have increased now that I cannot acquire these materials from my home and usual suppliers. I cannot perform this procedure for less."

The men discussed among themselves, then the giant spoke as if he served as a tribunal's commissioner. "If you fail and we find you are a charlatan, there will be consequences."

Eliezer whispered to Vidal, "Call this off."

Vidal agreed, he should not put up with threats, but he'd take whatever abuses they wanted to cast at him if it meant saving his community and family. "I will not fail."

The men looked to Marcos to deliver the final verdict and he was all too quick to tell them to pay Vidal. "Let me be finished with this illness."

"Then we will pay you your 10,000 reales." Padre Morales shook hands with Vidal. "You have the heart of a crusader, but the greed of a Jew. Something we will correct in the coming years." They agreed that Vidal would return to perform the surgery at dawn, as he'd grown tired from the day and needed to gather the supplies he did not tell Padre Morales he already possessed.

The streets of Málaga were vacant by the time he and Eliezer emerged from the priest's home. Candlelight and the smells of boiled chicken for supper came through the open windows of homes that lined the streets. A bird sang its evening song among the rooftops and the muffled sounds of laughter came from within houses. Vidal expected Eliezer to ask about joining the parish, but he instead remarked, "I recognized one of those men."

"They were stationed in Granada. It's not impossible we passed them in the streets."

"The man who answered the door, he was the one who whipped me."

"I find that a rather large and unlikely coincidence."

"He knew it as well. He recognized me."

"Wasn't it dark when the whipping took place? And weren't you whipped from behind? You could not have seen his face."

"Maybe it was his presence—or his stench. I recognized it as clearly as mother's rosewater."

"They smelled as bad as us. Perhaps he was merely present at your whipping." They turned a street corner and approached the archway in the city wall that led out to the sea. Only two days in Málaga and Vidal began to navigate it as if it were home. "If returning frightens you, I can perform the procedure alone."

"Tell me exactly what you're thinking with this plan, Father? I've never seen you perform a surgery before."

"This may be our only chance to escape."

"Are you doing this for the patient or the money?"

"I know I can perform this surgery. It's an incision, no more difficult than cutting and cleaning an infected blister."

"Removing the arrow could sever a tendon. If he's open too long, the infection worsens, or he loses blood. If we keep giving him opium, it could stop his breathing…"

All scenarios that Vidal had been reluctant to entertain. They passed under the sandstone archway out to the beach. Light from the nightwatchman's torch danced along the inside of the archway, and a pile of rubble lay at the ground where brick had broken off, eroded by the sea.

"Many things could go wrong."

"They will kill you if you fail."

"They're soldiers, not murderers. And this is not the first time a patient's family threatened me."

"You're a Jew and a stranger to this city. Nobody in Granada or Fez will be looking for you if you disappear. What's to stop them from punishing you if they face no consequences, especially when you charge such an exorbitant sum?"

"It is either this or we convert."

"An option you've already entertained."

"I'm surprised you did not bring that up sooner."

"I didn't find it surprising. The Mendezes are converting." This anecdote hung in the air between them as Vidal expected Eliezer to give his thoughts on the matter, but despite Tsipora's situation, the Mendezes had not come to Vidal for help and he could not concern himself with their plans. The Mendezes were one less family for Vidal to worry about.

"Would you prefer I didn't perform this surgery? Would you prefer we convert?"

Eliezer looked out at the crowds of people, tents, and wagons that lined the beach as if searching for someone in particular. "Do you think the people of Fez will treat us with any more kindness than the monarchs have done?"

"No. But they'll accept our faith." Vidal knew he was asking so much of his son, so much more than his father had ever asked of him at his age. The consequences for a failed surgery would be severe. He was already unsure if he should proceed with it. Was it right to keep his son involved? "You don't need to come tomorrow. I'll perform the surgery alone."

"That may be the case, Father. I don't know if I can be a part of this."

"Of course. Think about it."

Before they reached the wagon, Eliezer left Vidal's side and cut across the sand to venture along the sea water. Might he be debating on what he planned to do? As Vidal returned to their wagon, Bonadonna and their children had placed the iron cauldron over a firepit dug into the sand and skimmed boiling water off the surface with clay mugs—a tactic to make the water drinkable taught to them by Señor Curiel, the former head of La Alhambra's irrigation under the emir. He'd not spoken to his wife since their argument in the surf, but Vidal now approached her with such eagerness he could not contain the bounce in his step.

"Let us speak privately."

As the crowded beach offered no seclusion, Bonadonna ordered her children to keep the fire burning while she and Vidal spoke in hushed whispers on the far side of the wagon. Although another family from La Judería sat nearby eating a loaf of bread, Vidal hoped they would not overhear him and spread news throughout the rest of the beach of his possible opportunity and fortune.

The moment Vidal brought up the sick soldier, Bonadonna stopped him. "Don't you have enough ill to care for here?" By the time he finished his story, including the details about the payment and the opportunity to escape, she only said, "I am sick to death of you and your schemes."

"This is not a scheme."

"You expect them to honor their agreement? Even when your most loyal patients tore up their bill before your eyes as we left Granada?"

"Those patients weren't priests. He is a man of God. I know he'll keep his word."

"No, you believe he will keep his word. And your beliefs have brought us nothing but misery. This isn't a plan, it's a desperate attempt to avoid conversion."

"Conversion will not fix our problems."

"It worked for our daughter."

"Look at the scores of people on this beach. Why would they put themselves through this if swearing loyalty to the church would fix it?"

"Because they are shortsighted. Like you."

"Because they know it won't work! If conversion were the safest solution, the best solution for their families, they would do it. I doubt half of them will ever make it across the sea. Not a fraction even hold a profession they could leverage in exchange for escape. And the ones that do will be unsuccessful in meeting the patron who would pay them for it. I bothered telling you because God has blessed us with a chance to escape this place. Not just us, but our friends too, our neighbors. And maybe it is dangerous, but it is a blessing I do not plan to forsake."

"What about Eliezer? Are you dragging my son into this?"

"I've allowed him to make his own decision."

"So you'll go alone?"

"If he chooses not to help me."

"Can you do this procedure by yourself?"

"I may have no choice."

"We'll go with you, Father!" Vidal had not expected to hear the voice of Asher. His son and daughter stood behind him, barefoot in the sand.

"Absolutely not," Bonadonna said. "I forbid it."

Asher ignored his mother, a skill he'd mastered better than anyone in the family. "You're going to perform a surgery, no? Take me. It's my dream to be a surgeon."

"I'll do whatever you ask, Father," Iamila said. "I'm ready."

"Vidal, I forbid it."

Though he knew it would be unforgivable to bring his youngest children into such a dangerous situation, Vidal considered the option. Iamila was too inexperienced, she would be a liability. But if Eliezer refused to help, he would need another person. Asher served him well as an apprentice and never fainted or cowered at the sight of spilt blood.

"I know it's your dream," Vidal told Asher. "If you were older—"

"Please, you must let me do this. I won't let you go without me."

"Neither will I, Father," Iamila said. "I know I can be helpful."

Bonadonna looked at Vidal as if daring him to accept their children's proposition. He imagined if he said yes, she would not only wrestle him into the sea, but drown him. He'd ignored his wife's wishes many times in the past year, but he knew he could not ignore her now.

"I have a more important task for you both," Vidal said. "I need you to stay and guard the wagon."

"If that's what you want, then I'll guard it with my life," Iamila said.

"Not with your life. If someone tries to rob us, put up no resistance. I simply ask for you to watch it."

"I will. I won't let you down." With a mission and sense of duty handed down to her, Iamila left for the front of the wagon, to stand guard alongside the horse.

"Again with the women, Father?" Asher said.

"I need you to protect your mother and sister."

"But I'm a surgeon. I know it."

"And that's precisely why I forbid you to perform a surgery before you're properly trained. If surgeons were to know you performed a procedure in your youth, they'd never accept you as their apprentice."

"Do you take me for a fool?"

"Is that what I'm doing? Are you willing to stake your profession on it?"

"Is this because I struggle to suture? I've gotten better since the mountains, Father. I'm practicing. I'm ready."

"This has nothing to do with that unfortunate business with Señor Uziel—"

"I'll be thirteen in a month. You say I will be a man without a bar mitzvah, but still you treat me like a boy."

"If you were a boy, would I trust you to guard the wagon? If you were a boy, would I trust you with my wife and daughter's lives? Being a man means doing what is asked of us, not always choosing the option that most pleases us."

As Vidal climbed atop the wagon bed to rummage through the boxes and bags for his medical books, Bonadonna said, "I'll go with you."

Had he heard her correctly? "I thought you didn't support this idea."

"I don't. But if you're going to perform this surgery, you'll need help. I'm offering to be your nurse."

"This is not the time to begin a new profession."

"I raised your five children. Dealt with their ailments while you were away treating the sick. This is hardly the beginning of a profession."

Was Bonadonna truly offering to help or was this merely a new way to trick him out of leaving? "Why?"

"Like I said the night Eliezer was whipped. You need me. And if you're willing to wager a risk this big to save us, we should do it together."

Vidal jumped from the wagon and brought her into his arms. She smelled like the deepest crevices of an unwashed body, yet he could not remember the last time they'd held each other with such tenderness. "Thank you, Bonita." He kissed her.

"Promise me this will work."

"I promise. I just need to find my medical books to make sure I know how to perform this surgery."

"I sold off the books in the city center months ago." Vidal imagined Marcos bleeding out on the bed, the boy's heart ceasing to beat, his brothers-in-arms tearing Vidal limb from limb, and putting Bonadonna into bondage. If he failed, their children would convert and return to Catalina—or Asher and Iamila would be ripped away from Eliezer and placed in orphanages. He could picture his medical books, their spot on the cupboard shelf in the sitting room of their house. Why hadn't he packed them the moment he knew they would leave Granada? How had he not noticed their absence after Bonadonna sold them? "You've been practicing for twenty years, Vidal. You don't need your books."

"Right. We'll find a way to make this work."

As he sat in the sand with his stiff back against the wagon wheel, he ate a single uncooked carrot for dinner and tried to distract himself from whatever fate awaited them tomorrow. The wagon creaked behind him with the sound of Bonadonna climbing onto the bed to gather every blanket they could sacrifice as rags for the morning's surgery. Vidal looked down the beach at the seawater, dark and swallowed by blackness save for the moonlight that reflected off the foam. Women stood at the shoreline and spoke among each other as if they were meeting for tea after supper. Men waded in the sea submerged to their torsos; the moon accentuating the paleness of their shirtless bodies. Something seemed to catch their attention. They turned their backs to the sea and followed the direction of two figures who walked in the shadows of the wagon tents. When the figures reached Vidal and their faces emerged from the silhouette of surrounding bonfires, he realized he was looking at Eliezer accompanied by none other than Tsipora. The sight of them together made Vidal as worried as if they were being escorted by Malagueño soldiers.

"Father, I would like to accompany you to the surgery tomorrow."

"What is this? What's going on?"

"I will go to the surgery in exchange for the Mendez family's passage across the sea."

"The Mendezes? Avraham, all of them?"

"Yes, Father."

"They're converting. I'm sorry, Tsipora, but we must reserve the passage for people who wish to uphold our religion."

"If I may, Dr. ha-Rofeh?" Tsipora said. Light from a nearby fire cast a warm glow over her face, her cheeks appeared hot and flushed. "My father-in-law only converts out of desperation. If you give him the opportunity, he will take it. He wants to continue practicing Judaism."

"I'm sure many who are converting feel the same."

"Father, if it weren't for what transpired in Granada, Tsipora would be one of us now and her passage across the sea would be all but guaranteed after tomorrow's surgery. She's a victim of circumstance, we cannot forsake her."

"I am not suggesting we forsake her, I am saying this matter is out of my hands. I can only save who has come to me for aid."

"We will have more than enough funds to afford passage for the Mendezes."

"Dr. ha-Rofeh," Tsipora said. "I did not come to you before because I am a woman. I begged my father-in-law to speak to you, but he is too proud. You intimidate him."

"I intimidate him?" Vidal asked. Señor Mendez was a skilled blacksmith who worked with his hands, who forged armor and weapons from fire. Why would he be intimidated by a man who brought comfort to the sick and consolation to their families?

"Your intellect. He believes you will not consider saving someone as simple as a blacksmith."

"Do you not want to convert?" he asked Tsipora.

"How can I make myself accept things I've never believed in my life? It would be like waking tomorrow to convince myself that the sky is red and the sun is the shape of a square. I'll be lying to everybody for the rest of my life, and I doubt my devotion will convince many for long."

"You need me tomorrow, Father. This is my request. Save Tsipora by saving the Mendez family. We will have the funds."

Vidal could think of many people their new community needed in Fez more than a blacksmith. Scientists, engineers, architects—blacksmiths would be commonplace in Fez. For what purpose should he save the Mendezes? Rabbi el Barchilon likely thought the same. That traitor. Vidal was a doctor, it was not his place to triage the fates of who may leave, yet he had an obligation to save as many lives as possible. If circumstances were different, Tsipora would have become his daughter. Instead, she'd been sold off and forsaken by her father—a man he'd once called a friend, who abandoned a daughter without thought while Vidal had lost two. Whether her family was the most devout, the worthiest, did not matter to him. She deserved the chance to live a life his family could've given her, if only he'd caved to her father's impossible demands.

"Elie, a word in private?" Eliezer asked Tsipora to stand by the water. "I'm going to ask you this question once and I demand you answer me honestly. Are you having an affair with this woman?"

"No, Father not at all."

"Are you still in love with her?" His son said nothing. "Eliezer."

"I am."

"But nothing is happening between you two?"

"She'd be scrouged as badly as I if something happened."

"So you are saving this woman you love, who you cannot have, who belongs to another, simply to protect her?"

"Yes, Father."

Tomorrow he was going to cut open a boy without the tools or knowledge needed to succeed. Never mind the circumstances that led to this point, these were not the actions of the doctor he'd always imagined himself to be. "Then I believe, one day, you may be a better physician than I am capable of becoming."

Vidal called Tsipora back. "Assuming tomorrow goes well, we will pay for your family's passage across the sea."

Tsipora thanked him and curtsied, a sign of respect he'd seen her offer nobody—neither her father nor the rabbi—and Eliezer hurried to escort her back to the Mendezes to share the good news.

Though Bonadonna and Eliezer both agreed to help him in the morning, Vidal could not sleep that night. He lay beside his wife in the sand, listening to the symphony of snores from his family and those who filled the beach. He found it impossible to get comfortable, even though the sand was malleable to whatever shape he desired. His mind turned to Catalina. He'd planned to write her when he arrived in Fez. But if things failed tomorrow, she would never hear from him. He stood, grateful that sand did not creak with his heavy steps, and trudged to the wagon bed. He'd seen letter paper in his futile search for the medical books. Asher and Iamila slept beside each other at the rear of the wagon. Careful not to wake them, he lifted the tapestry above the back wheel and rummaged for a leather-bound folder of loose-leaf pages, a quill, and a vial of ink.

Sitting in the sand with his legs crossed, he wrote with nothing but moonlight to guide his hand. He began with his daughter's birth name, "Goyo," then crossed it out. He wrote "Catalina" on a clean page and began to tell her of their current situation and that if he failed in tomorrow's surgery, she might not hear from him again. But what if he was successful? What if he sent this letter but succeeded with the surgery? He'd have to send another straight away to explain things. Yet there was no guarantee the second would arrive with haste following the first. And if a second letter never arrived, she'd die of fright before he had the chance to compose a new message in Fez. That would not be good for the baby.

He turned to the next clean page. He would tell her only the facts and spare her all news of their troubles.

Dear Catalina,

It has taken nearly a month to cross the mountains to arrive in Málaga, but everyone in our family is in good health…

He continued to compose his letter and promised to write again when they arrived in Fez.

Chapter Twenty-Three

When they reached the priest's door, Padre Morales welcomed them inside. The twelve men sat in the living room, rubbing their eyes and foreheads to stay awake, sipping on tea and eating bread and fried eggs off of plates as if they were the ones who would need the energy to perform this surgery. Vidal wanted to request food for his wife and son, but did not desire to instigate any standoff that might call off the surgery. They needed the money and if that meant starving for a few more hours, so be it. Last night's carrot would stifle his hunger.

As Padre Morales led Vidal and his family to Marcos' room, the soldiers saluted them and raised their mugs as if welcoming guests of honor. Not even Catholics yet and the soldiers had already accepted them. Of course, Vidal had been a doctor long enough to know that the slightest error on his part could undo any amount of pre-established goodwill.

In Marcos' room, the boy shivered under the blankets and muttered unintelligible phrases. The candles that filled the room burned down to their stems, leaving melted golden wax on the stone floor. Vidal expected the sight to disturb Bonadonna, but she looked at the patient with a mother's concern. His wife was no stranger to a fever-stricken boy. He told her to prepare the towels and blankets so he could reach for them quickly, to tuck the tapestry under Marcos' infected shoulder, and place any rags on the ground to collect spilled blood. She set about the tasks with the efficiency of a veteran nurse, but kept her back to the door where the twelve men funneled through to stand on the far wall.

"Padre, I need a washbasin of boiled water for my nurse, new candles—these will all soon burn out—and the others must wait outside." Before the priest could speak, the man Vidal convinced himself was a giant announced that Marcos requested their presence. But Vidal knew this would be impossible, the soldiers would intervene the moment Vidal made an incision, and if he could not save Marcos, his family would never escape. "This is not theater," Vidal told the priest. "I cannot have an audience to watch my work. I must concentrate."

"How do we know he's done the job well?" asked the giant.

From the bureau beside the bed, Eliezer threw open his instrument case and the iron straps struck the stone wall. "You will know, for once we are done, your friend will be well."

Bonadonna hissed her son's name for speaking out of turn. To Vidal's relief, Padre Morales explained to the men that he alone would stay in the room to supervise the surgery. "Now bring fresh candles and hot water for the physicians."

The men caved to their priest's demands, and as the men carried in new candles, Eliezer brought the sponge dusted in opium to Marcos' nose and instructed him to inhale until the boy was too intoxicated to lift his head or take another deep breath. The giant carried in a cauldron of boiled water and placed it on the floor beside the bed. The hot water splashed over the rim and hissed as it broke on the cold stone floor. Padre Morales hurried the men out of the room and closed the door behind them. Only a flimsy wooden door, ill-fitting in its frame so that cracks of light came through the corners and sides, separated Vidal from the soldiers. When that door opened, Marcos would need to be on his way to recovery, or at the very worst still alive, if Vidal had any hope of ensuring his son's and wife's escape.

"Padre, how is it you plan to supervise and assess this procedure?"

"I don't." Padre Morales took the chair from the corner of the room and faced it away from Marcos' bed. "I have not the stomach for your profession. I will stay here and carry on my conversation with the Lord until you are through." He recited a Hail Mary as if Jesus himself were seated in a chair facing the priest. Did he plan on praying through the whole procedure? The prayers disturbed Vidal, for he needed God with him more than ever, and he feared that any connection he made with Him would be overwhelmed by the priest communicating from another faith.

Bonadonna readjusted Marcos' shoulder so it laid more firmly over the tapestry and Eliezer stood on the far side of the bed with the opium sponge in hand. Vidal began the procedure by washing the infected area with a rag soaked in water from the bucket. Once the skin dried, he slathered black salve across Marcos' shoulder. The methodical preparation was meant to lessen the chance of further infection, but was as much a way to postpone the inevitable act he was about to perform.

From his instrument case, Vidal brandished a scalpel no larger than the first digit of a finger but as sharp as the sword of King David. He stood over the naked infection and linen-infested wound and felt like a boy trying to make sense of a haftorah portion he'd never read before. Once he made the first incision, there'd be no going back. Blood would flow from Marcos' body, absorb into the tapestry and blankets, run across the floor to encircle the priest's boots. He'd never before plunged his knife so deeply into a man's flesh. What if Marcos awoke, screamed, and no amount of opium could subdue him? His friends would enter the room immediately to call off the surgery and give Vidal the deserved punishment.

He placed the knife at the peak of the scar—the botched stitching serving as his guide to commence the surgery—then slipped the blade into Marcos' flesh. To Vidal's great relief, the boy did not stir nor respond and only a tear-sized trickle of blood adhered atop the incision, but as he cut down the path of the scar, blood ran down Marcos' shoulder like water slowly being released from an aqueduct. By the time Vidal reached the base of the scar, blood had pooled around the soft crook of Marcos' shoulder so that the initial wound was no more visible than the bottom of the blackest sea. This was a terrible idea, unconscionable, idiotic. Vidal had cut open this man; what to do now? He wanted to drop the knife and flee the house, jump into the ocean and swim for Africa, anything to escape this situation. His face turned so red that he imagined drops of sweat would fall from his brow into the wound, infecting it anew.

"Bonita, dry the sweat from my brow." When she did not respond, he turned to see his wife transfixed on the blood as if it'd cast her under a spell. She stumbled forward in an effort to carry out Vidal's instructions, but her eyes rolled into her head and she fell backward as erect as a chopped tree. Vidal sprung for Bonadonna and blew air into her face. Blood from the scalpel stained her black dress. She'd seen many things as a mother of five—excrement, urine, vomit—but blood must have been a less common sight. Vidal whispered for her to breathe and was grateful that the priest was reciting an Our Father loud enough that he could not hear them. "You can do this. Focus on me. Don't look at the blood." She brought her hands to her forehead, breathing too hard to speak. From the other side of the bed, Eliezer called for his father's attention and Vidal was certain the blood had spilled on the floor. "Look at me. You can do this."

"I'll do it. I'll do it…" She fumbled to find the corner of the bed.

"Father!"

With Bonadonna balanced on the mattress, Vidal discovered the blood from Marcos' arm soaking into the tapestry, turning the dry thread's coarseness into the texture of a wet mop. If he lost blood at this rate, he'd be dead in a matter of minutes. Vidal ordered Eliezer to aid his mother while he tended to the patient. Standing over Marcos again, he no longer had time for fear or hesitation. He submerged his fingers into the pool of blood, felt for the cut, then pushed his index finger inside. The approach was most unorthodox, but he needed to find the arrowhead immediately, and he would find it faster by feel than digging around blindly with forceps. He asked God to help him find the foreign object, but the priest's words obstructed his ability to focus on prayer. He needed to find this object on his own.

To his relief, he encountered no nerves or tendons. A digit's depth into the wound, he felt the warm, rugged texture of the broad end of a Moorish arrowhead. None of the smooth texture he associated with bone. By feel, he realized scar tissue had grown around the wound to encase the arrow like a cocoon. He kept his finger on the spot like he was holding his place in the line of a book and called for Eliezer to bring forceps.

Eliezer stepped away from giving his mother a cup of water to retrieve forceps from the instrument case on the nightstand beside the bed. As he handed the instrument to Vidal, Eliezer looked down at the wound. "What the hell are you doing?"

Vidal ignored him, wiggling the forceps into the flesh formed around the arrowhead until the tip found the horizontally curved front of the arrow. The work must have had the potential to cause Marcos great pain, for his head rocked side to side on the pillow as if he were trapped in a nightmare. As Eliezer placed the sponge under Marcos' nose, Vidal clasped the jaw of the forceps tightly around the width of the arrowhead, preparing to pull the object free.

"Our Father, who art in heaven, hallowed be thy name…" The priest's prayers grew louder. "Thy kingdom come; thy will be done on earth as it is in heaven…" Whether Padre Morales' prayers were meant to bring him closer to God or merely distract from the procedure occurring behind him, Vidal could not be sure.

"I'm going to remove the arrow now." Vidal looked to his wife and son as if asking their permission. What if by pulling out the arrowhead, he'd sever a nerve or, heaven forbid, slash an artery? He was far from the heart, but the jugular was a mere digit away.

Bonadonna rose from the bed, took a cloth from her hand and patted the sweat dry on Vidal's brow. "I know you can do this."

"Are there any obstructions?" Eliezer asked.

Vidal submerged the end of his scalpel into the pool of blood. "None that I can tell."

"Proceed. Slowly."

Vidal clasped the arrowhead with the jaws of the forceps and pulled. Blood gushed from the wound as if attempting to make way for the arrow itself. As the broadside of the arrow snagged on fat and cartilage, Vidal cut a path for it with his scalpel like an explorer clearing a forest trail with a sword.

Once resistance alleviated, the arrow pulled free. Vidal lifted a shard of iron no larger than a coin into the air that dripped blood down his fingers and wrist. He dropped the arrow into a bowl he'd placed on the nightstand and the blood ran off it, returning the arrowhead to its original earth color. A collective sigh from his son and wife acknowledged a victory quickly cut short by the first drops of blood that fell from the bed to stain the white sheet that covered the floor. Vidal ordered Bonadonna to fetch the hot water and he proceeded to use the liquid and strips of cloth to clean out the wound, taking the edge of the scalpel and shaving off linen trapped in the skin.

Once Vidal stitched the wound shut, Eliezer placed a handful of garlic powder in front of Marcos' nose to aid him in regaining consciousness while Bonadonna gathered soiled rags and wiped away any blood that stained the floor. Vidal announced to the priest that they were finished.

The priest glanced over his shoulder. "Is he well?"

"I will need to monitor him to be sure the fever lowers. It should be safe to assess in a couple of hours. In the meantime, my apprentice and nurse will need to depart, as they have other patients in need of treatment."

"But what if Marcos needs their care?"

"I would have them called back. There is no need for them to wait in the interim."

When the priest opened the door into the sitting room, the men stirred from where they slept on couches, or looked up from the game of chess they played while seated on the floor. The giant rose to his feet in anticipation of news, but the priest assured them Marcos needed time to recover. Vidal expected his wife and son to pass through the room on their way out—gone from this home and safe for good, but Eliezer stepped off the path to the front door to meet the giant.

"We saved him. And when people ask how he got well, I hope you'll tell them who his physicians were."

The giant smirked as if Eliezer had made a joke he was debating whether to understand, then laughed and left the room for the kitchen without another acknowledgment of Eliezer.

Outside, the sun appeared over the crests of the houses. The ocean breeze kicked up a whirl of leaves on the street that'd fallen from the nearby oak tree. People were about, carrying baskets and wrangling their children, as they walked through town on their way to work or market. As Padre Morales waited in the doorway, Vidal hugged his wife and son. Every instinct told Vidal to leave with them. He'd already bumbled his way through a surgery without killing the patient; he should disappear before a failed recovery revealed his lies. But if he left now, he'd never get the money they needed and they'd be trapped all the same.

"You're sure you don't want us to stay with you?" Eliezer asked.

"Go back to the beach. I'm sure Iamila's having enough trouble handling your brother."

"Stay no longer than needed," Bonadonna said. "I'm proud of you. You did well."

"I'll see you both in a couple of hours. I'll be fine."

As he watched them walk beside each other down the street, disappearing among the other bodies in the crowd, he could not help but think that if God were not on his side, he would never see them again. They would forever await a father and husband who'd been sent on to a place from which there was no return. Was God on his side? He'd not prayed to Him during the surgery nor asked for His help. The priest had done all the praying in another faith. So what role had God played in his success this morning?

Padre Morales invited Vidal into his kitchen. Sunlight streamed in through the window and the walls were painted an attractive gold and orange. The giant faced away from Vidal, cooking something that smelled of salt and fats skewered over an open hearth. A circular wooden table was placed at the center of the room. Given that it was too small to accommodate the many friends of Marcos, Vidal deduced that this home had once been owned by a family with far fewer children than his own. A tattered and sun-damaged leather suitcase served as the table's centerpiece. Padre Morales lifted the case to reveal a treasure chest of reales inside. The coins were so abundant that Vidal could have submerged his entire fist into the pile and still not touch the bottom of the case. If he did not need it to ferry passage, the payment would've supported his family for years.

"A man in my parish deals in purchasing houses in this neighborhood. I can arrange a meeting with you and him after you convert. It would get you off the beach, some new clothes as well."

Was it best to lie? Vidal closed the case and brought it to his end of the table. "I would appreciate that."

"That is a great deal of money to carry around the city—you don't need me to tell you. Would you prefer to keep it here? As you can imagine, nobody is going to steal from a house full of soldiers."

"You are too kind. But I prefer to take it with me."

"Not all the money is for you?"

Did the priest know about the boat? Impossible. Vidal reminded himself the priest might very well be asking if he had debts. "I must pay back the credit I owe on the instruments and remedies I purchased for this procedure."

"I cannot imagine a doctor who lives on the beach has 10,000 reales worth of debt."

"Oh? Why do you think I cannot afford better clothes?"

The giant slid a sausage off its skewer onto a clay plate and placed it on the table before Vidal. "A token of our appreciation. You must be famished."

Vidal looked down at the rolled tube of pork, still cooking and marinating in its skin. He was forbidden to eat pig, an unclean animal. To bite into the sausage would be a violation of his faith, as shameful as conversion. "Thank you. But it's best I wait until after I convert."

"You'll be one of us in a matter of hours. What's the harm?" The giant's words did not feel like a test or a taunt, only a genuine welcome for Vidal to partake in the great cuisine of their shared faith.

Vidal had to admit he was starving. A surgery would do that to any doctor, especially one completed after a month of surviving off fruit, vegetables, and nuts. He'd already acted suspicious with the money. Would his ulterior motives be exposed if he refused the meal? The sausage looked succulent and juicy, encased so tightly that he imagined the meat would snap like apple skin once he tore into it. He was growing faint, on his way to passing out. Would it be so wrong to eat the pork? Only a taste?

Vidal requested a fork and knife. When he carved into the pork casing, little specks of juice exploded onto his sleeves and shirt. He impaled the end piece on his fork and inserted the forbidden meat into his mouth as unceremoniously as Eve took the fruit from the tree of the knowledge of good and evil. The sausage tasted like the darkest and juiciest chicken medallion. The grease that coated his tongue and cheeks assured him the meal was filthy, but his temptation outweighed his disgust. What good would starving do him? He was a man, he'd risked his life, succeeded in performing a miracle operation, and now he would save his family and others. Could God truly be angered with him for breaking kosher law once? If the soldiers had offered him anything else, he would have gladly accepted it, but pork was all they served.

"A cup of water, please." He slipped the next bite into his mouth. The giant instead presented him with a clay cup filled with grenache, saying it would pair best, and Vidal consumed the sausage and gobbled down the wine like a gluttonous Roman emperor.

He was burping the hot smell of pork when he returned to examine Marcos. He felt the boy's warm forehead and draped a cool washcloth over his brow to bring down the fever. Marcos regained consciousness as the morning continued, but babbled unintelligible questions and asked for his mother—who Padre Morales whispered had died while Marcos fought in Granada. Once Marcos could drink, Vidal gave him water and chamomile tea to help with the fever. He went through the necessary motions of assisting Marcos to recover, for the world did not exist outside this house until Marcos was well. He helped Marcos walk around the room and urinate into a chamber pot stored underneath the bed. The giant, of all people, took the urine and tossed it out the back window for them. Every hour that passed, he knew Bonadonna and Eliezer grew more worried, but despite what Marcos had put him through, at that moment, he was the most important person in Vidal's world. He needed to help him recover, he could not assume the boy would be fine and leave the way he'd done with Sarah.

Marcos sat up in bed by midmorning, his thoughts and speech groggy from the opium, but his body temperature cooled. Vidal allowed all of the men into the room, and they listened to Marcos with joy and approval as he remarked that he no longer felt chills and asked for someone to bring him bread. "Bread?" one of them said. "You need to get your strength back. You need meat!" He'd never seen the men interact with their sick friend and was surprised that these soldiers, these barbarians who destroyed the world he called home, could look down at this sick, weak boy like a little brother.

As Vidal bid them farewell, the soldiers thanked him by offering medical supplies: bandages, alcohol, tape, valves, canteens full of water, and cured pork rations. He accepted everything he could carry—even the pork, which he could sell—knowing it would be useful for the journey from the African coast to Fez. As he left for the door, the possibility of being free at least, of having survived this ordeal, he kept his mouth shut about further arrangements to convert. Padre Morales already assumed he'd see Vidal that afternoon; there was no need to lie about his intentions more than necessary. But as Vidal reached for the door handle, the priest grabbed his arm.

"Keep the medical supplies. But I warn you, take none of this coin to Africa." He'd come alone, the other men still talking with Marcos in the bedroom.

"I don't understand—"

"Spend it all. Keep nothing, not even what you can hide. I've heard rumors; sailors are taking Jews into the middle of the ocean and murdering them for their money. Some will even cut open their bellies to retrieve the treasures smuggled inside."

"Padre, I don't—"

"Travel safe, Doctor. And thank you for everything." Padre Morales opened the door for Vidal to leave. Had he been so obvious? There was no reason to continue to lie to the priest now as they parted ways. He gave thanks and stepped out into the bright sunlight of the streets, passing men on their way to work and women walking their children to the schoolhouses. He cradled the soldiers' gifts in one arm while he allowed the suitcase to swing in his other hand, so it did not seem evident that he was carrying a fortune, even when his instincts tempted him to forsake the rations and cradle the case in his arms like a baby.

He went forward into the streets, eager to seek refuge among his family on the beach. As he walked through Málaga, his surprise at the priest's kindness and understanding began to trouble him. How had he gone through with this procedure, one he was wholly unqualified to do, almost murdering a boy, just to acquire the money that would save his kin? Was that the kind of man he'd become? Putting strangers at risk to protect his own family? Even when conversion might have solved the problem all the same? He'd spared that boy of losing an arm—he should think himself a hero. Yet, he did not feel like a hero. More a sneak, a coward, a charlatan, for gambling with the boy's life. This was a miracle. God had been on his side. But had He? Vidal could no longer feel God's presence any better than he could feel the presence of Rabbi el Barchilon. The only interaction with a lord in that room had been between Padre Morales and his Christ. Vidal had acted alone. He had succeeded, but if that were the case, it was through pure luck rather than skill.

His stomach gurgled and bile emerged from his throat. He threw himself into the nearest back alley, put the suitcase between his legs and vomited a paste the texture of raspberries onto the stone slab of a chimney that protruded from the wall of a stranger's house. Everything he'd done, was it worth it? Once his stomach was clear, he put his hand on the ground and struggled to catch his breath.

Chapter Twenty-Four

Before returning to the wagon to rejoice in victory with his family, Vidal paid a visit to the captain. The captain was sitting on the bow of a beached wooden rowboat and the moment they agreed on the sum to deliver forty souls across the Mediterranean, Vidal offered the briefcase as payment. The captain said they were unloading cargo from Tétouan for the remainder of the day and would depart tomorrow morning when the waves of the sea were calm. Vidal looked out at the water and saw several ships hauling boxes and crates over their sides to be rowed back to shore. That the captain only requested half the payment to reserve his ship made Vidal believe he could trust this man, though he had no other choice.

When he returned to the beach, his family raced through the sand to embrace him among the tents and wagons of strangers. He knew the sight would make their neighbors grow suspicious, but with his wife and three children in his arms, he could only marvel at how he'd done something so despicable yet managed the good fortune of surviving and having his family embrace him as their hero. Though he wanted to laugh with joy, he kept his mouth shut so they would not smell the pork on his breath. He brought his family in closer, cherishing this moment. He'd survived to hold them again, their father who would save them all.

Eliezer and Asher wasted no time burying the briefcase under their wagon's supplies, so that if anyone attempted to steal the remaining reales, they'd be alerted by the sound of a thief upending boxes. As his sons worked, Vidal whispered to Bonadonna that they must abandon all of their possessions. When he confided that taking anything could mean fatal consequences, she needed no more convincing to start selling whatever possessions that might still hold value. Iamila was busy petting the horse's mane as they spoke and Vidal went to tell her that he should begin to wish María farewell.

At the wagons of the Pardos, Salomons, and Mendezes, he whispered that they'd be departing the following morning. The fathers cheered, the mothers and children embraced one another, but Vidal asked them to do so quietly. They needed to keep this information to themselves. Although he wished to leave an honest man, he knew they would have to slither away from La Judería as their rabbi had done.

"And the boat will take us to Fez?" Avraham asked when Vidal shared the news with the Mendezes in their tent.

"Tétouan. Fez will be farther yet."

"But without our wagons, or horses, or supplies, what will we do? How will we make the journey?"

In truth, Vidal did not know. The original plan had been for the rabbi's brother to meet them at the port and escort them to Fez, but he needed no reminder that no such welcome awaited them. "We'll find a way when we get to Africa," he said. "At least there, our faith will have no expiration date."

When Vidal exited the tent, Tsipora could not contain her excitement. She hugged him, and thanked him for saving them. Although this would be most unorthodox under any other circumstance, nobody, not even Vidal felt the need to push her away. He'd saved the daughter of his very old and very unreliable friend, a woman he'd prepared to welcome into his family for many years. Surely their all-knowing God would understand such an embrace.

But families from La Judería who surrounded the Mendez tent did not understand. The startling sight of Tsipora hugging Vidal was enough to generate the gossip that although unproven was true. As Vidal did rounds that afternoon, too excited to sleep, he felt the gaze and hate directed at him from other members of their caravan. Though they did not beg for or demand a spot on the boat, he could tell from the looks in their eyes that they prayed his ship sank.

When he visited the sick, he supplied their families with the offerings the soldiers had given him, the best he could muster as a consolation for not saving them as well. But why should he feel obligated to save them? They had not risked their lives and the lives of their wife and oldest son to perform a dangerous surgery, nor had they offered assistance at any point along the journey. For months, his family had provided free medical care to these people, even while trying to survive the pilgrimage through the Sierra Nevadas themselves. His family had earned the right to leave—they could've gone with the rabbi even—and if others remained hateful to the idea, he had not the medical expertise to cure their spite.

On the morning of their departure, Vidal completed his final rounds seated in the hot sand under the shade of the Curiel family's wagon and listened to Señor Curiel's heartbeat. An infestation of lice crawled in an assembly-line across Señor Curiel's blanket, but madness had so taken his mind that he felt no need to scratch. The old man mumbled unintelligible utterings and Vidal gave him lavender and sprigs of peony to ease his anxiety in this strange new land. He never expected Señor Curiel to survive the journey through the mountains, and was sure the man was too brittle to undertake the sea crossing. Yet, Señor Curiel's oldest son Isaac stood over Vidal, blocking the sunlight, angered that his family had not been selected for a place on the ship.

"How can you leave? You have too many patients here. They need your help." Although Isaac's words were selfish and filled with envy, that made them no easier to hear. From his medical bag, Vidal offered Isaac a generous handful of the bandages, herbs, and weeds issued to him by Padre Morales' soldiers. He explained how each item could keep Señor Curiel comfortable and requested that Isaac distribute supplies among others in their caravan. Isaac accepted the supplies with stern irritation, and as Vidal bid him farewell and left the Curiel's wagon, imagining the encounter done with, Isaac followed him. "How can you do this? How can you abandon us?" Isaac spoke to him as Vidal had spoken to the rabbi.

"We left Granada with 200. It was never my burden to deliver you all to Fez."

Isaac spoke over Vidal's shoulder as they weaved through the tents and wagons of their former neighbors. "I was the head of irrigation at La Alhambra. My skills are as valuable as a doctor's, yet you choose the family of a blacksmith over mine?"

"There is nothing you can say that would make me give you the Mendez's place."

"It's Shelomo's daughter. Your son is obsessed with her. I'll bet he begged you to take her."

The vein in Vidal's forehead felt like it might burst as he turned to face Isaac. "What would you have me do? Go back on my promise to the Mendez family? Or better, give you my place on the ship, so I can stay behind and die like the good doctor you all expect me to be?"

"A good doctor? You are a coward and hypocrite."

"If you know a way to deliver every man, woman, and child of La Judería to African shores, then speak. What is your solution? Tell me."

"Who are you to lecture me? You, who abandon us mere days after the rabbi's departure obliterated this caravan and its morale."

"I would part the Mediterranean for us if God would only bless me with the power He gave Moses. But He does not speak to me that way, and I can wait no longer to find another solution to save us. I wish you and your family nothing but health and luck—"

Isaac spat at his feet and because Vidal's boots were so torn from use, the hot saliva congealed into a space between his sand-covered toes. Vidal's hand trembled with such fury that he thought to slap Isaac, but he knew another punishment would sting far worse. "Farewell, Isaac."

He continued up the beach to his wagon with Isaac repeating after him that he was a coward and a hypocrite. Although Isaac no longer followed him, the words burrowed into Vidal's heart and mind to torment him no matter how fast he fled. Indeed, Isaac had a valid argument. What kind of doctor abandons his patients at their most vulnerable? How many doctors throughout history stood by their patients, even staying at their most ill patients' bedsides while foreign invaders sacked the city around them? Was it right to break that heritage, only to live in exile, filled with regret and concern for the fate of a community he abandoned? On the beach, he passed husbands and wives shouting at each other from opposite ends of their wagons, children with sand in their hair begging for food, and men looking out to the sea with the same hopelessness and desperation he'd felt less than a week earlier. If some jumped into the water to swim to Africa, the act would not surprise him. Why did he think he did not deserve happiness? That it was wrong to deliver his family to a land that would protect them and nurture their faith?

The sky overhead was a blank cloudless teal. Vidal looked up and prepared to ask God for an answer. What should he do? But for the first time, the act felt foolish. God would not reply. He would not set a bush aflame, nor crumble the walls of Málaga, nor raise high the tide of the Mediterranean Sea to drown out the Catholic invaders. He knew God was testing him, but how much greater could these tests become? Why could God never speak to him as He did to Adam, Abraham, or Moses? Even a single word to steady his heart? Was it possible—as pagans and heretics believed—that there was simply nobody there? And if that were the case, why was he putting his family through this nightmare to preserve a religion that was meaningless outside of his mind? Why had the new monarchs fought nine long years of war in the Kingdom of Granada and sentenced his people to exile if there was no God to observe their devotion? The thoughts seemed blasphemous; he should feel ashamed for even thinking them. But he saw no need to speak to God, as there'd been no need to talk to Him during the surgery.

He was so familiar with the layout of the beach that he found his way back to the wagon on instinct. When he arrived, Bonadonna was searching through the boxes and bags on the wagon bed for any last possessions they should take and Eliezer stood on the bed opposite her to stack the luggage in well-ordered piles. Iamila squatted in the sand to bury the firepit with her bare hands while Asher kicked away the grooves in the sand where they'd slept to make the camp appear as if nobody had rested there. Vidal wanted to speak with his wife away from the children. Was it possible she was right and that they should have stayed in Granada and spared themselves this misery? Did she want to go to Africa or would she rejoice in the idea of conversion if he suggested it? He could speak to his wife of many things, but to announce he was questioning his faith was not one of them. His doubts came about from weakness and exhaustion—he'd feel better when they arrived in Fez. He needed to suppress these thoughts, for they were nothing more than another way for God to test him.

Vidal worked in silence to help his family clean their plot of beach. This time, Asher needed no reminder for why they worked to clean something they would only abandon. When it became time to depart for the port, he reminded his children to carry only one possession, something small that could be hidden and held little value. Should it be stolen, he did not want them to resist or mourn its loss. They changed into their most rancid clothes that smelled of old piss and sweat. Nobody would come near them on the ship if they could not stand the stench, making them unlikely candidates for people smuggling fortunes in their pockets or bellies.

They left the wagon behind with its wheels half-buried in the sand; its bed stacked neatly with cauldrons, washbasins, clothes, and furniture they'd brought this far in vain. Bonadonna carried a loaf of maslin bread, Asher hugged the last blanket the family owned, Eliezer took his and his father's instrument cases—empty except for bandages—and Vidal held the tattered suitcase that contained their remaining coins for passage. Breaking his own rule, he hid a scalpel in his coat as well. At first, he thought Iamila carried nothing, then noticed an alabaster hairbrush in her hand.

"What's this?" He took it from her to examine the artifact closer.

"It belonged to Sarah."

He remembered combing it through Sarah's hair during their final moments together, the white gypsum so bright in contrast to her black curls. Although it hadn't cost more than a handful of dirhams, the way the alabaster reflected the sunlight deceived its true worth. "I cannot let you take this. It appears too valuable."

"It's all we have left of her."

"I know."

The alabaster only formed the brush's handle, molded together with wood that held horsehair bristles which clumped together through time and use. Although he preferred she travel without this, Vidal had heard of her strength when they'd sold the horse the day before. How she had not cried, but instead led the horse by its reins to a horse buyer who had every intention of using María to breed. He could not bear to let her lose one more treasure. He broke the alabaster off the end of the brush and handed her the wood and bristles. She looked down at the broken heirloom and at first, he expected her to give it back to him and leave in tears, but she seemed to fall in love with this old broken brush all the same, admiring it like a new toy as she caught up to her brothers.

Vidal stayed with the sharp piece of broken alabaster in his hand. Should he drop it? Throw it into the ocean? He did what felt right, kissing the alabaster's soft surface and burying it in the sand.

The Pardo, Salomon, and Mendez families waited for him at the stone walkway's edge. The sun reflected off the golden city walls, leaving them not a fraction of shade. The families bounced where they stood with a mixture of anxiety and excitement as they watched his arrival. Vidal now found himself as the leader of thirty-nine others, when the rabbi had led 200 out of Granada.

"Let us go forward, friends. If we can find our way off this beach, I know we can reach Fez."

They followed Vidal along the stone pathway toward the gateway into the city. Iamila walked beside him, and he pulled her close as she grasped the broken hairbrush in her free hand. They passed family after family of squatting Jews. The once-thriving neighborhood of Granada's Judería now only existed on this beach and it was startling for Vidal to think that in weeks, every person who lined the beach would be gone, either through fleeing to the Maghreb or remaining after the commencement of the decree to meet their fate. This beach would return to nothing but sand and surf, an empty place for families of Málaga to walk together after dinner outside the city walls, where within a generation, nobody would remember that so many had once occupied such a small strip of land. Vidal glanced behind them to the coastline beyond where they'd settled. The population stretched to the east end of the bay, where the distant hills of the valley spilled into the sea. There would be no miracle for them. No kind priest to enlist their skills at the most opportune moment. Had God allowed him to escape with his family so he could be a doctor in the new land? Or had God done nothing, and through fortuitous circumstances, Vidal helped others escape on his own?

They met the captain on the shores outside the city walls. The man wore a fresh white tunic and received Vidal's tattered suitcase with such anticipation that he almost dropped it for being heavier than he'd expected. He balanced the case on his thigh and unclipped the metal hooks to admire the silver of the reales inside that reflected sunlight onto his face.

The captain led everybody to two beached rowboats and pointed to a two-deck roundship anchored one hundred varas out on the water. Nobody from Vidal's family nor any other family had sat in a boat before, and the ability to sit above open water sounded as farfetched as the supposed miracles of Jesus, even if, as a man of science, Vidal understood why the boat would float. The captain and an accompanying first mate who smelled saltier than the sea offered their hands to the women and helped them step from the sand into the middle of one of two wooden rowboats. They instructed each person to sit a short width apart. "So the boat will not tip over," said the captain. He reminded everyone to stay seated. "If you stand, we could capsize."

He allowed the others to board first and once Vidal sat on a wooden plank at the stern of the rowboat, flanked by Bonadonna and Iamila, the first mate stepped into the bow as the captain slid the boat off the beach landing and into the water. The warnings of Padre Morales returned to mind. Vidal kept a watchful eye on the captain and first mate should they attempt to threaten his family and throw them overboard. Not that he saw any reason now that the captain had possession of all valuables.

The boat carried them out to sea, charging straight into waves that poured water into the boat and sprayed Vidal and his family with a salty mist. He leaned overboard to let his hand skim through the rippling surface of the water, feeling the ocean both push his hand against it, then pull him deeper out with the rip current that retreated with the waves. He could not see the seafloor and for all he knew, they were floating above the peak of an underwater mountain range that rivaled the elevation of the Sierra Nevadas. He knew humans could float, but if he fell or was thrown overboard, how far into the depths might he sink?

Once the rowboat arrived at the port side, deckhands aboard the ship draped a web of rope over the side and the first mate helped each person stand on the rowboat to grasp the rope and climb their way to the deck. The boat rocked back and forth on the water every time somebody stood, and Vidal put his hands on either side in a futile attempt to hold it steady. Once aboard the ship, he looked up at the towering masts wrapped with eggshell-colored sails that sailors unfurled to catch the wind like glorious curtains billowing with the breeze from an open window. The captain discussed the route on the upper deck beside a wheel shaped to look like the sun's rays. The wood on the ship's deck appeared weather-beaten and peeling from time. What sort of storms awaited them at sea?

As they set sail into the vastness of the blue ocean, Vidal brought his wife and children close. They huddled together at the stern, their backs turned away from the coast, as other families found spaces on the deck to call their own, where they could sit without being in the way of sailors and deckhands who ran to re-adjust the various pullies and knots that controlled the sails. He would need to watch these men, not even sleep, on their two-day journey to the far side of the sea. With his scalpel in his pocket, he was prepared to drive away any man who came near his family with impure intentions.

Eliezer tapped him on the shoulder and pointed to look back. Behind them, the ship was sailing away from Málaga to reveal a view of the city's docks, churches, houses, and forts. The mountain range they'd hiked through to arrive flanked either end of the bay, and beyond the mountains that encircled the city lay untouched land they'd never seen before and would never see again. But at the center of it all was the stretch of beach before the city walls that was overrun with Jews.

Throughout their journey, when he'd imagined boarding the ship, sailing away from Málaga to start their new lives across the sea, he'd imagined celebrations, hugs, tears, professions of love, a jovial affair. But escaping Málaga brought no such relief. The sight of the swarmed beach filled him with self-loathing. Would leaving be worth it? At least in Málaga, he'd known what evil consequences awaited him, but now they were traveling to a new land, where the fate of his family would be as great a mystery as the tongue in which the locals spoke. Was it only because of the warning Padre Morales had given him? Or did his body attempt to alert him of something else, something he overlooked?

Though Vidal kept watch of the strangers that sailed them to the Maghreb, he continued to steal glances over his shoulder. One last look at the land where his oldest daughter, pregnant with his first-born grandchild, still lived. One last look at his home, his country, his continent. One last look until the ship sailed into a low-hanging cloud of mist that engulfed his view of the city and the Iberian Peninsula retreated into memory.

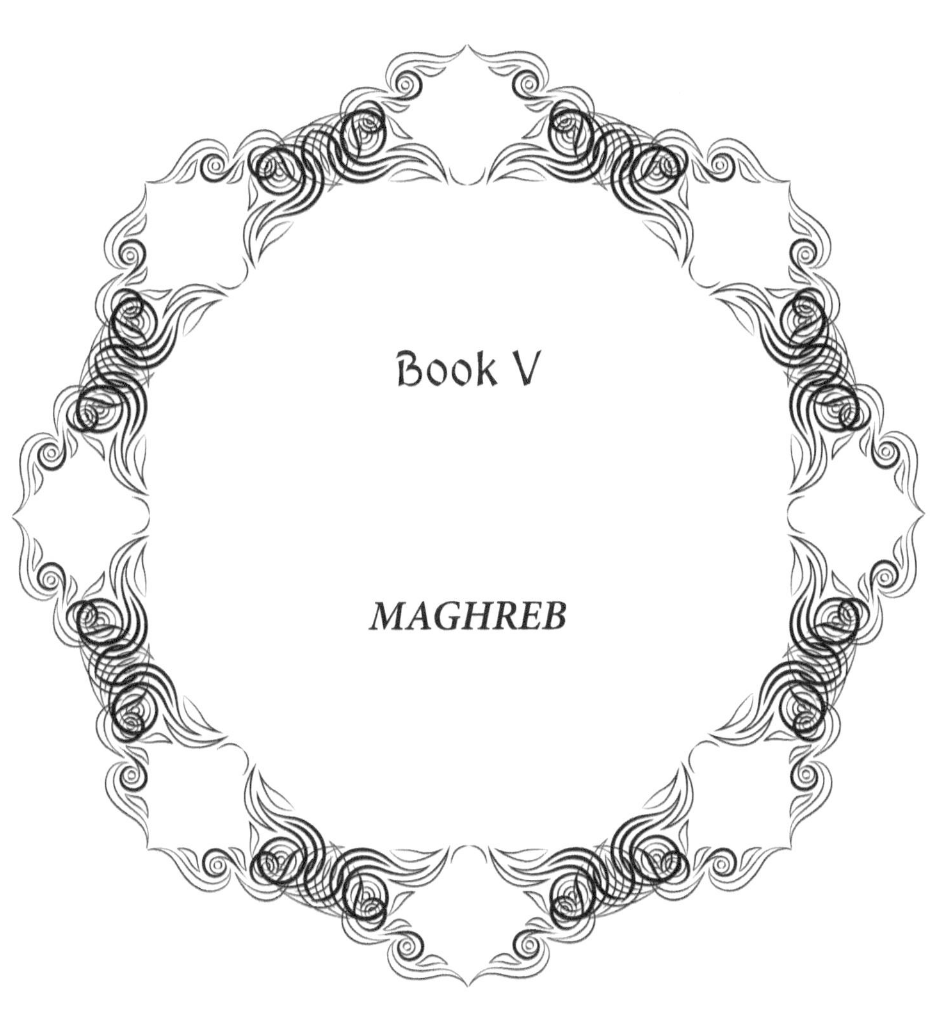

Book V

MAGHREB

Chapter Twenty-Five

The crow of a rooster woke Vidal before dawn. He lay on a straw bed and stared up at the stars through the little holes in the thatched hay of the ceiling. The first warmth of spring was already creeping into Fez and he took it as a good omen of the year that awaited. He heaved himself over the side of the bed, careful not to wake Iamila where she slept between him and his wife, hugging her straw pillow. With her eyes half-open, Bonadonna whispered she'd wake to make breakfast, but he told her there was no rush, as his stomach would remain asleep for several hours more.

He gathered his wool coat, wooden rake, and the linen tarp by the door, where his sons slept nearby among pillows and blankets on the wooden floor. His instrument case slumped covered in dust in the corner of this one-room shack they now called home. If he had the energy after picking the olives, crushing them on the neighbor's grindstone, selling the oil in the square, and the other myriad of chores awaiting him, he'd venture into town to solicit his services. But while not focusing on his practice would have irritated him in the past, waking before dawn to perform an act as methodical as picking olives gave him a sense of peace.

The front door was boarded shut by a plank of wood he nailed to the doorframe each night. Where at first he'd needed to use tongs to pull the nail loose each morning, the plank was so worn down from where the nail split it down the middle that he pried it open with one hand.

The darkness of the early morning, and the hoot of an unseen marsh owl filled him with calm. Behind his house, the city of Fez lay in darkness, save for the torches that burnt on city streets throughout the night, casting pockmarks of golden lights onto the sand-colored brick walls of the houses, mosques, and towers residing within the city's walls. To the south, no civilization, nothing but olive groves, stood between him and the grass-covered Atlas Mountains in the distance.

He unraveled his tarp beneath an olive tree and raked the orb-shaped picholine olives off the highest branches, where they fell onto the tarp like balls of green hail. In Granada, his family could barely cook with olive oil without alerting the suspicions of the soldiers. Now he cultivated oil himself, cooking without fear that its use would label him as a danger in his ruler's eyes. On occasion, he inspected an olive with his fingers. Was it hard as rock? Or soft around the outside and ripe for consumption? The act reminded him of diagnosing what ailment befell a patient by only feeling the beat of a pulse or the rise of a chest—though he doubted another doctor would make such comparisons. As light teased the appearance of the sun over a low eastern hill, Vidal's stomach grumbled, and he popped an olive into his mouth to stave off hunger.

That afternoon, he and Bonadonna ventured into the city to a square beneath the high palace walls of the Dar al-Makhzen, painted the color of beach sand and stretching such a distance in either direction the walls appeared to house an additional city within Fez. Bonadonna laid out a blanket to display olives cradled in muslin-lined baskets and clay vials of oil for purchase while Vidal stood under the sun on the wheat-colored bricks at the center of the square and attempted to entice passersby. People dressed in turbans, veils, and robes either looked at him like he was mad or laughed as if he were a court jester when they heard the accent he used to speak Arabic. A dozen other vendors sold spices, fruits, and tools atop blankets or beneath canopies in the square. He could not fault locals for passing on their olives. There must be vendors in Fez who'd sold the best olives for generations; why would anyone bother with his? Bonadonna had at first remarked to Vidal that nobody wanted to buy from them because they were

Jewish—foreigners as well—but after being threatened with the monarchs' penalty of death, how upset could either of them be with locals who ignored their business?

In six hours, they sold only two vials of olive oil—barely enough to afford bread, never mind the money to save for a home in the city. Once the adhan was recited from the nearby mosque's minaret and every person in the square kneeled on their prayer rugs—a practice that'd seemed unremarkable in Granada, but now made him feel at home—they packed up the blanket for the day. Despite the circumstances, Vidal placed the vials into a basket with such enthusiasm that he felt tempted to dance.

"If only I had your energy."

"It's a nice day, Bonita. The sun is out. It's getting warm again. It'll be our first spring in our new home."

"I hope you have this enthusiasm later when you go out in search of patients."

Vidal said nothing, only rolled the blanket closed to tuck it under his arm. He'd not gone out in the evening more than once a week to solicit his services to local synagogues and mosques. After the surgery in Málaga, he no longer felt justified in being a physician. But when she'd asked why he was not working harder to build his practice, he'd evaded the question. It was fortunate that Eliezer had successfully enrolled in the Al Qarawiyyin University and would soon become the respected physician of the ha-Rofeh family. "I assure you, our situation is temporary," Vidal said.

They walked beside the palace wall in the direction of Asher and Iamila's school. At the end of the square, where a keyhole arch marked their entry into the Jewish neighborhood, stood Shelomo Levin's new stall. The stall's tarp was woven from the tents that She-lomo and the rabbi's family had stayed in throughout the caravan, the plainness of Shelomo's beige tent hidden behind the majesty of the rabbi's emerald tent that faced outward to greet patrons. It was to Vidal's satisfaction that Shelomo had failed to procure a stall in the Medina, an ancient market that housed the most visited and successful businesses in the city, though Shelomo's new enterprise appeared more successful than their own. As the afternoon adhan concluded, a family who completed prayer rolled up their rugs and continued to the stall to purchase slabs of gazelle meat wrapped in cloth that smelled of blood. With Rabbi el Barchilon blessing each cut himself, Shelomo's new kosher gazelle meat had become a novelty in the city.

Shelomo called to them from behind a wooden table he set up to guard the entrance like a makeshift counter. "ha-Rofehs! How was business today?"

"Better than yesterday," Vidal said.

"If you're half as good an olive salesman as you are a doctor, I have no doubt they'll soon be importing trees from Marrakesh to keep up with demand." Shelomo asked them to wait and returned with an armful of cloth wrapped meat.

Bonadonna balanced a basket on her hip to accept it with a free hand. "We'll pay you back as soon as we can."

"Consider it an early bar mitzvah present for Asher." Their son's bar mitzvah was to occur that Saturday and the remaining families of La Judería were saving what money and food they could to feast in honor of Vidal's youngest son. His stomach grumbled at the thought of a long-overdue feast.

As they thanked him and continued to the children's school, Bonadonna asked Vidal why he believed Shelomo had discovered this new sense of generosity. "All this because we saved a daughter he hadn't thought twice to leave? Or do you think he feels guilty for abandoning us as well?"

"More likely a new way to flaunt his success."

"He is clever. Kosher gazelle meat. I'm surprised no local Jew thought of it."

"I'm sure they did. But Shelomo's from Granada, which makes his food a more exotic curiosity."

"If we were the only family who lived in the city, I wouldn't gloat as he does."

"Shelomo has gloated his whole life. Why do you care?"

"He has a house and we don't."

"Be patient. I won't have us selling olives on the streets for the rest of our lives."

They continued into Fes el-Jdid, or Fez's Judería as he liked to call it, and passed Stars of David chiseled into the stone of temple walls, smells of cooking oil wafting from open windows, and bronze cast mezuzot nailed to the thresholds of homes. As soon as they saved enough money, they planned to live there.

The school was built from sandstone beside the synagogue of Rabbi el Barchilon's brother. Two boys Asher's age were using water and rags to wipe away a word that'd defaced the side of the wall. הורחק, it said. Megorashim, written in crude and almost indecipherable blue paint. Hebrew was used outside of synagogue so rarely that the first time he saw the word, he'd nearly mistaken it for Arabic. "Expelled," it said. A reminder from the local Jews that their people were no more welcome in Fez than in Granada.

"We trade one form of hatred for another," Bonadonna said.

"Yes, but the king accepts us. That's all that matters here."

A humble-sized door carved from juniper marked the school entrance, a two-floor building painted white save for a tiled roof. The schoolteacher greeted Vidal with Asher in tow and explained that the boy needed considerable improvement with his haftorah portion's recitation if he were to have his bar mitzvah that Saturday.

"It's not the boy's fault," Bonadonna said. "He was well prepared before the Monarchs forced us out."

"I was speaking with your husband."

"I side with my wife. He's already been thirteen for half a year. At this point, a haftorah is nothing more than a formality."

"Was that everyone's attitude in Granada?"

"Apologies, it's been a long day."

"He must study," the schoolteacher said and left them with this demand as if Vidal and Bonadonna were equally his students in need of discipline.

As Bonadonna lectured Asher on the importance of his bar mitzvah, Vidal ventured off to find Iamila. She leaned against a wooden beam that supported the second floor of the school and looked up at a boy twice her height. The boy showed the first signs of a beard and spoke to her in Arabic. How well she understood him seemed irrelevant, as the look on her face made it clear she was thinking of something other than the words that came from his mouth. If he'd seen his daughter behave in such a way in Granada, he'd pull her away and scold her for speaking to a boy without a chaperone. But he could not be so aggressive in front of a Maghrebi.

He called his daughter's name sweetly and inserted himself between them. "I am Dr. ha-Rofeh. Who might you be, young man?"

The sound of Vidal's Castilian made the boy go silent.

"His name is Khalid. He works here."

"He works at a Jewish school?"

"He sets up everything for the Sabbath. With his family."

Vidal could not suppress his imagination. He pictured Iamila marrying a boy like Khalid, Iamila converting to Islam, Iamila baring Muslim children that he would call his grandchildren. Was he being irrational? Certainly. But his oldest daughter had done the same. Of the handful of families that trickled in from the shores of Málaga since their arrival, none came with a boy of suitable age for Iamila. And the local families, the ones who called him Megorashim, would not want her. Vidal thanked Khalid for watching after his daughter and told Iamila to say farewell as it was time to return to their shack.

He had no further time to dwell on his daughter's interaction with Khalid. Through the rest of the week, he sat on two wooden chairs outside their shack with Asher at twilight and attempted to have him memorize his haftorah portion as an actor memorizes a monologue in a play. It was the same story about Moses' twelve spies Asher had been assigned by Rabbi el Barchilon over a year ago and Vidal no longer had the patience to explain to the boy the meaning of the Hebrew he must sing.

That Saturday, Vidal sat beside Eliezer on the right side of the stage of the Ibn Zadok Synagogue. Along with a full congregation, he watched Asher stand at an azure tiled bimah and fumble through his haftorah for the final time. The brother of Rabbi el Barchilon breathed over the boy's shoulder and whispered for Asher to re-read the lines correctly.

Yet Vidal felt no embarrassment with his son. What man in this synagogue could imagine arriving in a new country at thirteen, with the need to relearn a language in six months, in time for a bar mitzvah imposed on him by the community? If the rabbi wanted to judge his son's pronunciation, let him. Besides, the haftorah portion that'd been selected for Asher was unremarkable, a short side story between Exodus and the crumbling of the walls of Jericho. How many people were only here because of the food?

On the far side of the stage, Rabbi el Barchilon sat in a chair with his eyes closed as if listening to music. They'd not spoken a word since Vidal's arrival. Did he fear Vidal would share with the rabbi's brother what he'd done? Certainly, Vidal was tempted. But he already knew that the brother would encourage forgiveness. Vidal had visited other synagogues in the city, curious to join a new temple, but the moment those rabbis learned he was from Iberia, they showed him the exit.

As Asher completed his recital, Bonadonna and Iamila leaned over the mechitza's wooden balcony in front of the other women. Bonadonna mouthed along to every word, on the verge of tears at the sight of her son finally becoming a man. And to think, she was the one who'd told Vidal to convert.

The party took place in the courtyard of Shelomo Levin's house. Unlike Tsipora and Avraham's wedding, this celebration was held after sundown. Tables and chairs were set up under the stars. Vidal was seated at the table of honor beside his sons, farthest from the exit to the street. As was tradition, a mesh net ran through the center of the party to separate the men from the women. He recognized it from celebrations past. Had they needed to travel all this way only to bring every custom with them?

On the other side of the net, Tsipora was wearing a white dress with a bump in her belly the size of an apple. The women kept approaching where she sat to compliment her and hold her stomach. If Eliezer had seen her in such a condition only a few months earlier, it would've driven him to madness—certainly away from his family and the community. But she smiled and glowed like a mother who was content and nesting. On the journey from

Tétouan, he'd noticed an affection and friendship between her, Avraham, and Eliezer like nothing he'd expected—as if they were a group of siblings. Avraham became a friend in their journey through the lowlands. Eliezer even worked with Avraham to communicate with the youth in the towns they passed to ask directions to Fez.

The party ate their fill of chicken, gazelle, salad, khubz, and tajine—a dish that put the tajine sold in El Albayzín to pity. The wine was drunken; the candles were lit with oil. After dinner, the tables were cleared from the center of the men's section. Asher was placed on a chair and lifted into the air by Vidal, Eliezer, Shelomo, and Binyamín as the men danced in a circle around them and chanted. The remaining members of the council of fifteen screamed where they danced in the perimeter as if they'd never sang above a whisper before, as no monarchs could stop their words now. The Pardos and Salomons pulled old men from their seats, anxious to bring everyone into the celebrations. While Vidal remembered being terrified of falling out of the chair the two times he'd sat in it before—his bar mitzvah and his wedding—Asher waved and shouted as if he were trying to stay mounted to a wild bull.

During a break from dancing, Eliezer disappeared to relieve himself while Vidal returned alone to the table. To his surprise, Rabbi el Barchilon approached the table of honor where he sat alone.

"Incredible news, isn't it?" The first words the rabbi had spoken to him since their argument in a tent on the shores of Málaga.

"What is?"

"From our old home."

"What news?"

"Of the discovery!" The rabbi might as well have asked if he'd heard news from Cathay; the man made no sense. "Some explorer was on his way to find a faster route to Asia, and he ventured so far off course he discovered a new world."

"World? What, he set sail to another planet?"

"Don't be preposterous; that's just what they're calling it. But they say there are islands, beaches, and jungles as far as any man cares to venture. The explorer returned with gold, spices unlike anything we've ever tasted, even natives from the land. Pagans with no knowledge of the crown, the pope, not even Jesus Christ himself."

"If that's the case, God help them."

"Of course, this happens the moment we leave. I'll wager Isabella and Ferdinand knew about this ages ago. They wanted to be rid of us before they told everyone."

"Why would they do that?"

"Make sure we did not all move there instead?" Indeed the thought of living in a land far from the crown or kings tempted Vidal, even if the concept of living in a jungle held no appeal. But would it be so different from living in a shack at the edge of town? "I'm surprised she didn't mention it to you."

"Who?"

"Your daughter."

"Iamila told you this?"

"Catalina. Or are we to call her Goyo again?"

Although he had no further information, these words from his enemy's mouth filled Vidal with hope. Rabbi el Barchilon was likely mistaken, it was not uncommon for even the most respected members of their community to lose their minds in their old age. But was it possible that his oldest daughter had changed her mind? That she followed her family to Fez?

"You must be mistaken. My daughter never left Granada."

"No, she's here. With Gabriel and Aznaro."

Vidal recognized the name only as having belonged to Gabriel's late grandfather. "Aznaro?"

"Your grandson."

Even if he were not on his fifth cup of wine, Vidal would have felt it impossible to stay composed. He shot up from his seat faster than a launched arrow. His body shook in a futile attempt to contain the excitement. It couldn't be. "Where did you see Catalina?"

"I didn't exactly see Catalina—"

"Is this some kind of a game?"

"I did see Gabriel. He came into the synagogue."

"What are you talking about? What are you up to?"

"I saw him this afternoon. Not an hour before the service started. He was holding a newborn, not three months old. I sent him to your house."

"Gabriel de Zaniçeras was never at my house."

"Maybe he is lost?"

"Then where was my daughter?"

"Outside, I guess."

"Did you see her?"

"No. But husbands leave their wives outside all the time when they come into temple."

"You take me for a fool?" Vidal grabbed the rabbi by the sleeve, and the wine on the table spilled over the tablecloth. Vidal could already hear the music and conversation cease around them. Every person in the courtyard turned toward him as if he'd called for silence to raise a toast. The rabbi's brother was already lumbering toward them, demanding the meaning of this quarrel and that Vidal unhand the rabbi.

"I will unhand him when an honest word leaves his mouth."

"You insult only yourself," the rabbi said.

"I do not want to hear another word out of your mouth. Deserter!" Vidal said. Rabbi el Barchilon's brother shouted at the rabbi to explain the meaning of Vidal's words as Vidal continued his interrogation. "One more time. Tell me the truth."

"I already did."

Vidal needed no more information before he started to call his daughter's name. "Catalina? Goyo?" He leaped over the net into the women's section of the party, and the women backed away as if he extended a broadsword at arm's length. There were many women at this party, some from parts of the Iberian Peninsula he'd not yet become acquainted with. Was it possible that in not expecting to see Catalina, he'd simply overlooked his daughter?

When he heard no response to her name, he fled the celebration, bumping into Eliezer in the corridor that led to the street. Eliezer was talking to another exile, a woman whose family had come from Cádiz. His son called after him to ask if they should fetch their medical bags, but Vidal ignored him, sprinting through the torch-lit streets of Fez. His new boots bent sideways at the ankles, threatening to give and sprain him with every step. But he'd gladly shatter every bone in his legs if it meant he could see Catalina again. Somehow, she'd chosen to leave Granada. Somehow, she'd convinced Gabriel to come with her. People turned their heads as Vidal raced past, for only young boys who delivered messages were known to sprint through the streets at such a speed.

A cloud of dust and dirt burst into the air behind him as he arrived outside his family's shack. The door stood open, the plank of wood leaned against the threshold, and the dim shimmer of candlelight came from within. It seemed a bit reckless to break into the house, but he remembered how depleted his family had felt when they wandered into Fez at the conclusion of the journey. Catalina would recognize this shack by the wooden mezuzah nailed to the threshold that'd once been on the door of their home in Granada.

The first thing he noticed upon entering the house was the sight of a toddler wrapped in blankets who slept alone on his bed. Vidal's eyes adjusted to the dark as he expected to see his daughter at the table, but only found Gabriel sitting alone. He looked filthy and unwashed, his boots and clothes as tattered as they'd appeared on Vidal when he'd arrived. Gabriel bore the stench of a man who'd spent too many days unbathed as he hiked through the lowlands, even as he needed to wear a winter coat to keep warm. When Gabriel looked up at him, the candlelight flickered to reveal a fear in his eyes far worse than the face the rabbi had made when Vidal accosted him.

Words were unnecessary to comprehend that Catalina was not with them. Neither lifeless pupils nor the stillness of a pulse were needed for Vidal to know that she was gone, for the same dread that'd overcome him the night of Sarah's death was as present in the room as Gabriel or his new grandson. Vidal sat at the table across from Gabriel and learned everything as the fire of the lone candlelight whipped and flickered between them with each blow that came from Gabriel's breath.

Chapter Twenty-Six

After the Act of Faith, Gabriel's priest advised him against gathering Catalina's remains for burial. But Gabriel told Vidal that he ignored the advice. "She'd atoned for her sins in the eyes of God. She deserved a proper funeral." Once they collected the remains from the inquisitors—what these remains were, Gabriel avoided describing and Vidal had not the heart to ask—the church refused their request to bury Catalina in the Catholic cemetery. Because she could not be buried with Gabriel's grandparents, she was instead interred under a tree on the farm of Gabriel's sister in Alfacar.

Before her death, Catalina had asked him to take Aznaro to her family, but he at first found this last request impossible to fulfill. Perhaps when the boy was older, but to deliver a toddler to Fez? Reckless. "Then the inquisitors came for my family." The Holy Office expropriated Gabriel's father for all expenses related to the imprisonment and execution of Catalina. His father lost everything: home, business, all deeds and titles, forcing the family to move to Alfacar. They never learned who'd accused Catalina of a false conversion, the Holy Office kept such accusations confidential, but he viewed everyone in Granada as a suspect. In turn, the community grew suspicious as to whether he and his family were devoted to the Catholic faith. They became pariahs, avoided on the streets by neighbors as if Judaism was as contagious as the black death. Even his mother turned against his father, cursing him for allowing their son to marry a Jew in the first place, his decision forever calling into question the piousness of their family.

Commissioners from Granada and captains from the monarchs' army would arrive unannounced at his sister's door on horseback to question Gabriel's father. They hinted that because Aznaro was born of a Jewish womb, he would be taken in by the Holy Office. "Our priest, Padre Leonardo, was the only one from the city who would still speak with me. He told me Aznaro would be brought up in a monastery." But as Gabriel remembered the farewell to his wife in a dungeon, the smell of burning flesh that traveled across Granada, the smoke that rose over the rooftops to eclipse the sun, he knew he could not surrender his son to the inquisitors.

"Gabriel, spare a father such details," Vidal said.

Gabriel apologized but continued to speak like a man who had waited for ages to share his story. With his father's blessing, he fled Alfacar on one of his brother-in-law's horses, carrying Aznaro and as much coin as possible to barter passage across the sea. Aznaro had been brave on the trip, crying rarely. As Gabriel had gone to Málaga several times on behalf of his father's business, he was no stranger to the passage through the mountains, but finding food for a child who did not yet have teeth proved to be the most challenging aspect of the journey. He paid for the milk of cows and goats in villages along the route, but after six weeks on the road, the boy was malnourished. "I trust his grandfather will nurse him back to health."

Vidal realized he'd not taken the opportunity to look upon his grandchild's face. But there could be no worse time for such an introduction, now that he knew his oldest child was gone from this world. Not as of that moment, but months ago, while he'd carried on with his life oblivious to her fate. Where had he been when they executed her? Picking olives? In temple at prayer?

"Did you write me about her death?"

"I only knew you could be found through the synagogue of your rabbi's brother. I could not send such sensitive contents with so little assurance it would reach you."

"Did she receive any letters from me?"

"Only one. From Málaga."

He'd written her twice more since they arrived in Fez. When no reply materialized, he simply blamed it on the slowness and unreliability of delivering a letter through a messenger. Should he have guessed that something was wrong? "I need to be alone."

"I'll take Aznaro."

"The baby can stay."

Once Gabriel left the shack, Vidal affixed the wooden panel and nail to the door frame. He could see Gabriel standing in the dirt beyond the holes in the poorly aligned wooden walls. The shack was so muted that he heard nothing but the soft breaths of the child on the bed. He peeled back the blanket that cloaked the boy's face. The skin clung tightly to the bones of the baby's skull that made him look far older than a mere five months. But the eyelids rested softly closed, as if he were not yet aware of what events transpired around him. Life had already ravaged his body, but perhaps it left his mind undisturbed. Did the boy look like his daughter? Impossible to tell with only the candlelight on the table.

Voices came from outside, up the path to their house. Through the slits in the walls, he could see Bonadonna walking with their children; Asher still dressed in his white prayer shawl and cap that caught the moonlight's reflection. They all stopped at the sight of a stranger outside and as Vidal came out to meet them, his wife exclaimed Gabriel's name with surprise.

At the funeral in the Ibn Zadok Synagogue, Vidal, his wife, and children—even Gabriel—each performed the kriah, tearing the ends of their shirts in mourning. After a ceremony where Rabbi el Barchilon recited the Kaddish for Catalina, the family returned to their shack to commence the mourning period of shiva. Gabriel lit the shiva candle on their table upon their return as the family washed their hands and faces in a basin outside the front door. Iamila worked to help her mother wash Aznaro's face. Though shiva required that all mirrors of the house be covered, they owned no mirrors, so Bonadonna draped a blanket over the window to block their reflection.

Forsaking the work and many chores they performed, the family remained seated on wooden stools inside their house for what would be seven days. Others from the community entered the shack with platters of fresh fruits and vegetables, tajine, hummus, falafel, and bread. When the woman who Vidal had seen Eliezer speak with the night of the party visited with a simple recipe of roasted eggplant, Eliezer went outside with her in the olive groves. Although this was not customary, neither Vidal nor Bonadonna bothered to stop him.

In the afternoons, when no community members visited, Vidal walked outside with Gabriel and listened to stories of what his daughter had been like after they'd left, how she'd loved Aznaro in the brief time she'd been his mother, and how hard she'd worked to transform herself into a devout follower of Christ.

"Have you considered whether you'll go back to Alfacar?"

"I must. I cannot abandon my parents."

"Have them come here. We won't live in this shack forever."

"Perhaps." After all the Holy Office had put them through, Gabriel's father still wished to reside in Granada and regain his titles. Vidal had always seen Ochoa as one of the proudest and most successful men he'd known. To hear Ochoa's fate made him sound weak, but Vidal could not fault him. If the monarchs abolished the decree at that moment and welcomed all Jews back into their kingdoms, their lands and occupations restored, he'd be a fool not to accept. "The trade routes are too controlled here. My father would never be able to rebuild his business."

"I can imagine. Even the olives are controlled."

"I will not be surprised if he wishes to venture to the new world."

After all that'd transpired over the past several days, he'd forgotten how the conversation with Rabbi el Barchilon began. "It won't be a new world for long. Not if your king and queen found it."

In the evenings, Bonadonna worked with Gabriel to care for Aznaro, eager to fatten him up with goat milk. She sat on the bed with her back against the wall and sang "La Prima Vez" to the boy as he fell asleep, the same song she'd sung to her children when they were young. In the mornings, Vidal examined the boy to ensure his head would not grow misshapen and listened for the sounds of healthy organs. He checked the uncircumcised penis for cleanliness and although he knew they should plan a briss following the conclusion of shiva, he decided to leave the decision to Gabriel. Throughout the examination, he kept the baby on the bed and diagnosed him as if he were paying one of his house calls, never holding the child as his wife or children did. How could he trust himself to hold this child, to care for it, when he'd allowed two daughters to die?

The night before shiva was to conclude, as the candle burned into a pool of melted wax on the table, Vidal lay awake on the wooden floor, having given his place on the bed to his grandson. He looked up at the stars through the holes in the thatched hay roof and found the idea of ending shiva the following day, of re-emerging into life, repulsive. His daughter was murdered and he'd sat in his house all week doing nothing. Was he supposed to move on with his life, as the faith guided him to believe? Not after he'd left Catalina to die, after he'd dragged his family to Fez only for them to suffer in new ways. He did not deserve a symbolic conclusion to his sorrow.

He gathered the supplies by the door and resumed work in the groves, raking clean the olives from the tallest tree. Work was no reason to break shiva and if anyone caught him, they'd say he was disrespecting his daughter's memory. But shiva would not bring Catalina back.

He swung the rake at the tree, attacked it; tried to tear its branches loose as if he were in a battle with King Ferdinand himself. He'd send it to its Catholic hell. Sentence it to death. If he had flint or tinder, he'd purify the tree as an effigy to the monarchs. To Moses, who had managed to save the members of his own exodus. To Jesus, who had been born a Jew but forsaken his own kind in the founding of a new religion. To the Jews who'd called for the release of Barabbas in exchange for Jesus' crucifixion, whose crimes remained punished to this day. But in the bark of the tree, in the deformed burl that protruded from its trunk, not so different from Vidal's nose, he saw himself. He swung at the father who had not been wise enough to save his daughters, as if all the pain his family had endured came not from a decree passed down by the Alhambra, but his own failures.

"What are you doing?" The voice was so high-pitched that for only a moment he thought Catalina was standing behind him. But when he turned around, he found Bonadonna hugging herself in a winter coat too thin to warm her as a cool breeze blew through the branches.

"Picking olives."

"You woke everyone up with your noise."

"I'm sorry."

"Is everything all right?"

"Yes, fine."

"We're not supposed to work during shiva."

"I know."

"Why don't you come back inside? You can sleep on the bed if you want."

"That's fine. I'll be along in a minute."

She took the rake from him and turned toward the shack. As he gathered the tarp, he looked again at the tree. It resembled no person, neither living nor dead. It was only a tree. It'd only ever been a tree.

"When I learned how urgent it was to leave, I asked if she'd come with us."

"You didn't," Bonadonna said. Vidal looked at her in silence. "What did she say?"

"She refused."

"Why did you never tell me?"

"What would you have said? It was scandalous to ask a Catholic wife to leave her husband—even though she was my daughter—how could I tell anyone? Goddamn it, I should've told you. You could've talked to her. You would've found another way to make her leave. Something that would've convinced her."

"We both know I wouldn't have done that. I would have used her refusal as vindication to stay. And if I'd gotten my way, my actions would've cost me dearly."

"Maybe if we stayed, we could've protected her."

"Or, we'd doom ourselves to meet the same fate. The piousness of our entire family would've been brought into question. They'd interrogate Iamila, Aznaro…" Bonadonna must have imagined a brutal vision, for she struggled to say more. Vidal brought her into his arms and stroked her hair, as he'd watched her do while soothing their children. "Ever since we found out about her death, I've been going over and over it in my mind. If we never let her be a nurse, if she never met Gabriel, if she never converted, this never would've happened. But then I tell myself that if she never met Gabriel, that beautiful boy in there wouldn't be with us now. God is testing us. He takes away two of our daughters to test us, and He rewards us with a grandchild to ease our suffering."

"Do you believe God is so cruel?"

"What else am I supposed to think?"

"We're supposed to love our God, not fear Him. That's what the Catholics do."

"But we were never truly meant to understand Him. That's why we devote our lives to the Torah. To try to comprehend why He has put us here."

Vidal felt a weight in his throat as heavy as the wagon they'd pulled through the mountains. The next words teetered on his lips. How little would Bonadonna think of him once he spoke them aloud? "What if we're devoting our lives to something that does not exist?"

"You're only upset. You wouldn't say such things if you were not in mourning."

"What if I left Goyo for something that isn't real?"

"Is that what you wish to think? That God is not real?"

"I don't want to think it. I want to remain a Jew. I want to believe. But I no longer feel Him by my side."

"Have you ever felt Him by your side?"

"All my life. Everywhere. I once spoke with Him as if He were a guest at our table or a member of our house. But since our time in Málaga I feel He has left me. Maybe He was never by my side at all."

Bonadonna looked him in the eye the way she looked at their

children when they'd come in the middle of the night fretting over a nightmare, only for her to assure them the nightmare had no relation to reality. "He is by our side."

"You must have your doubts. You advocated to convert."

"Are you so full of pride that you think you brought us to Fez by yourself? God is with us. This past year has made me more certain of that than I have ever been. How can you not see it?"

"What am I to see?"

"That we escaped a kingdom where so many others remained stranded."

"We escaped because I performed a surgery that could've killed a boy."

"We escaped because of your deep devotion to our faith. Because you refused to convert even when you had every excuse to do so. You followed your faith and it allowed you to save as many of us as you could. That's what I see."

Even if he questioned his own beliefs, he could not deny his wife's words. God had not intervened to rescue his family the way He rescued Noah from the flood or the Israelites from Pharaoh. God did not spare Vidal from burying a child the way He spared Abraham from sacrificing Isaac. Yet Vidal's steadfast faith, his decision to believe, to put his religion over the temptation of remaining a converso in Granada, had delivered his family to safety.

"And if another misfortune were to befall us," Vidal said. "If we must one day leave our home again, would you hold firm to this belief?"

"What was the story your father used to tell about the first Jews to arrive in Iberia?"

"They fled Jerusalem to escape the Romans."

"Nearly fifteen hundred years ago."

"That's what he said."

"And did they turn away from God?"

"Of course, not."

"They brought our people to a place where we could live for 1,500 years. And now you've taken us to Africa so we may have another 1,500. Even if it means leaving home again or that one day our descendants will need to face the same tests we've endured. Give them that chance, Vidal. Keep your religion alive for your children. Your grandson. Ferdinand and Isabella could not steal your faith from you. Do not take it from yourself."

Vidal looked down the row of olive trees to their shack nestled in the darkness. He'd given much thought to all he'd lost in the past year and in his misery forgotten how much he still possessed, waiting in his new home for his return. Why had he allowed himself to grow content with confining his family to this place on the periphery of town? Because of his selfish reluctance to practice medicine? His hesitation to continue worship? His perception of God would never be the same, but that did not give reason to turn away from Judaism. He must find a way to rediscover it and carry his beliefs forward, not only for himself, but for the children in his home who still relied on him. For the generations of Jews that would come after him.

He looked back to the tree he attacked, its bark ripped off, scratch marks sliced across its trunk. Why had he attacked it with such hatred? A great burden inside Vidal seemed to fall away from him, the way he felt when he laid down his bags for the first time inside their new home in Fez.

"I am so sorry," he whispered, pulling Bonadonna into his arms. "You are right. Forgive me, Bonita. I'm not myself."

"There's nothing to forgive."

"I brought us here and I have done nothing to help us move forward with our lives."

"It is all right, Vidal. No one blames you. We have only just arrived in Fez."

"I should have done more to protect you."

"You have done everything in your power to protect us."

"A wiser man would've found a better way."

"We do not have a wiser man, we have only you. Forgive yourself, you have done all a man in your position is capable of doing." She took his hands in hers. "Please let's return to bed. We'll need to conclude shiva soon, and after that return to our lives." A crack in her voice hinted that she struggled to move on from Catalina's death as he did.

"I'm very fortunate to have you for a wife."

"I'm blessed to call you my husband."

They kissed and for a moment he felt as if they were young again, as if they were not standing in an olive grove in Fez, but in their home in La Judería, when Bonadonna had come to him to share that she was pregnant with their first child. In that moment he had wanted nothing more than to protect her, to protect the children she would bear from any perils they might face. Why had he taken so long to remember that feeling?

He told her he would return home in a moment. "Good night, Bonita."

"Goodnight, my love."

She returned through the olive grove to the house and did not leave his sight until she was safe with the door closed behind her. Once he gathered his supplies, he returned to the shack. Inside, all his family was asleep again. He sat on the edge of the bed, where Iamila lay in a fetal position facing Aznaro with her body acting like a gate to protect him from falling onto the floor. The boy made soft cooing sounds; he kicked his legs and shut his eyes tight as if he were experiencing a vivid dream.

Vidal brought the baby into his arms and held him for the first time. At that moment, he made a vow, not to God, nor Christ, nor Allah, but to himself. He would let nothing happen to this child. He would protect Aznaro as he'd failed to do so with not only Sarah and Catalina, but his wife and children, whom he'd dragged across the sea. This boy would be the first of their family raised to carry them forth into this new world. He sang "La Prima Vez" to Aznaro and held him until the sun appeared through the windows, as the family stirred to begin their day, while he dusted clean his instrument case, and as he led his family in morning prayer to eulogize Catalina to signal the conclusion of shiva and a return to their lives.

Recommended Resources

In writing this novel, I drew from the following sources. I would urge anyone interested in learning more about Jewish and Spanish history to seek out these works.

To understand the history of Spain leading up to the 1492 expulsion, I relied on Teofilo F. Ruiz's *Spain's Centuries of Crisis 1300-1474*, Maria Rosa Menocal's *The Ornament of the World: How Muslims, Jews and Christians Created a Culture of Tolerance in Medieval Spain* and Yitzhak Baer's *A History of the Jews in Christian Spain*.

For a more direct understanding of the expulsion itself, Joseph Pérez's *History of a Tragedy: The Expulsion of the Jews from Spain* served as my most trusted guide. For information specific to Granada, Steven Nightingale's *Granada: A Pomegranate in the Hand of God* provided not only an in-depth history of the city, but also written accounts from people who journaled about the appearance of Granada around this time period.

The wedding of Tsipora and Avraham was one of the most challenging scenes to write due to the level of detail needed to describe a time period accurate Sephardic wedding. Anita Diamant's *The Jewish Wedding Now* served as a reliable authority in this endeavor.

For an in-depth understanding of medieval medical practices, I consulted *Medieval Medicine: The Art of Healing, from Head to Toe* by Luke Demaitre, which brings together different treatments and philosophies from the middle ages and cites many of the most prominent medieval physicians.

Several multimedia resources proved effective in helping me understand the expulsion as well. The website of the *Jewish History Alliance* breaks down the events surrounding the expulsion of the Jews into simple and direct terms. Podcast episodes from *Torah Café* and *Tides of History* served as great fact-checking resources toward the end of my research. Since there are obviously no photographs from 1492, the website of the *David Rumsey Map Collection* proved a valuable asset for historical maps and illustrations that gave me an idea of what the various locations in the novel might have looked like during this time.

I owe a debt to the inspiration of several creative works that helped me understand how to depict this event and time period. Marcos Aguinis' novel *Against the Inquisition* goes into great detail about the bureaucratic practices surrounding the Inquisition. Noah Gordon's novel *The Last Jew* provided a model for how to tell a story from the perspective of a converted Jew who remains in Spain. *The Dream of the Poem: Hebrew Poetry from Muslim and Christian Spain, 950-1492* and the play *The Celestina: A Fifteenth-Century Spanish Novel in Dialogue* by Fernando de Rojas provided valuable insight into the literature and attitudes of poets and playwrights who lived circa 1492.

For a more comprehensive list of resources consulted to write this novel, please download it at the novel's landing page here: https://www.historythroughfiction.com/south-of-sepharad.

Acknowledgments

My gratitude to the Mount St. Mary's University Creative Writing Program for supporting me throughout the crafting of this novel. I want to give a very special thank you to Juana Moriel-Payne and Johnny Payne who mentored me throughout the writing process. I'm grateful for my professors, fellow writers, and friends at the MSMU Workshop who read large portions of this novel, and provided me with their valuable feedback.

This book found a phenomenal editor and publisher with Colin Mustful. My thanks to him and the History Through Fiction team for championing the novel and working with me to see it through to completion.

Although this is my first novel, I've been writing for over 20 years, and I want to extend several long overdue words of appreciation to incredible teachers who guided me along the way: Karen Bender, Ron Darian, Dana Johnson, Susan Segal, Tom Jenks, Jervey Tervalon, Jody Agius Vallejo, and Bill Wishart.

My amazing and eternally supportive family of Weintraubs, Zimets, Baggs, McCammons, Cesareos, Harrisons, Salingers, Iglesias-Dublons and Hinckleys who always championed me to follow my dreams. A special shoutout to my parents, Andrew Weintraub and Mira Zimet, who proved you can make a living making art and helped guide me through my earliest creative projects; my step-father, Stewart Bagg, for his support; my grandma, Ellen Zimet, for her encouragement, and my grandpa, Sanford Zimet, who entrusted me to be the family member who'd carry our Jewish traditions forward.

The historian and author Teofilo Ruiz wrote one of the most informative books I read while researching this novel. When I reached out to him for feedback, he graciously gave me his time and provided me with expert details about 1492 Spain. My deepest gratitude to him for his kindness and generosity.

The novel is dedicated to my wife, Laura Cesareo, whose deep intrigue for medieval Spanish history is infectious. If she had not studied in Granada, and had not given me the chance to experience Granada with her, this novel simply would not exist. I wanted to write this novel for years, but was afraid of taking on such a difficult feat. Laura gave me the encouragement to finally put pen to paper.

About the Author

Eric Z. Weintraub earned an MFA in Creative Writing from Mount St. Mary's University where he wrote his debut novel *South of Sepharad*. Growing up in Los Angeles, CA, he comes from a family of filmmakers, writers, and educators stirring in him a passion for storytelling from a young age. His short fiction has appeared in *Tabula Rasa Review*, *Halfway Down the Stairs*, *The Rush*, and elsewhere. His novella *Dreams of an American Exile* won the 2015 Plaza Literary Prize and was published by Black Hill Press. His short story collection *The 28th Parallel* was a finalist for the 2021 Flannery O'Connor Award for Short Fiction. When not writing fiction, Eric profiles true stories of complex medical cases where he works at the Keck School of Medicine of USC.

www.ericzweintraub.com

Other Books by
History Through Fiction

Reclaiming Mni Sota:
An Alternate History of the U.S. – Dakota War of 1862
By Colin Mustful

The Education of Delhomme: Chopin, Sand, & La France
By Nancy Burkhalter

The Sky Worshipers: A Novel of Mongol Conquests
By FM Deemyad

The King's Anatomist: The Journey of Andreas Vesalius
By Ron Blumenfeld

My Mother's Secret: A Novel of the Jewish Autonomous Region
By Alina Adams

If you enjoyed this novel please consider leaving a review. You'll be supporting a small, independent press, and you'll be helping other readers discover this great story.
Thank you!

www.HistoryThroughFiction.com

www.ingramcontent.com/pod-product-compliance
Lightning Source LLC
Chambersburg PA
CBHW030140310726
48970CB00005B/1512